W9-AHH-473

Seeing Double

Born in Kingston, Jamaica, Patrick Wilmot is a graduate of Yale and Vanderbilt universities. He taught sociology at Ahmadu Bello University, Nigeria, for eighteen years. An outspoken critic of the military government of Ibrahim Babangida, he was kidnapped by security police in 1988 and deported to England. He is the author of several books of poetry and academic and non-fiction works including *In Search of Nationhood* and *Apartheid and African Liberation*. He lives in London and is a member of Transparency International. This is his first novel.

SEEING DOUBLE

Patrick Wilmot

THOMAS DUNNE BOOKS
ST. MARTIN'S PRESS
NEW YORK

THOMAS DUNNE BOOKS.
An imprint of St. Martin's Press.

www.thomasdunnebooks.com
www.stmartins.com

Library of Congress Cataloging-in-Publication Data

Wilmot, Patrick F.
    Seeing double / Patrick Wilmot.—1st U.S. ed.
        p.cm.
    ISBN-13: 978-0-312-34263-0
    ISBN-10: 0-312-34263-2
    1. Coups d'état—Fiction. 2. Petroleum industry and trade—Fiction.
3. Dictatorship—Fiction. 4. Africa, West—Fiction. 5. Satire. I. Title.

PR6123.I56S44 2006
823'.914—dc22

                                                            2006040195

First published in Great Britain by Jonathan Cape

First U.S. Edition: August 2006

10   9   8   7   6   5   4   3   2   1

To my wife, Makki, and my son, Nicolai,
and
to the memory of my friend
Ken Saro-Wiwa

COURTESY OF
THE NIAGRAN
TOURIST BOARD.

NIAGRA

BURTON HOLLY FARM

TEXAS

HIGHWAY 322

NIAGRA

XANADU

CRAWFORD RANCH

CHENEY VILLE

RUMSFELD TOWN

CONDOLEEZZA
TROUGH

SEA OF OIL

NEVERLAND

① Disposal Unit Special Republican
   Guard Barracks
② Mass Grave
③ Rock Castle
④ Elvis Statue
⑤ US Special Forces Barracks
⑥ John Wayne's Mummy (With Six Guns)
⑦ Prize Bull
⑧ Pretzel Factory
⑨ Oil Platform (With Black Hawk Helipad)
⑩ Karl Rove Bay
🍔 McDaudu's
🍕 Piazza Hut

Illustration: Elliot Thoburn

Contents

POLITICAL FOREPLAY: THE HOT NIAGRAN NIGHTS

HEALTH WARNING

The venue of this story, Niagra, attracted a lawsuit from the manufacturers of Viagra™, dragging the publisher to the World Trade Organization in accordance with provisions of the Trade Related Intellectual Property Rights (TRIPS) for copyright infringement. Argument that Niagra had historical antecedents, a fictional country named by the bimbo girlfriend of a colonial governor who got the spelling wrong after a dirty weekend at Niagara Falls, was dismissed by the company's lawyer echoing Henry Ford with: 'history ain't got as much material relevance to this here case as the hairs on a frog's back'. In case the WTO rules in favour of the manufacturers, readers are strongly advised to demand a coloured pencil from the publisher to blot out the offending word. *Or prepare to be fucked by the Pfizer Drug Company*.

The Attorney General has also ruled that smoking this book *is* hazardous to your health and that *not inhaling* will not count as mitigating circumstances in an American court of law. Readers are reminded that *all* characters are fictional, including Karl Rove who had hoped to be played by Charlie Bronson in the sequel to *All the President's Men* but will now have to settle for Tom Cruise. Nasser Waddadda, the Niagran Karl Rove, is definitely fictional,

as shown by his success in proving the democratic creden-
tials of his country's Dictator, the modestly named General
Abdu-Salaam bin-Sallah-ud-Deen bin Sani-Ibrahim al-
Daudu, The Life President of Niagra and Unique Miracle
of the Twentieth Century.

Under pressure from the Western Democracies, Nasser
advised the General to set up six political parties after the
number of fingers on his right hand, write their mani-
festos and fund each with fifty million dollars to avoid
their capture by unprincipled and corrupt moneymen.
Then, in a stroke of genius worthy of his mentor in the
White House, he advised all six to exercise their democratic right by nominating the General as sole candidate
to avoid the unseemly spectacle of violent and greedy men
fighting to the death in a game of winner-takes-all. With
this dignified and peaceful process of the Great Helmsman
competing against himself the outcome could only be the
recognition of Niagra as the Greatest Democracy in Black
Africa, if not the world.

But Nasser had forgotten that in addition to six fingers
on his right hand the General suffered multipolar personality disorder and, depending on the political climate and
the phase of the moon, believed he was Margaret
Thatcher, Idi Amin, Elvis Presley, the Emperor Bokassa,
Dame Edna Everage and Paul Wolfowitz. Besides, not
even God, who was suspected of creating Niagrans first
then spending eternity trying to correct His mistakes,
could remove ballot rigging and political violence from
the national character.

The result was the most violent election in the nation's
history as each political party took on the personality of
its leading character, promising to make each Niagran a
Thatcherite king of Scotland, Australia or rock and roll,
or to make their country achieve the Full Frontal
Dominance now enjoyed uniquely by the United States
of America which allowed that country to fuck any
country which dared to say 'No!'. Dame Edna, who

finished marginally ahead, was disqualified by the Electoral Commission for complaining that three of her rivals were dead, one was a partially-real woman though *gaga* and the other a member of the Bush cabinet. So the General was advised to cancel the elections, declare a state of Emergency and elect himself Life President by Decree.

Which was alright then, because just before the letters of denunciation and threats of sanctions were despatched from Western capitals, Nasser Waddadda announced the discovery of huge quantities of oil off the coast of Lidiziam which made his country a more valuable piece of real estate than Iraq. The result was invitations from the White House, Buckingham Palace, the Elysée and Chancellor's office, with promises of the Congressional Medal, Honorary Knighthood, Iron Cross, and Legion of Honour. His portrait appeared under the heading of 'New Democracy' on the covers of *Time*, the *National Review* and *New Republic*, and editorials in the *Washington Times*, *London Times* and *Sunday Telegraph* praised his 'brilliant statesmanship' and 'profound courage'. And George Bush declared him the George 'Dubya' Washington of his country while Tony Blair went one better, dubbing him the Peter Mandelson of our times.

Literary critics such as Harold Bloom, who argue that if this character did not exist it would be necessary to invent him, are reminded that according to the First Protocol of the Abuja Convention the only *necessary* being in the universe is the General himself. If after all these warnings, readers persist in mistaking this fiction for reality, they hereby deprive themselves of the protections of the Geneva Convention and Kyoto Protocol and are liable to be detained indefinitely in the appropriately named Camp Climax in Guantanamo Bay, Cuba, where fat Castroite mosquitoes will bite their naked asses.

This book is best read hot, to the accompaniment of Bob Marley's 'Get Up, Stand Up', played at such volume that the neighbours bang the ceiling with baseball bats, shouting 'turn that foreign shit off, you fucking scuzbag foreign-loving faggot'.

Do not pretend you have not been warned.

PROLOGUE

THE TRAGIC FLAW OF A MAN IN BLACK

A fine dust rose through the mist which in the early morning sun separated into gold and silver. But the man in the Police sunglasses and purple Thierry Mugler shirt with brass studs saw nothing of this transformation because his castor-bean eyes were focused on the hunched, dirty old man approaching the border fence about fifty metres away. His inability to appreciate the beauty of the rising dawn was not helped by his proximity to his American 'partner' from Special Operations whose idea of sartorial elegance was a t-shirt of such spectacularly offensive floral design it attracted disoriented bees and jeans so old no self-respecting cart pusher would be caught dead in them. Did his commanders honestly believe that a man whose ponytail was kept in shape with a conditioner suggesting air-freshener in a lower class brothel was the best instrument for capturing Al-Qaeda operatives trying to cross the Nigeria/Niagra border? Fortunately there was minimum opportunity for conversation because one ear was plugged with his radio connection, the other with one arm of a Walkman. Unfortunately the other arm was left hanging so innocent bystanders suffered the collateral damage of 'Shove your hand down my blouse again, / These ain't no plum tomatoes'.

While this may have well served a bunch of rednecks near a fictional town called Crawford in Texas, it was out of tune with a stretch of border between two 'failed states', described by their own Secretary of Defence as 'a clear and present danger to the security interests of the United States of America'. On this the Secretary need not have worried because Nigel 'Doc' Holliday's cover was completed by a medium sized box of Wrigley's chewing gum, an MI6 rifle adorned with a 'Homer Simpson for President' sticker, an Uzi sub-machine gun, a Ruger Blackhawk .357 pistol on his right hip, a Rambo hunting knife on his left, a ring of grenades like green star apples round his waist and a bunch of urine yellow RPGs hanging louchely about his torso like dinosaur eggs painted for a Jurassic Easter.

Mustapha would not even have noticed the grey bastard struggling across the stretch of no-man's land in slow motion if he hadn't reminded him of the central character in his adolescent novel, *Magic Fountain*, which Heinemann had rejected on the grounds that the 'narrative was too disjointed, the characters not credible enough, the setting too futuristic, the plot too apocalyptic, the dialogue too scatological, and generally unsuitable for Heinemann's major audience in schools and colleges'. While severely pissed at Heinemann at the time, he was now happy at the rejection, not even recognizing then that the title was stolen from Thomas Mann's *Magic Mountain* and Ayn Rand's *The Fountainhead*. Even at seventeen he should not have been so naïve as to mix the decadent conformism of Old Europe with the raw individualism of a hyper-power destined to achieve Full Frontal Dominance over a world of sheep-like nations. What kind of sick shit had led him to imagine a loser like the grey bundle of rags slinking toward him existing in the same Nietzsche/Ayn Rand world of American tycoons and

Darwinian generals who rubbed the noses of no-hopers like the grimy jackass in the shit bucket? How could the slimy turd co-exist with the golden, crew-cut nuclear warriors who left fire in their wake?

Because of the dire state of the continent, every educated African had a book in him to show that a new, better world was possible. And Mustapha was no exception, bursting with a real swashbuckling, literary semtex-charged rollercoasting cauldron of a book, peopled by gigantic egos capable of parading the same stage as the heroes of *Atlas Shrugged* and *The Fountainhead* who would do for Niagra what Ayn Rand had done for a vigorous, thrusting America which rolled over lesser nations on its way to glory, without apology or excuse. He looked at the old loser and felt the power swell up inside him, beyond the narrow confines of morality and feeling, beyond good and evil, to that rarefied, austere pinnacle of creation where World Historical Individuals like General Daudu, Richard 'Mr Dick' Burton and Lord Conrad Black did as they willed, while the undifferentiated mass suffered as they must.

But he was brought back to earth by the memory of the new man at Heinemann – called the 'Exchequer', or 'Chancellor', because of his resemblance to a former Chancellor, so striking they could be told apart only by his goddess daughter with her 20/20 vision for spotting trends in expensive *nouvelle cuisine*. When Mustapha had presented an outline with characters representing the ideas of Friedrich Nietzsche and Ayn Rand, 'Exchequer' had asked what he thought of Al-Qaeda and the coming clash between Western and Islamic civilizations on the battlefields of Africa. But even this was not considered a suitable topic for his novel as the man still thought the African writer had an obligation to present mythical peasants and workers living in communal bliss, a bunch of angelic faggots wishing the best of all possible worlds for other brainless wonders, rather than animals engaged in a brutal struggle for survival, willing to rip off each other's heads and stuffing them down their throats. Africans were no different, and probably a whole lot worse, than other races which triumphed. Even Earl Grey, moping like a tuft of silk cotton without its own means of motion toward him, probably beat the shit out of his wife, buggered his sons and squeezed his daughters' plum-sized tits till they screamed bloody murder while reciting verses from the scriptures and thinking of defecation.

His poor parents had always pressed on him the importance of making money so they could make the neighbours look like shit and his father, who had a primary school education, smashed his head with his belt buckle when he caught him writing shit he could not understand, which confirmed his suspicion that he had given life to an abomination against the Most High, a fucking man-woman. They wanted him to join the customs or immigration, the runners-up for the national sweepstake to the military because they didn't think he had the balls to become a soldier and commit grand larceny on a national scale. But Mustapha had his personal ambition which was not for money but power, the root of all one could desire, including wealth, sex and fame. So he opted for the Security Service, in whose shadow he could hold feet to the fire, forcing the arms to rise in surrender, study the psychology of terror and measure the extent to which an enemy gave in to his fear.

But he was no psychopath and took no pleasure in inflicting pain. His limited experience with enemies of the state was that they yielded far more easily to the fear of injury than the defiance or at least the numbness which derived from its actual infliction. He remembered his Ulster Protestant tutor in Political Philosophy at St Anthony's who, in alcohol induced hallucinations, railed at his Republican 'enemies' and Loyalist 'friends' alike for killing, maiming and torturing each other, rather than using the threat of such horrors to gain advantage in cynical compromises and tawdry accommodations of interest because *the power to hurt was more effective when held in reserve*. And his slim muscles, toned to perfection by their own internal tensions, shivered with self-satisfaction in his black Ginochietti linen jacket, Ungaro jeans and £1,500 Hermes belt, its hand-made silver buckle with an image of Tantalus splayed, at the consciousness of his own rightness. His Lobb boots shone so brightly he could see his face in them if he did not already keep, fixed permanently in his mind, an image of Patrick Vieira, the Arsenal football captain, ruthless and machine-like in a million-dollar suit straight out of *Reservoir Dogs* and with the will and resolve to slice the fucking ears off Manchester United and Chelsea football clubs. Whenever he indulged in his favourite sport of shopping he was driven by the image of those muscles toned in the hot sun of the Senegalese *niaye*, the incredibly long legs bursting through the Chelsea lines, the indomitable brow.

Shopping, not terror, was integral to the philosophy of the security service and Idi Amin's reign in Uganda demonstrated that shopping was superior to terror, in fact a continuation of terror by other means. During his stay at Buckingham Palace – a gentle giant balancing two royal corgis on those enormous platforms of hands – Amin lacked the intellectual sophistication to realize that the same Agency which supplied the *Chateau Margot*, artichoke hearts and lobster bisque to the Royal Table also garnered the silk shirts, single malt scotch whiskies and expensive *eau de cologne* for his boys in the State Research Bureau who did the business on opponents in the dimly lit 'chicken coops' below his own Presidential Palace. But neither did his Royal Hostess understand the psychology of shopping and the role it played in the political stability of African military dictatorships which made such sterling contributions to her civil list.

Every Friday evening at nine without fail a DC9 left Stansted airport for Kampala stuffed with orders from the Field Marshal's Men in Black which they needed to maintain their sense of purpose and restore their equilibrium after inhuman exertions spent teaching sense to the Enemies of the State. Before their spectacular break over the issue of Weapons of Mass Destruction, Israel and Uganda maintained such intimate relations that the academic Professor Jana Herzovogina, inventor of the Wonder-Bra, was allowed to study these specialists in the State Research Bureau at close quarters. The Professor, using an admittedly self-selected sample, found that 'optimists' looked forward with anticipation to the arrival of their 'gifts' and were generally more pleasantly inclined toward their charges while the 'pessimists', anticipating disappointment, acted in a truculent and insensitive manner by beating the shit out of them. But the most shocking finding was the charges' vicarious identification with their specialists and the feelings of envy over who got the brightest silk shirt or most stylish designer shades, as men about to die competed with each other to see who could have the deepest, most satisfying, final lungful of Givenchy's heady *Eau Sauvage*.

On trips to London to liaise with his English counterparts, Mustapha took his bosses' lists to collect Brioni suits and matching shirts, belts, socks, shoes, ties, boxer shorts and hankies from Rossini's. At first he had wondered why they paid the huge mark-ups when they could send him to Rome and still save money at the source. Why did they refuse to buy a simple safari suit for less than £3,000 when they probably had a closetful they never wore? Then he realized that paying more was the whole point, you did it because you *could*. Marshal Mobutu paid ten thousand dollars to a Lebanese contractor for a six hundred dollar bottle of *Chateau Petrus* because the inflation made it taste a thousand times richer, to make him worthy of his name Mobutu Sese Seko Kuku Ngbengu Wasa Banga which meant *the warrior who leaves fire in his wake, who emerges triumphant from a thousand battles, the cockerel who fucks the hens till they bleed.* This was *power*, to do what you wanted without considering the cost, not battering the head of some poor bastard who had no 'information' worth knowing. Three thousand pounds could probably buy a bigger mud house for the grey wonder over there, his four wives, twenty kids and countless hangers-on, if he rose above the instincts of his type to marry more wives and breed even more children. The money could prevent his wives dying from cerebral malaria, vesico-vaginal fistula or malnutrition and provide a future for their children through better education and healthcare. But the point was he couldn't stop you spending the dough on useless safari suits or £10,000 alligator skin attaché cases, from screwing his wives and daughters, or even his young sons if you were that way inclined. Naïve liberals thought people whose noses you rubbed in shit would rise up and try to fuck you but the truth was they dunked their heads even deeper in it to hide from the source of their pain before lining up to kiss your dick or crawling away to die. They knew nothing of the power of shopping, the true aphrodisiac, the Viagra of Niagra, for which the Generals and Field Marshals had the formula, not the WTO or the Pfizer Drug Company. A whole industry of servile Europeans had sprung up to massage the egos of the new African Big Swinging Dicks and Masters of the Universe, suitable reparations for slavery and colonialism despite the objections of the British PM who argued that slavery, like nazism, was legal in its day. So Mustapha had no qualms of conscience when he crossed the road from Rossini's to buy from the Hermes flagship store two £1,000 belts, some £250 ties and a bunch of £200 silk scarves for the undergraduates he maintained as informers at the General Daudu University of Niagra. Already he had a Zero Halliburton suitcase stuffed with underwear from Janet Reger, La Senza, Myla, La Perla and Agent Provocateur

for the women he would fuck when he returned, including
the widows and daughters of enemies of the state held in
the rat holes under the Presidential Palace, before he set
the dogs on them. He recalled his first marriage when he
suffered bouts of nausea and self-doubt after his boss gave
him a Pathek Phillipe watch and he thought it signalled
the end of his career, a vote of no confidence in his ability
to create fear. There was no sign of gold, the strap was
leather and the dial was plain as the eyes of the dull fool
he was watching as they waited for Justice Saleh's son. It
was only when he found the £15,000 price tag in the bottom
of the case that he realized 'Pathek Phillipe' *meant* something – that he was valued as a human being by his superior. It did not even phase him when he got to know that
his C-in-C wore a million dollar watch with a platinum
band and more diamonds, rubies, sapphires and pearls
than on his C-in-C's mother's coffin, made by Gaddafi's
personal watchmaker in Lucerne, a fucking irony in a
nation hosting the worst timekeepers in the world. He was
not bothered, because he recalled as a boy reading a self-
help pamphlet titled *Men are led by Baubles* about using
such coveted symbols to focus one's ambition to get to
the top. And on this score Niagra was way ahead of America
despite their disparity in military and economic power. On
his course to study Al-Qaeda operations at CIA
Headquarters with thirty-one other Africans, he had
mastered the techniques of gratuitous swearing, putting
'fuck' before every 'p---' and 's---' but learnt nothing about
shopping. And it amazed him that a country boasting its 'Full
Frontal Dominance' had no equivalent of Rossini's in
Washington and he doubted if Laura Bush had the ability
to blow $100,000 in a Paris boutique in the time it took to
say 'War, Motherhood and Apple Pie', a talent bequeathed
to any harlot who hit the jackpot and married some fucking
leader of an African basket case.

Mustapha's exultant mood was lowered, however, when
he recalled the sudden tragedy of the man he had once

considered making the hero of his own updated version of *Atlas Shrugged*. Hamidu Baggadudu was marked out as a future Nobel Laureate in economics when, only a senior at Yale, he wrote an article for the *American Banker* titled 'The Need for New Thinking in the World Bank and IMF', described by Joe Stiglitz as 'without precedent in the annals of economic thinking'. By changing the International Financial Institutions' mission statement from 'austerity' to 'poverty alleviation', Baggadudu argued that they would fuck left-wing assholes like Samir Amin, Walden Bello and Iain Duncan Smith who could not be seen to oppose programmes designed to improve the lives of the world's poorest losers. Stiglitz marked him out as World Bank material and followed his progress at Harvard where he enlisted for both the Ph.D. in Economics and MBA after graduating *summa cum laude* from Yale. At the Bank he was an instant success, designing programmes of such complexity Third World rulers could not fuck them up because they had not a fucking clue what they meant. But his stay was short-lived. Huge deposits of oil were discovered in Niagra and the Bank and Fund decided they needed their own man in place to prevent the megalomaniac General from blowing the whole fucking windfall on himself and his bunch of lame cocksuckers and their retinue of whores.

Baggadudu arrived on the scene shortly after the British Prime Minister had come for the state opening of the Afro-Disney Theme Park at the beginning of Africa's Development Decade. The entourage included the CEO of Equitable Life to teach Niagrans how to save, and of British Aerospace to show them how to screw their Nigerian rivals with Hawk aircraft and be recognized once and for all as the Greatest Black Power on Earth. The General had been so impressed with the Premier that he consulted with Nasser Waddadda on how he could establish his own pension fund so he would not be a burden on the state after he retired. He felt humiliated about depending on birthday presents of twenty million Euros from German Construction companies, Belgian chateaus from French oil companies, twenty-five million pounds from British arms companies, and fifty million dollar 'consultancy fees' from the Burton Holly Corporation on each Thanksgiving Day. As a proud African General he felt diminished by these episodic contributions to his 'pension fund' and it was his talent spotter Waddadda who pointed to Baggadudu as the man to design a coherent strategy to assure his long-term financial independence by converting his country into a cash machine.

The young economic magician did not disappoint. First he negotiated an agreement at the IMF for the release of a loan of ten billion dollars on the condition that Niagra take steps to reduce its thirty-five billion dollar debt. Ten billion of this was owed to the Russians who were so desperate for cash they had created bonds to sell the debt at almost any price. When Baggadudu arrived, the asking price was thirty cents to the dollar and his first move was to plant stories in the *Financial Times*, *Wall Street Journal* and *American Banker* that the Niagran economy was on the verge of collapse which had the desired effect of halving the price of the bonds on the first day. He advised the General to buy when they reached their floor of five cents to the dollar, through a bewildering array of Special Purpose Vehicles and International Business Corporations his City of London lawyer, Mr Rodmill Thompson, had set up in Nauru, the Cayman Islands, Grenada and the British Virgin Islands. Then Baggadudu began the process of ramping up the prices by planting stories in the financial press that a truly tough programme was on the way to restore macro-economic equilibrium. The currency was devalued, interest rates doubled, exchange controls relaxed, privatization accelerated, subsidies on gasoline and fertilizer removed, and cost recovery programmes introduced for previously free services in health, education, welfare and pipe-borne water supplies. The predictable riots erupted, sixty-seven people were shot, the *Washington Times*, *Wall Street Journal*, *Jerusalem Post* and the London *Telegraph* praised the Niagran financial authorities for their will and resolution and the IMF released the ten billion dollars as promised to reward the regime for its courage in reducing the debt burden and liberalizing the economy. The bonds rose to 55 per cent of their par value but a secret Financial Decree allowed the government to repurchase them at par and, at a stroke, the General Daudu Pension Fund was richer by $9.5 billion.

Then the London media began a feeding frenzy about the 'Steal of the Century' after the newsletter *Africa Confidential* revealed the financial architecture of a scam so elegant it would later be used by Enron, Global Crossing and Parmalat. Again Baggadudu was called upon to protect the good name of his General and rose superbly to the occasion, taking on the leader of the baying pack from the BBC World Service, called 'Florence' after the royal bull terrier which shared its mistress' talent for savaging anything that smelt common. As a special treat, the Men in Black in State Security played sped-up versions of her voice to secure confessions from men who had survived extreme measures such as 'crucifixion' and Florence lunged as Baggadudu stepped into Bush House looking like a laid-back, more athletic version of Tubbs from *Miami Vice*. But she was thrown on the defensive when he accused her of racism for not condemning the same methods used by Burton Holly, Hollinger International, News Corporation and twenty-four corporations on which members of the BBC's own Board of Governors sat as directors. He showed her the organograms, read out some figures and resisted when she tried to cut him off as he mentioned the name of the General's lawyer who played tennis with the Prime Minister and was his adviser on the Financial Action Task Force on Money Laundering. By the time they were finished Florence had been so neutered she looked more like a tabby than a bull terrier and the economist felt exalted having fulfilled his duty to his General. But in such great moral battles there could be no victors or vanquished because as soon as the Fat Controller saw that Florence had lost it, allowing the 'arrogant Black Prick' to mention the name of companies owned by the Chairman of the BBC, he pulled the interview and replaced it with a recorded programme about drunken Niagran soldiers wiping out an entire village, with the odd name of Lidiziam, after drugged-up youths had killed seven American missionaries who had only come to help their poor people.

But then at the height of his glory tragedy struck the young man as hubris led him to think that because he was an economic genius he knew more about the sociology, psychology and politics of *shopping* than his General. Niagra was chosen to host the Summit of the African Union and the General hoped to win the coveted Order of the African Spear, awarded to Heads of States who blew more than $500 million during the week of discussions/celebrations. Baggadudu's job was to convince the IMF and World Bank that this expenditure, greater than the combined budgets for education, health, housing and social welfare, would have no impact on monetary aggregates. So high was the young man's prestige that the General, in all innocence, asked him to pick up 'something simple' that he could wear to impress his colleagues with the necessity to lead lives of such exemplary humility that the suffering masses would appreciate the need for self-sacrifice in making the continent great again. And this misplaced faith was to lead to what became known in Niagran folklore as *The Parable of the Fifteen Hundred Pound Suit.*

Boosted by this mandate our young hero went about the task of procuring the *simple* suit with the same panache that he approached negotiations with his former employers, or on first dates at his *alma mater* where he had acquired the title of 'Barracuda Mark II' after the legendary Jamaican who could do the limbo dance between the spread legs of six drunken female undergraduates with one can of Schlitz balanced on his forehead and another down below. The original Barracuda was alleged to have introduced industrial strength marijuana to the campus which some blame for the obsession of more famous undergraduates with Weapons of Mass Destruction in other people's countries, especially those found to possess enormous quantities of oil. Like Dick Cheney, Barracuda dropped out of Yale but, being of a Rastafarian rather than Episcopalian persuasion, he could not become Presidential Chief of Staff, Secretary of Defence, CEO of Halliburton, Vice President or a royal pain in the ass to every other world leader but the Great Helmsman, General Daudu, his very favourite after the General pulled his country out of OPEC which Cheney said distorted free markets with narrow, self-serving, politically motivated decisions. Mustapha recalled the legend of Barracuda after reading in the Nigerian *Spicy Girls* about a Niagran superstar singer and her Rasta boyfriend who lived in a shack in the late Bob Marley's village, vowing to burn down the American Embassy in Kingston after the Defence Secretary threatened to invade the 'country with two hundred and fifty thousand troops and a coalition of the willing, and install Ahmed Chalabi as Minister of Petroleum, if your Parliament has the temerity to legalize the evil weed'.

Baggadudu first checked out Brioni suits at Rossini's and other expensive boutiques on New Bond Street, trying to visualize a *simple* General Daudu in the extraordinary selections of styles, fabrics, colours and shades. Noting the prices he then flew to Brioni's HQ in Rome where he hoped to make them an offer they could not possibly refuse. He had settled on a casual style evocative of the African savannah, part safari, part English blazer, with a touch of Texan cowboy and Argentinian polo player which would not be out of place in a Las Vegas brothel. The simplest fabric was a 50 per cent silk, 40 per cent cashmere and 10 per cent wool mix whose soft texture would soothe the General's piles, especially when highlighted by twenty-two carat gold buttons embossed with his image imposed on the map of Africa to highlight his boast to *dominate his environment*. Knowing his master's superstitions about primary colours, he chose shades ranging from *eau-de-nil* to a rich forest green, then proceeded to bargain with Brioni's finest using techniques learnt from the campaigns of Genghis Khan, Atilla the Hun and Donald Rumsfeld.

First he used the race card, pointing out that the illustrious Italian tailors could not afford to keep ignoring the 130 million black people who made Niagra the Greatest Black Power on earth. Then he appealed to their competitive spirit by pointing to the glories of their ancient city, recounting that fine Romans such as Quintus Fabianus Maximus, Cunctator and Scipio the Younger had once kicked ass in Africa, defeating the preposterous Hannibal and destroying his second rate capital, Carthage. Now the even finer Romans at Brioni could again achieve glory in Africa by out-styling the pimping Francesco Smalto who built suits for lesser African leaders in Congo, Gabon, Gambia, Togo, Malawi and the Central African Empire. Dressing the General, the Great Bull Elephant and Lion of Africa, the continent's undisputed Leader, would add feathers in their caps superior to the plumes of the Republican Guards who ponced around important public places like carnival masquerades. His proposal was that Brioni build ten suits in the shades he chose for fifteen thousand pounds in cash and the Head Tailor, proud of his schoolboy exploits in translating the ablative absolute of Virgil's *Carthago delenda est*, was thrilled to comply.

Returning to Xanadu after completing his mission, Baggadudu awaited his master's judgement with the same anticipation he had experienced when confronted with Catholic virgins at Albertus Magnus College in New Haven and was not disappointed as the General looked enraptured, viewing the shades of green he had seen in a dream after his marabout from Nwadibou predicted he would be the queen of the ball and great shining star of his own African show. This young man would go far as he understood how to obey orders, capturing his demand for *simplicity* to a 'T'. But then Baggadudu took the first step on a lethal descent of ten thousand miles, violating the first rule of Niagran protocol that *no one volunteers information to the General*. When he volunteered that the 'suits cost only fifteen thousand pounds' he mistook the General's alarm and his strangled cry of *'Each?'* as a signal that they were simply too expensive and *volunteered* further that it was for the whole fucking lot.

A man of General Daudu's coloration turning blue was a mystery to all but the experienced courtier Nasser Waddadda, who was summoned to evacuate his master to a private clinic in Bonn after the portable blood pressure monitor he kept with him showed a catastrophic rise and he could feel without looking that his haemorrhoids were inflamed. Weakly pointing out the suits to his own Karl Rove he whispered '£15,000' to which Waddadda queried *'Each?'*, his master barely managed *'No, all!'*. The master strategist showed commendable restraint because he recognized the necessity not to look *more* shocked and disgusted than his master who was trying to come to terms with his disappointment that this young man in whom he had shown such confidence had repaid his generosity by trying to kill him. *A fifteen hundred pound suit!* How could he face his colleagues who flew in tailors on chartered Concordes or Presidential 747s to build suits which captured the spirit of a poor, devastated continent, destroyed by natural calamities and the rapacity of white slave masters and colonialists? He would have nightmares, from which he would probably never wake, about Presidents Bongo, Eyadema and Sani Abacha of the hated Nigeria, dressed in million dollar suits built by Francesco

Smalto from gold and diamond thread, pointing to him and laughing – 'this is the man who said he wouldn't be caught dead in a £1,500 suit!'. Thanks to the false economy of the foolish boy he would probably have to spend an extra hundred million to be sure of the Order of the African Spear.

Because of the sterling contribution Baggadudu had made to the General's pension fund, and to rubbishing his critics at the BBC World Service and other Western media, Waddadda took the extraordinary step of not having him arrested and shot for attempting to overthrow the General, and even allowed him to collect his pre-signed letter of resignation and apology which acknowledged his failure to live up to the expectations of his Leader, and to request Jerry 'Lewis' Gotchakka, the Minister of Information, to announce his regret at accepting the resignation of one who had showed such promise. And the young fool, not wishing to play the starring role in the General's next 'coup plot' drama, left the country in disgrace the same day to become the lone dark star at the Yale School of Management where he spent his time in abject melancholy dreaming of the Glory that might have been.

Liberals who feel sympathy for his tragic fate should reflect that this was not his first failure to understand the General's sense of values. On his return from a trip to the City of London, General Daudu had admired Baggadudu's collection of Ted Baker safari shirts that he picked up in the circular fronted little shop with its pastel blue ambience on the High Street as he drove to fuck a young American analyst at Goldman Sachs who lived next door to a decrepit rock star on Richmond Hill. He had *volunteered* then that they 'cost only £89.99 each' and obviously misinterpreted the General turning completely white as a personality switch in his alleged multipolar disorder syndrome. As a renowned international scholar he had an obligation to do the research which had already been written up in volume three of the magisterial *The African*

Leader's Transcendent Dress Sense by Professor Sterling Payden of Harvard University, the foremost Africanist in the West:

> The African leader has not caught the Western disease of believing that he should descend to the level of his subjects. Nowhere is this truer than in the African leader's sartorial evolution, which follows the course of nature where the peacock inspires his inferiors with his glorious displays of tropical sunsets. Unlike the degenerate Westerner, the African leader does not hide his plumage, or conceal himself in the disguise of mediocrity. Outdressing the Leader, or especially his First Lady, is accepted as an act of lèse-majesté worthy of capital punishment, a denial of the rank order created by God. The poor African has no desire to replicate misery by wishing to see his leader dressed in foul rags. As the veil between God and his subjects the African Leader has an obligation to look like a million dollars, to let his people transcend their poverty by identifying with a Vision of splendour second only to the Almighty in the sumptuary flamboyance of his attire.

Thus, despite his personal sympathy for the young man's tragedy, Mustapha had to reflect that Baggadudu set back the work on his *magnum opus* by months. While Sophocles, Aeschylus, Shakespeare and Goethe created heroes who destroyed themselves through tragic flaws, they had not had the misfortune to know these people personally. Oedipus and Faust may have learnt wisdom through suffering but Baggadudu should have accepted from the very beginning that *no one knows more than the General*. Far from ending with wisdom, his suffering continued with the knowledge that he was stuck in a Connecticut limbo, while lesser Niagrans accompanied the General on triumphal state visits to Washington, London, Paris, Bonn and Beijing.

So Mustapha's quest for a suitable hero shifted to Richard 'Mr Dick' Burton who earned the name 'Spear' from the instrument he used to fish the head of Patrice Lumumba out of the acid vat in the Belgian mining company for display in his secret society at his *alma mater* in New Haven. As Chairman and majority shareholder of the Burton Holly Corporation which controlled oil, construction, pharmaceutics, arms production, agriculture and holdings in every strategic sector of the world economy, he had more power than any president. Here was a hero worthy of Ayn Rand, Hegel's World Historical Individual who collapsed the difference between the Idea and Concrete Reality, the Nietzschean Superman who transcended the weakness of the human all too human.

But the true Hero without the hint of a tragic flaw was surely Justice Nafiu Saleh, father of the man he was waiting to apprehend at the border. What other African man would have the guts to sentence his only son to death *in absentia* and order his name to be put on top of Niagra's TEN MOST WANTED? Even more remarkable, he condemned his pregnant daughter-in-law to the same fate, effectively causing the end of a line that had lasted a thousand years. When he went for his briefing, Mustapha expected to see a grieving and broken man but was almost frozen by the cool of this courteous gentleman of the old school who was just ushering out a lawyer from the American Supreme Court who had come to consult on military tribunals of which Justice Saleh was the world authority. He appeared apologetic and solicitous for the task that faced him, having to arrest a man who had abandoned his leader, his God, family and nation to pursue atheism, materialism and secularism. He warned that his son had become so evil that he had adopted the Sufi mysticism of his useless uncle Aminu Saleh which allowed him to shape shift into the little people like they had in Cameroon. Had Nietzsche met Justice Saleh he would never have spoken of the Magnificent Blond Brute, the blue-eyed Nordic warrior but of a sleek ebony fighter who, in a thousand battles, emerged triumphant.

Mustapha's reverie was broken by the roar of the white refrigerated truck with the black skull and crossbones which crossed the border every Monday, Wednesday and Friday. It belonged to Green and Branch, a subsidiary of Burton Holly, and transported toxic waste into lawless and corrupt Nigeria because of General Daudu's respect for the environment. Leftists who claimed the truck belonged to the supposed 'Disposal Units' which got rid of the bodies of rioters and coup plotters lived up to their reputation for lying. How could any sane person believe that Burton Holly would transport frozen bodies for medical dissections, juju concoctions or organ transplants by private hospitals in the UK?

If the decrepit petty trader in his frayed kaftan had been able to look up, rather than concentrating with such intensity on each spot he placed his stick, he might have wondered why the man with the delicate artistic hands was displaying a smile of such self-satisfaction, an almost beatific vision. Mustapha was thinking of what Doc Holliday would have done to such a man in the time before he, Mustapha, had been posted to the border as a liaison when the Special Forces were at the height of their paranoia. On the rare occasions when he loosed himself from his ear-harness, the Doc had explained why he treated everyone crossing the border as a potential Al-Qaeda terrorist: 'Look, Mustapha, nothin' personal, you understand. You know you're not one of 'em but if I was one and knew how the white man treated my folks the past five hundred years, I would want to kill every fucking redneck I come across. So when I see one of 'em my first instinct is self-defence. I must kill him before he kill me.' Patiently Mustapha had explained to the Doc that not all nappy hair was proof of Al-Qaeda, and now he seemed almost nonchalant about unsmooth facial hair.

In a way Mustapha wished this had been the man they were looking for, the renegade son of Justice Nafiu Saleh, 'Comrade' Rabiu Nafiu, alias 'Robert Nesta', 'John Lennon', and a host of other stupid foreign names to make his father, the General and all the Men in Black hunting him look fucking stupid. The idiot, Rabiu, reading too many second-rate novels about the apartheid Bureau of State Security and Portuguese PIDE, would expect muscle-brained goons slamming his face against the metal border fence while the shackles and 'crucifixion' machines cut into his wrists and ankles and the smell of flesh scorched with high voltage electricity was dispersed by screams so inhuman it made him clam up, incapable of telling the truth. Instead, as a fellow man of letters, Mustapha's first move would be to ensnare him in some narrative from which he could not escape. Greene's *The Power and the Glory* was almost ideal, with the relentless *mestizo* playing the role of nemesis like Iago, or the Anglo-Saxon Grimm in Faulkner's *Light in August*, pursuing their prey with greater efficiency than any predator on the great plains of Africa. He was not ashamed to take on the role of the irredeemably hateful yellow man with his incisors like fangs, tracking the anti-hero Whisky Priest whose flaws were painted so sympathetically they could be taken for medals of honour. The important thing was that, like the *mestizo*, he got his man in the end. He always did, even when they didn't know it *was* the end. As he imagined the man coming level he could feel the American's hatred rising like the dust and the mist to envelop him but Mustapha turned his head away because, in his mind, the rank smell of stale sweat, an unwashed penis and slept-in clothes was already too much for his delicate, artistic constitution, even with the protection of Chanel's *Allure pour homme*.

As he looked at Nigel's rucksack while he embraced the two other Special Forces men from the truck, Mustapha once again marvelled at the technical efficiency of the world's only superpower: designed by another subsidiary of Burton Holly, the thick outer skin was made from material designed for the prototype Jupiter Icy Moons Orbiter to survive the heat and pressure of the colossal planet, with thirty-two megabytes of memory to keep hamburger buns at ideal humidity, atmospheric pressure, and a temperature of 76 degrees Fahrenheit. But its pièce de résistance was the vacuum-packed, genetically modified sausage which resurrected itself, grew its own bun, and smothered itself in ketchup, relish, onions and *American* mustard when exposed to the atmosphere and tropical sunlight.

THE FAKE AGONY OF A CROSSOVER DRESSER

Rabiu refused the temptation to feel elated because the man he was presenting to the Man in Black waiting for him at the border was too old, too exhausted and beyond care to afford such emotional luxuries. The weight of four wives and twenty children, of irregular income, taxes, tributes, humiliation by officials at every turn, and the demands of religion, all the pain a character in his position was expected to suffer, should have reduced fear to submission and resignation. His wife Kikelomo had always teased him about his lack of imagination, his inability to put himself in the place of others, to *act*, rather than just *be*. That was true and, despite the advice of Captain Jaja and Isaac to empty his mind before he confronted his would-be interrogators, he thought of her now, how she had acquired the reputation of being outrageous and uncontrollable because she had the courage to act out what she knew or felt to be true or right. Even telling stories to their children involved such a metamorphosis they always ended up seeing the characters she portrayed rather than their own mother. Jaja, a trained interrogator himself, had cautioned that the best ones – and they put the very best at the border to catch so-called 'intellectuals' – could get into your head and see the man you were trying to hide. But Kikelomo was like gravity, a force of nature, and he could as easily get her out of his mind as fly above the Niagran and American he saw like ghosts across the empty stretch before the border post.

But in other respects he had obeyed Jaja and Isaac to the letter. He still held his cap in hand so they could see the grey of him all over, from the shivering hair and frosted eyebrows, his yellowing, slept-in clothes and cracked plastic sandals which blended with the gold of the dust and mist incandescent in the morning sun. He had not slept for twenty-four hours and the all-night journey on the back of the sputtering Vespa had drained him of years of his life, his spirit and upright stance. He left the dead insects among the dust and bits of leaves in the whitened tufts of his hair to convince them he was a mere floating piece of nature, detritus of a harsh, unforgiving world, not a man, husband, father, or friend with cares beyond the fate the Almighty had assigned him. The pains in his joints were not just of weariness but of age and the stick was no prop but needed to keep him from succumbing to the drag of earth and the overwhelming temptation to weep. But as a Marxist-Leninist he knew the image he was projecting was due to concrete, material conditions of physical fatigue, not some inner artistic spirit which allowed 'method actors' to assume the persona of whomever they chose. On the far side he could barely make out the green and white of the Nigerian flag on the twisted pole, fluttering like a wrinkled leaf above the featureless prefabricated gunmetal buildings. But he could not afford to see that far ahead.

Without looking up he could sense the eyes of the American on him, full of hate but also fear, and imagined the strains of Big Bill Lester, Floyd Tillman, Darryl Worley and Ernest Tubb being pumped into his one ear like 'whites' into the Jem Hadar of *Star Trek: Deep Space 9* whose mission was to bring death and destruction into all corners of the galaxy in defence of the great Dominion.

Like these synthetic sci-fi warriors the Special Forces seemed mass-produced and tailor-made, machines of war which made war necessary, with their uniforms of pony-tails, t-shirts, jeans, hi-tech gadgets, surfeit of weaponry and addiction to the beat of honky-tonk and the Redneck Anthem. In the outskirts of empire such as Afghanistan, Niagra, Nigeria and São Tomé they could feel free, unencumbered by the need for uniforms or codes of conduct, their genius for terror and racism liberated and allowed to bloom. How would he feel after days and nights in a hot metal container with unending strobe lights, hallucinogenic drugs, and pumped-up volumes of Toby Keith's 'Courtesy of the Red, White and Blue'?

But it was the Niagran dressed like Will Smith in *Men in Black* who interested Rabiu more. This one was typical, unlike his classmate Joseph Mammamia, the perverted genius whose craving for security and stability meant that he constantly switched sides, ever in search of the centre of power. This Will Smith lacked the edges of the gifted Joseph who changed ideological coat at the slightest change of tack but used the same slogans to proclaim his eternal loyalty. This one was one-dimensional, typical of the children of the *nouveaux riches* whose only loyalties were to designer clothes, Jeffrey Archer, James Hadley Chase and reality television. He remembered the ones in university who might as well have worn uniforms, with sunglasses all hours of the day, Calvin Klein *eau de toilette*, Dennon stereos and an obsession with Chinese food, considered a status symbol because it was expensive and scarce.

Although Jaja warned him about negative thinking and Kikelomo would have killed him if she knew he contemplated failure, he could not help fretting about what would happen if those two got hold of him. If they let him pass he still had to go through the hell of Nigerian Customs and Immigration which would strip him of everything of value but he still tried to balance the 'choice' between the music of Martina McBride and accelerated disco lights and the attentions of his countryman who would be particularly solicitous when he learnt that he was not just a hated 'radical' but also a member, however rebellious, of one of the detested 'Old Families', the so-called 'Feudal Oligarchy'. Comrades without his connections who had gone to SS Headquarters for a 'chat' spoke of being 'softened up' by 'Idi Amin', 'Mutt' and 'Jeff' and other specialists who asked no questions but tried to live up to their American-inspired mottos: IF FORCE DOESN'T WORK YOU'RE NOT USING ENOUGH! And LET THEM HATE US AS LONG AS THEY FEAR US!

It was after this baptism that the 'convict' graduated to the smooth operators like this 'Will Smith', whose smell of new silk and after-shave masked the stench of blood, electrocuted flesh and soiled clothing, while they administered American-designed psychometric tests after watching the softening up process through two-way mirrors. He had escaped relatively lightly in his own previous sessions because he suspected the gorillas were too scared to inflict lasting injury on the prodigal son of the Hanging Judge. He remembered now feeling embarrassed that he had nothing to show for his sojourns in the dungeons below the Rock Castle and was even tempted to invent battle scars and traumatic memories until Kikelomo, whose friend was married to the boss of the interrogators, told him the list of questions he had been asked. He was less apologetic now that he would face nemesis naked and alone, as his father must have signalled his abandonment by placing his name on Niagra's TEN MOST WANTED list. 'Will Smith' would be all over him, full of hate and envy for what his father's money could not buy, perhaps willing to get his hands dirty by coming in at the softening up stage. This possibility was enhanced by the incident last night when they had stopped to pee and heard his former comrade 'Vladimiro' being interviewed by the Nightingale from the BBC World Service from his luxury hotel in Davos where he had been sponsored to the World Economic Forum by the Soros Foundation, which had made the remarkable discovery that Marxist-Leninists of the most extreme variety made the best capitalists. Vladimiro said he was sure Rabiu's father had hidden him in a safe house owned by Burton Holly because, despite his radicalism, dialectical materialism showed that 'blood was thicker than water but money was thicker than blood'. The BBC presenter was called 'Nightingale' after comics among the Men in Black swore that her voice was more effective with the truly tough cases than explosive cotton buds.

He would have to add all this to his manuscript, for which he had hoped to sign a contract with Heinemann, after one of their editors had praised it for its 'rigorous commitment to objectivity, its admirable balance between conflicting forces, its understated moral conclusions, and the quiet potency of its depiction of the undemocratic leaders ruling the author's nation'. He had planned to write his novel in Fulfulde when the Central Committee of his party had decreed the 'Indigenous Language Policy' to rouse the masses against imperialism. But he found that the language had no words for 'dyspeptic Vietnamese pot-bellied pig', 'kleptocratic parvenu', or 'megalomaniac psychopath whose self-awarded medals weigh more than his brain'. Educated Fulani women had no time to read the language as, like all other rich Niagran women, they were so obsessed with reality television that when the latest version of *Survivor* ended there was a massive run on Prozac and the General had to promise further concessions to Burton Holly to get emergency supplies so that the cowardly Nigerians would not choose the moment to attack when his entire officer corps was demobilized by the sexual depression of their wives. The men were even worse because they waited in agony for the state-of-the-art pornographic videos from the small Finnish town of Ivalo, involving frolicking Danish *au pairs*, a frisky moose with enormous antlers and an acrobatic Dachshund called Fred. And the nomads who spoke the language were still illiterate despite the billion dollars spent since Andrew Martian, in the fifth volume of the General's *Autobiography*, proved he was a pure Fulani, who could trace his ancestry back through the Prophet Mohammed and every other important person in history to the Pharaoh Akhenhaten who invented monotheism. By the time Rabiu decided he could not write in Fulfulde the Communist Party of Niagra had received a grant from the Soros Foundation and decided that English was the best language in the new global order.

But things had changed at Heinemann after 11 September 2001 when they brought in the 'Chancellor' to exercise tighter fiscal control on inflated hallucinogenic images and he rejected Kikelomo's manuscript *Revelations in Paradise* as 'unsuitable for schools and colleges', on the grounds that it 'portrayed incest, torture, lesbianism, marijuana smoking, cannibalism, promiscuity and childbirth out of wedlock', despite the positive assessments of three readers, one of whom argued that 'the writer has the potential to make the first genuine advance in African literature since the tragic early death of Dambudzo Marechera, author of *Black Sunlight*'. When the Chancellor came to interview potential authors in Xanadu, he had come to Rabiu's office, where the sight of his beard seemed to unnerve him, though it was a few hairs short of Osama's.

'You know the Queen is sent a copy of our books, Mr Nafiu', the Chancellor began, flipping through the pages of his manuscript. 'How do you think she would feel, surrounded by her corgis while she eats cornflakes from her royal tupperware, to read this passage about a man she entertained at a state banquet with her best claret, as old as her husband, and caramelized toad-in-the-hole on a bed of cherry pips: "despite ten billion dollars in stolen funds and millions spent on braids and medals, the

General remains what he has always been since his conception in the rainforests of nearby Cameroon, a dyspeptic Vietnamese pot-bellied pig whose snout is never far from the national trough". The Chancellor had looked up and for a moment Rabiu feared he was going to check his beard for evidence of Al-Qaeda.' He had been rescued by a plumpish lady from Harvill Press who swore that not *all* English publishers were so many chapters short of a bestseller, and that she would consider his manuscript if he was willing to 'Ali Campbell it up a bit,' and write in a language even more obscure than Fulfulde.

Just then Rabiu was woken from his reverie by the roar of the Green and Branch refrigerated truck with the black skull and crossbones, which government and Burton Holly spokesmen claimed transported toxic wastes into lawless and corrupt Nigeria, but which he knew was part of the 'Disposal Units' which collected the bodies of political prisoners, demonstrators and alleged 'coup plotters', so that in case the General and his American friends fell out and he was hauled before the International Court of Justice, there would be no evidence to link him and Burton Holly to crimes against humanity.

The American Special Forces soldier approached his comrades who stepped from the truck and did high fives, releasing strains of Roy Acuff's *Great Speckled Bird* which had the same effect as the sound of the Nightingale and exploding cotton buds on his eardrums. He congratulated himself on his acting ability as the Americans concentrated on their sizzling, mustard-smothered hotdogs and 'Will Smith' hid behind *The Power and the Glory* as Rabiu stumbled past them through no-man's-land toward the chaotic Nigerian border.

BOOK I:
LEGEND

BOB MARLEY'S SURREAL CONCEPTION OF THE 'REAL'

'Bob Marley' sketched the faces into his notebook as if his life depended on it and, as the faces gained life, he tugged at his locks or stroked the green, black and gold of the tam perched on his head like the crown of the King of Kings and Lord of Lords, Elect of God, Conquering Lion of the Tribe of Judah, His Imperial Majesty, Ras Tafari, Haile Selassie I. He was trying to capture the pictures of NIAGRA'S ONE HUNDRED MOST WANTED pasted on the wall of the biggest post office in Black Africa, to paint them on the curved ceiling of the rotunda of the newly liberated Rock Castle, replacing the frescoes of the General's state visit to Graceland. This had been a resounding success, unlike the visit to Madame Tussaud's which almost led to war between Niagra and the United Kingdom over the ownership of the Elvis waxwork and was saved only by the diplomatic intervention of the Duke of Edinburgh. Those who could not fit on the ceiling would be painted onto the walls to cover the Playboy bunnies drawn by General Daudu's favourite conceptual artist who was flown in each month from London after he had achieved great fame in transforming High Art into Elephant Shit and been lauded by Lord Scraatchy.

Bob Marley lit up his sketches with whiffs of the

sweetest *sensimila* from Brotherman's private supply which
flowed into his brain like a stream of pure, fresh honey,
imagining the intense, electric colours of the luminous
paints he would use to make them live again. Joy and the
dope killed the pain in his side from the spear point of
the Roman soldier and the Second World War bullet in
his leg from the rifle of the mad policeman. From his late
father, the greatest sign painter in the history of the
country, he had inherited a little paint box with the red
slogan, 'more real than the real, more human than human'
and he remembered the slogan even after the box was lost.

The removal of Daudu's government, which had made
smoking the sacred weed a capital offence, added to his
sense of freedom and well-being as each puff lifted him
up to heaven, almost as high as Nine Mile, to visit the
tomb of the greatest Reggae Superstar of all time. He was
wearing the first tam his woman had knitted him and it
hung loosely over his locks, caressing his intense copper-
coloured forehead with a softness that was light and warm
in the wind blowing above the square at the centre of
Xanadu, the capital city of the most populated, most
vibrant Black Country on earth.

They were still living on the street then, long before
Ahmed bought her the machine to make woolly hats which
she sold in the main market to provide a roof over their
heads in the compound of the meat seller, his mentor,
whose wisdom saved them from the horrors of the sulking
capital, crouched to pounce on the unwary and undead.
When he closed his eyes to let the weed create his new
world, he could see her fingers moving like delicate, cocoa
brown magic wands, coiling the green, gold and black
threads into a new creation for the religion of Jah, Ras
Tafari. If he stopped breathing, closed his ears to the sound
of the city and shrunk his skin to block its touch in the
wind, he could feel those soothing fingers on his cheeks,
warming his heart and mind as they crouched under old
plastic and cardboard in the shadow of the General

Daudu Flyover. And he never ceased to wonder that among the odours of old sweat, stale piss, shit and rotting carcasses, she still managed to have the freshness of new rain on buds of yellow bellflowers when the timid sun emerges to light, droplets still clinging like glass beads to the leaves of fever grass. Somewhere in the depths of his mind he heard her hum the opening lines of Aretha's 'Natural Woman'.

Before the soldiers came to her village, Agbani had grown up with a family who loved her and, when offered the meat seller's hospitality, had found it easy to leave the streets to provide a home for herself and Bob Marley. She had a history, a legend, she knew who she was. After her doomed hope of bearing children, she wished for nothing more than to bring his mind home from the street, freeing it of its recurrent nightmares to give him the tranquillity that surpassed understanding, of being at peace with himself and the world. When she saw his brows knotted in anguish she was always there with the soothing hum of 'one good thing about music, when it hits you feel no pain'. But she never pressed him to stay at home, because he had belonged to the street so long, it was now part of him, just as the brown dove belonged to the air, or the crayfish to the rivers in the lands from which her ancestors were driven. As long as he could paint those images so full of life and the living she was content. How could she press him when even she, who had done so well in school while her parents were still alive, had to be guided by the gentle wisdom of the meat seller as to who he really was?

The man told her of Bob Marley's 'father' who found him in front of a mosque, a sign painter and righteous man called Revelation because of his striking depictions of flaming lions, eagles, vultures, horses, griffons and the Great Whore – based on General Daudu's moon-faced, fat-assed, midwife mistress – which still adorned the backs and sides of a multitude of buses and lorries all over the country, years after he had been shot while painting the doors of a new hotel by soldiers chasing students demonstrating against the appointment of the General's illiterate First Lady as Chancellor of the University of Niagra, the biggest in Black Africa. Trouble had started when the students found out that because of the woman's illiteracy, Nasser Waddadda had hired a body double, an African-American woman trying to make it big in country and western music, to read the acceptance speech for her award of the Doctor of Letters and Humanities (*Honoris Causa*).

Revelation had brought up little Bob Marley, treating the foundling as a gift of God, the child he and his wife had strived in vain to produce for years. He said that Bob Marley was a prodigy who could whistle tunes he had heard only once, or draw, from memory, the most complicated picture he had seen his father painting, but he had a problem with words. When he copied a rearing black horse with flames rushing from a mouth red as fresh palm oil, he reproduced the accompanying words as just another picture. *Leave Am For God, God Dey, Man No Be Wood, Monkey Dey Work, Baboon Dey Chop*, and *Khaki No Be Leder* were just like the claws of a lion, or an eagle's beak, without reference to anything beyond the signs. To teach Bob to read, Agbani needed to have him hear the sound of the words then link them with the pictures in his head by drawing them as his mother had done when teaching him to speak.

That is how he learnt to 'read' the posters of NIAGRA'S ONE HUNDRED MOST WANTED he now perused, linking their harshly drawn faces to their crimes and the rewards for 'information leading to their capture'. They all, according to their posters, had 'thick lips, untidy beards, broad noses, wide brown eyes, a good set of teeth'. He had already finished sketching Ngũgĩ wa Thiong'o, Jack Mapanje, Ken Saro-Wiwa and a few other foreign Africans added to the list on the advice of Nasser Waddadda who told the

General 'it will make you look good with the new American administration'. His reason being that the men were *'shifty, bearded, bug-eyed and foreign'*, all characteristics of Al-Qaeda which showed that they posed a clear and present danger to the re-election of George 'Dubya' and the moral certainties of Tony Blair. By showing the will and resolve to screw them properly, Niagra would receive loads of money as reward for the great crusade against terrorism and would not suffer sanctions when they went ahead with plans to wipe out another six villages in the oil-rich Delta, *even if they kidnapped the President's mother.* In response to the American Ambassador's threat to 'invade the country with two hundred and fifty thousand troops and a coalition of the willing' the General gave firm assurances that there were no plans to snatch the old lady at this point in time as it was not in the security interests of the Great Black Republic of Niagra.

Bob Marley's eyes scrunched up as he stared at 'Fela', the most celebrated armed robber Niagra had ever produced whose picture had remained in its position of honour years after another Fela had been captured, tried and shot in the National Stadium, before a mob of 100,000 driven to a frenzy by giant Dennon loudspeakers blasting the latest offerings of Garth Brooks and Floyd Tillman. There were rumours that the executed Fela was not the real one but a man who had asked his friend to turn him in to gain the reward for his starving wife and children, only for the million dollars to be collected by 'Slick Willy', the General's brother, a part-time actor who worked in the claims office, and the friend threatened with the same fate as an accomplice if he pursued the case.

Agbani had told him how the armed robber had earned the name 'Fela' and it was then that he began to wonder who *he* was, how he came to be called 'Bob Marley' in a country where men with dreadlocks were considered lunatics and the Reggae Superstar was banned in favour of country and western stars like Martina McBride and countless praise singers who sang in local languages and used plenty of drums and other traditional instruments to eulogize the Great Leader, the Unique Miracle of the Century, the Margaret Thatcher of Africa, the recently removed Life President, His Excellency Abdu-Salaam bin-Sallah-ud-Deen bin Sani-Ibrahim al-Daudu. According to the most authoritative version told by the meat seller, Bob Marley's mother was Aishetu, a beautiful, fair-skinned secondary-school girl, daughter of a powerful aristocratic Chief Judge from the North of the country who was the General's eyes and ears among the judicial barons of the Capital City. Aishetu fell madly in love with her classmate at the elite Federal College, an assistant in his uncle's shop which sold both *original* and locally-made spares for Peugeot and Toyota cars and pick-up trucks. When she became pregnant she fled her father's house before he found out and sent his orderlies to kill her and her infidel defiler. She lived with Chukwu in his little room above the shop while her stomach grew, but his uncle threw them out when he feared that Nafiu Saleh, the Hanging Judge, would avenge his disgrace by shutting his shop and driving him out of town. Besides he had become fed up with the loud reggae music and the constant, pungent smell of the foul weed, which Chukwu claimed was smoke from made-in-China mosquito coils.

As both young people had taken the precaution of helping themselves to what they considered deserved portions of their family wealth, they managed to survive the rest of the pregnancy and the first months of Bob's life by living frugally, except for the generous supply of the herb their religion demanded. Little Bob was a wonderful child but did not appear entirely normal – while he seemed completely aware of what went on around him, he hardly responded to flashing lights or loud noises and refused to look you in the eye. Then came the shock of the real Bob Marley's death and they were faced with the moral dilemma of whether to stay at home and take care of their beloved son or fulfil their religious duty by going to Nine Mile to pay homage to the great reggae singer, number one Disciple of the King of Kings and Lord of Lords, Haile Selassie I.

Young Bob Marley had seen pictures of the multitudes at the funeral, and searched for the mother and father who had wrapped him in a thick bathtowel and left him with the note saying 'Respect. Please take good care of little Bob Marley.' He imagined them in the Caribbean paradise now, enjoying fish from the sea, herbs from the fields, and wild peppers all colours of flame, and always the haunting rhythms of frothing blue waves slashing the shore and returning to the sea from whence they came, for ever and ever and ever. Whenever he saw photos of Sade and her Rasta boyfriend, he thought that's how his parents would look now and often daydreamed of Sade stroking his locks and cooing in his ears 'I gave you all the love I got, / I gave you more than I could give, / This is no ordinary love.'

It was Agbani who first pointed out the striking resemblance between Fela and the great Nigerian singer, Anikulapo-Kuti and Bobby could see this now, except that the late singer did not have the biggest smile in Black Africa like his namesake. This Fela was a footballer with the Black Stallions and also a part time alto sax player with the Niagran All Stars but turned to armed robbery after he was shot in the leg by a mobile policeman, called *Kill and Go* in Niagra, who caught him in bed with the woman called the *Mother of God* because Prophet Oluwole, the disgraced evangelist whose church bordered the National Brothel, would shout at the height of their sexual ecstasy, 'Holy Mary, Mother of God, what are they doing to that poor girl'?

Unlike his fellows who preyed on the weak, Fela concentrated on government offices, preferably the most well guarded, and thrilled his audiences with the music of his *guitar boy* which sprayed the golden 7.65mm bullets like notes against the hulking armoured vehicles, the so-called 'elephants' in gunmetal. Whenever the soldiers or policemen thought they had him cornered, he would empty a box of mint-fresh $500 notes in the already congested streets, causing the greatest traffic jams in history since the fixed chariot races of Emperor Caligula.

After Fela, Agbani's favourite poster pin-up had been the Doctor her uncle told her about who had written a book called *Heroes* and was condemned by Jerry 'Lewis' Gotchakka, the General's spokesman, who said that Niagra 'was not big enough to have more than one Hero'. The only person on the 'Wanted' posters he knew personally was Brotherman, the Dean of Rastamen in Niagra, who was alleged to have taught Fela Kuti and a host of younger musicians to play the saxophone, trumpet and trombone, and the 'fusion' music which blended the rhythms of East, West and Southern Africa and the diasporan Africans in the Americas and Caribbean. He also produced on his small farm an organic herb so pure and strong musicians would stop over on their way from other African countries to concerts in Europe and America to collect the stash that made their music glow.

Bob Marley could hardly recognize his poster now, the picture was of a younger man whose eyeballs you could see because they were not yet drowned in the red of the Holy Weed. There was also one of Wole Soyinka, the Nigerian Nobel Laureate, who earned his place in the spotlight when he failed to dedicate his autobiography, *Ake*, to Salome, the General's Liberian girlfriend, although she was a twelve-year-old 'consultant' at the time of writing, providing consultancy services to relief workers and UN Peacekeepers at the old wild west Laredo Hotel in Tubmanburg. His picture was only removed after an exchange of angry diplomatic notes between the General and his Nigerian neighbour who protested that the distinguished author deserved the honour on his own country's NIGERIA'S ONE *THOUSAND* MOST WANTED list.

Suddenly Bob Marley noticed that the herb was losing its sweetness, his hands were damp and beads of cold sweat clung to his forehead, as if afraid to fall on the bare concrete frontage of the post office. This had started when they first left the street, after he got tired of waking Agbani with his nightmares and decided to live them out while awake, but had stopped after the new government told them they were *free*. His ears twitched as the sound of a siren grew out of the far distance, reminding him that above the post office, occupying the length of one side of the square, was a portrait of General Daudu, listed by the Guinness Book of Records as 'probably the biggest hoarding in the world'. Although he could reproduce the minutest detail of the illuminated, laminated medals which covered both sides of the General's Anderson and Shepherd tunic, the brilliantly polished teeth in the perpetual smile and the hint of rouge on the gigantic cheeks, he never looked up.

When the poster was first put up people appeared awed by its majesty and the General was thrilled by the American PR firm which recommended it after its great success in promoting snug-fit Pampers baby nappies. But like everything in Niagra this story had a history. Scraatchy and Scraatchy, which held the Pampers contract, had lost the Niagran account to Shille and Coulton after forgetting the General's birthday. The American firm, with the backing of the Burton Holly Corporation, not only remembered his birthday present but the E*id al-Fitr* present for Nasser Waddadda, the Easter present for Jerry Gotchakka, and the compliance officer, in accordance with Federal Anti-Discrimination statutes, insisted on presents of talismanic fetishes so animists in Daudu's administration would not feel left out. When the *Sentinel*'s Delroy Gower pointed out the cost of the poster and people began to make rude gestures, shout 'Thief!' and cover the steps with spit, plain clothes men started infiltrating the angry crowds to beat up, arrest and torture those impressed the wrong way by the Sacred Likeness of His Miraculous Highness. Now people tended to gaze at their feet as they entered the post office, although they kept their necks coiled to snap upward in salute in case they were accosted by Men in Black for not showing respect.

The other problem was the huge black birds which lined up atop the poster like the black silhouettes of Russian MIG29s, British Hawks and American F16s, which had been mothballed after the air force was implicated in an aborted coup and its pilots seconded to America to help fight the war against the Goddamn Madman Saddam of Eyerack. Serbian pilots who now flew the planes to celebrate the General's birthday used the hillside shanty towns for target practice to make up the hours they needed to keep their licences as well as celebrate the great victory of Srebenica and make space for the First Lady's housing development. Lined in ranks facing north, the birds' use of their daytime roost as a toilet facility caused rumblings about subversion in the Rock Palace and the firing squads were brought out to restore the dignity of the nation. Again crowds gathered until some were killed by ricochets or smothered in tail feathers of the birds which, like teenage girls at heavy metal rock concerts, seemed to increase in numbers in the excitement created by the full metal jackets of the MI6s and AK47s. When this did not work, Hind MI24, Alouette and Huey Blackhawk gun ships began to sweep out of the leaden skies of Xanadu to blow the shit out of their enemies and Bob Marley recalled the mushroom clouds of black wing feathers and the grey tufts from the triangular breasts rising toward the past and present gods of the General and his entourage. An air of crisis permeated the Rock Palace as the constant skirmishes with vultures were slowly destroying the poster, disgusting foreign investors and making the administration look stupid. Andersen Consulting's recommendation that they plaster it with Thames Water mixed with remnants from fish and chips shops was rejected out of hand on the grounds that it was not worth the £5 million asking price.

It was the General's enormous midwife mistress, with cheeks like binary stars and hips capable of holding the head of the Nile waters in the Mountains of the Moon, who suggested that they destroy the remnants of the old cattle market which were left on either side of the square, above which the vultures used the vantage of the giant poster like sentinels on a rocky outcrop in a Ronald Reagan cowboy movie. But, as an international statesman who recognized the imperatives of globalization and the full frontal dominance of the USA, the General knew that he could not commit an act of destruction, however benign, without consulting his allies. He therefore dispatched Nasser Waddadda to Washington. Waddadda returned with a 500 page questionnaire which requested your 'name, geo-positional co-ordinates and serial number' and read: 'If your country has enormous quantities of oil please turn to page 307' where it read: 'You are in breach of UN Resolutions regarding possession of Weapons of Mass Destruction. You will be invaded by two hundred and fifty thousand American troops and a coalition of the willing and Ahmed Chalabi will be installed as your Minister of Petroleum.' It was accompanied by a note addressed to 'My Dear Nasser' on pale yellow paper with a border of pastel blue decorated with delicate flamingo pink J-DAM bombs disguised as butterflies and signed 'from Wolfie, with all my love'.

Although Nasser Waddadda agreed that this was the most insane government since Caligula made his horse the Trent Lott of the Roman Senate and that a trained chef had to attend cabinet meetings to tell the President the difference between his Vice President, Defence Secretary and the fruitcake, he still cautioned that Niagra had to stand shoulder to shoulder and ass to ass with its great ally because if the Americans were planning to destroy the world, it was necessary to do so with style and *in the best possible taste*. An argument which the British

Prime Minister accepted 100 per cent when the General requested 150 modified Hawk Trainers to 'kill some cows which were farting up the place with huge quantities of methane gas, causing global warming and made him incline towards signing the Kyoto Protocol against the advice of Karl Rove'. Concerned about the effect of 150 planes on the regional balance of power the PM informed the Nigerians of the request of their mortal enemies next door. They promptly ordered 300 of their own. Explaining the efficacy of the balance of power to the BBC's Mad Axman, the PM said: 'Look, Jeremy, the concept *works*, if it hadn't been for that fucking Serbian student with his socialist ideas about getting a free lunch from the Archduke of Westminster, we would have had peace in our time since 1914.' Questioned further about the wisdom of extending the ranges of the 600 planes to two failed states in a volatile region the PM, overcome with moral outrage, wiped the sweat from his upper lip and snarled: 'You BBC people know that the majority of the populations of the two countries are concentrated near their common border. This includes women, children, old men and pets. The range was extended to avoid these populations of innocent people. A British Prime Minister with such exquisite moral sense could not possibly be seen to be associated with a policy resulting in the deaths of women, children, old men and pets. Come, come, Jeremy, I didn't know the Beeb had descended to such depths!'

The Serbian pilots who flew the Hawks to gain command of the skies before the cows were attacked had spent the previous night drinking single malt whiskies looted from the hotels of Dubrovnik, singing sad songs about the tragedy of their existence, and watching *Top Gun* and *Days of Thunder*. But they could not decide who should be Tom Cruise in the bovine drama about to unfold until ground control informed them that the real Tom Cruise was not much taller than a gypsy and in a chore-ographed act of triumphal suffering worthy of their ancient martyrs they crashed into each other, hoping that this act of self-sacrifice would win sympathy with international public opinion which, since that misunderstanding between the Serbian student and the grasping Archduke in Sarajevo, had come to the conclusion that Serbs were a bunch of fucking homicidal psychopaths willing to commit genocide in the time it took to assassinate a Swedish Prime Minister.

The French, brilliant in their Yves St Laurent tunics and haute couture helmets from the house of Givenchy, had prepared for battle by debating with Bernard-Henri Levy, dressed in an astonishing azure silk blouson, the existential angst of brazing a bunch of stray cows in a capital choked with hillbilly cuisine. They praised the foresight of their President for insisting that the Niagran government supply at least two French restaurants with the maximum number of Michelin stars before answering their requests for weapons of mass destruction and orchestrated the tips of their elegant Alouette helicopter blades to etch incandescent images of Baudelaire, Rimbaud and Verlaine in the leaden, tropical sky. With such heroic ambience could works of new Antoine de St Exupérys be far behind? Then horror struck as they looked down at the vision of gastronomic hell their choppers were heading for and cursed the Americans who had bought the entire Niagran general staff with hundred dollar bills stuffed into metal Samsonite suitcases to lay the most treacherous ambush in the tarnished history of modern gastronomic warfare. Their eyes almost burst from their Pierre Cardin goggles as they gazed on the biggest fast food emporium in the world, a Pizza Hut bigger than Notre Dame, a Burger King the size of the Stade Française, a Wendy's one could mistake for the French Embassy and a McDonald's so colossal that God and St Peter debated whether the arches should be taken up into Paradise since they were more golden and serene than Heaven's Gate. And so the French, defeated once more by their culinary enemies, were forced into their most humiliating retreat since that incident at Dien Bien Phu in 1954.

Once again the heroic General Daudu was forced to fight alone, providing material for at least two additional volumes in Andrew Martian's *Autobiography*, tentatively titled *No Sacred Cows*. As in his previous monumental battles against the street children, taxi drivers, pupils who refused to wear uniforms with his portrait, nurses, university students and lecturers who insulted his First Lady, doctors who refused to surrender wounded coup plotters and demonstrating harlots who refused free service to his soldiers, our hero was forced to stand alone, without a friend in the world but resolute in his solitude, which should inspire an epic poem by Jerry Gotchakka, the information minister who doubled as Poet Laureate. And so one bright, balmy morning in the middle of spring, despite lack of air cover and limited artillery fire, the brave warriors of the First Marine Commando stormed the water troughs to prevent the enemy swimming ashore while two brigades of elite Death's Head Commandos with tanks, APCs and self-propelled 155mm artillery ambushed several herds of cattle, goats and sheep, killing hundreds, capturing thousands, and barbecuing the others with Ukrainian laser-guided flamethrowers and Lee and Perrin's sauce then bulldozing the burnt bones to prepare the site for condominiums modelled on the General's hacienda complex in Fort Lauderdale. A most elegant solution which earned its author, the General's obese mistress, the highest honour of a grateful nation, the monopoly to import frozen fish from Denmark and Norway. To celebrate this revolutionary triumph in nouvelle cuisine, domestic gods and goddesses all over European and American television trumpeted the virtues of the *patina of braised cow manure drizzled with balsamic vinegar and extra virgin olive oil served with risotto and ciabatta on a bed of buckled asphalt.*

* * *

As the sound of the sirens grew Bob Marley tried to suck the juice out of the herb as fast as he could and the blood was almost bursting his eyeballs as his locks shook around his ears and neck like blooms of cats' tails. He had already chosen a thick metal cauldron filled with solid asphalt behind which to hide and was holding in as much of the smoke as he could in anticipation that it would betray his hiding place. Sometimes strangers unfamiliar with the culture of Xanadu sought shelter in the Post Office or the National Cathedral only to be chased, tear-gassed and beaten with gun butts on the very sound premise that they would not run and hide if they had nothing to hide.

He choked and gagged, swallowing the rest of the weed when he saw a medium-sized, genetically modified American pig (called Daisy, for the sake of argument) stroll like an over-eager German tourist from the passage between the Central Bank and the world's biggest McDonald's, its pink snout raised in an expectant smile as if saluting the power of the General. It must have been one of the hundreds of thousands liberated from the farms of military officers by members of the Animal Liberation Front after the change of government amid the universal celebration of Freedom. Like her namesake in *The Great Gatsby*, Daisy's voice suggested money and the GM bacon of her breed was of such exceptional purity that men in search of English or American breakfasts, like Fitzgerald's hero, Jimmy Gatz, would pursue her green light to the end of any dock. It was available to White House consumers as the *Finest All-American Back Bacon, Product of Crawford, Texas,* and from Harrods Food Hall, before the falling out with the Palace, as the *Finest English Bacon, Sold Exclusively by Harrods, Purveyors to Her Majesty, the Queen.*

All morning Bob Marley had been confused by the presence of General Daudu's picture, which had been the first to be torn down by the workers after the former Supreme Leader had flown to one of his palaces in Morocco to give his family time to recover from their trauma while his estate was being refurbished in Palm Springs. The plan had been for the National Union of Sign Painters to fill the space with heroic images of the masses and Bob Marley had been given a spot to cover with heroes from the African diaspora in the Americas, the Caribbean and Europe. As he sketched the ONE HUNDRED MOST WANTED his mind had been filled with photos of Frederick Douglass, W.E.B. Dubois, Malcolm X, Marcus Garvey, his namesake Bob Marley, Fidel Castro and other revolutionary Africans which he would use his paints to make *more real than the real, more human than human*. Now here was a spanking new photo of the General with the stench of foul-smelling adhesive. And his confusion was compounded when he heard the sirens because one of the first decrees of the Transition Government was to ban this symbol of people made mad by power.

The fastidious pig had a dainty walk like a chameleon, twisting its hips like the General's wives and mistresses who were deployed *en masse* on Independence Day and competed to see who could stay upright in the tightest skirts made from the latest, most fabulous Holland brocade by dressmakers of genius, from as far away as Nouakchott and Timbuktu, in the latest mermaid style. The torque running from the ankle joint to the cruciate ligament of the knee and then up to the hips and ass was estimated by Professor Yoram Goram of the National University to be equivalent to the gravitational pull of a black hole of three million solar masses at the centre of a whirlpool galaxy. He argued in a paper aimed at the Nobel Committee in Stockholm that while the String and Membrane Theory might be compatible with certain aspects of general relativity it failed to explain how the asses of the General's women could twist under such pressure as to defy the laws of fashion, sanity and gravity. He hid his resentment at not getting the prize and agreed with Professor Payden in his monumental work on the transcendent dress sense of the African leader that the General's wives were influenced by Stephen Hawking's *Brief History of Time*. No woman wanted to be upstaged in her dressing and African First Ladies, as the most evolved of their species, adopted Hawking's concept of singularity as the most effective means of achieving uniqueness. According to this concept, phenomena such as the Big Bang, Black Hole and J-Lo's ass defied the laws of physics, common sense and even good taste, explaining why light slowed down in the proximity of Ms Lopez's posterior so that men spent a longer time looking at hers than at an old trout like Ann Coulter's. Had he been white he would have got the science spot on *Celebrity Big Brother* where Hawking reformulated $E=MC^2$ as E=Jordan's embonpoint, M=Jenny's royal midriff and C=the cosine of the curvature of Edwina Currie's ass.

The pig had almost made it across the square when the first black armour-plated Lincoln Continental of the convoy surged into view and Bob Marley was whimpering and shaking convulsively as he tried to shrink himself behind his refuge to escape the coming rain of bullets. His sense of unease continued to rise, seeing black American cars instead of green Mercedes 500s and Humvees and Bradley Fighting Vehicles with white men in t-shirts with ponytails and beards like the Taliban instead of the crop haired, clean shaven ones in polo shirts from Israel they'd used before. The pig, like the General's women, seemed intoxicated by the scent of power and its walk became increasingly pretentious, flamboyantly exaggerated as it twisted its hips and fat ass in provocative curves and wiggles designed to make the blood of even the most sedate and considerate killer boil.

These feelings of resentment and outrage were increased by the cavalier way in which it sauntered, flaunting its blonde hair, pink skin and suggestion of blue around its eyes which smacked of an infatuation with things European and suggested an identification with

Nietzsche's 'magnificent blond brute'. How could scholars have identified this metaphor for the 'Superman' with the *lion*, an *African* animal which *slept* twenty-three hours a day and then spent the remaining hour fucking or posing for David Attenborough's wildlife programmes for the BBC when the pig was so German, all too German, a model of Teutonic efficiency and industry which *ate* twenty-three hours a day and spent the remaining hour boasting what beautiful bacon it would make?

To this porcine evocation of racial superiority was added the element of class as it was rumoured that the former 'Life President' fed his pigs with leftovers from *La Petite Maison*, the French restaurant at the Rock Palace hotel (owned by the second cousin of his third wife in partnership with the Lebanese twin brothers who organized the massacres of Sabra and Shatila) which received the coveted three stars from both Michelin and Gault Millau, confirming its status as *the finest French restaurant in Black Africa*. Selections from the menu on Valentine's Day show just how pretentious, spoilt and capable of provocation this fucking pig was:

> Brouillade de truffe noire Tuber Mélanosporum et sa salade de Nice; Trilogie de foie gras de canard des Landes, confit au chou vert cuit en terrine au Muscat; Terrine de Venaison aux coings parfumée au genièvre; Turbot de Bretagne en filet, Pied de Mouton et réduction de jus de viande; Filet de boeuf de Salers épais, à la façon Rossini, sauce truffe; jambonette de grenouilles à la purée d'ail et au jus de persil; and Noisette de chevreuil d'Alsace façon Rossini, galette de Polenta à la farine de châtaigne. [Editor's Note: There is also an excellent English menu, from which we recommend: Caramelized Frog, Wild Liquorice, Bizarre Salad, Orange Vinaigrette; Dory with Almond Aromas, Basmati Rice, Sour Caramel baked on a Fier Stone; and Langoustines, Candied Grapefruit Rinds, Virtual Eucalyptus Semolina.]

Discerning readers may legitimately ask what so many pigs were doing in a country where 50 per cent of the population were Moslems and 99 per cent of the rest hated this filthy animal almost as much as they did the General. When Congress passed the African Growth and Opportunity Act the Americans generously offered the African superpower the opportunity to export centrifuges for enriching uranium, components for the Jupiter Icy Moons Orbiter, Osama-proof pacemakers for the VP's ticker, or pork products.

Since Niagra had systematically dismantled its industrial capacity and imported toothpicks from China, refined petroleum products from Ivory Coast and used ladies' underwear from Thailand and the Philippines, it wisely chose to export streaky bacon, a favourite of the American Defence Secretary who threatened to 'invade your country with 250,000 American troops and a coalition of the willing, and install Ahmed Chalabi as your Minister of Petroleum' after the Canadian Prime Minister ventured that Breton clams with sun-dried tomato might possibly have less cholesterol than the American bacon, tomato and lettuce sandwich with pickle, relish and mayo.

At the same time a huge schism had arisen among Evangelical Christians about whether Viagra was God's answer to their prayers that the Congress have a permanent Republican majority so that the Party would rule for a thousand years, at which point the Iraq Survey Group would find Don Rumsfeld's Weapons of Mass Destruction, signalling the end of time and the beginning of Armageddon, when it would be okay to fuck the French and all the other liberal, Osama-loving queers of Old Europe and beatify Ted Bundy, Rush Limbaugh and Kenneth Starr.

But the ecclesiastically more conservative faction, represented by the *National Review* and the *New Republic*, argued that while Viagra was American and therefore divine, using it sent the wrong signal to liberals who could argue that they were not satisfied with the equipment God gave them. The second cousin of Andrew Card's mother-in-law's best friend said that Charlton Heston argued persuasively that when God ordered Republicans to 'Go forth, multiply and replenish the House and Senate,' he didn't say to use a fucking calculator.

A more *natural* solution was the humble pig, entirely created by God without the help of Mr Darwin, which had a corkscrew dick, increasing its sexual coefficient of efficiency, and resulting in divinely sanctioned multiple orgasms of fifteen minutes' duration each. In addition, since the President said that 'those who are not with us are against us', it would be easy to identify friends by the number of pigs they raised since the Al-Qaeda faggots would not want a bunch of fucking pigs shitting on their prayer mats, *would they?* And thus it came to pass that Niagran military officers were required to own pig farms before they could be promoted above the rank of Captain.

Christian security men in the convoy whose salaries had not been paid for a year and who could not, therefore, afford to buy a helping of *Noix de St Jacques blanches d'Erguy, fondue de poireaux perpetuels* or *Hedge Woundwort Soup, Iced Wilted Eschalottes* or *Hint of Back Bacon* from *La Petite Maison*, saw the flamboyant posturing of the pig as a racist and class-based provocation and, unmoved by its supposed aristocratic lineage, opened fire. But the pig's teutonic mind had absorbed Heisenberg's Uncertainty Principle at the quantum level, allowing it to be in two places at the same time and avoid the bullets by wriggling free of its destiny.

And this provoked the Moslem snipers on the roof of the Central Mosque who, not understanding the two-timing, double-spacing of the pig at the subatomic level, thought the Secret Service men were letting it live to defile their space, and fired into the convoy, drawing cannon and shell fire from American Bradley Fighting Vehicles which accidentally landed in the French embassy where the diplomats had just sat down to a light meal of *shoulder of lamb with raisins, vegetable tajine, lettuce heart with lemon, cheese, apricot sorbet and red fruit,* to be washed down with a *Pouilly Fume 1998* and *Chateau Latour 1988.*

Snipers atop the National Cathedral took umbrage at the fire from the mosque, seeing it as religious discrimination and they too opened fire, outraging the Special Republican Guards in the barracks surrounding the Rock Palace who thought AK47s and M16s were for sissies and tried their hand at bacon making with lethal, egg-shaped RPGs. Meanwhile American Desert Hawk Unmanned Aerial Vehicles circling overhead spotted a potential Al-Qaeda target on the route. Professor Herzovogina, in her ground breaking *Fuzzy Wuzzy Wuzn't Fuzzy Wuz He?* the bible of the Special Forces in Africa, had argued that Al-Qaeda could always be recognized by their fuzzy beards and, these images being fuzzy, Black Hawk helicopters and Warthog gunships were called in to level the target with Hellfire missiles, 20mm cannon, and .50 calibre machine gun bullets. The firing went on for five hours and when it ended even the ashes were vaporized. Although the Niagran *Sentinel* would later claim that the 'enemy' were sixty-seven orphans heating water for their baths in the building, the American Secretary of Defence was smiling as he showed the fuzzy satellite images on the Fox Network, later joking on the *Tonight Show* when Letterman showed the list of 'Ten Things You Didn't Know about the Al-Qaeda Beard', the first being that it didn't look like Wole Soyinka's.

Bob Marley closed his eyes to douse the flashes of fire, tightened his earlobes to blot out the staccato of machine guns, and shrunk his body down to the size of the smallest atom to ward off the eyes and full metal jacketed 7.65mm shells of the assorted killers. But the inflationary power of the weed expanded this one atom into one hundred billion galaxies of one hundred billion stars each, in a parody of Stephen Hawking's interpretation of the

Big Bang and speculative theory of the role of black holes in the formation of spiral galaxies and the First Lady's indomitable ass. Then when the universe of light and sound reached the outer limits of infinity it collapsed under the force of its own gravity and its molecules became peppers and tomatoes and Bob Marley found himself collapsed in his own sweat on the cold concrete, a victim of the primordial slime, with not an atom intact.

Long after the final car had passed and the last bullet sounded he peeped from behind the cauldron and saw the children fighting the brown mange-ridden dogs with ribs sticking out and cawing vultures with wings raised in salute for the flattened carcass on the asphalt smouldering from the friction of hundreds of speeding tyres and tons of armour plate. Bacon-making at its finest, which, due to the powers of the WTO in hijacking Third World inventions through the TRIPS, might one day grace the food halls of Harrods, Fortnum and Mason and celebrity TV shows. In the old days he might have been there with his *Outkastes* fighting with the children for their meal of the day but even then he had refused to eat the filthy pig, in accordance with the rules of Jah. As the last child fled with an ear [Editor's Note: No connection to Shakespeare's 'silk purse from a sow's ear'.] and was chased by a pride of whining dogs, the vultures surrounded the spot, silent as the spent bullets littering the square, as if paying tribute to the not-yet-dead. *This was no ordinary pig.*

He shivered when he saw the white truck with the black skull and crossbones which they said captured children for adoption in America. Across the square was a smaller poster of a man, polished brown pipe held casually near his open, smiling mouth, advertising the 'Black Gold' from General Daudu's farms. It was Slick Willy, his younger brother who played him in the twenty-four part series of his early life, adapted from Volume III of Andrew Martian's *Autobiography* and sponsored by McDonald's, the Lone Star Bakery and Dr Pepper Cola. The huge caption above

his walnut brow read 'Put It In Your Pipe and Smoke It!'
Bob Marley's eyes were fixed on Slick Willy's smile and
he did not notice when the vultures took flight at the
approach of a lone Humvee blaring Toby Keith's 'Courtesy
of the Red, White and Blue' like explosions on the Fourth
of July from gunmetal speakers big as the fucking world.
Besides Bob Marley's rhythms were pounding inside his
skull to kill the memory of the wounds in his side and
leg: 'One good thing about music, / When it hits, you feel
no pain.'

TONE PAINTINGS OF A MAN OF YELLOW

When Revelation found the child outside the Bullrush Hotel next to the Holy Trinity Cathedral it was wrapped so tight in the thick white towel it was unable to move its limbs. It was very early in the morning, the mist had not yet risen and there was dew on the baby's forehead like beads on a new vine, its eyes wide open but looking past him, like a little old man, with not a cry or tear. From the Paradise Hotel behind the Cathedral, which he had just left to watch the moon above the skyscraper housing the Ministry of Defence, he could still hear the strident sounds of Fela Kuti's tenor sax playing 'Shakara Oloje' and see the electric pinks, blues, reds and yellows of the transparent blouses and hobbling skirts of women who had not found full-night customers and were now dancing with each other, eyes squeezed shut, dreaming of the inexperienced boyfriend or abusive uncle who had *done it to them* and sent them on their way to their long nights in the Hotel of Paradise. Was this child the product of a night of terror, with a father's hand crushing the breath out of a young girl's mouth and nose as she was speared and torn apart like the celebratory lamb during harvest time? Or a mistake when a customer promised double for a *ride without a raincoat* after she had taken the birth control pill manufactured in the factory owned by 'Big Mama', the First Lady, from chalk and icing sugar? Revelation always went to the Paradise on Sunday nights to hear Brotherman play the old 45s he collected from all over the diaspora, and tonight he had concentrated on the build up of Jamaican music for the celebration of Bob Marley's ascension to the home of Jah, the Most High, featuring the trombone of Don Drummond, the tenor sax of Tommy McCook, and the alto sax of Bertie King. So powerful was the DJ that Revelation decided to come up for air when Brotherman took a break to build a new spliff and make acquaintance with his wife for the night.

He held the child close to his chest, loosed its swaddling clothes, dried the dew on its forehead, and listened to the faint sounds it was making as if trying to mime the notes of Fela's saxophone which suddenly rose to a crescendo then descended into those deep troughs where the dancing girls would begin to swoon and the tears roll through banks of eye shadow like the Black River in flood. Despite the chill, Revelation freed its arms and legs and he thought he could see gratitude or at least relief in its eyes like bright reflecting pools as it paddled its legs and tiny hands reached for the waning moon. He felt the growing warmth of his own body, touched the reddish brown forehead to see if it too was losing its chill and, for a moment, thought he saw consternation as the shadow of his hand passed over the image of the moon. Maybe it was the music which had made him so tranquil and he began to understand just what the late Bob Marley meant when he sang *'One good thing about music, / When it hits, you feel no pain.'* What would he do with this child?

The outline of the Police Headquarters, called Rock Fort by the British, hulked in the distance but he ruled that out at once: by the time he was halfway through explaining that he had found a baby outside the Bullrush, he might have already been beaten to death. If he survived he could be thrown in a cell, charged with kidnapping and left there to rot until some relative borrowed money from a loan shark, with jewellery or home as security, and bribed with enough to share with the police all the way up to the Commissioner. And he had no relatives to speak of except his wife Ngozi. The nearby General Hospital was no good either as Men in Black lounged outside the reception and the emergency ward to pick up injured students, armed robbers, demonstrating workers, dissidents, hostile journalists, striking teachers, coup plotters, or the other usual suspects. And he ruled out surrendering the baby to the convent attached to the Cathedral because of the time he spent with the Irish Christian Brothers who punished him constantly when he, although 'whiter' than they, refused to bend his knees to blond, blue-eyed God the Father, Son and Holy Ghost, the Blessed Virgin Mary, Mother of God, angels, saints, and the holy Fathers who ministered to boys in the daytime and the nuns at night.

When his stepfather, who married his mother 'out of pity', got drunk he would beat him, telling him that in the old days children like him would have been condemned to the spirits of the Evil Forest. His own father had abandoned them, complaining that after twelve years of barrenness, countless prayers at the white man's church, and a fortune on *juju* men, it was plain wickedness on his mother's part to give birth to a monster. But he could see her now, holding his tiny reddish-yellow hands, watching his white hair and eyebrows, repeating over and over 'Thanks be to God, His Son Jesus Christ, and His Blessed Mother Mary, for this little miracle, this precious gift that your daughter, a sinner, does not deserve.' And that's the name she asked the holy father to confer on him at the baptism, *Deogratias*, the gift of God. And he kept that name until his customers, amazed that he could paint their hidden visions with such raucous epiphanies of the most intense colours that they seemed more *real* than the real, conferred on him the title *Revelation*. That was when praise went to his head and he wrote the slogan on his paint box: more real than the real, more human than human.

There was a tiny cry and Revelation thought he detected the slightest hint of reproach when he realized he was holding the child too tight. His mind was made up. His wife too was having problems conceiving but he knew it was not her fault, that the cause must have been with the men of his family who either fired blanks or bullets with white smoke and no colour. Ngozi was a good woman who had married him against the violent protest of her wealthy parents who disinherited her for daring to marry an evil spirit, an outcast. She tolerated his infrequent contributions to their budget, caused partly by his drunkenness and womanizing, partly by the fear of some potential customers that the figures he would paint on their lorries, mini-buses, clubs, bars, brothels and hotels might reveal truths they preferred to keep hidden. At first he drank the viscous *ogogoro* to blot out the nightmares that afflicted him when awake but noticed that it put some colour into him. The blood would flow to his skin under the pressure of the raw alcohol but coalesce into blotches that made him seem even more monstrous and then he started smoking the *sensimila* from Brotherman's farm to smooth out the tiny petals of blood and make him look human again.

It was the first time he saw a video of Yellowman, heard the hoarse rhythms of the songs the musician used to draw beautiful women to him, that Revelation decided that a creature afflicted like himself could become a man. Not only did his figures become sharper, his colours more vibrant and explosive, he found himself spending more time with Ngozi, with less need of the women in the Paradise Hotel and able now to convince his customers that the truths his paintings revealed of their secret visions would free them of their torments and make them want to fly. So he would take this gift of God to his beloved Ngozi but would not call him Deogratias after he himself had given up the name and the white God who neglected him despite his lack of colour. He could not call him Yellowman because there was colour in *his* skin and, besides, he had begun to tire of his hero's constant boasting of the number of women he could have, how they could suck on his yellow all night and still scream for more, how he would reduce them to things designed for his pleasure to make him feel more like an all-powerful man. More and more his paintings had been inspired by the quieter but more intense rhythms of Bob Marley, his worship of a black God more in tune with nature and the African reality, with its love for life, joy and children and respect for women, other men and the aged, encapsulated in his *'One love, one heart, / Let's get together and we'll be all right.'*

He had become a full convert early one night without a moon when he staggered past two policemen and, not hearing their 'we get pickin, wetin you get for we, Niagra oyibo', kept going until they recovered from their astonishment at his brazen effrontery and began to try out their new American-style batons on his skull. When he woke up in the A & E room of the General Daudu Hospital he swore that it was the pounding of 'Buffalo Soldier' from the giant speakers of the Paradise Hotel which had brought him back from the dead. And whenever Ngozi's head was torn apart by the migraines which came on each month she failed to conceive, he found the only thing that would bring her down and make her whole again was tea made from ginger, fever grass, neem and fresh ganja leaves, with the lyrics of Bob's 'No Woman, No Cry' played on his little Philips radio. And so after opening the towel and checking in the dying light of the moon to make doubly sure what sex it was, he touched the earth, and then the now warm forehead and anointed the baby Bob Marley, paraphrasing for the last time the scripture which, like the songs of

Yellowman, he no longer believed, *'This is my beloved Son, in Whom I am well pleased, hear ye Him.'*

The mist had almost disappeared and it was beginning to lighten as the sun replaced the moon over the Ministry of Defence when the three men appeared with women he recognized from the hotel. Their clothes hung loosely from their bodies and they looked like they had been through a hurricane with sweat stains marking out strange countries and continents on a map of weariness and pain, the stench of alcohol, urine, local perfume and the holy weed so concentrated he thought he could see drops of liquid distil from the rankness. But their eyes were awake and hard, focused on the infant he held so closely in his arms. They had seen the Albino leave the hotel alone and now here he was with a white bundle of perfection.

Almost every day the papers ran stories of children stolen and killed for rituals to make men rich, or women to get pregnant and snare rich men, of university professors to be made ministers, lieutenant colonels to be made military governors, brigadiers to be promoted generals, and generals to replace the General. There were rumours of marabouts telling Maryam, the General's senior wife, that only the blood of the newborn could make her husband get rid of the fat, slovenly moon-faced bitch he had been fucking since he was a starving sergeant-major, and of Daudu collecting the live bodies of premature babies and the still-warm foetuses aborted by students in the university teaching hospitals, and fucking madmen and mules to restore his virility, cure his piles and prevent UN sanctions for his violation of human rights. Some said there was a whole industry for capturing children for adoption in Europe and America, of 'Prophets' and 'Evangelists' using children's body parts in get-rich-quick schemes for housewives abandoned by husbands destroyed by a worthless currency, who sought to live like 'Big Mama' and her friends. There was a story in the *Weekend* about a Prophet Oluwole who told women to bury their live babies and watch them rot and count the maggots, each of which would equal one hundred American dollars in the prize they would win in *El Gordo*, the Spanish lottery.

The leader of the group from the hotel had a glass eye which he shielded with the black felt hat he wore at a rakish angle. But his good eye was more powerful than the Hubble Telescope and he could see into corners of the human soul people did not know they had. He came from a family of witch-sniffers and he could detect even the minutest trace of evil, could tell if a man or woman had even a little finger which crossed the line into the dark side, to harm the weak, the lame and abandoned.

But coming level with the Albino, piercing him with his one good eye and absorbing the smell of Brotherman's weed, he could find no impurity in the man, and recognized the child as Nazarene, the Redeemer, and the Albino as his protector. From the loving way Revelation held his child and the way the baby kicked and touched his cheek they knew that this was no child-killing contractor for the ogres of the Rock Palace. So they saluted the loving African father: 'Respect, brother. Make you take good care of the pickin, Niagra oyibo! God dey.'

After the shock of seeing her dishevelled, now sober husband clutching a smiling baby, and having decided what they had to do, Ngozi made the sign of the cross and forced Revelation to kneel with her and thank the Lord for this precious little miracle for which they had prayed so long. She would leave that very morning for his home-town where she would say she had given birth and was taking the child for them to see and give Revelation the chance to find a better, brighter place. While she was gone he would tell the neighbours she was pregnant and gone home to protect the child, as a babalawo had told them it was a jealous girlfriend in Xanadu who was causing her to have miscarriages. When she came back with the child no one would doubt them as Bob Marley didn't look like he would be a big baby.

During their absence Revelation stopped drinking completely, gave up his women and worked extra hard to make money to pay down on a one-room house on the outskirts of the biggest slum in the capital and, with the help of friends and some grateful customers, he put on an extra room and prettied up the place with paintings of sugar cane, weed, pawpaw, mango and sweetsop trees. He could hardly recognize them when they returned, Ngozi was no longer skin and bones but had bloomed as if she had been really pregnant and had actually given birth to the lively little boy she held so tightly to her breast as women tried to hold him to show the universal love the African felt for the child.

And that was the problem: she didn't want him out of her sight for even a second because she was afraid someone, maybe the real mother, would come and take him away. Something about him made her feel his blood family were really important people and when they came she would be powerless to hold on to him. Exasperated Revelation had to appeal to the beliefs he no longer held to get her to loosen her hold on little Bob and give him room to breathe: if she had so little faith perhaps Jahweh would take His child away since He was the real Father of us all. So she let go, just a little bit, but he could see the tension in her body when the baby was out of sight, ears pricked up to hear his slightest cry, always neglecting herself to make sure he had the best their poor household could offer.

Bob Marley started trying to draw before he could walk or speak, with pieces of charcoal or the crayons Revelation used to sketch his designs for customers before he painted them. Ngozi was reluctant for him to go to school in case his powerful family recognized him and had them arrested for kidnapping their child. She had finished secondary school and could teach her son to read and write when he was ready. But Revelation insisted and she appeared relieved when the principal of the nursery school sent for them to say that there was something wrong with their child, that he was incapable of learning, that when they asked him a question he tried to draw the answer rather than reply. From a desk drawer the young woman took a pile of exercise books and they could see the other children's with their crude a,b,c,d,e and 1,2,3,4. Bob Marley's sheets were covered with pictures of the teacher and his classmates. Then the woman took her into an adjoining room and showed her the life-size drawings: 'The other children see themselves and try to touch them because they look so three dimensional and so real and start to cry when they can't. Then at night they see the drawings in their dreams and wake confused because they look for their images instead of themselves.' It was better they kept him at home.

So Revelation decided that just as his own father had taught him to carve and paint from the time when he could hardly hold the tools, Bob Marley would become his apprentice and succeed him when he passed on to join his father in whatever place old painters practised their arts. At first a reluctant Ngozi dressed her son in his finest clothes and he was proud to carry the little box with his father's brushes, paints, thinner and scraping knives, with the slogan *more real than the real, more human than human*. On the *molue* buses decorated with his paintings people stared appreciatively at the proud father and his quiet, well-behaved boy, their only regret that if the sins of the fathers had not been visited on the poor man whose colour God held back, he would be the spitting image of his seed.

At first the boy just sat watching quietly, his eyes and hands absorbing every stroke Revelation made. Then he started following with chalk drawn on a slate and when his father was convinced by his sureness he let him put a touch of paint here and a little daub there to a ripe fruit on an orange tree, the long black hair on a mermaid, the eye of a stray jackal hunted by hounds. He was very good with eyes, even better than his master, able with a single touch of black or brown paint to suggest anger, fear, hate or loneliness. So by the time he was about nine years old Revelation would make the design in consultation with the customer then begin the picture and leave it for little Bob to finish while he sat in the shade sipping fresh palm wine. Their biggest job was to paint the panels for the dance hall of the new Paradise Hotel which was built further away from the centre of town after the former one had been knocked down, together with the old cathedral, in order to extend the office building owned by Mama Maryam which stood between the Ministry of Defence and the Central Bank. The new owner, who came from her home town and was rumoured to be her cousin, wanted a Garden of Eden without a snake, with local trees and animals, done with fluorescent paint so that dancers stepping to the tunes of Garth Brooks, Don Williams, Jim Reeves and LeAnn Womak in the darkened hall could be thrilled with highlights of pomegranates and ripe bananas and the eyes of crocodiles, wild horses and big cats.

Bob Marley first created the sky and the earth with all its crystal streams before putting in banana, palm and mango trees and then, when the animals had settled down, he would draw the people. He was putting the finishing touches to a panel with a lion on its back playing with a baby antelope between its front legs when Revelation began to hear noises he could not make out. Little Bob was oblivious, as if he was not of this earth, his dry lips parted and the red tip of his tongue slightly extended, his fingers moving so fast the paint strokes were blurred into a single image. Revelation could make out shouts now but not what they were saying as Bob Marley put an almost invisible stroke of black between the red of the mouth and the white of the huge teeth against the light brown of the tiny hoof which seemed to be playing a tune with the threatening ivory. Now he could hear what sounded like 'doo doo' and he marvelled that his son had modified his own design but so subtly that he had not noticed it till now. He had gotten one of the lion's front paws just a little further forward so that it was bigger than the baby antelope and seemed to protect it with its shadow and his father wondered what kind of painter his son would be when he got to be his age. Whatever was happening was coming nearer and he could make out that the shouts were about General Daudu. Bob Marley was moving his hand with the brush above the panel and when he saw the eyes of both lion and antelope they appeared to be following the tip of the brush and the approaching sound.

He was about to put the final stroke to the right eye of the lion when Revelation turned to see a multitude of people rushing from Maryam Daudu Boulevard into General Daudu Way, pursued by two lorry loads of *Kill and Go*, the mobile policemen who preceded the Disposal Units and were addicted to the Congo music of Papa Wemba while enjoying goat-head pepper soup. The younger, better dressed protesters who looked like students were shouting 'Up your yansh, General Daudu!' but most looked like shoppers, cart pushers, traders, market women, housewives and beggars whose eyes were wide and white with fear, their mouths frothing from exhaustion, their noses running out of the pressure of lungs full to bursting as they strove to stay out of range of the killing 'pop, pop' sounds.

When Revelation saw an old woman with a green straw basket fall and a girl in jeans hold her forehead as the blood flowed beneath her hands into her eyes and down over her nose into her mouth then further down to stain her yellow blouse with the red horse and polo player on the pocket he stood up to put his body between his only son and the hunters pointing their rifles from the jungle-green lorries. As they came closer their aim seemed to improve and now it was mostly the young students shouting 'Up your yansh, General Daudu!' who were falling but he saw the neck of a one-armed old man with a burlap sack over his shoulder snap as his head exploded and the stick with which he was trying to propel himself away from danger acted like a rocket to launch him into paradise. Then Revelation saw the huge black face of his nemesis, the policeman from their hometown who had pursued him obsessively from the time he heard he was engaged to Ngozi. He held binoculars which looked like a toy in his hand and was lost on his face as he pointed to the target and shouted the name of the marksman who would despatch the chosen one. Then he saw the huge black finger point at him. The face of the young policeman grew out of the distance, fixed relentlessly on him like long-lost brothers renewing their old acquaintance from before the beginning of time. His face was angelic, fine, oval and narrow, the image of the delicate young saints and angels he had seen in all the religious books from the time he spent with the Christian Brothers from County Kildare and he was smiling as he took aim and Revelation watched the trajectory of the bullet as the light reached him, then the revolution of its bright cylindrical motion, the thud of its impact and only later the sound. Perhaps in another life, in another universe of infinite dimensions, in another time of hope and deliverance when his son would have created his new world of images, he would have been able to draw its blinding path, absorbing its movement into the trajectory of his own life, into immortality.

Painting always exhausted Bob Marley and as he rested from his labours, satisfied with his work, he did not hear the final 'pop' behind him or see his father fall. From a nearby kiosk selling sugar, Maggi cubes, Peak milk, soaps, Dr Pepper Cola, batteries and cigarettes, a young man in a grey kaftan fled, leaving Fela's 'Zombie' gnashing like teeth on his ancient ghetto blaster.

NGOZI: THE LADY WHO LIVED THE BLUES

After the ascension of her one and only Yellowman, Ngozi lost her golden glow as she no longer took pleasure in preparing the delicate combination of herbs, vegetables and spices with which she put the special colour in her cheeks to match those which haunted his pictures and were reflected in the blinding snow of his skin. She stopped toning her firm body with the precious oils from white lilies of the valley and sweet unguents from her people's most famous medicine man. Bob Marley was still there with her, but while he seemed to need her physical presence and enjoyed her touch on his head or shoulders, his only interest was his late father's paint brushes which, now that Revelation was no longer around to restrain him, seemed to take control of him, producing wild, incoherent images she could not understand, but which gave her a warmth that she had felt only when she had been with Revelation, her infinitely precious, everlasting love, when their two hearts beat as one.

True, the portraits her son made of the men who came to court her, despite her attempt to put them off by wearing black, were easily recognizable, though he would add some tiny detail which disconcerted them as if they recognized something in themselves they had tried to hide. Ngozi always marvelled that he had inherited this talent from Revelation although they were not of the same blood and was grateful that, without realizing it, he was protecting her from the unwanted attentions of men who failed to respect her desire to mourn in peace the only man she could ever love but whose absence left her too weak to resist their unwanted money, attentions, crude laughter and bad breath.

But there was one man who would not be denied. Sergeant Ogwu was called 'Idi Amin' by fellow policemen at the Force Headquarters and by hardened criminals who confessed spontaneously to offences they could not possibly have committed as soon as his huge shadow blotted out the naked electric bulbs shining through the bars of their 'interrogation' cells in the dungeons below General Daudu's Rock Palace. For the new type of felons, the so-called 'political prisoners', the stubborn ones, the subversives, students, man/women, radicals, enemies of the state, spies, anti-government elements, atheists, communists, anti-Americans and Antichrists, it did not matter as the State Security had their confessions typed in triplicate with key words underlined in red for the judges and their American advisers even before their arrests. Idi Amin had had his eyes on Ngozi even while her husband was alive. During drinking bouts at the Paradise Hotel he would complain to his fellow policemen about what he saw as the terrible injustice of this useless little outcast winning the hand of such an outstanding natural beauty from one of the best families in their area whose ancestors were once powerful traditional chiefs who fought the white man to a standstill. But he was deterred by the fear of albinos in their culture and this was reinforced by his friend, James 'Killerman' Obi who warned that Revelation controlled such a powerful *juju* that he could shrink Idi Amin's balls and tie his prick into a corkscrew like a genetically modified American pig's. So even now, long after the Albino was dead, he held his

crotch for reassurance every time he thought that way
about his very special lady.

Not even James Obi knew that he too was an outcast
in their society and, even if he did, would not talk, or even
think about it, in the fearful hulking presence of his friend.
Idi Amin Ogwu never thought of himself as an outcast
and considered it an injustice that some time in the distant
past a wicked ruler had enslaved his people and cursed
them as unworthy to be citizens of their own country for
all eternity. *God* had cursed Revelation and his type, denied
them the colour of redemption in this life and the next,
made it obvious to everyone with eyes to see that these
were men apart, inferior beings, unworthy to possess treasures like his noble lady, Ngozi.

At first he actually liked Bob Marley, liked the intent
way the child bent over his pieces of cardboard to produce
the spectacle of colours which were at the same time
disturbing, incomprehensible and intoxicating. Instead of
being disconcerted by the portrait which made him look
even more like Field Marshal Idi Amin Dada, the former
King of Scotland, he was so proud of the likeness that he
gave the boy a dollar and pinned the portrait above his
desk in the Force Headquarters where it attracted such
comments as, 'Me never know you so ugly, Sgt Ogwu, you
fit pass Idi Amin sef for ugly ugly!' At which he would
beam like a hippo in a pool of mud after a full lunch and
decide to show off the finest set of teeth this side of the
mud banks of the Black River.

When she first saw the drawing, the Israeli adviser,
Professor Herzovogina, was so struck by the likeness that
she sat down, tapping the ashes from her cheroot onto
the raw concrete floor and reminisced, with a faraway look
in her shrunken eyes, about the colossal teddy bear of a
man. The spectacle of a Field Marshal playing elephant
with their four grandchildren clinging like toys to the
endless expanse of his back had brought tears to her
husband's eyes. Crawling on all fours he bent his left arm to

look like a trunk which coiled around the little ones, bellowing so realistically that they fell helpless to the blue carpet of their living room, their bright laughter hiding the wet in their pants. This had been during the good times when the lilting, almost Elizabethan rhythms of his voice brought tingles to their spines as he told those unforgettable stories about his work with the Mau Mau rebels in Kenya, as part of the pacification programme by the King's African Rifles which tried vainly to bring civilization and order to these people who lacked the intelligence to understand what was being done for them, or the gratitude to appreciate it. Like this man, Ogwu had a gentleness that belied the menace of his size, a refined sense of humour which seemed lost and out of place in a face opening like a huge tunnel with the guffaws which started in the elephantine gut and travelled light years through the columns of rough granite that were his teeth. The sergeant was telling her about a child belonging to his intended, called Bob Marley, who made the drawing of *him* and suddenly she realized it was the work of a mere boy, not a cartoon from *Haaretz* or the *Jerusalem Post* which reflected the bitterness they all felt after Marshal Idi sold out to the enemies of the state of Israel and started doing bad things to his people.

Idi Amin Ogwu basked in this reflected glow of artistic achievement in his 'family' and gave the boy little treats of fruits or sweets he picked up from traders in the market or paint from the Lebanese Emporium. But then he began to notice the striking likeness of the boy to his dead father although he had his mother's fine golden colour, if just a shade darker, as if God in his goodness had added some brass to spite Ngozi for sleeping with that Satan whose death by police bullet proved that he was indeed the Antichrist and Enemy of the State. He knew the mysterious ways of God, who visited the sins of the fathers on the second and third generations, and was sure the curse of the Albino would return after skipping this generation to haunt the line. If he wanted to marry Ngozi, to add to his two wives and many other mothers of his children spread across the full extent of Niagra where he had been posted, he could not have this constant threat of potential embarrassment hanging over him. At first he told Bob Marley to go and play so he and his mother could discuss some important adult matters. Then he sent him to the market to buy things and locked the door so that when he returned he would stand outside knocking and pleading for his mother to open so he could give Sgt Ogwu his things. At first he could hear the low pleading and then the subdued cries after the sound of a slap, imagine the tears down his mother's perfect cheeks, the longing in her eyes for her beloved son, then silence.

Ngozi wanted to protect the boy, but the bullet which blew out her husband's brains had also destroyed her will. When his people, who had mocked his whiteness, disowned and disinherited him, arrived to claim his property – long after she had gathered her resources to give him a fine send-off – she had not resisted but had taken her personal possessions and those of Bob Marley to move to a room-and-parlour in a tenement owned by a customer whose mini-buses Revelation had painted with his finest slogan: MONKEY DEY WORK, BABOON DEY CHOP. It was only when they tried to take his paint set that she put her foot down and said it belonged to his son, at which they sucked their teeth and said, 'How Niagra oyibo fit born brown skin pickin?' It was to continue paying the rent that she had accepted the job to cook at the police barracks offered by Sgt Ogwu, one of her and her late husband's townsmen, but it was her total loss of will and self-respect which allowed him to take over her body and the rest of her life and cut her off from the son who God in his goodness and wisdom had gifted her.

It was a very bright day after a week of unbroken rain when Sgt Ogwu strode beaming into their parlour clutching a brown paper parcel with Holland Wax for her and a white kaftan with blue and red embroidery for Bob Marley. She stared at the marks like small coffins left by his police boots but her eyes quickly shot upwards to regard the big mango tree so laden with green fruit and the clinging rain water that several branches had cracked and threatened to fall. The Sergeant's teeth lit up the parlour till the room shone almost like the sun outside and his hand covered the boy's head with room to spare as he bent over his square of old cardboard, drawing a lion chasing a baby antelope.

'Make you put de new kaftan for pickin, Mama Bob, dey get nice Taiwan paint for market. Bob self he need fresh air. Not good boy pickin stay for inside house all de time wid im modda.'

'Come and let me dress you up nice, Bob. Sgt Ogwu want to take you out. See you paint almost finish and you baby antelope not complete.' For the first time since she was a widow she felt a little life in her body and she looked at the fierce concentration of her son, then at her hands to see if the blood was flowing again in her pale, thin fingers.

In the market Bob Marley's hand was lost in Sgt Ogwu's which had battered so many opponents in the past on his way to winning successive heavyweight championships in the police force – until he ran out of opponents. He kept waving and laughing with all the traders he stopped to greet until some were emboldened to joke that Goliath should watch out for little David, even though he didn't have his slingshot with him! To which Ogwu replied, 'Bob no be David, him be good boy who obey him elder like good Christian. No be like him late Albino fadder. Come, Bob, see de Syrian sef wid de paint you want.'

Ngozi could not understand why Ogwu wanted to send her son to the far north to deliver his package when police vehicles went all over the country every day. But she was so happy he was beginning to warm to Little Bob and wanting to take care of him that she simply dried the boy's tears, assuring him that the trip would be lovely and that they would move to the new home Sgt Ogwu had promised when he returned.

'You're a big boy now, Bob. Revelation is watching over you, wherever he is now, and will be so proud of his only son, who will one day join him on the right hand of his Father.'

'At him age I don walk hundred mile wid police to track down cow tief. Beside, when him come back him can buy all de paint him want wid dis!'

In his palm the ten-dollar note looked like a postage stamp with the smiling face of General Daudu with his rouged cheek and mascara eyes.

'You'll be alright, Bob, you're a big boy now,' his mother reassured him, holding him against her shivering body with the smell of fresh water lilies, yellow bellflowers and new rain. Sgt Ogwu frowned and sucked his teeth: 'No wonder de boy soft soft pass woman,' he growled.

The bus Sgt Ogwu put him on was big and shiny red, the back and sides covered with his father's painting of palm trees surrounding a water hole in the desert and men covered from head to toe in blue, bent over to drink from the hole with their camels, their long swords resting against the trunks. Painted boldly on the right side in shiny black was the motto GOD'S JUDGEMENT, NO APPEAL. He watched Sgt Ogwu's face tighten till his eyes almost closed to shut out the images as his boot made a dent like a grave when he kicked the sign, swearing at the unrelenting, eternal stain of his dead rival and his deformed progeny.

The bus conductor stood his ground when Idi Amin marched the boy to the head of the queue which scattered in panic as if he intended to enter the bus without paying. He even attempted to return the giant's bright smile but was fascinated by the boy, almost his own age but much smaller, who was sizing him up like a tailor taking his measure, surgically removing his soul to tinker with dark recesses he did not know he possessed.

The conductor did not see the giant walk to the front of the bus and tried to make eye contact with Bob Marley who continued to stare intently, seeing nothing but absorbing everything, leaving him empty and disoriented as he found himself almost compelled to retrace his short life which began in Denver where his father was a Ph.D. student in microbiology and his mother a computer programmer. His father was granted a post-doctoral fellow-ship to Yale and had even paid a deposit on a small house until the family saw General Daudu, accompanied by the vice-president of the United States, addressing the Oil Summit in Houston on the Fox network which postponed an episode of *The Simpsons* to cover the speech of the Great Helmsman of Niagra. After Richard 'the Jackal' Burton, Chairman of Burton Holly, gave the eulogy to the 'greatest statesman the world has known since Cal Coolidge' the General brought his audience to their feet more times than the President's State of the Union Speech as he urged Niagrans in the United States to return to make their homeland and Africa great again. His father recognized Jerry Gotchakka, a classmate from primary school, who kept handing his President large white hand-kerchiefs from a green Harrod's bag each time the concern for his nation overcame him and his eyes overflowed. The President would then hand these to his ADC who handed them to a Man in Black who locked them in a Chubb safe as there were rumours that the vice-president wanted to clone his DNA so America would have another friend in Africa. The reporter from the *Washington Times* was so overwhelmed by the statesman's exquisite moral sense that when the assembled oil men wept as they sang 'Danny Boy' along with him, he half expected the flint-hearted vice-president to burst into Martin Luther King Jr.'s 'I have a dream' speech. 'I have a dream. I have a dream of one day owning all the world's oil.'

Patriotically the conductor's father had called his head of department at Yale to express his regret and relocated his family to the General Daudu University, the biggest in Black Africa and engine house of the continent's glorious future development. Their first shock was when they received their initial bank statement, informing them that their $15,000 savings had been changed into Niagran dollars at the official rate and were even more shocked when their bank manager showed them the letter of authorization with signatures more *theirs* than any they had ever signed. His father was saved by a concerned kinsman when he saw their estate car being driven by a captain in the Presidential Guard and sought advice about going to the police. They received no compensation for their lost personal effects because insurance companies had threatened to call the police when they went to buy cover for their shipment to Niagra. Six months after their return there was the scandal of the 'missing $9.5 billion', the Niagran dollar fell by 67 per cent on the parallel market and the bank where his mother worked collapsed after the General's brother failed to repay his $30 million loan. Then the university was closed indefinitely over the affair of the General's illiterate wife being made chancellor, soldiers drove lecturers from their university homes, their children from the staff school, salaries were stopped and their bank accounts frozen.

Mikey was lucky to get the conductor job through his mother's townsman who owned a fleet of buses and he was well liked because he was bright, friendly, fair, hard working, and performed a small miracle by making Niagrans queue. Until Idi Amin, that is. Because of his fascination with the boy whose eyes never left him Mikey had forgotten about the giant until he heard screams from inside the bus and saw passengers jumping from the doors, covering their mouths and weeping. Then he saw the driver who was almost six feet tall suspended like a rag doll from a black hand thrust just outside the front door. He was completely covered in blood which flowed in torrents from his head until the hand which held the neck of his gown from behind pulled back then thrust forward and the man was released from his gown, flying through the air into the dust as the smiling Idi Amin followed into the fading sunlight. Meanwhile the driver rose from the dust, parted the curtain of his blood to inspect the source of his agony, grabbed the stick from an old man who fell into a woman's basket of mangoes and struck Mikey repeatedly screaming, 'Wicked boy, after all I do for you, you tryin' to make Sergeant Ogwu kill me!' He prostrated before the smiling Idi Amin, screaming 'Sorry, sah! Is not my fault, this boy come from America with him trouble, make you no kill me, sah!' Idi Amin Ogwu was a man of exquisite moral sense, as incapable of doing an unjust act as his name-sake: this boy, as the driver rightly said, had been spoilt by America and it was not his fault he had no sense, demanding that a man like Sgt Ogwu pay. It was the duty of the foolish man who had never left Xanadu to put him right and the sergeant's smile became cherubic, almost grandfatherly with satisfaction, until he saw Revelation's portrait of the baboon which ate the fruits of the monkey's labour, its smirk of satisfaction illuminated by the radiance of its crown. The change in his features was like a volcano erupting without warning and the kick he aimed at the baboon was misinterpreted by the driver who thought he was still annoyed at the conductor's effrontery and applied more of the old man's stick to his head.

The bus left in the evening in a convoy with a police escort and travelled very fast to avoid armed robbers and Bob Marley watched the speeding landscape with blurs of broken down shacks and twisted trees for a while before falling asleep. He dreamt of the cosy little house they lived in before with the smell of his mother's sweet cooking and his father's paints and his own little room with all the pictures he had drawn, shaping the visions which came to him in the night. His body shook and he moaned in his sleep, earning a prod in the ribs from the woman next to him with a red and green cloth bag and blue food carrier on her lap, from which she took meat, fish, yams, rice, plantains and countless vegetables throughout the night. When he first got on the bus he had studied the unfamiliar setting, the arrangement of the seats, the different sizes and shapes of people, the loads, the big side mirrors, and the clothes of the driver, conductor and security man with a very big gun. There was a nurse on the bus who had dressed the wounds of the two men and other passengers had helped them find new clothes after Sgt Ogwu left. At first they had wanted to be hostile to Bob Marley but his eyes, which bored into their souls, told them he was an innocent. The light was mellow and he was regretting that Sgt Ogwu had not allowed him to take his paints so he could get it all into pictures. He had shut his eyes to record the images for later when suddenly the lights went out and when he opened them he had to suppress the screams he had in nightmares as the biggest woman he had ever seen began to flow over him onto the seat. Even if she had the whole seat to herself some of her would have flowed into the aisle and when she sat down he ceased to exist as he was absorbed into her folds which were endless but light as a sponge. In the process of sitting her hand was rising to her mouth with a ball of pounded yam, stockfish and palm oil, and when she was seated the hand kept moving to her mouth, setting off waves in the universe of her body which made him feel seasick. Each time he dreamt of food and the hunger woke him she had a new variety of food on its way to her mouth, as if the food carrier were magical, without a bottom, or a new version of Noah's Ark, with varieties of every manner of meat in the world. Sometimes his dream of a new home was overwhelmed by images of their present dwelling whose memories floated above the shadow of the house they lived in before. The tenement was rectangular with little rooms and parlours on three sides and toilets and baths on one of the narrower ends and, in the centre, a standpipe and a shack for cooking which was always full with the buzzing of the shiny blue flies from the pit latrines. Sgt Ogwu had bought his mother a kerosene stove so she could cook in the parlour and during the night the smell of the rare spices she used blended with the odours and shiny colours of the paints and thinner in his dreams. As the bus sped in the night outside the visions he evoked, he saw the new place Sgt Ogwu promised they would move to when he returned from the North. It was a small stone house whitewashed bright and light under the zinc roof of blinding green like young palm fronds just shooting into the noonday sun after light rain. The walls of his own room would be white at first before he completed on them the scenes of paradise he was painting with his father when he died.

'Wake up, bwoy, journey done finish!' The woman was shaking him with one hand while cleaning her mouth of palm oil with the back of the other which still held a piece of yam with fried goat meat on top. He followed her, clutching the parcel, and when they got to the steps he was so eager to see what was outside that he bumped into her trailing buttocks like twin hills, slowing the sweep of her hand to her mouth with the last piece of goat meat and yam.

'People nowadays doan teach dem pickin manners!' she complained.

It was early but the motor park was already crowded like those of Xanadu, the dust much thicker, the air drier, the smells more pungent with ginger and ground pepper, and more of the beggars, who were far more numerous, were cripples. The Blue Men here squatting in their soiled, faded gowns, the rusting handles of their dull swords

jutting limply from the scuffed red leather of worn scab-
bards, looked less alive, less real and human than the brilliant images of his father. Then he saw a herd of mangy
camels being driven by three boys no bigger than himself
toward a big open space some distance away full of sheep,
goats and cattle, and flocks of the huge, nasty black birds
so thick they cast shadows over the animals waiting for
slaughter in the light of the rising sun.

'You be Bob?' This must be the policeman Sgt Ogwu
told him to look out for. He looked like a shrunken version
of the sergeant, his uniform like clothes on a line but not
as smooth, sagging like the skin around his twisted mouth
and red, pained, almost mournful eyes, whose black irises
floated like flint in two pools of rancid blood.

'I am Bob, sir, Sgt Ogwu said to look for you.' The
policeman was already off, walking fast through the crowds
which parted for him and the boy, trying to keep up, almost
tripped over the stock of his old Lee Enfield rifle.

'You, driver, come!' He beckoned to a thin brown man
in a blue danshiki and loose brown trousers with maroon
flowers leaning on a battered grey taxi with LEAVE AM FOR
GOD painted in crude maroon letters on the back.

'Make you take dis boy to Mallam Aminu 'ouse,' he said,
handing the driver a slip of brown paper stained with oil.

'Is not the route I go take,' the driver said, handing back
the paper.

'Dis be police work,' the man said, gripping the rifle
more firmly.

'But –' the driver began but the rifle butt in his stomach
stopped him as he doubled over and only heard the boot
smashing his left brake light when he straightened up and
saw the gun pointed at his back tyre.

'I beg you master, make you no vex wid me', he was on
his knees between the policeman and his tyre, his hands
clasped in prayer, trembling. 'I go take the boy wherever
you want, *oga* masta, sah.'

'Just take am where I tell you, leave am dere, don wait

for am.' The driver rushed into the taxi whose engine was already running and cursed the boy in Igbo for not moving fast enough to get out of range of the drunken policeman they called 'the Vulture' because of the frequency with which he pecked at their pockets on the roads around the motor park.

'Get out my mota quick quick!' the taxi man screamed at the boy who held the parcel against his chest with one hand while rubbing his head with the other to kill the pain from bouncing against the bare metal of the battered inside when the driver flew around the many corners like a bird trapped in a maze.

The house before which he stood was like the one in his dream, except much bigger, its walls of white stone topped by a black border where the gutter ran off the water from the red slate roof. There was a lawn in front, smooth and green as the *ase oke* his mother wore when they visited his father's grave, there were pink and yellow flowers he had never seen before, and in the back he could see a garden lush with laden mango, orange and pawpaw trees. Next to the house, separated by a low hibiscus hedge, was a field where hundreds of men in white kept bowing, touching their foreheads to the ground then straightening to wipe their faces with both hands, while chanting to the measure of their nutmeg coloured beads. In front there were huge fires where men in blue stirred huge steaming cauldrons with giant ladles.

So absorbed was he in the beauty of the house, pained that he had not brought his paints to bring them to life, that he did not notice the reddish-yellow little dog barking at him till he heard a sharp *'Barkono!'* and its whine as it ran and lay with its head between its paws in front of the man who had come to the gate.

'Is what you want here?' asked the man in the long white kaftan and red fez.

'I have a parcel for Mallam Aminu from Sgt Ogwu, sir.'

'Mallam inside restin, give it me.'

'Sgt Ogwu said I must give it to Mallam Aminu,' he said, clutching it more tightly to his chest, both hands like a shield, and the man opened the gate for him, kicking at the dog who ran to sniff the parcel.

He had never been in a room so big and he was wondering how long he and his late father would have taken to paint some fine scene of crystal streams and lush fruits and magic flowers and brown doves on the bare white walls when he heard the tall grey-haired man whose bare feet were silent on the thick blue carpet say, 'Hello, young man, I hear you have a parcel for me! What's your name, little man?'

'I'm Bob Marley, sir, I have a parcel from Sgt Ogwu.'

'O, you're named after that Jamaican singer – where's the dreadlocks, and who's Sgt Ogwu?' He was smiling at the boy who looked so small in the big red chair and the ill-fitting kaftan as he opened the parcel. Bob Marley wanted to tell the nice man about his dreadlocks, which Brotherman told his father should not be cut because it was the sign of the Nazarene, the Redeemer, but Sgt Ogwu told his mother he looked like a madman and wanted to cut it but she started crying, throwing herself between him and the giant man with the scissors. But later he told him to come to the Lebanese shop where they sold the paint he needed and when he got there a white man held him while Sgt Ogwu shaved his head with the straight razor which smelt of linseed oil. But his mother said he should never tell on people, and he didn't want to get the sergeant in trouble.

'Sgt Ogwu is a police, sir, he visits my mother every day.' He saw Mallam Aminu struggling with the twine which was tied so tight it cut into the parcel like a wound. Mallam Aminu was thinking of the real Bob Marley who he met as a young man when he went to Moor Town in Jamaica to celebrate the anniversary of Marcus Garvey, the man who had influenced Nkrumah, Nyerere, Azikiwe, Neto, Patrice Lumumba, Nelson Mandela and all the other African leaders who took the continent seriously. The singer had a vague resemblance to this little boy who was studying every item in his parlour with such intensity and he recalled the song which reminded him so much of his followers who were united around the command of Allah to protect the weak, nurture the poor, give justice to the innocent – *One love, one heart, / Let's get together and feel all right.* ' Although some of his more traditional followers objected, saying the man was an infidel and hemp smoker, he insisted on playing it before rallies, and the crowds became more resolute in their determination to throw off the yoke of their oppressors. He always remembered the scene at the Ward Theatre with the High Priest of the Order of Niabinghi, whose pipe was bigger than his head, the strength of the herb enough to remove his head which he saw floating, an out-of-body experience he had never been able to repeat even with the help of the deepest Sufi mystics. He was still fighting the knots, humming silently to himself as he wondered what had been done to the boy to make him so like a statue, but one full of all the life that Allah had breathed into men and women from the beginning of time.

He called Shuaibu to bring a knife but untied the last knot as the man entered, saw him turn pale, and barely heard the strangled cry as he lifted the bloodstained white kaftan from the open parcel and gripped the edge of his desk to stop himself from falling.

'Is Mallam Nuhu's things,' said the younger man harshly, approaching Bob Marley with the butcher knife, a clenched fist, tightened mouth and suddenly black eyes.

'Leave him alone, Shuaibu!' Mallam Aminu shouted, 'Can't you see he's just a boy? It's not his fault. Stop crying, little man, no one's going to harm you in this house!' He looked accusingly at Shuaibu who recoiled at his master's rebuke. 'Where did you come from, Bob?'

'From Xanadu, sir. Sgt Ogwu put me on a big bus which drove all night and a police at the motor park put me in a taxi to here.'

'All the way from Xanadu? Tell the taxi driver to wait, Shuaibu, Bob will need a wash and something to eat.'

'Driver he gone, Mallam,' Shuaibu said in Hausa.

'Gone?' the Mallam asked, then in English, 'How you getting back home, little Bob?'

'Sgt Ogwu made the conductor give me my ticket, sir.' He brought out the bloodstained ticket and Shuaibu took it to Mallam Aminu who had sat down and was holding his white head in his hands, thinking of the son whose corpse the General had still not allowed him to see. Why did the man behave like this? When he was a stable hand in his father's household, Daudu, then known by his Christian name, Daniel, used to kill small animals with Mallam Aminu's younger brother Nafiu, starting with insects, then graduating to lizards, rabbits and finally cats and dogs. But while Nafiu hated all living things, and enjoyed killing them, Daniel was tormented killing what he loved, and would insist on burying them with wild flowers and crosses of white, then singing to them with that ethereal voice of his, hoping to bring them back to life – he had to *kill what he loved* because whatever he loved was a symbol of his self-hate. Mallam Aminu knew how much he loved his son Nuhu and Rabiu, the son of Nafiu, whom he still pursued like Satan himself. There were rumours that he kept the corpses of his enemies in display cases in huge refrigerated trucks where he sang 'O, Danny Boy' to them in the dead of night, hoping they would rise again to sing along with him. It was because of this bizarre behaviour that some of his European and American friends spread the falsehood that he was a cannibal who ate his victims' testicles to drive his warrior spirit. The irony was that they worshipped his brother Nafiu, 'the Hanging Judge', who initiated his friend Daudu into his ritual of mass killing. Just then these pagan thoughts were banished by the roar of his followers shouting 'Allahu Akhbar!' to signal the end of prayer.

'One way,' he said. 'Let me see the return ticket, Bob.'

'This is the only one the conductor give me, sir. He and the driver were bleeding.'

'It's all right, Bob, you need some rest before your return journey,' he said, then in Hausa, 'Let him have a wash then give him food and tell Patrick to drive him to the motor park to catch the bus at six.' He was removing things from the box, studying each one, a torn, bloody pair of white trousers, a shiny ballpoint pen, a black comb with several teeth missing, an empty brown leather wallet, a copy of the Koran and a notebook with the front cover torn off and blood-stained pages covered with squiggles like hieroglyphs.

Bob did not sleep as well on the return journey and he was yawning when the bus arrived at the motor park and he looked through the tinted windows for his mother or Sgt Ogwu. All night he had fallen in and out of sleep, blending dreams with images of awakening as he thought of the kindness of Mallam Aminu and, after the initial hostility, of Shuaibu, who warmed to him and did for him even more than his master ordered. Even the dog Barkono became very friendly though he was driven out when he tried to share Bob's food.

When he got off the bus he looked around and even called out and started to run towards women in brightly coloured, nicely cut Holland wax dresses who seemed to resemble his mother at first but, on closer inspection, looked nothing like her. She was nowhere in the hazy smoke from the distant garbage dump which glistened in the morning sun, punctuated by the rhythms of Fela's 'Original Sufferhead' and the shrieks of motor park touts. Despite the contents of the box which he told Shuaibu to put in his study, Mallam Aminu was a jolly old man, teasing him about his hair and again telling him he had to grow dread-locks if he wanted people to keep calling him Bob Marley. As the sun rose higher he found an old tyre in the shade to sit on but made sure he could see the whole park when his mother came. Mallam Aminu had asked him how he learned such good English and he told him of when he was younger and could hardly speak at all, only painting with his father, and how his mother would sit him down when they sent him home from school and go over each word, again and again, until the sound was like a picture in his mind. She also taught him to say 'Sir' and 'Mam' to older people and how to eat with a knife and fork. He would do anything to make his mother proud.

When the sun was right overhead, he wiped his brow on the sleeve of one of the nicely sewn kaftans Mallam Aminu had given him, ate a bit of the fried yam, and took a sip of the sweet, cloudy drink Shuaibu called *kunu*. He would not touch the lamb marinated with delicate spices and dusted with pepper whose smell was tearing at his insides and making his mouth water because he wanted to save it for his mother, to show her how kind and good a stranger could be. Mallam Aminu had sent Shuaibu for a suitcase of clothes he said belonged to his youngest son, now in secondary school, who had outgrown them. He had watched as Shuaibu held up the kaftans and trousers, setting aside those which were almost new and would fit him, and he thought of paints bought with Sgt Ogwu's ten dollars, which would match their bright colours, as the servant put them in a small brown suitcase.

In the middle of the afternoon he began to worry that his mother might be sick and decided to find his way home which was not that far away and was fixed in his mind like the images of Mallam Aminu, Shuaibu and Barkono that he promised to draw and send them as soon he arrived in Xanadu. He picked up his little suitcase and the plastic bag with the food and drink and headed in the direction of home, thinking all the time that the 'Paradise' his mother talked about must be like Mallam Aminu's household, so there was no need to die first in order to get there. Paradise was especially for young ones like himself, she said, telling him of Jesus' saying: *'suffer the little children* . . .' He could not finish though, because just then a minibus so overloaded that the chassis almost touched the ground crashed through a puddle and drenched his beautiful clothes which he had hoped to surprise his mother with. The bus was so filthy he could not read the second half of the legend EVERYBODY WANTS TO GO TO HEAVEN BUT —

When he arrived at the house it was just as he feared, no one was there. Sgt Ogwu must have hurt his mother and he sat in front of the door wondering how he would find her in the huge General Daudu Hospital. Next time he painted Idi Amin he would put horns, fangs and claws like the devils haunting his dreams. Then he thought that she might not be there but in one of the many smaller hospitals in the vast capital city. But the General Hospital was a start and he had picked up his things to start his quest when he heard the woman call his name. It was the landlord's wife.

'Is what you doin here, Bob? Is why you not with you modder an dat Idi Amin?'

'Good afternoon, mam. Sgt Ogwu sent me on a very far journey to take a parcel to a very nice man, Mallam Aminu, in Arewa City. I come back this morning but my mother was not there, I thought she was sick, and was just going to the hospital —'

'Dey not here, Bob, dey —' Just then the landlord shouted, *'Yemisi!'* and the woman froze as if struck. 'Stay out of other people business, you hear. I don't want trouble with Idi Amin or any other police.'

'But what de boy go do, Alhaji?'

'Is not what the boy go do, but what can *we* do if his people don't want him.'

'Is wetin you de talk, Alhaji, you know Ngozi love de pickin pass self.'

'You don't need to tell me, Yemisi, I see how she sacrifice for her child. If she agree to leave him behind it must be because she fear Idi Amin would harm him.'

'Yes, she don cry like pickin wen him drag her into de police lorry.'

'Shut you mouth, woman, can't you see the boy's about to bawl his eyes out? Come, Bob.' He opened the door, took the boy's hand and led him into the empty rooms where he had lived with his mother since his father died and his uncles and aunts took away their house.

'They said they would wait for me to come back, sir, I thought my mother was sick.'

'Your mother's fine, Bob, maybe they had to move sooner. You know the Force Headquarters where Sgt Ogwu works?'

'Yes, sir.'

'He can't go dere, Alhaji Garuba. You know Idi Amin don transfer, you know wetin *kill an go* can do am.'

'You should worry about what they will do to *us*, Yemisi. We don't need police trouble, we get plenty of our own. At least Idi Amin *pay* all the rent he owe . . . Here, Bob', he placed a new $10 bill in the top pocket of Bob Marley's kaftan. 'When you get to the HQ you ask them where Sgt Ogwu is, tell them he's with Ngozi, your mother, who used to cook at the barracks.' Bob could see him squeeze his eyes shut to keep in the tears as his hand stroked his head in the soft warm fez Mallam Aminu had given him. 'What you saying, Bob?' he asked, bending to hear the near whisper. 'Mama gone,' Bob said.

Outside the gate he saw for the first time the rotting mountains of rubbish smoking in the heat under the whirling shadows of the circling vultures, the holes filled with green water in the twisting, unpaved streets, the dry, broken standpipes, the fallen poles which would never carry electricity again, the squealing pigs driving the chickens away from the small mounds of children's shit, and the places now so bare and cold because his mother was no longer there. Above, the setting sun splashed the sky with its brilliance, painting it with colours more radiant by far than neon or his paints or wild peppers or the most ravishing Holland wax. He would have liked to capture the scene on paper but Sgt Ogwu had taken away his box of paints as well as his mother. When he heard the revving of an engine his body shook, looking for a place to hide, as he feared the white truck with the black skull and cross bones was coming to get him.

HOMICIDE:
LIFE ON THE STREETS

From the top of the broken watchtower of raw concrete, Bob Marley surveyed the waste of the sprawling city with its anonymous millions seeking hope in the rising dust and roads leading nowhere flooded with unfit, overloaded vehicles bearing the signs of his father, Revelation. Without his paints he could not bring them to life and he felt, in his thin body and head made light by the sweet, cloying herb of Brotherman, that fate had condemned them to anonymity in the dark, hot kingdom of Xanadu. Some day, after completing the visions of Agbani's nightmares, he would do justice to them, possessing them as they now possessed him. Smoke rose like incense from the burning mounds of garbage and pyres of cattle dead from an unknown disease so virulent that the Disposal Units had to shoot the starving crowds to prevent them eating the carcasses and dying, putting more pressure on Burial Units overwhelmed since the latest coup attempt when interrogators from Israel and South Africa were joined by Britons and Americans equipped with sound synthesizers, exploding cotton buds and computerized crucifixion machines.

The Lone Star Bakery, between the Ministry of Defence and the National Mosque, gave out free bread to needy

Evangelical Christians who flocked to its distribution centres despite scientific rumours that it *disappeared your dick*. It was part of the charitable foundation set up by the Burton Holly Corporation after Niagrans in the USA wrote a petition to Congress complaining of its role in devastating the environment with its socially irresponsible policies. Besides free bread made from wheat grown on its heavily guarded Eden Farms, it supplied medical treatment, drugs and counselling for victims of HIV. After collecting their loaves the sick were given free transport to the hospital, free hot meals, and even stop-offs for shopping. But the most attractive incentive to converts were the hermetically sealed coffins for the departed, which prevented prophets, apostles and jujumen from using their body parts to manufacture miracles. There were also rumours of France, Germany and other countries of Old Europe exporting corpses for medical experiments, or for students to dissect. The coffins, designed by a Burton Holly high-flyer who was also a *Star Trek* fanatic, were modelled on Spock's casket from 'The Wrath of Khan', with the outline of the Stars and Stripes superimposed on the slogan BURTON HOLLY IS GOOD FOR YOU.

Outside the bakery stood a colossal billboard, second only to the General's, with a cowboy pointing his giant six-gun with the caption – EAT ME OR ELSE! It was set before the column which towered above the mosque with a helipad doubling as a platform from which American and Niagran Special Forces bungee-jumped on Sunday afternoons after receiving their weekly supplies of food, water and designer gear in giant C5As and, after watching them, Bob Marley absorbed them in his dream where he sat on the right hand of his father and jumped through cyclones of all colours passing through the nightmares of the multitudes of the undead then seeing the white plains of his father's skin below, bright and wide as all the world, his mother waiting to save him in her circling arms until, just before he felt the fragrant cushion, the hands of Idi

Amin Ogwu were reaching out to arrest her and he switched to a new nightmare of the gigantic monolith at the centre of the city holding up the sprawling Presidential Palace dominated by the white statue of Elvis Presley with its crown of forest green.

When the black cloud appeared suddenly, blotting out the sun, his eyes twitched and he saw again Esther's nightmare of the locust swarm hovering above the ring of flames around her encircled people, arms raised to the soldiers in the black sky, about to die. He had left the others sleeping off the effects of Brotherman's *sensimila*, *ogogoro* and blistering afternoon sun when his mother invaded his dream through the enigmatic portrait his father painted of her in heaven above the shoulder of Orion in the night sky. Perhaps she was there somewhere in the city, one of those he was doomed never to paint again. Through the pictures stored in his mind he could evoke her and Revelation in their little house with the vegetable garden and the brilliant sharp odour of paint but just as their pictures became most radiant and she reached for him with her saving arms the dark shadow of Idi Amin floated again above her and he woke with screams struggling through torrents of cold sweat. The others were so far gone they were unmoved by his screams but he needed light and air so as not to dissolve in the power of his 24/7 nightmare.

After leaving the house that day he had gone to the Force Headquarters as the landlord suggested, to look for his mother. There was a long queue and when he got to the sergeant at the desk he saw that the man was even bigger than Idi Amin and before he had even finished saying, 'Excuse me, sir, please, where are my mother and Sgt Ogwu,' the officer had leaned over the desk and opened his mouth which was violently red round his black teeth and so wide Bob Marley jumped back to avoid being swallowed. But there was a corporal behind him who wrenched away the small suitcase Mallam Aminu had given him, opened it, and was saying, 'Dese one will fit my pickins well well! You small boy you be big big tief.'

'I'm not a thief, sir. My mother said it's a sin to steal, the things are from Mallam Aminu, sir, he's a very good man who lives in a nice, big white house in Arewa City, sir. His steward is called Shuaibu, sir, and he has a dog called Barkono.'

Bob Marley had turned to address the corporal so he could face him while he spoke as his mother had told him it was polite to do. He had lost sight of the sergeant but his shadow seemed to be growing, blocking out more and more of the light from a broken window as it flowed past him and onto the corporal. When Bob Marley turned his attention to him once more he saw that he was bent almost double over the chipped brown desk and had increased in length as his mouth opened wider and wider till it looked like a cave, his tonsils hanging red magic lanterns. He was not breathing out and Bob recalled Revelation's tale of the hippopotamus, which his mother taught him to spell, standing on the bottom of the Black River and eating the fat yellow green grass not needing to breathe in and out because the river was its home where it was free to do what it wanted. His father had painted on the back of a bus owned by a man called Uncle Sege, embittered by the number of times he was attacked by armed robbers and robbed by police, a hippo whose body was dwarfed by its mouth opened so wide it could swallow heaven and earth with the caption MAN NO GO FEED ON GOD WORD ALONE. He remembered how as the painting neared completion it grew and grew till it filled the world and he had to grow himself, absorbing all that was, and would ever be, to avoid being swallowed. The body had arched like the sergeant's till it got to the head which was thrown back by the force of the extending upper jaw and it was now the boy saw just how big the sergeant's front teeth were. It was just then as he inched imperceptibly forward to see how he would draw the mouth if he had his paints and brushes that the man chose to breathe out as he said, 'Na be you sef call my offisa tief, small boy?' The breath rushed out like a torrent denser than water from stale *ogogoro* and lab alcohol from the Force Headquarters clinic and Bob Marley felt himself ascending like a bird on a thermal from where he could see his mother running from Idi Amin's huge hands. His head pulled back before the sergeant's mouth could digest it and he said, 'No, sir, your friend is not a thief but he's taking the nice things Mallam Aminu gave me.'

But the sergeant had lost interest in him and grabbed the clothes from the corporal and was stuffing them in the suitcase which was not much bigger than his hand. 'Make you give me dis evidence, corporal, is you de only man fit born pickin?'

'Na be me see am first, sergeant, na be me get right.'

The sergeant sucked his teeth and pushed the corporal away, holding up the boy's clothes appreciatively, and counting the number of boy children he had of the age that would fit them.

'*Right?*' he asked, morally offended, holding up an enormous fist which blotted out the rest of the light. 'Come make I show you *right!*' But the corporal had moved out of range of his fists and *ogogoro* breath and Bob Marley had taken the chance to dodge through the crowd to where he knew not when another hand reached out to collect his little red fez from Mallam Aminu and when he ducked, willing to sacrifice this too to escape, a skeletal hand implanted itself in his kaftan between his neck and shoulder and a voice from a great height roared, 'Wetin you get for parcel, small boy?'

The private was so tall that when he straightened up Bob Marley's feet were off the ground when he mumbled in a strangled voice, 'It's yam and fried lamb from Mallam Aminu's house, sir.'

Spittle dribbled from the policeman's mouth and, from

that gargantuan height, made a 'plop' on the bare head of the boy whose feet were now back on the ground as the man's hands were otherwise engaged tearing open the parcel. 'Yam be my favourite food,' he said filling his mouth with a handful then holding up a piece of the meat to the broken black sunlight, tilting his head back before placing it on the frothing, half-eaten yam like a sacrificial offering. 'Na be ondly big man self chop meat so fine,' he said as the rain of spit plopped on the bare concrete, Bob Marley seeing it coming and ducking out of the way.

'I'm sorry, sir, but the meat is for my mother. I told Mallam Aminu I would give it to my mother, sir.'

The shock and horror on the man's face was caught in the fractured beams from a dirty skylight and Bob Marley feared he was going to burst into tears from the effron- tery. Clearly distraught, a half chewed gob of yam and meat escaped but less than halfway to the bare concrete floor one thin hand reached out like a chameleon's tongue and speared it like a fly. Although he had two eyes the boy could swear the outrageous suggestion had shrunk them into one and he looked to be sharpening his teeth as they ground together in preparation to eat him after the silence of chewing the rapidly diminishing lamb.

'Na ondly you mama get mout, boy?' One free, oil- stained hand was already reaching out for him when Bob Marley decided to run without his suitcase or food or cap but with the clothes still on his back and the fifty dollars from Mallam Aminu, the driver, and the landlord in his pocket heading he knew not where. When he burst out of the police station a cloud was just shifting from the face of the sun.

As he woke the black cloud moved above the unfinished watchtower and he heard the voice of Charlie Bronson calling his name like a *muezzin*. 'I soon come,' he shouted before descending.

The room where the five boys hid was so dark that only the glints in their eyes showed when the light from the spliff was reflected as it passed round the circle. The uncompleted compound sprawled over almost an acre of land set on a low hill with spectacular views all the way to the lagoon and the Atlantic which foamed in the distance like froth in a boiling pot of new yam. It had belonged to Daura Okontino, an over-ambitious drug dealer executed for allegedly financing a coup attempt, and became a rendezvous for the tougher elements of the city, including Prophet Oluwole, a suspected ritual killer, a favourite with the General until a rival spread the rumour that he knew when the Life President would die. In a swift response, which showed his understanding of the American concept of 'reinforced pre-emptive strike' from the Vietnam War, the General successfully predicted the time of the Prophet's death: ' *As soon as my Disposal Units get hold of his ass!'* Before his demise, however, he had managed to scrawl in red paint: I WILL EXECUTE GREAT VENGEANCE ON THEM WITH FURIOUS REBUKES; THEN THEY SHALL KNOW THAT I *AM* THE LORD, WHEN I LAY MY VENGEANCE UPON THEM. The place had been a shanty-town before the Brigadier commanding the armoured corps married Okontino's sister. The day after the wedding the Brigadier's tanks and bulldozers levelled it so his brother-in-law could have a place fit to live. The First Lady liked the young man's enterprising spirit and allowed him to merge his operation with hers to avoid harassment by American DEA agents and her husband was so impressed with his acumen that he put him in charge of all operations East of the Oder-Neisse Line. When the Brigadier's new wife was caught fucking a townsman she said was her 'brother', Okontino was charged with treason and committed suicide by firing forty-six fifty calibre bullets at himself from a range of thirty metres. [Editor's Note: The reporter who used 'suicided' as a verb was 'disappeared'.]

The reddish glow lit up Bob Marley's narrow face, framed by his locks and beard, until Charlie Bronson grabbed his wrist and shouted, 'Make you no finish the governor weed, Bobby!' He shouted to be heard above the boom of Fela's 'Zombie' from the big ghetto blaster hanging from a hook on the wall, took the spliff, and when he inhaled the paper showed brown against the welts of his lips under his thin moustache.

'Governor? I think say na General product we get here.'

'General own na for export ondly. Dis be grade two weed,' Charlie Bronson said. Kilimanjaro took the spliff and blew the white smoke above their heads where it trailed through the empty doorway and the endless corridors toward the watchtower which the late drug dealer had designed in the shape of a crown. 'Weed be weed,' Kili said, 'na like woman self, we take am where we fin am, no like Bob ere who tink woman na be queen.'

'Shut you mout!' Charlie Bronson shouted.

'Waffor? Na troot my mout talk, Bob Marley no wan touch odder woman cause he tink say im woman pass our own. You no fit shut me up, man.'

'We ere to relax before we go work de street, man, make you leave Bob alone,' Mr T boomed from his barrel chest, bent over with his hands cupped around the spliff to keep in the smoke, exposing the shine of his scalp with the hair down the middle.

'Who be dis socall "Bob Marley" to say make I leave am? Na be foolish man de worship woman who can't –'

Balloon sat next to Bob Marley and grabbed his wrist so hard that the plank with the bent nail aimed at Kilimanjaro's head fell on the cracked, uneven floor. With the other hand he grabbed the spliff from Mr T who had taken hold of Kili's ankles while Charlie Bronson squeezed his wrists as if they wanted to stretch his already elongated body. Balloon pounced on him, pressed his knees into his stomach, gripped his throat with his right hand while slapping him with his left and blew smoke into his

face from the spliff clenched in his teeth until Kili retched.
'If is suicide you wan, go stan ousside Rock Palace an say
General Daudu Mama na dancer like im wife. Promise
you go leave Bob Marley in peace.'

Kili bit his lips as Mr T and Charlie Bronson pulled his
legs and arms while Balloon tightened both hands around
his neck till he felt his eyes popping out. 'Promise?' they
asked together and Balloon loosened his hands so the 'Yes!'
could escape in a thin, metallic whisper.

The record stopped as they left Kili alone to crawl with
his back to the wall, rubbing his neck as he replaced
'Zombie' with 'Shakara Oloje', Fela's tribute to Glory-Bee,
the other sister of the late drug dealer who had fallen out
with her partner, General Daudu's junior wife, and died
of natural causes after selling her story to *Newsweek* magazine. They knew Bob Marley hated the song because Glory-
Bee was from Agbani's area and only Kilimanjaro
complained when he switched to 'Redemption Song'. The
others pulled closer to Bob Marley and Balloon said, 'You
got to take it easy, Bob, you don wan dem hang you for
murdering boy like Kili.'

'Is troo, Bob,' Charlie Branson said, 'you know say you
get fine fine woman, we all jealous you because na you
she choose.'

'Wid dat kin woman very soon you no fit stay for place
like dis. See ow soon she don leff de street,' Mr T said.
'See how nice you look, boy, you face shine and you clothes
starch and iron.' He ran his hand over Bob Marley's khaki
shirt.

'Is wen we goin eat?' Kili asked from his corner and the
others turned to look at his ghostly outline.

'Na troo I tell you say na only food self go get Kili attention,' Balloon said. 'Na by bread alone him fit live.'

Kilimanjaro sucked his teeth and made a gesture the
others couldn't see, but which meant 'your mother didn't
know which of five men was your father'.

'Jus see dis balloon man self talkin bout food.'

'Na tape worm inside stretchin him body like elastic,' Mr T said.

'Worm inside you ass, man, dis governor weed don tretch my tommy like drum. I say make we go eat before Military Guvna pig done chop all de food.'

'You never need herb to make you tommy suck food like sink hole, man.'

One of their gang, who had just been expelled from school with forty-two of his mates when a nude drawing of Candace, the General's teenage girlfriend, was found on the wall of their dormitory, had got a dishwashing job in the five-star Hyatt-Regency Hotel part owned by the First Lady. 'Jairzinho' saved some of the leftovers before army jeeps collected them for the Military Governor's pig farm. He was called 'Jairzinho' in homage to the Brazilian striker whose iconic goal against the Italians set the 1970 World Cup alight. By the time he was fifteen he had already played for the under-17 and under-21 national teams. On the wings his running at defenders so unnerved opposing teams that they assigned two men to take him out of the game. But they could not catch him as he already ran the 100 metres in 10.3 seconds and Arsene Wenger said they were playing him out-position, that he was the best natural striker he had seen since the great Brazilians and Marco van Basten, one of the three Dutchmen who, with Ruud Gullit and Frank Rijkaardt, made AC Milan the best football club in the world in the late 1980s.

Candace's father, who had been nicknamed 'Pele', was a legendary footballer who lost both legs in the Civil War and had not been paid his pension for years so his daughter had to work part-time in a Lebanese shop to help the family. Gabriel, the elder by eight minutes of the Lebanese twin brothers, saw her there and was so enamoured with her beauty he decided to have her at all costs but was persuaded by his short-sighted brother Emile to keep her as a surprise for the President if Niagra won the African Cup of Nations which he spent $400 million to stage. Such a beauty, Emile

warned, could attract powerful Niagran rivals and it made
good sense to make the sacrifice. The brothers bought
Pele a two-bedroom house in the Low Cost Housing
Scheme sponsored by the British Department for
International Development launched by the Prime
Minister when he came with delegations from British
Petroleum and Shell to sign agreements for rich ultra-deep
blocs offshore from the village of Lidiziam.

The brothers built Pele a shop and got him a Guinness
distributorship through the First Lady. Niagra won the cup
in the National Stadium built by the brothers' construction
company (which sub-contracted the work to Green and
Branch) and they presented the General with Candace,
together with the title to the refinery in São Paulo, which
they obtained at a bargain from their friend, the mayor.

When Candace was collected from the school in a presidential Mercedes 600 accompanied by six APCs, the boys
drew cartoons of her doing things to herself with a huge
empty bottle of stout with the caption GUINNESS IS GOOD
FOR YOU! Expelled for such a treasonable offence, none
of the boys could be enrolled in any other school, work,
live at home, or obtain a passport. It was through a chef
who was a kinsman that Jairzinho got the dishwasher's job
and discreet appeals by Arsene Wenger and Fabio Capello,
the renowned football coaches, almost led the General to
break diplomatic relations and declare war with France
and Italy.

The boys looked up when they saw the Black Hawk
helicopter heading for the tower at the Lone Star Bakery
and were just entering the sunlight with the curl of the
surf in the distance when they saw the boy with the limp
struggling up the hill. He was a beneficiary of an expired
polio vaccine purchased by the First Lady's company, the
Better Life for Children Project.

'Is Brotherman boy. Wetin he wan dis time of day?'
Charlie Bronson asked.

Kilimanjaro sucked his teeth again and glared at Bob

Marley. 'Is why you ask such foolis ting? Na only Bob Marley Brotherman get time for dese days.'

'I tink say you promise you go leave Bob alone, Kili,' Mr T said, stepping toward his over-stretched friend.

'Im alone aready, man. No my business wetin he go do.'

The boy must have heard them and looked up from his laborious climb at the crew who looked like they could start rolling the cut stone for the half completed wall down on his head if he said a wrong word. 'Na Bob he want. Brotherman say make he come quick quick.' He gasped the words out as if they were his last breath but turned to hurry down the hill as soon as he saw Bob Marley had got the message.

'Stay cool,' Bob Marley said. 'Greet Jairzinho, give him the new herb. Make you save me some small "special" from the First Lady, maybe some French or Italian.'

'Go well, Bobby, and greet Brotherman for we. Come on, Kili, man, is why you never say bye-bye to Bob?'

'Go well, Bob Marley, an stay well. God de,' Kili said.

Bob Marley stopped to stare up at the hill where a forlorn stake was topped by a blue CD cover tied with strips of white linen. It was the grave of Harry, one of their lost comrades, the Voice who people said was sweeter than spring water, than fresh honey in the comb, than life itself. When Harry had sat on the hill where he was now buried, on mornings when the sun rose from beneath the sea to pierce the mist and smoke rising from the burning pyres of Xanadu, people stopped what they were doing, nightmares turned to dreams of sunlight, and young maids saw visions of the angels they would marry. It was their golden age as passersby stopped to listen and threw them money, fruits, clothes and wild flowers. A blind seer who shared their leftovers of bread, cheese and cold meatballs from the Danish Embassy predicted that Harry would live forever because a grateful God would reward him with immortality for bringing peace and tranquillity to the troubled nation with his golden voice. But a weeping prophetess had lamented that God was angry that men could love one of His creatures so, for the gift He had bestowed on him, when they had rebuffed His Sacrifice of His only Son, showing less interest in His Divine Attributes than reality television.

After he left the police station Bob Marley had wandered aimlessly until exhausted, dehydrated and disoriented he began to see visions of his mother and father in the mirages floating in the perpetual haze of dust, smoke and the souls of the dead in Xanadu. When he saw the gang, led by Agbani (who was still called Esther then), patrolling outside the Lebanese Emporium to collect rotting fruit before the jeeps arrived, he thought they were part of the haze surrounding his parents. Esther shook him while Harry tried to find out who he was. Kilimanjaro fed him water and stale bread and cheese that the boy who swept the store risked his life to put out for them. When they voted on whether to admit him into the *Outkastes* it was Kili and Harry who supported Esther, the Balloonman was neutral, while Mr T and Charlie Bronson were sceptical that someone so strange and fragile could survive life on the streets. He did not know then that Kili would have followed Esther's lead, even if it meant his death. While the others respected her and obeyed her orders to share everything, not taking from those as poor as themselves, Kili loved her. When they found the fifty dollars in his pocket the others wanted to buy fresh food and drink but Kili, Balloonman and Harry supported her suggestion that they hide it to be used in emergencies.

Harry was named by his mother, who had fallen in love with Harry Belafonte when she heard him sing 'Island in the Sun' about the Jamaica she had left at fourteen to join

her parents in Brockley, South East London. Chukwuemeka was his grandfather's name, given him by his Niagran
father who was orphaned in the civil war and brought up
by Catholic missionaries. His mother Joyce was an average
student but hard worker and became a nurse at the
Hammersmith Hospital in West London where she met
the brilliant but laid back Niagran medical student,
Chinua. Working extra overtime Joyce helped her man to
finish his studies and they were married in the
Hammersmith Registry Office a month before Harry was
born. While they were making good money they both
wanted to return home. Chinua was a proud Niagran who
thought that despite its problems his country was the best
in the world. Joyce's parents were disciples of the Pan-
Africanist Marcus Garvey whose ambition had always been
to return to Africa. After qualifying Chinua specialized in
gynaecology, they worked for two years, saved all they could
and returned to Niagra where they both got jobs at the
General Daudu University Teaching Hospital. But Chinua,
better qualified than his Dean and Head of Department,
wanted to set up his own clinic and after three years they
pooled their savings to rent a surgery in a building owned
by the fourth wife of the second-in-command of the Third
Marine Commando. Joyce's parents mortgaged their house
in Brockley to loan them the money to buy medical equipment in London.

For the first few years they lived an almost idyllic existence, the handsome, brilliant and dashing husband, the
pretty, quiet, generous, hard working and polite Sister
Joyce who, in addition to her nursing duties, organized
the administration and finances of the clinic. Joyce did
not complain when her husband's 'people', about whom
he had never spoken, started showing up to ask for school
fees, rents and other favours, or even to live with them
while they looked for jobs or places in school. She accepted
his explanation that this was African tradition but said no
when they turned up with a young girl not much older

than their son, claiming she was the wife the elders of his
clan had chosen for him from birth.

She said this was one African tradition she could not
accept but did not give him an ultimatum when he said
that his people would put a horrible curse on them if he
violated this sacred family tradition. All she asked was that
she be allowed to leave with her son. But Chinua said this
was another sacred tradition, that a woman, especially a
foreigner, could not be given custody of a Niagran child.
When she finally threatened to make trouble, to call on
both the British and Jamaican embassies, he reluctantly
agreed, insisting that she was still his only real wife, and
that he would be visiting them regularly in London.

Chinua had kinsmen in security at the airport so the
car drove on the tarmac right up to the plane but when
Joyce stepped out two women escorted her up the steps,
threatening to handcuff her, while the car drove off with
her son. Chinua was weeping when his son returned and
found more reasons to weep when he saw the life he had
built with his soulmate crumble. The nurses who had
restrained themselves when Madam was still around now
insulted his patients and shirked their duties, thinking it
was enough to sleep with the master. He was an excellent
surgeon but knew nothing about administration or finance
and the 'brother' he employed, on the rare occasions he
was sober or on duty, seemed competent only in awarding
himself colossal expenses and advances.

His new wife tortured a younger relation they employed
as a house help, forcing her to work from dawn to midnight
cooking, cleaning, ironing, shopping and gardening. She
was obsessed with reality television, insisting that they get
a huge satellite like her friends, and was supported by her
mother who joined them to teach her how to be the perfect
wife. The mother had become an aficionado of high-tech
Finnish porn which reminded her of the rows of bare
chested maidens parading on the bank of the great Black
River, watched by the ravenous King Me Swatem wrapped

in his leopard-skin cloak, his hat of albino colobus monkey-fur with grey parrot and eagle feathers, shield of alligator skin, ivory-handled spear tipped with white rhino horn and necklace from twenty-four of the seventh vertebrae of baby lowland gorillas. As one of the maidens herself, she had watched the mud wrestlers below, wondering if she would be the king's prize or a leftover for his warriors.

She warned her useless son-in-law that her daughter was a *Niagran*, not a foreigner from a country where they allowed mad people with matted hair to roam the streets, singing insane songs and smoking Devil's weed. How could he expect her daughter to watch *Dynasty* on a 20-inch set when her friends married to *privates* watched Richard Rowntree in *Shaft* on 42-inch ones? She warned about that son of his alone in the house with his young, pretty wife when even she, a mature woman, felt like taking her clothes off when he opened his mouth with those enchanting, sorcerer's songs, bewitching even the wild flowers that grew around the house.

Harry, who had learnt his father's language, was soon able to carry on a conversation with his stepmother and her mother but when he tried telling them that his people came from St Elizabeth, Jamaica, where many slaves were Ibos, it merely increased the older woman's hatred and alarm since the only slaves she knew in her language were outcasts (*osus*) who normal Ibos were forbidden to marry.

As the clinic fell deeper into debt Chinua could not pay Harry's school fees and his mother-in-law became nasty at having this foreigner in their house. She blamed him for his father's inability to buy the latest video recorder and surround sound TV and stereo to watch her favourite Indian films and Papa Wemba music videos. Chinua did not believe her when she accused Harry of going into the bathroom when her daughter was in the tub but he could not contradict his mother-in-law, an elder, and for the first time in his life he beat his son who left the house, followed shortly after by his wife and her mother when he lost his clinic and drank so much he could not perform in bed. Eventually, when a distant cousin married a major and he was able to get enough bank loans to set up a chain of clinics, Chinua started looking for Joyce and Harry but found the world was bigger than he thought. Joyce had suffered a mental breakdown when her letters to Harry were returned and she got no satisfaction from the British Foreign and Commonwealth Office, which was indifferent, or the Jamaican High Commission, which was positively hostile.

After the massacre of the 129 students protesting against his illiterate wife, the General was certain the UN would pass sanctions and dreaded telling his First Lady she could no longer sip tea with the Queen of England, nibble bacon, lettuce and tomato sandwiches in the White House, or try to make small talk with Frau Helge, Marlene, Greta or whoever the German Chancellor was married to at the time. He was particularly aggrieved about the libel of his 'illiterate wife' and wept as he complained to the UN Secretary General that the First Lady chaired a book club which studied the writings of Jeffrey Archer.

But Nasser Waddadda pointed out that there was no word for 'impossible' in any of the 450 Niagran languages. First he approached members of the Security Council with the latest seismic maps off the coast off Lidiziam, which showed that the American satellite data passed to Burton Holly underestimated the reserves by a factor of five. Then he met with Foreign Ministers from the Caribbean in a luxury hotel in the British Virgin Islands and advised them to set up International Business Corporations in the Cayman Islands to which Niagra would sell its super-sweet, low sulphur content, low specific gravity crude at a discount of 7.5 per cent which would then be sold on to their governments at the full market price, providing enough money to pay for birthday, Christmas and Easter presents for their leaders. Only the Cubans refused, explaining that Fidel did not *do* birthdays and as leader of the sole remaining official atheist state could not possibly celebrate Christmas and Easter. The Commandante would, however, vote against sanctions against Niagra to make the Yankees and English look like a bunch of fucking dickheads.

Harry had found the *Outkastes*, the first people to make him feel at home since his mother was snatched from him. He left his father's house with just a few possessions, copies of Achebe's *Man of the People*, Orwell's *Animal Farm* and Salinger's *Catcher in the Rye*. His mother had bought him the CD of the King's College choir so he could practise the *Laudate Dominum* which made all the women weep when he sang it in the church choir. And he took the Dunhill white linen slacks she had bought him on the final Saturday of the Harrods sale when he was just a year old. She remembered in Jamaica how white linen was revered and when she saw the beauty of these trousers, reduced to only £9.95, she dreamt of her son in them when he grew up. Harry knew that he would find a way to leave the country one day and wanted her to see him in them, to see her dream come true as she pressed him in her loving arms. But the day came when he would sacrifice this dream to save Bob Marley from the spear of the Roman soldier.

The General had been persuaded to attend the Italian National Day celebrations by the promise to meet his favourite porn stars, whom he watched unfailingly on a satellite channel owned by Silvio Berlusconi. Besides, the Italic Oil Company had just been given oil rights taken from Arbusto after the State Department criticized Niagra's human rights record. Although the Embassy was surrounded by a division of the Presidential Guard hours before the event, a garden boy had sneaked the *Outkastes* into the grounds the day before and hidden them in an outhouse from which they could see the show as well as get spaghetti bolognaise, meatballs seasoned with tarragon, fettuccine, prosciutto melon and Parma ham, which he would steal from the kitchen.

Because the leftovers would be fed to the General's pigs which were genetically modified to produce low cholesterol pork bellies, the Italians flew in the world famous Professor Toto Riina from the University of Palermo. The entire diplomatic corps were in attendance as well as the oil ministers of Kuwait and Uzbekistan, and the Jamaican security minister who came to finalize the sale of his country's sole refinery to General Daudu's Black Gold Company. The dignitaries were warmed up with Rossini's 'Barber of Seville' while giant video screens showed scenes from Roman history beginning with Romulus and Remus, the Colisseum, the Venus de Milo, the Mona Lisa and Silvio Berlusconi singing 'O Sole Mio' when he was a crooner on an Italian cruise ship surrounded by sunglassed men in roomy Franco Aldini double-breasted suits.

Harry gave a running commentary based on the things his mother had taught him from her self-help books. The porn stars acted out a sketch called 'Fine Young Cannibals' in which the missionaries were played by topless dancers while the cannibals were bodybuilders in blackface wearing head gear of turkey feathers and loincloths which threatened to fall off when they thrust toy spears sheathed with condoms in the national colours at the 'missionaries'.

But in the middle of the show the General received a message from the American Embassy that a coup attempt was in progress and decamped, leaving an astonished gaggle of diplomats and porn stars and enormous quantities of food. Children who had waited outside the security perimeter hoping for titbits after the jeeps had collected the leftovers for the General's pig farm suddenly found they had a free run at the fusilli tricolore in pesto and braised linguini surrounded by kalamari rings.

They rushed into the vacuum created by the retreating troops of General Daudu's army but were confronted by a line of Roman soldiers in plumed helmets, red and white tunics, and patent leather thigh boots which highlighted the brilliance of their ceremonial swords. The porn stars, determined that the show must go on, clambered up to the balconies and started throwing meatballs, tossed salad, garlic bread and spaghetti down at the street kids who fought until they were covered in tomato sauce and balsamic vinegar.

The dignitaries clapped, shouted the slogan 'Forza Italia' of the AC Milan football team and threw glasses of asti spumanti and chianti into the crowds. But some of the bodybuilders were from the Italian Communist Party and took this opportunity to climb the highest balcony and piss on the bourgeoisie below, drawing outraged cries of 'uncivilized bastards' as VIPs brushed down their Balenciaga gowns and Armani suits and retaliated by hurling medium-rare tournedos rossini up at the disgusting reds who, enraged at this gross bourgeois exhibitionism, dropped their loin cloths and bared their bottoms, creating a diplomatic rift when the French cultural attaché projectile vomited into the bodice of the British Ambassador's wife who spent pleasant summer evenings watching extra-strength Finnish Art Movies with Brigadier Rabiu, the Commander of the Special Presidential Republican Guards.

Then the bored Roman soldiers, disgusted by the in-discipline of the civilians, picked up the discarded spears of the 'cannibals', removed the peppermint flavoured condoms and fixed to the naked tips sirloin steaks wrapped in Parma ham and smothered in ripe parmesan cheese drizzled with garlic butter, sprinkled with oregano, dill and thyme, which they thrust at the kids who jumped to reach them. But the soldiers were all over six feet tall even without the three-inch heels of the boots and the silver helmets whose black plumes shivered in the evening wind, and when they pulled back the spears above their heads there was no way the kids could reach them. Then the *Outkastes*, who could not find their garden boy friend, huddled and decided that if Bob Marley, the lightest, climbed on the shoulders of Kili, the tallest, they would have a competitive advantage.

This worked, they got the steak, but the neighbouring soldier, astonished at the inventiveness of the children, swung round, his steak flying out into the crowd which tore at each other to get at it, and the tip pierced Bob Marley's side. As he slipped from Kili's shoulder the spear point came out and the others grabbed him and ran, bewildered that no one was following to finish them off. But before they got to the hospital they were met by nurses who warned them that the soldiers had orders to shoot anyone approaching, given the statistical probability that anyone needing treatment might be a coup plotter. They said Bob Marley's wound was not critical but that he would bleed to death unless they could find bandages fast. But before they finished saying it Harry was running as if a Disposal Unit was after him and he was ripping the linen trousers into strips as he ran back out of breath.

Bob Marley lived and recuperated, fed by Esther with chicken soup, matzo balls and gefilte fish 'liberated' from the Israeli Embassy by the son of a cleaner.

He turned back to look once again at the remaining strips of linen tied round the CD cover of the King's College choir blowing in the wind above the grave cold as the day his side was pierced by the Roman soldier. The same wind was blowing in the bare parking lot of the 500 room Hyatt-Regency Hotel which had been emptied, except for sixty-five Evangelical Christians, for the twenty-fifth birthday party of Major Emeka Nzeribe of the Armoured Corps, a favourite of the General. The guest of honour was the Jamaican Foreign Minister who had arrived a week earlier to sign a new oil agreement. The Lebanese twins, Gabriel and Emile, supplied two container loads of *Mateus rosé* and fifty 'models' from Peru, Thailand, the Philippines, India, France, Albania, the United Kingdom and Brazil, procured through Francesco Smalto, the tailor who did similar service for the President of Gabon.

An additional ground for celebration was the purchase of another refinery for the General from the First Lady of the Ivory Coast so that the last refinery in Niagra could be shut down, thus assuring him and the twins the monopoly of supply. [Editor's Note: This is confirmed by the latest issue of *Energy Compass*.] The Collection Units came early so they could start drinking the *rosé* and smoking the genetically modified *sensimila* with armoured units and Death's Head commandos guarding the venue because of the General's presence. But the *Outkastes* came even earlier, smuggled in through the pantry by Jairzinho.

The Major, an avowed nationalist, insisted on African food, and all evening Harry could smell the *egusi* stew, his father's favourite, which his mother had learnt to cook in London, buying the crushed melon seeds, bitter leaf, spinach, goat meat, periwinkles, dried crayfish and yam flour in the Shepherd's Bush market. When the waiters brought out the leftovers in boxes to pack in the jeeps, Harry could bear it no longer and broke through the first line of drunken soldiers, grabbed the box of *egusi* stew with goat meat and pounded yam from a waiter and almost made it to the narrow passage which led past the swimming pool, through the garden of hibiscus, frangipani and white lilies of the valley, and home. His mother had showed him a picture of Michelangelo's *Pietà* in a supplement of the *Guardian* and now he thought he saw her in the shining marble with empty arms but it was only the metallic grey of the packing box.

The young commander struggled to stop himself from weeping at the sheer audacity of this convict: for thirty

years soldiers had had one hundred and thirty million lives
and three hundred billion dollars to do with as they pleased
and here was this bare-assed street kid trying to *fuck it
all up by stealing the First Lady's pig feed*. (He was not to
know that the First Lady would be so upset at the thought
of her pigs eating African food that she had to be comforted
by the French Ambassador's wife with a screening of Alain
Resnais' *Last Year at Marienbad* with Ibo subtitles.)

The first volley whistled above Harry's head into the
rooms of the Evangelicals. As the soldiers' eyes focused in
the dark they saw the white of the box with the fluorescent label of the General's *Black Gold* company and they
kept firing even after the box stopped moving, screaming
that they'd shoot the waiters if they didn't collect the First
Lady's pig food *with immediate effect* and the trembling
waiters threw up and wept as they collected some of the
boy's shattered brains which in the recessed lighting was
hard to distinguish from the crushed melon seed in the
egusi stew. The Disposal Unit also found some stew where
the brain should have been and docked the soldiers a
week's pay for dereliction of duty when they calculated
that only twenty-three bullets of the 512 fired entered the
boy's body, a kill ratio of only 4.492 per cent.

SERGEANT PEPPER

Brotherman's mud house was deep inside the forest outside Xanadu and after the minibus ride which lasted about thirty minutes Bob Marley and the boy walked another hour before they saw the blue smoke coiling out of the grey thatched roof. He had owned a shack once, on the site where Okontino started his palace, among the small-timers who had 'captured' the hill and started a settlement for the debris of old Xanadu. The brethren was one of the first Rasta in Niagra and the first to plant ganja on a modest scale to supply the herb of God. But when General Daudu came to power he signed Decree 33 making cultivation a capital offence and persuaded the American Drug Enforcement Agency to invest hundreds of millions of dollars to eradicate the evil from the land.

Launching raids against small producers like Brotherman, the General and his friends cornered the market, using the grants to buy American fertilizers, tractors, trucks and airplanes to mass-produce and market the drug across the Free World in a model of neo-liberalism celebrated in a monograph by Milton Friedman. The most infamous act of the General, according to veteran hemp smokers, was not the alleged ritual sacrifice of his first son to gain promotion, the massacres of school children

who refused to wear uniforms with his image, the torture
of nurses and doctors who had the temerity to go on strike
during the visit of Margaret Thatcher, the murders of his
father and best friend to prove he was not Cameroonian,
or shaving the heads of the Niagran Union of Journalists
executive committee with broken bottles because they
failed to buy a full page ad to congratulate him on his
birthday, but the introduction to the Niagran market of a
genetically modified strain of weed developed by the CIA's
Dr Friedrich Gottlieb to make Niagrans the happiest
people on earth.

Brotherman sat with his back against the mud wall
under portraits of Haile Selassie, Count Ossie and Alhaji
Mamman Shatta, meditating on the smoke trailing through
the open door and out into the small patch of sugar cane,
runner beans, pumpkins and a lone cashew tree before
the house. But the scene was dominated by the faded
poster of Dr Delroy Solomon's mother, a golden woman
with the high cheekbones of the Akan and broad face and
curved eyes of the people who once roamed the Caribbean.
A haunting tune by Roberta Flack and Donny Hathaway
was playing on his little short wave radio, on which he
listened to the BBC World Service, Radio Moscow and
the Voice of Jah, from the small Rasta community in
Ethiopia.

Rumour had it that Brotherman and Fela Anikulapo-
Kuti had once had a contest to see who could build the
biggest spliff and that Brotherman's winning entry was on
display in the Physics Lab of the University of Niagra to
prove, through the maintenance of structural integrity for
an object whose volume/surface ratio exceeded xy, that
African gravity defied the White Man's Laws of Physics.
Bob Marley was peckish and checked out with a bamboo
ladle the three-legged iron pot on the fire where pieces of
yam boiled in the fish soup with red and green peppers
floating above the coco yams and squares of pumpkins
from the new vines which ran riot between the guava,

mango and plum trees behind the house. Brotherman still had the sax he used to play in the backing bands for visiting singers but had given up after the fiasco with Jimmy Cliff when a rival promoter bribed the Chief Judge and Gorilla, the Chief of Police, to arrest the Reggae Superstar unless he agreed to play for him. Which explains why the original Bob Marley, the Lion of Nine Mile, refused to play in Niagra, his natural African home, and chose instead to sing for Bob Mugabe, the uncool Zimbabwean, that most unmusical of men.

Scientific rumour held that Brotherman tempted Fela, the Nigerian pastor's son, away from the life of a lawyer or doctor when he took him on the hill overlooking Xanadu and with real Jamaican *sensimila* blowing like a hurricane of hot wax through his astonished mind and flaring nostrils, taught him to play the sax with notes so far above the sky and the throne of the Almighty that Fela spent the rest of his life seeking to recreate them through countless jam sessions, twenty-seven wives, and Kilimanjaros of the holy weed. Now Brotherman grew just enough for himself and his friends and was reduced to the humiliating position of selling inferior shit from the farm of Cecilia, the Military Governor's wife, with whom he had a thing when she danced at the club where he played to eke out his living as an occasional DJ.

But at least he was safe from arrest and torture as long as the weed he sold was 'legit'. Was it not the same trick practised by the White Man, precursors of the General Daudus of Africa, who destroyed the stills and banned *ogogoro* so people were forced to drink inferior, imported English gin?

'You still not coverin you head, Bob,' he said.

'Esther knit me a tam, Brotherman, but I leave am at Okontino.'

'She a fine woman, Bob. Is how she doin?'

'She fine, man, she get we a place, soon we both off the street.'

'People from good family like you and she don belong for street, Bob. She a good Rasta woman.'

'You know she won't agree for dreadlocks, Brotherman, she love me, she love we way of life but she want she hair the way she born.'

'Look, Bob, Rasta is of the inner being, the way of the righteous. You an me we see locks and tam and weed as the righteous path. Esther wan to keep you off the street, keep you alive to love an comfort she.' He gave the spliff to Bob Marley whose eyes were already seeing two of everything, sent the boy for fresh palm wine, went outside and came back with a package wrapped in dried banana leaves.

'Dis for dat righteous student leader down by the University, some of dem looking for de true path, man, dey need guidance. Dis be me own good stuff but if Babylon stop you, make you say na Cecilia shit. You look like a ungry man, Bob, I hope say you no angry man too!'

'True, Brotherman, I ungry but not angry. We goin to look for Jairzinho at the hotel when you send Ade for "Fort Okontino".'

'Food soon ready, man. Blow smoke for a good appetite.'

'A don need weed foh dat, Brotherman, and I aready check out de fish tea.'

Bob Marley climbed the rock overlooking the lagoon which surrounded the university to see where the security men were hanging out. The students could always spot them because of the slavish way they copied what they considered the latest campus fashion, wearing genuine, brand new Tommy Hilfigger t-shirts and jeans when poor students wore second-hand, made-in-China replicas which were hand washed and hung out to dry but never ironed. They also wore genuine designer shades which they polished frequently unlike genuine students to whom some smudge was a sign of style. The ones dressed like Rasta were the worst of all, with artificial locks, manufactured tams and joints which seemed professionally rolled in genuine Rizla paper and burned evenly like the one in the face of the Marlboro Man.

Their favourite spot was near the entrance under the portrait of General Daudu, next to the advertising hoarding for *Black Gold Smokes*, the tobacco monopoly part owned by BAT and the China Tobacco Company. Bob Marley squeezed tightly on Brotherman's package under his shirt as he smiled at the 'Rastaman', General Daudu's brother, smoking a Sherlock Holmes pipe under the tobacco advert with the PUT IT IN YOUR PIPE AND SMOKE IT caption. When he heard the twig snap he swivelled on the rock and saw the drunken policeman trying to sneak up on him.

It was hard to judge Sergeant Barkono's age because no one could tell which lines on his face were due to age, which to pure alcohol, *Black Gold*, fake prescription drugs or sheer meanness. As a veteran of the traffic police he acquired a reputation for the record jams he caused and the sums he passed up to his superiors and was moved only when commercial drivers threatened to strike during the visit of the American Vice President. Now he was shouting, 'Polis! Stop, or I fire you. Bloody loonatic!' as he struggled to regain his footing, using his old rifle as a crutch.

Bob Marley scrambled down the rock and began to run a zig-zag course through the woods, which the students used to escape when the Disposal Units raided the campus, and thought he was making good progress as Barkono's shouts and stumbling over the hidden tree stumps appeared to recede. Then he threw himself to the ground when a bullet sank into an acacia tree just above his head and crawled on hands and knees for about fifteen minutes until he rose to climb over a wire fence and another shot exploded in the ground near his foot and the leaves flew into the air like brown doves.

He resumed his crawl in a new direction but two shots

gouged out the bark from a young cedar tree just ahead and he was overwhelmed by the odour of the raw sap. He felt relieved when he rose and burst into the clearing near the hole in the fence which he could use to get to the room of Akintunde, the student leader. There was just a narrow fringe of trees, then the space outside the perimeter fence, and he would be free, lost in the chaos of 'temporary' buildings and multitude of fake and genuine Rastas at the General Daudu University.

When he felt his right leg give way under him and his mind go blank he thought at first he had stubbed his toes on a rock or stump but then he heard the crack of the bullet and felt the numbness all over his body as he twisted round and fell on his side where he had been speared by the Roman Soldier. He could not tell how long he was out but when he could see again Barkono was sitting on a rock with Brotherman's parcel open, eyes squeezed tight as he sighed, *'Dis be sweet, sweet, shit!'*

Then Barkono noticed Bob Marley had opened his eyes and was trying to raise himself on his elbows and he grabbed for the rifle which slipped from the rock as he tried and failed to get to his feet. But the joint was held firmly between thumb and forefinger and the breath he drew was so deep the flame blazed red like his eyes or the fires of hell this young lunatic would soon be feeling. But the sweetness of the weed cleansed his mind of such wicked thoughts, mellowed his grim spirit and he felt so relaxed that some of the lines of his face smoothed out.

'Wetin dey call you, boy?'

'Bob Marley, sah.'

'Dat no be Niagra name, you mean say country fit import mad people now?'

'No, sah, I man be Rasta, I just goin to de University.'

'So you one of dem student troubling gofment? Soon as I finish I goin fire you.'

'I no be student, sah, na my frien I go see.'

'Not student? Maybe I forgif you for dis good weed. From where you get am?'

'Cecilia farm, sah.'

'*Cecilia?*'

'Yes, sah, de Guvna junior wife.'

'You mean say na Cecilia weed I don smoke now now?'

'Yes, sah, I man only massanja for am.'

Barkono had sprung to attention and saluted at the name Cecilia and was screaming for Allah, the General, his wives and Military Governors to forgive him, his hands on his bald head as he had hung his helmet on the bayonet which now lay in the dust.

Cecilia and General Daudu's latest wife had been dancers at the *Big Bamboo*, the club owned by Emile, the younger of the Lebanese twins, who had returned to their country from Niagra in the Civil War and given the order for all the children in Sabra and Shatila to be massacred so they would not live to avenge their parents. Emile had taken the young girls to Major Nzeribe's birthday party and the General had loved them both but after painful deliberations he decided on Cordelia and gave her mate to his favourite, the slim-wrist Military Governor of Xanadu. But the women had remained so close that when the First Lady of Xanadu took exception to the playing of 'Cecilia' on Radio 1 FM she was able to persuade her friend, the First Lady of Niagra, to obtain an amendment to Decree 258, so the song was banned on private as well as public radio stations, which were prohibited from playing any other music but Blue Grass and country and western.

'Wetin I go do, Bob?' Barkono wailed. 'Make you help me, Bobby, my frien.' Bob Marley kept floating in and out of consciousness as the blood flowed out of the hole in the border between his thigh and right buttock and his mother picked him up in her redeeming arms and he smelt the perfume of jacaranda and frangipani and the fresh-ness of new rain in the radiance of flame trees as she reached out across circles of fire to hand him over to Esther. 'Take care of my beloved son,' she cried as Harry led the chorus of the angelic choir singing the *Laudate Dominum*.

'Help me, Bobby, my frien!' Barkono was shaking him, now flat on his back, his face drained till it was almost blue, his glazed eyes full of the empty sky. 'Wetin I go do, my good frien, Bobby?'

Life flickered briefly in his eyes and his face twitched as he saw Barkono's face close to his, tears drifting down his cheeks into the spittle which flowed from his hemp-flecked lips. But he was unable to dodge the flow and the torrent was on him like gum arabic and he was being dragged into oblivion by its viscous tide, back into Esther's dream with the burning bush, the growing shadows, locust clouds and, above them all, the field of torches and candles above Harry's white coffin.

After they had collected the remnants of Harry's body, Bob Marley told them to take the fifty dollars to help buy a suit and coffin to bury him in and hundreds of people donated to the children of the streets and they found a second-hand suit of white linen and a friend of Brotherman built a coffin and they had enough left over to buy a few torches and candles and others donated food and fresh palm wine for a wake and someone from the University contacted CNN and the BBC and after General Daudu banned the funeral, the ambassadors from the US, Japan, China, Russia and the EU countries issued a joint statement saying that 'as representatives of the civilized world which cherishes fundamental human values of charity and goodwill we cannot be seen to openly condone the massacre of innocent young children'. Although the General's specialized units were scowling at every street corner, they left the children alone to bury their comrade amid a sea of torches and candles which the *Guardian* described as 'the sky at night with all the stars transposed to the mean streets of Xanadu'.

Bob Marley felt himself going, let go and was floating up to the lone grave on the hill when he felt the hand on his shoulder shaking:

'Take am, Bobby, make you tell Cecilia Sergeant Pepper say sorry.' The policeman took a small brown packet from his boot and tried to replace the weed he had taken from the banana leaf to roll his joint. 'Wetin you say, Bob?' His ear was so close to Bob Marley's lips they almost touched.

'I can't move, sah.'

'Cyan move? You be strong young man, Bobby, my frien. Is why you cyan move? Na be Rasta hair mek you weak?'

'You fire me foot, sah, me leg don die.'

'Me fire you, little Bobby? For the sake of Almighty Allah and my Commanda-in-Chief, spare the life of the Massanja of Cecilia. Come, Bobby, make I take you for Genal Ospital. Make you tell Cecilia say na armed robber fire you leg.' He had rewrapped the banana leaves and stuffed the package back under Bob Marley's shirt, then picked him up and carried him on his shoulders, binding his hands in front with a dirty handkerchief to prevent him from falling. When he got to the entrance of the University Barkono stood in the middle of the road and threatened to shoot the first taxi driver who refused to stop. 'National Security Matta!' he shouted, pulling the students from the taxi.

At the hospital he picked up Bob Marley again and, with his bayonet thrust forward he kept shouting 'National Security Matta!' at the terrified nurses who dropped bed pans, urine samples and expired drugs, abandoning food trolleys, laundry bags and saline drips until they led Barkono with his unconscious passenger on his shoulders into the operating theatre where Dr Adekunle was performing an abortion on a secondary school student.

When Sergeant Pepper aimed at the foetus on the tray with the rusting tip of his bayonet the doctor told a nursing sister to finish cleaning up and led the mad policeman and his burden into an adjoining theatre with a hole in the middle of the operating table. 'Is National Security Matta, Doc!' he kept shouting.

When Bob Marley woke from uneasy dreams he found a hand on top of his, which was even smaller than his own.

'Esther!' he began to whisper but she put a finger to her lips and covered his mouth with her other hand.

'I'm Agbani, now,' she said.

She was wearing a new tam and leaned over the edge of the bed to raise his head and put on his own. He opened his mouth to speak but again she stopped him, moving her lips as if to say, 'There'll be time enough for words, Bobby, my eternal love.'

BELOVED

by Agbani Jaja (Formerly known as Esther)

The first time ever I saw your face I knew my prince had come, the smell of rain was in the air, blooms were shooting from new vines in the raw earth below the battlements, and I no longer needed heaven with you, my love, filling the immensities of my longing. You were my resurrection, my light after the dark nights, and I became Woman once again in your sight. There you stood on the ramparts of Okontino's Folly, your locks streaked with gold from the sun, more radiant by far than the longings of my youth. No gold was as precious as the rags adorning your frail body, my love. Who needed a home, riches, security, when you stood so upright above the cities of illusion, negating them with undesire? Who knows the measure of a man, who fit to judge that you are not the greatest of your kind? Certainly not the ones who cast you down, crushed you into nothingness, not knowing the force of my love was stronger than death. I arose and opened for you like the lily of the time to come, my heart and hands were filled with longing for you, your locks waved at me like the ocean into which the rivers of my love flowed, your head bathed with my tears.

I looked up to you and you were Akhenaten on the walls of Amana, I wanted to be your queen, to bathe in the radiance of your being. Together we would ride the sunbeams into the future, mock Death in the Valley of the Kings, become Isis and Osiris, on dark rivers without beginning or end. I am Nut, I am Eve, I am your Woman, I am, I the Shulamite who tasted the wine of your kisses, now and forever and ever, because I am who you resurrected from oblivion. I am Esther, your Queen, I will protect you, my love, smite the enemies who cast you down, crushed your innocence. And now for you, my love, I have become Agbani, Queen of the worlds and the clear running streams, whose beauty is greater than the power of all gods, who lives for your radiance and the fragrance of the sacred lily which is your frail body. Now I bring you forth, my Bob Marley, like the son I cannot bear, I will love you, shield you from evil, and cast down your enemies into the pits.

I am your endless love, you are mine, you are in every breath I take, my brown dove, my perfect love, you are what I sought in every dream of the warriors of my heart and my land, behold I went down into you, into the green of your valley, to see what had conquered death, and found your lips like jasmine, dripping with the sweet dew of love. I flew with the doves that were your eyes, back into the streams and valleys of my lost land, and your hands raised me up, your legs were the cedar beams elevating the house of my fathers from the rubble till its roof touched the sky. Now not even its eternal, fragrant waters can quench my love for you, my first, my endless, my everlasting love.

In the light blue pyjamas with 'General Hospital' stencilled in black on the shirt pocket Bob Marley stirred on the mat in the corner of the hut away from the waning sunlight which seemed to hesitate before sliding through the opening. Agbani put aside the cap she was knitting and lay beside him, stroking the lock above his right ear and taking in the smells of the new, sun-dried clay blocks, the white plaster on the walls, the dried cow dung mixed with earth to make the floor warm and smooth. She waited for him to turn and then put both arms around him, pressing his face into her bosom to give him her love and her strength. 'Forever I will hold you in my arms, my endless love,' she whispered. The doctor had told her he needed sleep so his wound would heal and gave her the little blue tablets to be taken with meals twice a day but Brotherman came with his herbs and she remembered as a child among the creeks and rivers of her lost land accompanying her late grandfather to collect the medicines for malaria and jaundice and spear wounds, telling her to remember these ancient cures of her people even if she went on to study the healing powers of the White Man's medicine. Bob Marley's colour was coming back slowly so his skin looked less like his late father's and now he hardly had the fevers which made him shake in the long nights or the dreams, which made him scream, of his mother and Idi Amin. His arms tightened around her, his lips were moving, he groaned as if there were words inside he could not express, and she reached over him to the clay pot to fetch water with which she wet his cracked lips. 'Esther,' he was trying to say and she mouthed in a whisper, 'Remember, I am now Agbani, for you, my love.'

The smell of the fresh fish tea coming from the pot on the three grey stones outside the hut drifted into his dreams of luminous paints as he helped his father create the Garden of Eden, his mother waiting for them with the smell of palm oil and fresh spices and soap, and him proudly resting the box with their paints outside the door so she could embrace him. Agbani returned from stirring the pot.

'You awake, Bob?'

'Is that you, Esther?'

'Agbani, Bob. My dead grandmother's name.' She had come into the hut and was wiping her hands on her apron. When they first met he could not understand what she was saying and had to use sign language but now her words were clear pictures in his head as if he were talking to himself. 'Why you asking if it's me? How many woman you have to make you fish pepper soup?'

'How many you go allow me, Agbani?'

She lifted his head and fed him the water brackish with minerals from the spring and so cold he felt his teeth numb and his skin rough with goose bumps and the pains in his side and leg that would not go away. She felt his pain and hummed their song to draw it out: 'One good thing about music, / When it hits you feel no pain.' She told him of the mermaids' song from their area which the river nymphs sang to tempt unfaithful lovers, and how surprised she was to hear Roberta Flack sing 'The first time ever I saw your face . . .'. Then she replaced the tin, rested his head down, lay next to him and pulled his head between her breasts. 'How many you want?'

He pressed his head into her, feeling her hard like green mangoes and said, '*These* two will do for now.'

'They'd better. Brotherman brought the fish and this one to gut them with,' she said, holding up the knife and grabbing his pyjama pants. 'Is not just the fish this can cut!'

He held her hand and said, 'Madwoman! You worse than Barkono!'

'You hear what happened to him?'

'No, he didn't wait around after dropping me in the hospital.'

'Brotherman said that after he left you he went to a palm wine bar and drank *ogogoro* till he started seeing ghosts of the people he had killed and screaming that he wanted to kill them again to win favour with the Governor and Cecilia. Then he saw a patrol coming up the hill and thought they were coming to get him for wounding the Messenger of Cecilia and fired off a shot which missed but hit a broken lamp post and the patrol responded with all 160 bullets in their magazines killing him and the proprietor and wounding six customers. They said after the first shot he flung his hands out to the sky and was screaming, "Bob Marley, my frien and brudder, make you sing a song for poor Barkono to kill the pain."'

'O my God, Esther –'

'I told you I'm Agbani now. When I saw you there on the table under the light and the dirty green sheet I took back my African name so I can protect you.'

'*You* protect *me?*' he asked, holding up a little fist.

She held his wrists and swung her leg over to straddle him. 'Yes, you idiot, but I can't protect you from myself if you keep provoking me!'

'I surrender, I surrender!' he shouted, hiding the pain in his laughter, then more softly:

'*Agbani*, she who is wiser and more beautiful than the world and all the waters of desire, whose goodness surpasses understanding, child of Jaja the King! Agbani, my beloved, my every breath, our two hearts beating as one, two doves in flight, one but not the same, my endless love, no tears can quench my love for you.'

'If that's what you want it to mean, that's what it means.'

'That's what it means to me, Agbani, my woman, my queen, my sweet waters of desire, my lily of the valley, my new vine with yellow bellflowers dripping with my love for you.'

'Let me bring you the soup before it boils away.'

'Okay, my love, but make haste, that news about the dead policeman is draining my appetite. I feel it was my fault.'

'Don't,' she said, and he'd never heard that edge to her voice before. 'You don't know how many people he robbed and killed, how many women he raped. Ever since he took you piggy-back to the hospital with your blood all over his torn khaki people have been coming up to tell me how lucky we were and how many workers, students, beggars, homeless people and girls from the local hotels he'd finished. Brotherman said they came to him with their tales of horror at the hands of this murderer. Some of them brought money and food for us till you get better. Don't feel sorry for him, Bob Marley, he shouldn't have tried to play God with you. If you hadn't lied that the weed was Cecilia's, you wouldn't be here provoking me to finish the job he started!'

After the fish soup she stripped off his pyjamas and washed his body with hot water, the faint smell of fish mingled with scents of honeysuckle, lemon and fever grass. Then she oiled him and sat him up on the new mat, a gift from the meat seller, and fed him his herb tea with honey, cinnamon and pounded nutmeg. When he heard the water pouring over her body in the new moonlight outside he thought of fresh rain and waterfalls pouring into the valleys where her love had conquered death and when she came in fresh from her bath, smelling of wild flowers, their bodies would again be together as one. *This was no ordinary love.*

THE BLIND SEER
OF XANADU

Through the pale smoke rising above the brazier Alhaji
Suleiman the meat seller watched the slight figure of Bob
Marley squatting on the tomato-shaped rock, legs crossed,
arms folded across his chest like a Native American warrior
contemplating the remnants of his country, or Lord
Buddha meditating on the Nothing That Is. Business was
slow and he had concentrated the live coals at the centre
of the cut-off metal pan, with the sticks of *tsuya* at the
edges of the home-made grill so they would not take time
to roast when a customer came. For Bob Marley he felt
the same love as toward his own sons, perhaps deeper,
certainly on a different plane in terms of refinement. In
normal circumstances his eldest son should be doing the
job Bob did but he had gone to the Military Academy and
was now a Captain. But he had other sons, some in school,
some working on his farm, others herding cattle with his
relatives who had chosen to follow the ways of the ancestors and remain in the bush.

When he first started at this spot long before
Independence, the house behind was a club for European
civil servants and it had taken them time to appreciate
the subtle spices on the flat strips of meat which had up
to a dozen ingredients – groundnut cakes, ginger and

various types of pepper, including the very hot *barkono* which reminded the evil ones of hellfire. The road was a dirt track then, which the Europeans plied on horseback, bicycles or dusty Morris Minors. Now the place had become a busy Press Centre and the dirt track a major highway jammed with traffic for most of the day. So he needed a boy like Bob to run down when a car stopped to take the order and deliver the sticks of meat. And it never ceased to amaze him that Bob Marley could remember each face, the order they made months ago and the amount they should pay, but could not make change.

While the meat seller scrutinized him, the squatting figure had not twitched a hair, seeming to absorb like his mother's milk all that floated around him in the clear November sun which bleached the streaks like honey in his hair. It was not just the inability of one so obviously intelligent to calculate change which made the older man wonder. He was probably near twenty but had the innocence and bearing of a fifteen-year-old, which his dreadlocks and wispy hair did not belie. At the same time there was something ancient and ageless in his profile, as if a bronze statue of him had been cast thousands of years ago and only occasionally came to life. He reminded the meat seller of his ancient ancestors, hooked noses and stone faces burnished by the Sahelian light, who had left their homes in Egypt, Yemen and the *Fouta Djallon* to spread their harsher brand of Islam to neighbours further south. Like Bob Marley they never looked you in the eye, though in Bob's case you always felt he could see right inside your soul and would one day paint it for all eternity. He had adopted the strange religion of his namesake but if that was the way Allah chose to reveal himself it was okay with the meat seller. Allah be praised for His mysterious ways. Besides, Bob never preached to anyone, sought no converts. His dedication to the music of his idol was between him and his loved one, Agbani, and his pictures were beginning to attract the attention of the wider world.

Look at the magnificent mural he had painted of Mallam Aminu's household in the front of the meat seller's house! Bob had seen a faded poster with the saintly Mallam the first time Agbani, then called Esther, had brought him round. It seemed he had met the man venerated by all scholars, modern and traditional, in West Africa and the girl helped him tell the full story of the horrible trick Idi Amin Ogwu had played. Only the goodness of the saint had spared the boy from certain lynching. It was Agbani who suggested the meat seller buy Bob some paints and brushes so he could reproduce the scene at Mallam Aminu's home and he had wept when he saw the immortal goodness of the man emerge on his wall, with even the happy little dog Barkono appearing to be suffused with his eternal sanctity. On separate panels were the portraits of his followers at prayer and of his dead son, Nuhu, whose corpse was still on display in the General's glass-fronted freezer. But most striking of all was the portrait of Mallam Aminu in the Ward Theatre in Kingston Jamaica surrounded by Rasta men led by the High Priest of the Order of Niabinghi with his gigantic ganja pipe.

Now he thought of Bob's father, Revelation, whose pictures and sayings on vehicles all over West Africa were becoming legend. There were so many stories about him, his beautiful wife and their gifted but doomed child who had to paint what he wanted to express. There was a blind seer once who, in exchange for a stick of *tsuya*, pieces of red onion, tomato and extra *yaji*, told fabulous tales all the way from the lands of the Arabs to the wild forests of the South where the little people climbed giant trees in search of honey, trapped monkeys and racoons in nets of vines and stunned antelopes with wooden darts.

The blind seer told him of the man so white you could see his bones through his skin, whose pictures were so real that some people refused to be painted by him so they would not bare the secrets of their souls and be confronted with their double. Not appreciating that his talent and lack of colour were gifts of Allah, the man resorted to alcohol and harlots, neglecting his divinely beautiful wife who could not bear him a son. Then one night in the depth of his drunkenness, after he had debauched himself in the city's most notorious brothels, the Spirit of Allah descended upon him in the form of a shining cloud where he lay comatose in front of the Central Mosque. Allah warned him to amend his evil ways and take care of His gifts and when he awoke he found the child in his arms with the name Bob Marley penned on the white sheet wrapped around him. The cloud had almost disappeared but there was still a bright haze, brilliant in the dawn. Then he remembered the words the Angel Gabriel told him in his drunken stupor of the destiny of this child, the Redeemer whose birth signalled the coming end of the world and of his mission decreed by God to paint the souls of all who had lived because there was no longer space to resurrect them as flesh from the dust. On the last day when the final trumpet sounded God would breathe life into the pictures of those who were just, who nurtured the poor and protected the weak, so their images would be displayed on the walls of Paradise. But the unjust, the General Daudus of the world, would be melted down into the primordial slime and buried with bacon fat in the grease traps of McDonald's. At this point the blind man seemed exhausted and confused and Alhaji Suleiman would give him an extra stick of meat with all the trimmings, plus a cold Fanta.

The meat seller smiled to himself as he saw Bob respond at last, his lips moving silently to the words of his master's voice, '. . . don't worry about a thing / every little thing's gonna be alright', coming from the Press Centre. Of course he could not believe every rumour, even though the blind man had predicted the death of the first Life President and the rise to power of the present one. But Allah would not allow words to reach the ears of his servants that were totally false. So it remained for the faithful to seek kernels of truth in the most bizarre tale. And it was an incontrovertible fact that Bob Marley was special. How else to explain the fact that he was the spitting image of his father when he was a foundling? Or his ability to draw pictures when he could hardly walk and to know at an early age such wisdom that it overwhelmed his speech? It is written that pain and fear were the beginning of wisdom and how he had suffered! How could someone not protected by Allah have survived the death of his father and the cruelty of a murderous stepfather before years of life on the streets where children disappeared daily at the hands of ritual killers to make charms for the powerful, or were shot by the General's Disposal Units when an important visitor was expected? Idi Amin Ogwu was known to have killed many more people than Barkono and to have earned the confidence of his superiors who promoted him to the rank of 'special interrogator' for what they considered their toughest cases.

And see what Bob's guarding spirit did to the late Sergeant Pepper! Nurses at the hospital said that while Bob Marley was being operated on to remove the bullet, Barkono was rolling on the floor in his bloodstained khaki uniform begging Allah's mercy for the wound he inflicted on His Messenger. On his knees he told anyone who would listen how Bob Marley kept disappearing when he fired at him or, when he saw bullets about to enter his body, a flaming hand like an Olympic torch would reach out to stop the speeding missiles. On the night he was shot, bystanders claimed he mistook the patrol for the Angel Gabriel and his attendant spirits and, running towards them with his bayonet raised in salute, the soldiers cut him down.

Only Allah could have put him in the care of the divine

Agbani. Why else would He spare her, when all around her had fallen, except for His own Divine Purpose? From something like a madman, almost like an animal roaming the streets, she had transformed him into a man who now looked like an immortal statue on a basalt plinth. Body and clothes were now almost spotless, his beard and locks were neat, she knitted those beautiful tams he wore and bought him nice, almost new, leather sandals. Even more important, she had improved his reading and taught him to write simple words that before he could not understand. Now all Alhaji Suleiman waited for was for her to teach him addition and subtraction so Bob could make change for his customers! But in her precociously wise way, with a secret smile like one of Bob's portraits, she would mutter and sign to him, 'Time, Alhaji Suleiman, in time all things will come.'

Major Ahmed Abdullahi arrived in his staff car, a green armour-plated Mercedes, his driver, with shaved head sporting a shiny new cap, staring straight ahead. The major looked taller in uniform and, when he stepped out of the car the starched khaki made his movement stiff, as if he was nervous about approaching Bob Marley and the meat seller. Usually he drove himself in his beat-up blue Volkswagen Beetle, sometimes with other junior officers, including Sabo, the meat seller's son. Then he had looked more relaxed, joking and shadow boxing with Bob Marley after greeting them. Bob had already run toward him, shouting 'Major, Major, Major,' and Ahmed patted him on the head and embraced him like he would his young son, even though their ages could not have been that far apart. The old man never failed to smile at the depth of Bob's joy each time he saw his friend, contrasting the first time a soldier had come in uniform after he started working some years ago. Then his face had broken into pieces, the dreadlocks shivering like snakes, his mouth open as if rendered mute by the size of his scream, his body twisted and tensed for flight. The meat seller had shouted for him to stop, saying this was a friend, but had not been surprised after Bob's experience with Sergeant Pepper and what the soldiers had done to Agbani's village and their friends. Besides, soldiers who normally came to the Press Centre arrived in lorries and Bradley Fighting Vehicles and started firing even before their feet hit the ground. At first the press boys had plastered over the bullet holes but had given up and renamed the place 'Swiss Cheese Cottage'.

'How many times I have to tell you to call me Ahmed, not Major, Bob?'

'That's true, Bob,' the meat seller said in a bantering tone, 'Ahmed is more than "Major" now, he's a Lt Colonel!'

Bob Marley's forehead creased in puzzlement and Ahmed self-consciously patted his new pip as he squatted to greet the old man with his fist raised in obeisance, '*Ranka ya daidai*, sah,' then bent to grasp the proffered gnarled, smoke-stained hand with both his own. The old man did not rise to greet him as even privates expected of civilians nowadays and he marvelled that a soldier in such an important position still respected the practices of the old ways.

'Congratulations, Ahmed, thank Allah and serve his people, protect the poor, the weak, the lame. Congratulate your friend, Bob!'

'Congrats, Ahmed,' Bob Marley said, looking up past his eyes which were shadowed by the peak of the cap, 'but you've always been a big man!'

'Don't mind Alhaji, Bobby, he's just making fun of me. I hear the press boys playing your song.'

The sounds of 'Redemption Song' came from inside as they watched a group of reporters rush to their bus to cover the press conference where the General's spokesman, Chief Jerry 'Lewis' Gotchakka, was due to explain why democratic elections were out of the question despite the threat of sanctions by the USA and European Union.

'I've brought you some more of Bob's tapes from London,' he said, signalling to another soldier whose face had been hidden by the tinted windows in the back seat. This one wore a black beret and dark glasses, his huge feet shook the ground and his solid muscles almost burst out of his short-sleeved khaki shirt as he saluted and handed over two red Virgin Records plastic bags and a roll of canvases.

'Here, Bob, take this, there are books for Agbani.'

'She thanks you for the last ones, said she hopes I'll soon be able to read like her.'

They were now playing 'Get Up, Stand Up!' in the Press Centre and Ahmed tapped his feet to the beat.

'That's good, Bob, these days people must read and write to know and protect their rights. And I have good news about your paintings in London – they were very excited about the ones I took to the Africa Centre and the Tyburn Gallery of African Art but suggested you try painting on canvas rather than old cardboard.' Bob Marley had spread the canvases on the ground and his face shone as he inspected the new set of paints and brushes and the brilliant wrapper and matching head-tie for Agbani.

'Someone at the Africa Centre paid £300 for the paintings, they were so impressed and wanted to see more. A Mr James Pulger hopes to visit you when he comes next month on a British Council tour. Here – I've opened a savings account for you and Agbani at the HSBC branch near the Press Centre here. You can use it to finish your little house.' The Lt Colonel's hand was trembling as he bent to hand over the little red book, then he turned to collect his *tsuya*, handing over a new $100 bill.

'No, Ahmed, after all you've done for Bob I can't take this – besides I have no change,' protested the meat seller.

'Keep it for Bob, sir, he and Agbani can make better use of it. For *uwargida*,' he said as he handed the other plastic bag to the meat seller whose eyes widened as the

force of the colours of the Holland wax hit him. Now *he*
stood up and held the hand of the younger man with both
his own.

'*Na gode*, Mallam Ahmed, *na gode da yawa*, the blessings of Almighty Allah be upon all your undertakings. I
thank you, *na gode, na gode da yawa. Allah Ya taimake ka!*
May Allah let His light shine upon you, give you long life
and increase your wisdom and compassion for the weak
and abandoned like little Bob Marley here.' Alhaji
Suleiman's eyes were dry but under the shadow of his cap
the colonel knew what was moving inside. They watched
his car drive off – it did not use its siren to get out of the
jam.

BEHOLD, THE
REDEEMER COMETH

Bob Marley was almost screaming as he ran toward the hut, almost falling as he struggled to hold all the things in his arms. The old man had told him to go home to Agbani, using the excuse that he wasn't needed as business was slow. But the meat seller had seen how excited he was, very unusual for Bob, and wanted him to share his joy with his wife as soon as he could. Besides, knowing how little Bob thought of anything but paints and brushes, Alhaji Suleiman was afraid he would lose the fortune Ahmed had brought them which could change their lives for the better after all they had suffered on the street. And he wanted to be alone to contemplate why the newly promoted Lt Colonel had come to his place in uniform in his official car, with a bodyguard strong enough to lift the world on his shoulders, at that time of day when all the reporters had rushed off to the circus of the Rock Castle like a bunch of excited schoolboys. He had felt like sending Bob with a message to his son but could not deprive him of this opportunity of freeing Agbani of her nightmares.

'Agbani! Agbani!' Bob Marley kept shouting. In one of the books Ahmed had brought her from a previous trip to South Africa, by a woman called 'Head', about something like 'electricity', there were stories about how illiterate peasants and children had been taught to grow beautiful vegetables in wild, apparently infertile soil. He had helped her dig the trenches between the beds to carry the water from their baths and cooking and had gone to the market where Alhaji Suleiman bought meat to collect the cattle, sheep and camel dung to enrich the exhausted soil where Agbani transplanted the seedlings she had grown in plastic bags. Now he was so enthused, in such a hurry, that the cabbage, green beans, carrots, beetroot, tomatoes, onions, peas, lettuce and peppers in all colours of flame, passed in a blur before his eyes like his incomplete painting of the source of the Nile on the Mountains of the Moon which he had seen in a supplement in the *Sentinel* on Women Pharaohs of Egypt.

'Agbani!' he shouted as he burst through the doorway.

'Agbani is my name, madman. Why are you shouting it like that?'

The words were pouring out like a torrent of frothing water and difficult to separate as he tried to hand everything to her at once and ended up with it all on the floor now covered with straw mats dyed red, green and black. Wheezing breathlessly he handed her first the box of paints and brushes, then the bank book, then the Holland wax. The books were Ngũgĩ Wa Thiong'o's *Petals of Blood*, Sembene Ousmane's *God's Bits of Wood* and *White Genesis*, and Hama Tuma's *The Socialist Witch-doctor*. He glanced at her eyes, kissing the lids to prevent her tears falling. Then she held him and his arms were around her, their beating hearts as one.

'Your friend Ahmed is not like a soldier, not all soldiers are devils.'

Over her shoulder she could see the wall covered with his images of the funeral of the singer Bob Marley on the ascending slope of Nine Mile which seemed to jump from the hill in flares of bright colour to dance in the dull flame of their old lantern which they could replace with an electric bulb now they had a bit of money. The brethren

covered the hill like a thick carpet of many colours but
he had made each one so alive she could smell the sacred
herb rising in swirls of thick smoke cut by the blinding
light which flowed from the tomb in the little stone house
at the summit. Each tam was different, the dreadlocks
individualized, some thin like Bob's, others thick as her
wrists, the faces of all colours and shapes under the
banners of the heroes, His Majesty Haile Selassie I, the
Honourable Marcus Moziah Garvey, Nanny, Queen of
the Maroons, Sam Sharpe and Paul Bogle. The High Priest
of the Niabinghi Order was there with Mallam Aminu who
was the only one not smoking the sacred herb because
his Goodness was of a different order. Their friends from
Okontino's Folly were all there, transported by Bob's magic
paints from the unmarked grave where the burial units
had bulldozed them after they had been shot in the demonstrations against the American Vice-President who came
to sign oil contracts for new blocs off the coast of
Lidiziam. Harry and Jairzinho who were killed earlier were
there too and if she reached out she could touch their
sweating bodies, smell the odours of their blood, of the
hard work and cramped spaces to which they were
condemned, feel their weariness and pain. She could
recognize each one of them if he or she came into their
hut now, know exactly where in the picture Bob's tiny
hand had placed them. And in the centre, dominating the
scene as if she were the Creator, was the anguished face
of Sade as her hands reached out for the brown dove
which flew beyond her grasp to join the spirit of the
greatest reggae singer of all time. Behind her a huge bald-
headed man seemed to be pulling her back, to restrain
her longing for the dove. Agbani could not hold her tears
any longer and Bob dried her eyes with his hand, whispering, '*Hush, little darlin, don't shed no tears*'.

Then he remembered the canvases on the floor and
tried to untie them but he had knotted the string too tight
when he retied them and was now panting as he fumbled

with the roll. Agbani was on her knees now, holding him to give him strength to complete all the pictures he had stored in his mind which at moments like this made his face twist and his locks shake. Again she looked above his head and, as the wick of the lantern flared with the kerosene running low, she saw her village burst into flame and she was there again, pristine and alive as at the dawn of creation, all its colours and noises and smells of fresh fish and stale coconut flesh and peppers and cut new vines in the mists above the creeks resurrected with a precision that was *more real than the real, more human than human.*

Across the entire wall he had painted the images she described just as he teased from her throat the words she could not say, first the streams which were the basis of their culture as people of the rivers, their gods of creation to which children were committed from such an early age that they felt as much at home on water as on land. When she saw how he blended the shades of blue and green and ash and silver she found herself rushing to stop the water flowing onto the mats and, intoxicated, swam with dancing lacquered fish, mermaids polished like green sunlight and brown mother hippos smiling in a circle of their young. The lianas reaching from the overhanging branches were alive like the green snakes playing with children and Bob put their reflection in the moving waters at just the depth she remembered. Then there were the whitewashed houses of her relatives and her father's servants and she smelled the steaming dishes of *egusi, edikang ikong*, crayfish and periwinkles as they called in the passing children and visiting teachers for a meal.

It was when she got to the great house her people had occupied for countless generations that she always lost control. Maybe it was the depth of her feelings which had impelled him to craft the stilts on which the house stood with such strength as to bear its weight for all eternity. The cedar beams supporting the roof held the power of the tall warriors who once entered its portals, swords and

shields aloft, filling the cavernous interiors with songs of
defiance at the white devils who threatened to bring the
snake of greed into paradise. Her ancestor had been Great
Chief then, had inspired them, fought alongside them,
sworn to die with them. But swords, spears and clubs
could not hold out against Gatling guns forever and he
had been banished to Sierra Leone and then the
Caribbean. Some governors of the islands with a shred of
humanity had persuaded their superiors in the Foreign
Office to let the old lion return to his homeland to die
and be buried alongside his ancestors. And they allowed
the family he had taken from Africa and the one he had
acquired in the Caribbean to accompany him on his long
last journey home but no government from that time to
the present had ever trusted her people. Her own father
had refused to take the religion of the White Man but
was a fanatic about his education, becoming a teacher and
doing the unthinkable of teaching the children of those
considered his 'slaves' in the olden times, bending to enter
their huts to persuade them that with education their
young would no longer be obliged to bend their knees to
him and his kind. Exhausting the rooms of the great house
for his teachers he had built extensions so no child in his
domain would be without wisdom. He used to be with her
all the time in her nightmares until Bob brought him back
to life and she could see him without dreaming, taller than
the major but with Ahmed's steady gaze which looked out
at all that was and would ever be, for ever and ever and
ever. Maybe it was Bob's feeling for his friend, almost like
a son's, which had made him put touches of Ahmed in
her father, a tiny droop at the corner of his left eye, the
shadow of a scar on the line of his lower lip.

She was his favourite and she could remember hearing
him tell her mother, after she had done so well in the
school as a child of six, 'This is my beloved daughter, the
jewel of my eyes, more precious than all my hopes and
my possessions'. The family portrait was framed by huge

cedar columns, the beams above the veranda completing the square. She could not understand how Bob Marley had managed to put in details she had not remembered telling him, like her tiny bell-shaped earrings and necklace of cowry shells and her father's snuff box of polished mahogany to the fore of the picture. Her father sat in the chair carved from a giant *iroko* tree, with her resting on the right arm, her twin brother on the left, as the sun passed its zenith then began its long last journey home. On the floor, painted on old cardboard, were other scenes from the village before and after its destruction which he extracted from her mind and brought to life in the radiance of fresh paint.

Bob was holding up the canvases and chattering about Ahmed being made a colonel and how good he looked in his staff car and his new uniform. But she did not want his head filled with the new images he would create on the new spaces so she blew out the lamp and pulled him onto the mat. They were so exhausted that they fell asleep as soon as their bodies touched the ground, forgetting to change into their night clothes. When she reached the depth of sleep the nightmare began again, first the burning bush, then the swarms of locusts blocking out the sun. When they dispersed and the sun came through again she saw they had turned into soldiers but now, instead of landing with their guns aflame, they remained suspended in the air as if unclear about what to do next, and when the screams came in the night it was from outside, not from their own dreams.

'Bob Marley! Agbani! Come quick, come and see your friend on the television!' It was Ali, the meat seller's grandson.

Ahmed's portrait was on the screen and Marley's 'Get up, stand up, / Stand up for your right' was vibrating from the tinny speakers of the old black and white set. The old man embraced Bob, lifted him off the ground and spun him round and round, with the strength of a man half his age. Some of his grandsons, from the corner where they huddled in the reception room, watched their grandfather with eyes wide and mouths open. Alhaji Suleiman was like a divine being even to their parents, and to see him behaving like a youth, dancing with the young Rasta with the shrouded, sleepy eyes and overwhelming sting of weed, was like the eighth wonder of the world.

Then Ahmed strode in, the camera having difficulty getting all of him on the screen, and settling for a frame from heart to head, in the same uniform he wore earlier. His eyes were clear as his words as he addressed the people.

'Fellow Niagrans, my name and rank are not important in this message I have been mandated to present to you by a coalition of civil society groups and the Military Committee for Democracy. Even as I speak the former dictator, "Life President" General Daudu, and his family are taking off from the national airport after meeting with democratically elected representatives from all the military formations in the country. Two C5A transport aircraft have been provided to take the General, his wives, constant companions and eighty-seven children to one of their fifty-four houses in the United Kingdom, United States, France, Switzerland, Monaco, Saudi Arabia, Senegal, Morocco, Nigeria, Ivory Coast and South Africa.

'The Niagran people, disgusted with the looting of the national treasury by the General, his family and his favourites over the years, may be excused for showing anger at this generosity. It was not a decision that was lightly taken but the consensus was that bloodshed should be avoided, that this man should be peacefully removed from the scene without fear for the welfare of his family or himself. This decision is driven by the humane principles which motivated our action. It is our hope that General Daudu and his friends will not mistake this for weakness, and will reciprocate by not seeking to disturb the peace and tranquillity of our country.

'We do not need to repeat here the catastrophe caused by years of economic incompetence, corruption, repression and the destruction of all the institutions and noble traditions of our martyred nation. Niagra now has more political prisoners than the United States, our hospitals have been turned into mortuaries, our schools into brothels and criminal enterprises, our roads into death traps, our houses of worship into bureaux de change. Even armed robbers complain that banks were robbed before they arrived on the scene – by their managers who grant themselves "loans" they will never repay.

'As I speak, democratic representatives from civil society and the military have spread out over all the country to sow the new gospel of political freedom, economic regeneration, social liberation of all oppressed groups, cultural and religious choice. It has been decided that sufficient time be given to draft a new constitution, form political parties and organize free and fair elections, but that this time should not exceed one calendar year. None of these representatives may participate in the new political order except as citizens, and the military members will resign their commissions as soon as democratically elected civilians are installed in office. For the meantime, the country will be run by a committee of twenty from civil society and the military, of whom at least five must be women. My colleagues have elected me as co-chair of this committee, together with Chief Patrick Chukwuemeka Ajegunle whose election was annulled by General Daudu five years ago on the grounds that one of his great-grandfathers was not born in Niagra.

'Fellow Niagrans, democrats who organized this change of government are motivated by the highest ideals of all mankind as embodied in the fundamental laws and beliefs of all societies whose citizens enjoy economic security, social equality, political stability and cultural and religious freedoms. Our new social order will be governed by laws not men, by the people's consent rather than blind obedience obtained at gunpoint. We want equality before the law and dignity on all occasions, for all our citizens, regardless of their class, gender, ethnicity, culture, religion, age, or sexual orientation, and will defend their right to air their views, however unpopular these may be.

'Fellow Niagrans, in military academies here and overseas our spirits thrilled not just to drums, bugles and trumpets but the military beat of cries for liberty, equality and fraternity. We too believed that all men and women are equal, that leaders require the consent of the governed, that no ruler has the right to alienate or frustrate their opportunities to pursue happiness, gain material advantage, live in peace and improve their lives, experience progress and guarantee a future for their children.

'As for the dead and the "disappeared", we have returned to their families all the bodies kept as trophies in cruel and bizarre displays in the ice coffins of General Daudu's glass cases, and will employ every means at our disposal to identify the occupants of the dungeons under the Rock Castle, the anonymous victims hidden in unmarked mass graves, the children taken from parents about to die and adopted by childless couples of the former regime.

'Fellow Niagrans, this is just the beginning, a new dawn after nightmares of terror and repression. We have taken the first step in the journey to peace and progress but the next ten thousand miles is all yours. We must help the weak on this great journey, raise the fallen and place the lame on the shoulders of the powerful. But no matter how humane or compassionate or generous we may be, I know that some of us will fall, never to rise again. For us immortality will always be in the minds of those who remember the multitudes who sacrificed themselves that others may live and prosper.

'The Struggle Continues. Keep hope alive. Long Live the People's Republic of Niagra.'

The old meat seller had not released Bob Marely during the speech and when it ended, with 'Get Up, Stand Up!'

restored to full volume, he started jigging again. 'I told you, Agbani, the blind seer was right, our little Bob is truly special. See how he inspired his friend Ahmed, who will make him something in his government. He'll replace the American pornography on the ceilings of the Rock Castle with pictures of poor people trying to survive, farmers, craftspeople, herdsmen, students working at their desks or in their parents' fields.'

One of Alhaji Suleiman's younger grandsons had got up and started dancing, tentatively at first, then bolder but after a time the others pulled him down and all were laughing with the old man and his two young friends. In the glare of the single light bulb the luminous paints on the mural of Mallam Aminu's household shone like the new dawn around his blessed smile and the old man knelt with raised fist to salute his mentor. Then they heard the sounds growing out of the distance, the high pitch of fifes, the throbbing drums, clashing cymbals, the occasional wail of a trumpet, then tambourines and human voices.

People were awake again as if the dawning of new life were growing out of the dark night, windows and doors were thrown open, releasing the suppressed joy that would fill the earth together with the rhythms of Mamman Shatta, Fela Anikulapo-Kuti, Bob Marley, Youssou N'Dour, Angelique Kidjo, Don Drummond, Leroy Smart and Jimmy Cliff. There were cries of 'Allahu Akhbar' but these were filled with joy and the promise, guaranteed by the face of the Unknown Soldier, that there would be no threat to other believers or unbelievers.

The old man grabbed Bob Marley and Agbani by the hand and, with his grandsons and the rest of his house-hold in tow, they merged with the multitude of cart pushers, the destitute, the white-robed scholars of Islam and prophets of Pentecostal churches, men in animal skins, women in electric coloured miniskirts, masquer-ades, the unemployed, the lame, *almajirai*, low paid workers, civil servants, soldiers without guns and the students they had previously been ordered to shoot, musicians competing with each other to bring joy to the people, not the pot-bellied businessmen and women, the brigadiers and generals, the ministers and permanent secretaries, the fat professors who used to spray them with brand new stolen $100 bills. This was the 'moment of the morning cataclysm / when the embryo burst the earth damp with rain'. This was 'the resurrection of the seed / dynamic symphony of joy in men and women'. This was the time of Pablo Neruda, Agostinho Neto, Josina Machel and all the poets dead before their time. *This was the time of the new beginning.*

When they fell onto their mat exhausted, as the sun began to rise above the huge baobab tree, Agbani's nightmare began again. But when the burning bush went out and before the sky could be filled with black locust clouds, there was a blinding light and the resplendent petals of white lilies floated down onto the glory of her lost village, no longer ringed with flame. *And not even the waters of the sacred river will quench my love for you, my endless, my everlasting love,* she sang in joy.

BOOK II:
GET UP, STAND UP!

THE UNQUIET AMERICAN

When the door handle turned Rabiu Nafiu shoved the handwritten manuscript under a map of Africa on his desk at the *Daily Sentinel*. He could not understand why his hands were moist and shaking, why his heart was doing a talking drumbeat against his straining ribs. This was not his weekly column, 'From the Soap Box', which he understood was required reading in the Rock Palace, according to his wife Kikelomo, classmate of Fatima, wife of Colonel Rabiu, favourite of General Daudu, who commanded his Presidential Elite Republican Guards, home of the feared 'special units'. It was not even one of the 'subversive' pieces his boss and former classmate, Joseph Mammamia, suspected he wrote for the *Red Bull*, under the assumed name of 'John Lennon', a clear allusion to *Vlad Lenin* according to Joseph.

What he was writing was pure fiction, which not even the fevered imagination of Jerry 'Lewis' Gotchakka, the Minister of Information, could confuse with fact. He had, in fact, been working on a poem to commemorate the anniversary of the death of Nuhu, his classmate and first cousin, at the hands of the Presidential Guards, who the Minister had accused of being both a Communist *and* Islamic Fundamentalist, in addition to being a disciple of

Dr Delroy Solomon, their lecturer who taught them about
the African origins of calypso, reggae, jazz and all other
music of the diaspora. As all Niagrans knew, the real reason
for the massacre of Nuhu and his five comrades was the
refusal of Nuhu's father, Mallam Aminu, to accept the
post of Minister of Sports, Women's Affairs, Information
and Culture, in the coalition government the Americans
insisted the General put together before he could be
rewarded with a state visit to Washington. Luckily Nasser
Waddadda had produced new seismic maps showing even
more oil in the deep trough off the coast of Lidiziam and
the visit went ahead.

The seriousness of the appointment was indicated by
the fact that instead of hearing it on the radio like all
other ministers, Mallam Aminu had been informed by his
younger brother Nafiu, then Chief Judge of Xanadu, who
took personal offence at being once again outshone by his
other-worldly brother who, without the trappings of office
and the power of arms or money, had more influence and
prestige than a government with the power of life and
death over all its citizens. The 'Hanging Judge', as he was
called even then, felt that his reputation was threatened,
since it was an axiom he had established with the General
that he *always got his man*. And since not even an absolute
Life President could be seen to murder a living saint, it
was argued that deprivation of his favourite son would be
even more painful than the death the great scholar did
not fear.

Part of the problem Rabiu had been experiencing was
trying to integrate his poetry into a prose work such as
his *Dancing with Satan*, given his aversion to the practice, which was reinforced by the supervisor for his masters
at Amherst who sneered that 'Lousy poets often seek to
cover their inadequacies by sneaking their lousy poems
into their fiction or drama, which they then condemn as
the work of a *character writing lousy poetry*! What a con
job major-league assholes like Tennessee Williams and

William Faulkner try to pull on the paying public!' But revolutionary poets like Pablo Neruda and Agostinho Neto had the ability to transcend the distinction between prose and poetry, and Dr Solomon had tried to show why their verse, like calypso and reggae, could tell stories, sound fantastic and also mobilize the people for action. The poetry of Neto and Josina Machel had been put to music to drive the guerrillas in their fight against imperialism and to illustrate what he called the failure of intellectuals in air-conditioned offices to speak to the homeless beggars on the streets. Rabiu pointed to Neto's poem 'Friend Mussunda': 'To you friend Mussunda / to you I owe my life / And I write poems you cannot follow / do you understand my anguish?'

So ever since Nuhu's murder Rabiu had sought to produce the definitive verses to immortalize his cousin and drive the progressive forces to certain victory over the General and his Gorillas. So far he had written a single stanza and even this he could not fit seamlessly into the passage of his manuscript, where a long-haired Nuhu with his pale, oval face and talismanic beret with star exhorted the masses: *wherever death may surprise us let it be welcome . . .*

Remembering this now, years later, Rabiu Nafiu's own 'poetry' still seemed prosaic next to the words of his more gifted cousin, who was immortalized by their teacher in a calypso which placed third in an annual contest in Grenada. He had just finished the stanza when the turning lock fractured his thoughts and brought him back to the concrete prison of his windowless office:

> Will you hear us in the morning
> After your long night of dreamless sleep
> Will you hear us in the empty stillness
> Of the spent bullets
> Will you hear us, Nuhu,
> In the imperishable silence

Of the wind
Blowing a futile bouquet of dust
Into the yawning ground
Mothers wept
On the steps of the mortuary
As the sentinel blew taps
Will you see the live green
Of the resurrecting savannah
The brilliance of the dew
On the ravishing petals of flame
Washed in the sunlight
Of the wasted dawn . . .

When he saw who the visitors were he grabbed the picture from his desk, held it close to his chest, then slipped it on top of the manuscript while keeping his eyes fixed on the two men. Joseph Mammamia would have over-shadowed anyone he came with because of his height, the way he showed his teeth in a wide, intimidating smile, and his narrow, basalt eyes, which reversed the gladiator's salute by urging enemies of the regime, 'You who are about to die, salute the General'. When they were students Joseph had been the most radical, *the* revolutionary, the black beret with the biggest red star perched on the Kilimanjaro of all afros, parading the *Little Red Book, The Wretched of the Earth, How Europe Underdeveloped Africa, Thomas Sankara Speaks* and other revolutionary scriptures the way his ances-tors had paraded the Koran of the conquering Arabs and then the Bible of the insipid Europeans.

He had attached himself closer to Delroy Solomon than Delroy's Gary Dourdan hairstyle and, at rallies for the freedom fighters of Southern Africa, when the doctor para-phrased Nkrumah that 'Niagrans can not be free while South Africans are slaves', Joseph's arms were spread widest to embrace the distant comrades, his voice loudest with the slogans of the revolution – '*Amandla!* Power to the People! *A Luta Contínua!* Victory is Certain!'

'This is Comrade Rabiu, Mr Armitage, our revolutionary in residence! *Vitória é certa*, camarade!' His smile was so expansive Rabiu pressed back into his chair as if to avoid being swallowed. Joseph had not been present the day the Disposal Units waited in ambush for the students marching against the Defence Pact with the Americans and targeted Nuhu and the other leaders. Even Delroy Solomon, who had the innocence of a lamb because he was as saintly as his hero Mallam Aminu, appeared surprised that his star pupil, who led the chants before the rally and drove on the others with the power and purity of his revolutionary rhetoric of *the Fatherland or Death*, had disappeared before the shooting started. Rabiu survived only because he was shielded by the corpses of Nuhu, Lasisi and Gwuso Ksahall.

'Impossible,' Mr Armitage said, 'this *can't* be the son of the Attorney General!' The American Consul was a man of absolute certainties but no match for Joseph's. 'Not all chips are from the old block, sir, you've surely heard of the demon seed, the *black* sheep of the family. Can you imagine this atheist disciple of Karl Marx being the grandson of the greatest Islamic scholar West Africa ever produced?'

The Honorary Consul's whiny voice went up an octave as he remarked plaintively. 'But Justice Saleh,' (he pronounced it 'Sally') 'is a close friend. He was at Harvard Law a year ahead of the President, and if he had been American he would have been in the Supreme Court ahead of Sandra Day O'Connor, who shares his economy in legal drafting.'

Very true, Rabiu thought, recalling the article by 'John Lennon' in the *Red Bull:*

Justice Nafiu 'Sandra Day O'Connor' Saleh must be the only judge in history to enjoy wearing the wig and gown off the job when he arrests and confines at his own pleasure comely young men and women in luxurious government guest houses, upholding the principle of equality before the law by refusing to discriminate on grounds of sex, race, ethnicity or religion. Our 'Hanging Judge', or 'Chicken Hawk' as he was known in Roxbury, pursues young flesh with the same tenacity as he swoops on the enemies of the state for his master the General . . .

He was smiling but this went unnoticed by the Honorary Consul whose eyes were boring into Mao's *Selected Works*, and by his managing director, who was gloating at the portrait of the General above his desk.

Joseph's first act after taking over from Delbert Gower, who died of 'natural causes', was to place outsized portraits of his master in each room and open space of the building, which was only fair since the ban on the *Sentinel* was lifted on the condition that he was made MD with the mission to purge all the 'undesirables' before the government took it over. But although Rabiu was the most 'undesirable' of all the 'undue radicals', he was still the son of the Hanging Judge, and Joseph's neck was already too long to risk having it stretched some more. Maybe he had just reminded himself of this because he rubbed it and the gloat froze on his face.

When he entered the office the first day after spending a week 'chatting' with State Security to 'help them in their enquiries' in explaining how Gower had managed to attach the extremely sophisticated bomb to the chassis of his car while his hands were cuffed behind his back and, even more subversively, managed to shoot himself in the back of the head after being blown to pieces by a kilogram of C4 military explosives, Rabiu had seen the picture and almost exploded himself. Although the Men in Black used a blank in the Russian Roulette phase of the interrogation out of deference to the son of the Attorney General, this had not spared him the need to dry clean his trousers in the 'Asabra Same Day' monopoly owned by the First Lady and the Lebanese twins. In a blind rage Rabiu had taken the portrait from the wall where Joseph had placed it so he would be forced to look at Daudu's pig eyes each time he raised his head from his computer screen. He had thought of smashing it or throwing it out the window onto the General Daudu Boulevard below until common sense told him that not even Joseph's fear of his father would prevent him from sacking the perpetrator of such sacrilege and handing him back to the Men in Black. So he had placed it against the wall behind a bookcase.

When Joseph came to gloat about Rabiu's 'holiday' with the SS, and to see how much weight he had lost in the 'microwave' under the Rock Palace, his googly eyes had spun in disbelief at the empty space and just barely managed to launch the strangled cry of 'Where . . . ?' He followed Rabiu's gaze and saw the gilt edge of the sacred icon peeping from behind the bookcase. There and then he had called for the carpenter to *screw* the portrait to the wall so this madman, Hanging Judge or no Hanging Judge for a father, would not tempt him to murder again. In self-defence Rabiu had moved the desk so the portrait was behind him, but Kikelomo had sworn never to enter his office again in case she suffered another miscarriage or gave birth to a demon child.

The consul was wheezing as if full of compressed air, which finally exploded: 'So many books on revolution, Dr Mammamia, isn't this dangerous for a government publication?'

'First Amendment rights, Mr Consul, you know Niagra is the America of the African continent, we do believe in free speech and the rights to life, liberty and the pursuit of happiness! At least *some* of us do!' His protruding Adam's apple pointed at Rabiu as if to indicate to Mr Armitage that such libertarian instincts did not apply to radicals but the Honorary Consul was not amused, seeing no need for jocularity in the face of such extremism. Mr Armitage was not a jocular man and, even if he were, jocularity would have a hard time making an appearance in his Russell Crowe eyes which seemed to have been pasted on his

Humpty Dumpty head with its crisp new Panama hat by unsteady hands, which then loosely attached it to a pumped up Sydney Greenstreet body. Graham Greene's title might be thought applicable to the Honorary Consul, except for that author's ambiguity about evil, which stemmed from his Catholic obsession with original sin.

There was not an ounce of original sin in Armitage's ample Protestant body, which was covered by a double-cuff Van Heusen shirt, ivory links and linen suit of such blinding white it made his Panama look beige. Was he a Colonel Blimp? Not likely, since no one who knew the consul would accuse him of the bumbling inefficiency which characterized the British figure of fun. No. Mr Armitage was like a larger-than-life cartoon, the Balloonman, who pursued what was considered Good by his government with such robust, Ian Paisley zeal that the rest of the world could be destroyed in the process.

This full-blooded Protestant without original sin and his sacred nation requisitioned the saying of the Prophet Ezekiel with less humorous intent than Samuel L. Jackson in Tarantino's *Pulp Fiction*: 'I will execute great vengeance on them with furious rebukes; then they shall know that I am the Lord.' Of course, in the cartoons the destruction was repaired by the stroke of a pen, there was no such state as death or loss and the happy characters lived happily ever after. Not so the village of Lidiziam and its two thousand dead.

That was when the *Sentinel* was the Niagran paper of record, Delbert Gower had won a PEN award for his courage as an editor and Rabiu's column on Lidiziam, written under his own name, had been picked up by the London *Guardian* and the *International Herald Tribune*, attracting favourable comment from Basil Davidson, Noam Chomsky, Edward Said and Samir Amin. The appearance of Rabiu's name on a slim, self-published volume of poetry entitled *Nightshade* seemed to have reminded the Consul of his heinous record and, for the first time, he removed his eyes from the offending titles and pasted them on the man cringing behind the small gunmetal desk.

'It was *you* who wrote that libellous article about Burton Holly,' he bleated, the words escaping like air from a child's balloon.

'Before my time, Mr Consul, the press was not free then, but the prisoner of foreign ideologies and programmes which denigrated the Open Societies of the Free World with their commitment to freedom of the individual, not the double-speak of Political Commissars like Comrade Rabiu here,' Joseph rushed in.

He was bent over the desk like a praying mantis and Rabiu leaned even further back to escape the shower of spit, which had a structure as complex as the Hale Bopp comet. When he was 'Comrade' Mammamia and firing on about the need for permanent revolution, he had replied to mean-spirited malcontents who complained about his rainbow showers that 'No weapon can be spared against the enemies of the revolution!'

'That article led to a congressional hearing and wiped a billion dollars from the value of Burton Holly stock.' Armitage seemed on the verge of weeping and Rabiu looked around for a bucket to hold his tears and Mammamia's spit. Burton Holly had made Armitage a scapegoat for the massacre but had paid him more in compensation than the two thousand three hundred and eighty-four dead of Lidiziam who were not covered by its insurance policies, voided by 'acts of war'. Was this the young troublemaker who had led to further loss by Burton Holly when a slanderous article appeared in the *Nation* that its charitable foundation was repeating the Tuskegee Syphilis Trials in Niagra by testing genetically modified wheat and fish from its Eden Farms on recipients of its free loaves and fish, medical treatment and burial programmes, which allowed scientists at its medical complex in neighbouring Nigeria to do post-mortems on smuggled corpses? He was sure Rabiu was the one who wrote the story about Burton Holly presenting on behalf of Major Nzeribe to the charity of his choice, the First Lady's Niagran Society for the Prevention of Cruelty to Children, a birthday present of a Samsonite suitcase with a million dollars in unmarked bills. And to rub more pepper into his wounds, after the Security people had forced the paper underground, this boy had written that the best birthday present of all was the Vice-President pulling the Major's files from the FBI, DEA and CIA.

Thanks to his childhood friend, Dick Burton, Armitage was still a director of the Lone Star Smelting and Drilling Company, which had a monopoly on drilling boreholes and oil wells, collecting scrap metal and refining minerals throughout the territory of Niagra. And as President of the Burton Holly Charitable Foundation he controlled a budget of billions, invested in everything from bakeries to farms, oil distribution and newspapers, which allowed its parent to pay less tax in Niagra than a street cleaner. Rabiu explored the drill bit eyes in Balloonman's face to see if there was even the trace of a memory of over two thousand souls.

FROM THE SOAPBOX

THE DESTRUCTION OF LIDIZIAM
by Rabiu Nafiu

David Attenborough, the British naturalist, described the village of Lidiziam as the 'original garden of Eden, the closest to heaven on earth' he had ever seen in his long and distinguished service at the BBC. The genetic diversity of its flora and fauna were unequalled outside the Amazon rainforest and it had several varieties of water lilies that were unique. So were the purple and magenta orchids, the new vines with yellow bellflowers which grew from the nests of rare white egrets and brown doves in the forests of liana suspended above streams so clear that young girls braided their hair in the reflection.

A study conducted by an American-trained Niagran microbiologist before the university was closed down showed that the area was endowed with an incredible storehouse of medicinal plants which the local people used to cure jaundice, hypertension, glaucoma, migraine, obesity, diabetes and acne. Their women suffered no ill effects from the menopause and while traditional healers did not claim to be able to cure AIDS, they had medicines which alleviated its symptoms. That's why reports that refrigerated trucks from the Burton Holly Foundation were collecting samples to patent were credible.

This idyllic site was not, however, occupied by people contemptuously described by the *Wall Street Journal* as 'From the Stone Age'. Its two thousand inhabitants had the highest literacy rate in the country, thanks to its enlightened chief, descendant of King Jaja, the outstanding nationalist leader who fought gallantly against British colonialism. One of the first graduates to achieve a first class degree in English from the nation's premier university, this distinguished poet received the prize of the Association of Niagran Authors for his *Lianas in the Mist*.

Not content to keep his educational achievements to himself, the Chief set up an innovative scheme in which each educated citizen of Lidiziam was given the responsibility to ensure that at least ten of his neighbours would achieve his or her level within two years. All public spaces, including his palace, were converted into classrooms and, whereas in the past honours were given to swimmers or mud wrestlers, the *Orders of the Sacred Liana* were now reserved for scholars. With improved education, infant mortality decreased dramatically, employment rose and couples began to postpone starting families until they were able to provide a future for their children.

Outside Lidiziam, however, more powerful men had found that the village possessed even more valuable treasures below its land and waters than above. A *Resource Indicator Satellite* from the Hughes Corporation discovered petroleum reserves more bountiful than Iraq's and a quarter as cheap to produce at fifty US cents per barrel. Appraised of these new riches by a smiling Minister of Information, which would have given the villagers per capita incomes above those of Kuwaitis, the Chief called a general assembly of his people, who politely declined the opportunity to 'better themselves', thus challenging the axiom that it was 'good to be rich'.

They had seen neighbouring villages where oil spills had poisoned the soil and waters and ruined the fish, where flared gas created perpetual hellfire, where people, driven to desperation by lack of opportunities, tapped into exposed pipelines which exploded and incinerated them. Young women prostituted themselves with oil workers while young men were massacred by Disposal Units of the Presidential Guards when they dared protest that their resources were being extracted to pile up the fantastic riches of Xanadu's Generals, leaving death and destruction in their wake.

The government's plans to remove the entire population forcibly were rejected by the oil companies already smarting from the international revulsion engendered by the hanging of the eight environmental activists and campaigns for transparency in the industry being pursued by Global Witness and other NGOs over finance in Angola. The Chief had already contacted his friends in the ANA who mobilized support from Amnesty International, PEN, Greenpeace, Global Forum and other anti-globalization activists.

The villagers were assured that with such international support not even the Niagran government could so blatantly deny the will of its own people. But they were unaware of the even more determined will of the new CEO of the Burton Holly Corporation, who saw no reason why the preference for genteel poverty by two thousand major league assholes, undoubtedly incited by communists and Islamic Fundamentalists, should interfere with the right of the American people to life, liberty and the pursuit of happiness in their Sports Utility Vehicles.

According to John Pilger, the Australian journalist, in the London *Daily Mirror*, Burton Holly contracted out to its subsidiary, Green and Branch, a study on how the oil could be extracted covertly and with minimum environmental damage. Although it was strenuously denied by Bobby Golightly, Burton Holly's spokesperson, that there were 'security options' outlined in an annex marked for the 'Eyes of the CEO Only', subsequent events appear to confirm Pilger's claim that a 'Search and Destroy' mission had been sub-contracted to Danlev, the Israeli Private Military company, and Victor Bout, the international arms dealer, whose clients included Jonas Savimbi, the Lord's Resistance Army and the Iranian Ayatollahs.

A special oil platform was built by the Hughes Corporation, creator of the Glomar Explorer which the

CIA used to retrieve the Soviet nuclear sub, to drill under Lidiziam without the people knowing. As readers of Shakespeare and Steinbeck know, however, the super-highways to hell are paved with the best-laid plans of mice and oil-men. Pressures built up by the covert drilling released foul smelling gas into the pristine air and oil slicks into the translucent waters. Healthy people were succumbing to respiratory illnesses and dead fish floated on rainbows of oil.

When the people caught the white men collecting samples at dead of night, they were fired on by crew-cut retired Navy Seals and Special Boat Commandos who killed four villagers, whose angry comrades retali-ated by beheading the seven Burton Holly employees. Now the secret 'Security Option' was put into effect. According to *Africa Confidential*, the London-based newsletter, the British extended-range Hawk jets, American Black Hawk, French Alouette and Russian Hind MI24 helicopters, plus Niagran leased CI30 trans-ports, were flown by Serbian pilots recruited by Victor Bout on a subcontract by Danlev and Executors Outsource because Niagran pilots were still out of favour with the General.

On the day there was brilliant sunshine and the first the villagers might have sensed that trouble was coming was the brief waning of the light and what looked like burning bushes as the Hawks and helicopters fired incendiary shells into the leaking oil around their village, creating a ring of fire like the ones they used to herd the wild rabbits which threatened the grasslands where rare Agbani antelopes roamed. Then the CI30s disgorged the Niagran parachute regiment, just withdrawn from Kosovo, who, in their green parachutes, must have appeared to the villagers like a locust cloud.

Unfortunately none of this can be confirmed because not a single villager survived to tell the tale. Not knowing they were about to die they could not have given the gladiators' salute, *Ave, Imperator Daudu, morituri te salutant*. But die they did, with not one left to envy the dead. Trapped by the ring of fire, they gathered round their chief who, because of his height, was the first to fall as the Serb gunners did target practice to earn their special bonus. But by the time they completed their assignment and flew out in formation to celebrate at the Xanadu air force base there were still enough villagers left alive for the parachutists to torture and rape before killing.

Rabiu remembered being violently sick when he read the account of a Cameroonian student who had stumbled across the massacre a week later but was rebuked by Kikelomo who showed him the file on massacres she was building for her new take on the 'White Man's Burden'. In 1864 the *Colorado Times* reported that one hundred and sixty-three indigenous American women and children were hacked to death at Rock Canyon by the pride of the US cavalry: 'They were scalped, their brains knocked out, the men used their knives, ripped open women, clubbed little children in the head with rifle butts, beat their brains out and mutilated their bodies. Men cut out the private parts of women and exhibited them on sticks, stretched them on their hats and saddle bows, cut open pregnant women and scalped their unborn children.' The commanding officer was Colonel Walker Carlyle Winthrop Burton, who later struck oil on the site to lay the foundation for the company that would one day rule the world.

The Honorary Consul was suddenly quiet, his Humpty Dumpty head as if put together again by a more steady hand and becalmed by memories of the red mist of the souls rising above the former glory of Lidiziam. He was contemplating the forty volumes of the Yale *Shakespeare* on the shelf of this unfortunate young man, who might have turned out better if he had spent his formative years in New Haven rather than the middle-class desert of Amherst. His melancholy increased when he saw the picture of the three boys and thought of the glories that might have been. One was this young man here who had

betrayed the promise of his father; the other, a preposterous imitation of Che Guevara, down to his weedy beard
and the red star on his black beret, was the renegade son
of the fundamentalist Aminu Saleh, which proved his
thesis that if you scratched an Al-Qaeda fanatic you got
to the Marxist under his skin; the tall one was Major
Abdullahi who had played basketball with Michael Jordan
and now coached a team of street urchins. He wondered
about such a man being so close to General Daudu but
Nasser Waddadda had assured him the Major was in
Military Intelligence, one of his most trusted operatives.

'One for all and all for one.' His eyes were almost misty
as he remembered the *Apostles*, his own gang of three,
from the time they were six and played in sandboxes in
their summer homes in the Hamptons. Even at six Ricky
was the Man, the one who pulled the wings off insects to
show that it was possible to remain silent and expres-
sionless while experiencing the most intense pain. Later
he graduated to frogs, then hamsters, then cats and dogs,
and even his displeasure at being proved wrong when the
animals refused to be silent did not alter his belief that if
you wanted to impose your will on others and dominate
your environment you had to immunize yourself to the
pain you felt, or especially that which you inflicted on
your enemies. By the end of the third summer there was
a garden of corpses of slain animals, a cemetery of the
will which they decorated with the stars and stripes and
the skull and crossbones of the pirate flag. He remembered the tears he locked inside till he almost burst,
pressed by his fear of retribution from Ricky and comforted
by the stoicism of Porgy who went along with whatever
he could not stop. At Andover, then Yale, Ricky was recognized as the leader of men who got straight As without
much effort and was so good at football and hockey he
was scouted by professionals in both sports.

Porgy was a mediocre student but made the baseball
team while Armitage himself was excellent in literature

but had to settle for tennis. Although he wanted to join Scroll and Keys, the secret society for those like him with literary pretensions, he followed the others into the Society of the Sword and Cross (even now he was not allowed to use the real name) which collected the skulls and bones of vanquished enemies and he remembered Ricky obsessed with the skulls of Geronimo, Emiliano Zapata and Frederick Douglass in their brilliant glass cases, seeing in them fellow victims of the US government which had fucked them like it did the Standard Oil Company. Ricky thought if you absorbed the spirit of your enemies you would be invincible. They read *Atlas Shrugged*, *The Fountainhead*, *Beyond Good and Evil* and *Thus Spake Zarasthustra* but it was Capote's *Breakfast at Tiffany's* which cemented them in the path they had chosen from childhood. He and Porgy were fascinated with Holly Golightly but Ricky *loved* her with such a passion that the others sometimes forgot she was a mere fiction.

They had a dream to one day rule the world and all its oil and Holly was integral to that dream. Ricky was from an oil family which had fallen on hard times and never forgot his father's lament that the greatest crimes in history were not committed by Nero, Caligula, Attila the Hun, Genghis Khan or Hitler but by his own American government which had broken up the Standard Oil Company of John D. Rockefeller, his distant ancestor. He had attempted to restore the glory of the past but ended up with the minnow of Burton Oil which the parvenu John Paul Getty had offered to buy for fifty million dollars.

Ricky would change all that, paying tribute to his heroine by naming his octopus of a conglomerate Burton Holly and his only daughter Holly Burton. Beside his two comrades, those were the only two loves of his life although only the company reciprocated, not just in the colossal scale of its profits but in fulfilling his dream to impose his will on the rest of the world, to make and unmake presidents, rewrite laws he did not like, wage war on the

unwilling and find new sources of oil to satisfy the
unyielding thirst of America for gasoline and of Holly
Golightly for ever new adventures.

Porgy would have settled for vice-president in Burton
Holly but was pressed by Ricky to become President of
the United States. And he, Marceau Armitage, had agreed
to become his pro-consul in the chaotic but oil rich
Sodom of Niagra after deciding that his literary ambition was an impossible dream. Literature was about
choice, about picking out of all creation the characters
and settings that would satisfy his fancy. As a religious
man who believed in God and Richard Winthrop Payne
Walker Burton's power to make real the American Dream,
he could not presume to make this choice, to edit the
vast canvas of their Creation. And who, sitting on the
can, would be willing to read a 9,000 page account of
the smell of your Aunt Barbara's chocolate-chip cookie
when you were a six-year-old in short trousers eating
your own shit? The memory produced an anguished smile
as enigmatic as the Mona Lisa's and twice as likely to
be misunderstood.

His benign look at the top of Rabiu's head, which threatened to crease into the hint of a smile, appeared to alarm
Joseph whose eyes hardened into the bottle caps of *Sun*,
his favourite beer before he became a teetotalitarian
Christian fanatic. A former comrade, who studied
Hydrology at Caltech, had calculated that he was the only
creature in nature who could consume enough liquid to
swim in, a first for African physics.

Now he was hurrying his guest along. The inspection
was over. 'We have to leave before we get contaminated
with extremism here, Consul!' he said, trying to nudge
Armitage toward the door. But a forty-volume dose of the
Yale *Shakespeare*, the epiphany of the *Three Musketeers*
and the memories of the Sword upon the Cross had
reduced the fear of this danger and his eyes were as friendly
as they could possibly get. Without original sin this

Moslem boy could have the evil of Marxism burnt from his soul by his noble Father, Justice Nafiu Saleh, the Lord Chief Justice, Solicitor General, Lord Privy Seal and Attorney General of Niagra.

After they left Rabiu looked at the article again. He had been able to use his own name then and even his picture with an afro. Perhaps it was true what his friends had said, that Kikelomo was so good for him he was growing younger. He had had to change his pen name to 'Robert Nesta' in honour of Dr Solomon after his father said the General was whining that he shared the same name with the commander of his Special Presidential Guards who complained that his marabout from Marrakesh had been told by a blind seer from Sierra Leone that sharing a name with an unbeliever was sinful because in the transmigration of souls what went round came round and he didn't want to end up writing articles critical of the government and having his balls cut off and stuffed up his ass.

Then he retrieved the picture from above the manuscript where he had hidden it to protect the memory of his friend from the men whose mere presence would sully it. He still felt the pain in his arm where Kikelomo clung to him as she stared at her sister who nestled as if half asleep in the easy embrace of her husband, Dr Delroy Solomon, who wrote the reply to the *Economist* after its African affairs editor referred to the villagers of Lidiziam as 'luddite' and 'antediluvian' for refusing to be rich. Although his eyes seemed so close there was something in them which spoke of infinity and it was only after Kikelomo pointed it out that Rabiu noticed Delroy's striking resemblance to the African-American actor Gary Dourdan. Their two children looked more like Kikelomo than their mother, and the thought of them now spending their holidays with Mallam Aminu inspired Rabiu to complete the poem to the memory of his uncle's lost son:

Will you see the lilies of the valley
Now buried in the shadow
Cast by the death-stained green khaki
Of the euphoric legions of night
Schoolmates wept
On the steps of the mortuary
In the cruel greyness of the dusk
Why are you silent, Nuhu,
Speak to us
Reach out to us, comrade,
Touch the hands of your brothers
Can you not feel the weight of our grief
It is time, let us go home
With your shattered breastplate
And your brain frozen blue
And the sweep of your eye
On the slant of the rain
It is time, it is time
Let us go
We all wept
On the steps of the mortuary
For our brother
Who has gone before.

He took one last look at the picture and almost wept out
of regret that Kikelomo, Antonio Maceo, Josina Machel
and their unborn child were not there to join him in sorrow
for what they had lost. But he could not weep or feel
emotion in this mausoleum of his dreams suffused with
the Honorary Consul's odour of *Obsession* and Joseph
Mammamia's cologne, which reminded him of embalming
fluid, and he was overwhelmed by Neto's lament, 'Now do
you understand my anguish?'

CRIME SCENE INVESTIGATION

Before Kikelomo saw Gary Dourdan in the popular American television crime series, her recurrent nightmare had always been without structure. In it she had pursued the indistinct figure of Dr Delroy Solomon, her brother-in-law, husband of her elder sister, Omolare, as he spun in the type of vortex one sees in graphics of typhoons or hurricanes, or in the better class of science fiction movies to which her husband Rabiu was addicted. In the manner of dreams he was solid and substantial at one minute only, as the cliché goes, to disappear *into thin air*. In between he would take on the shape of some unknown person who was vaguely familiar, even a suggestion of Rabiu, or a hint of the profile of King Jaja whose enormous statue once towered above the ancient rock at the centre of Xanadu, from whence his gaze traversed the Atlantic Ocean and Caribbean Sea to the paradise islands which had once given refuge to him and his family, and later given birth to the nomadic wanderer who washed up on the shore of the destiny of her life. Blinding light alternated with darkness as the figures surged in technicolour in a hunt on dimensions her mind could not grasp, Isis and Osiris changing places then merging so the world could be. But while she was the pursuer, she had the feeling of being

pursued, trapped, unable to escape, except through the
screams which woke her husband who loved her so much
and instead of whining at being aroused would have the
towel handy to dry the sweat drenching her body, water
to quench the fires inside her and loving arms to lull her
back to uneasy dreams.

Gary Dourdan changed all that with his rolling walk
which stopped short of being a swagger, his calm, eternal
grey eyes, and those big hands which could span a basketball and had inspired her with bitterness and ecstasy when
her sister brought him to their little house and introduced
him as 'Dr Solomon' and he had patted her perfectly plaited
braids and drawled, 'So this is the beautiful little Kikelomo
you told me so much about!' It was not that Gary Dourdan
looked like her brother-in-law – he *was* the Delroy of her
nightmare and when he walked off the screen toward her
she felt herself pulling back so he would not pat her head
again and reduce her to the quivering fifteen-year-old who
longed in vain for the love of her sister's husband.

Now she looked forward to her nightmare with the same
anticipation as she awaited the logo *CSI*, resenting the
quizzical smile and know-it-all conceit of William Peterson
(homage to McGarret in *Hawaii Five-O*?), whose image
delayed the appearance of her beloved, her shining star,
her infinite, extraordinary love. Of course she was in
charge of casting in her dream so Peterson's character
Grissom was demoted to a bit part, to clumsy assistant
with leaden dialogue, confused body language and trite
gestures who misplaced evidence, misinterpreted clues,
mixed up cases and created such a mess that only the brilliance of Gary Dourdan as Warrwick Brown, the Chief
Crime Investigator, could sort out and pat his lowly assistant on the head to show that he was magnanimous and
had no hard feelings. Her people thought that bowlegged
men were stupid and Grissom confirmed this.

She was especially careful with the women characters
who were not even given screen names but confined to

their own and kept well clear of their boss with whom they were bound to fall in love. In the series she suspected that Marg Helgenberger had slept with Warrwick although the evidence was thin and deliberately confusing. Jorja Fox, who had not slept with him, definitely wanted to, always sidling up in that furtive way, so he could look down her pathetic cleavage and smell her American perfume. Kikelomo particularly enjoyed it when Warrwick refused to take the bait, walked away, or patted her shoulder with what he considered the mild affection of a colleague but which the pout of her thin lips and tightening of her squared jaws indicated that she thought was condescension. Why else would she try to get Warrwick in trouble with Grissom over a gambling habit which was no fault of his? Or why her constant tension, sideways glances and shallow breathing when they were in the same scene? In her dream Kikelomo dressed Marg in severe, navy blue power suits which could never turn on a laid-back character like Warrwick while Jorja was given hippy chic clothes in line with her quirky obsessions with alternative therapies, queer diets, Northern California lifestyle and environmental hang-ups. She made doubly sure the women never appeared alone with Warrwick, and their make-up was so minimal their lines and wrinkles showed! And in a cruel twist she had Grissom lusting after Jorja who had a lesbian fix on Marg! Meanwhile, like a Philosopher King, the unattached Warrwick was able to devote his entire energy and love to solve the great puzzle of the Unidentified Victim.

The badly burnt creature lies curled up on its side on the slab, knees bent, arms open wide as if it had been holding a beach ball. Grissom thinks it is a gorilla until his anthropologist girlfriend takes measurements and, on the basis of the ratio of arm to leg lengths, concludes it is a biped, definitely Homo sapiens. Warrwick agrees and asks Marg to examine the body and tell him what she thinks. But all she can venture is that it is a Caucasian male about six foot to six foot five, and thirty to forty years old. According to Warrwick the Vegas police claim that the victim has committed suicide by setting himself alight but Jorja Fox says this is unlikely because the evenness of the burn indicates that someone has carefully spread the inflammable liquid over the body, including the palms and the soles of the feet. It also appears that the clothes have been stripped off before ignition, unlikely for a man preparing himself for death.

It's Marg Helgenberger who notices the bullet holes which have been reduced almost to pinpricks by the flames but she can't tell if they are entry or exit wounds until Warrwick points to one in the back of the skull which has made a neat hole like a dime so it looks almost as if it has always been there, as if the man had been born with the proverbial hole in the head. Are these wounds and the burning still compatible with suicide asks Warrwick? Yes, replies Jorja Fox, but someone else must have attacked the body after death, indicating great passion for revenge, perhaps a serious grudge, envy or hatred for some slight. If the body is identified it would be possible to find the killer, or defiler of the corpse, who probably felt thwarted or shamed by the 'suicide'.

Was there a suicide note, did the police authenticate it, or refuse to pursue the case because of it? They should certainly examine the other bullet holes to determine points of entry and exit, as even the one in the back of the head does not rule out suicide unless cause of death is established definitively. Warrwick can see Grissom's girl is eager to make a mould to see if they can identify the victim and, although he is sceptical, based on the failure of her previous work to identify the perpetrators, squeezes her shoulder in encouragement and lets her get on with the job.

Although she was the director, Kikelomo could not get the action to proceed beyond this point, as if the Scriptwriter had refused to let her see the ending because He did not trust her not to leak it to John Lennon of *Red Bull*. It was at this point in the dream that she started to moan in frustration and grind her teeth as she tossed and turned and the patient Rabiu would hold her in his comforting arms and whisper, 'Darling you're having that nightmare again.' And she would bury her face deeper in his chest, feel the child moving inside her and pray that this time she would bear him their own child to give comfort to the two orphans of her sister Omolare.

DANNY BOY – OR THE GENERAL IN HIS ELVIS COSTUME

General Abdu-Salaam bin-Sallah-ud-Deen bin Sani-Ibrahim al-Daudu was born plain Boma Cumo of a *Maguzawa* father, as the indigenous people of the Hausa Kingdoms of West Africa were called, and a *Bata* mother, the so called 'Little People' of the Cameroon rain forests, whom western anthropologists libel as 'Stone Age Pygmies'. While his father was a strapping six foot one in keeping with his origin on the sun-scorched savannah, his mother was a diminutive four foot seven, a height considered genetically advantageous for negotiating the hazards of the rain forest, climbing very tall trees to garner fresh organic honey, trap monkeys in nets of vines and featuring on the Discovery Channel or David Attenborough's excellent wildlife specials. In keeping with Aristotle's maxim that the golden mean is the measure of all good fiction, the future General came out a well rounded five foot four, an ideal adaptation, as we shall see, for all situations, enabling him, in his own words, to *'dominate his environment'*. Like many short men with a Conrad Black complex he had a compulsion to fuck everyone else in the ass *'before they do it to me'*.

His first opportunity to prove his mettle came when his father, Coma Cumo, went to work as a gardener for an

Anglo-Irish academic who specialized in the unpublished
poetry of W. B. Yeats and was not averse to singing a ballad
or two while having a warm bath after a breakfast pick-
me-up of Irish whiskey. The young Boma who fetched the
hot water for his bath would wait outside and mime the
words of his songs of longing. His favourite was 'Danny
Boy' and Boma's rendition of this in perfect pitch when
he was only six years old so impressed his father's master
that he gave him the name Daniel and raised his gardener's
salary from fifteen shillings to seventeen and six.

The ambiguity inherent in the poetic sensibility of an
Anglo-Irishman specializing in the schoolboy musings of
a great poet had other repercussions on the Cumo family.
While his Englishness dictated that he look down on the
local brew enjoyed by the *Maguzawa* during their celebrations of the *Bori* spirits, his Irish enthusiasm for inclu-
sion led him to invite the elder Cumo to his maudlin
deconstructions of the hidden meanings of *Finnegan's
Wake*, over bottles of made-in-Niagra over-strength
Guinness stout and Irish single malts. Unfortunately the
Maguzawa liver is not genetically programmed to assimi-
late the Irish brew and Cumo senior soon found himself
crooning maudlin Irish ballads to the great *Bori* spirits in
the sky.

Young Boma's mother was then taken in by a four-foot-
eleven tailor of Manama called Daudu who had searched
many years for a woman shorter than himself and his
adopted son got a job as a stable boy in the household of
the great Islamic scholar, father of the saintly Aminu Saleh
and his brother Nafiu whom detractors later called the
Hanging Judge. Impressed by the manner in which the
boy could calm the most violent tempered beast by
whistling 'Danny Boy', the Grand Khadi treated him like
a son and, when he expressed his desire to join the army,
the old man pulled strings to overcome his failure to meet
the minimum height which the English had introduced
on the grounds that it 'just isn't sporting to be so short

that it isn't possible for the other chaps to spot you and blow your fucking brains out before you do it to them'.

As a soldier young Daniel was just as successful as in his earlier incarnations as crooner of Irish ballads and stable boy. At Fort Bragg his American instructors were impressed by his genius for deception, which found its apotheosis in the absolute brilliance of his Elvis impersonations. This won him contests from New Jersey to Las Vegas, earning him an all-expense trip to Graceland and the Grand Ole Opry, where he met Big Bill Lester and Ernest Tubb and developed his lifelong love affair with country and western music. From then on his ambition was to become General, Head of State and Commander-in-Chief of his country's armed forces, so he could honour men like Elvis who had been a source of such inspiration in his life.

In America he had also become attracted to the preaching of Father Divine and spent hours watching films of his sermons, his mansions and cadillacs, and the vast multitudes of his poor followers who made him his fortune. On his return to Niagra Captain Daudu fell under the influence of Prophet Obafemi Oluwole who bore a striking resemblance to Father Divine, including his gold lamé gowns from whose huge sleeves his long, thin fingers flashed and trembled as he shrieked that the 'Wrath of God will descend like flaming eagles on the heads of those who fail to stuff the gold envelopes of the Risen Christ with Holy Dollars dedicated to the expansion of His glorious Tabernacle of Light'.

The Captain was so impressed with the Prophet's piety, dedication and business sense that he donated one tenth of the salaries of the men under his command in accordance with Prophet Oluwole's Commandment that 'the Workman is worthy of his hire and only payers of the tithe will enter the kingdom of heaven'. He was less impressed with the prescription that in order to attain the rank of General and seize power in ten years he would have to sacrifice his first born, rape a mad woman, sleep with a black donkey and give away his Elvis paraphernalia. After berating the Prophet for his cruelty and insensitivity, he explained the central position Elvis held in his life as his talisman, *raison d'être* and Guiding Light, the man who brought him in touch with his feminine side, gave his life focus and led him on the narrow path to the Power and the Glory. As a devout Christian he could not be so ungrateful to Elvis. Prophet Oluwole agreed, but in return for remaining faithful to the King, he would have to convert to Islam, and take at least five names, corresponding to the five corners of the American Pentagon and the letters in E-L-V-I-S.

When General Abdu-Salaam bin-Sallah-ud-Deen bin Sani-Ibrahim al-Daudu seized power from his mentor General Caleb Calloway, he wracked his brains about how to immortalize the memories of those who had done so much to ensure his emergence as the *Unique Miracle of the Twentieth Century*. Passing Decree 419 to ban all music except country and western on public radio was derisory. Replacing the staid national anthem *written by a menopausal British spinster* with 'Ain't Nothin But A Hound Dog' was hardly a tribute to the King. And the biggest McDonald's in the world looked like just another place of worship next to the National Mosque and Cathedral, which were themselves only the *second biggest* in the world after the duplicity of the goddam madman Sadam and the whinging of the Pope. How could he style himself the fucking *Dominator of his Environment* and *Master of the Universe* if he couldn't express the depth of his Gratitude to Elvis?

His opportunity came when the eaters of live monkeys and dead fish from the riverine areas killed the seven Americans who came to bring them the wealth and security of proven oil reserves making him look bad before the US President and British Queen who had promised him State visits. After making a 'proportionate response' he would tear down the statue of their so-called 'National Hero' from the 'Rock of Ages' and replace it with one of Elvis bigger than the fucking Statue of Liberty. According to the foolish academics from the area the so-called 'King' allegedly fought against the British who came to impose 'Imperialism' on his people until they locked up his ass and carted him off to a primitive Caribbean island full of sugar-cane eating wastrels and monkeys.

[Editor's note: The Amuz Rock at the centre of Xanadu was estimated by geologists to have been formed at least 500 million years ago when a unique alignment between our planets and stars on the shoulder of Orion caused a massive eruption in the earth's crust which explains its earthy, ruddy colour even today. Over millennia, rich, wind blown soil collected on top and dense foliage grew to give the appearance of a jungle in the sky, accounting for the so-called 'Hang Up Gardens' of European folklore. The Amuz Rock is accepted by most experts as the geographical centre of the universe although this is disputed by Stephen Hawking who argues that it is unlike the black hole singularity hypothesized in his monumental *Brief History of Time*.

In an interview with the celebrated *News of the World* the Lucasian Professor of Mathematics at Cambridge argued that the only place in the known universe where gravitational forces exceeded that of a black hole was the fashion singularity in the Niagran city of Xanadu when the President's wives wiggled their big, tight-bound asses as they paraded their love for National Independence on the fourth of July. Another sceptic is Grubman Peacock who argues convincingly that the rock, because of its resemblance to the flat-top Aztec pyramid, the mastabas of Nubia and the temples of Angkor Wat, was obviously constructed by very tall white men with blue beards, as there was no evidence that rock builders of such exquisite skills existed in sub-Saharan Africa 500 million years ago.

What is indisputable, however, is that all the people of Niagra, from the earliest times to the present, argue that this is the origin of the human race, if not life itself. Tiny crystalline spheres, not unlike sequins, reflect light, appear to contain water and sometimes look green, which would suggest the three essential pre-conditions of life. Because of their belief in its sanctity ancient Niagrans worshipped at shrines there but refused to build temples, dwellings or farmhouses. And it was not until British colonialists arrived that the sacrilege was committed of building the Rock Fort as the seat of administration, a zoo to exhibit the spectacular wildlife that roamed freely there and a replica of White's Club to provide R&R for the better class of civil servants. But the wrath of the gods, or perhaps dysentery, taught the buggers a lesson they would never forget and their fossilized shit on the north face is still visible from the Space Station.]

Even after Independence nationalists refused to use the follies of their colonial masters and it was only after consultations with a representative sample of marabouts, *sangomas*, *babalawos*, blind seers, medicine men and witch doctors, that it was decided to erect the statue of King Jaja, recognized as the purest example of National Resistance. That is, until the coming of General Daudu and his Homage to Memphis and Las Vegas. The General's resolve to make some architectural rearrangements was strengthened on his state visit to Madame Tussaud's when an incident occurred which went down in English and Niagran folklore as *The Day the Duke of Edinburgh Played the Diplomatic Card by Pouring Crude Oil on a Troubled Waxworks Museum*.

When he came face to face with the effigy of his hero, General Daudu was so overcome that he prostrated and embraced Elvis's ankles while planting wet kisses on his blue suede shoes. An embarrassed Nasser Waddadda gently pulled him to his feet, slipped a bundle of Harrod's white Egyptian cotton hankies into his trembling right hand and discreetly pointed to the 'Do not touch the exhibits' sign. In his most soothing Karl Rove whisper he explained that this obeisance to the *white* King of Rock and Roll could be exploited in the local *Voice* newspaper by black extremists like Diane Abbott, Paul Boateng and Ann Widdecombe.

When his offer to purchase the waxwork was refused, a distraught General, gesticulating wildly, denounced the cultural imperialism of perfidious Albion, Nasser whipped up seismic maps of new-found oil deposits off the coast of Lidiziam and the Attorney General presented his English counterpart with his interpretation of UNESCO's protocol on the need to return stolen colonial artefacts which had just been published in the *Harvard Law Review*. A summary which appeared in *Platt's Oil Digest* argued that the Elvis statue counted as a colonial relic of Niagra because of the seminal role the King of Rock and Roll had played in the formation of the Life President of the country, that *Unique Miracle of the Twentieth Century*. The Brits should therefore give it up so as not to fuck up the oil market. And it was at this point that a hack from the *New Statesman* swore that he overheard the Duke turn to his wife and say, 'Look, Lilibet, would it placate the African gentleman if we gave him Eddie instead? Surely he would prefer a real prince to the waxwork of some fucking Redneck "King" who had to sing for his supper rather than marry a real queen?'

This was the third insult the Brits had inflicted on General Daudu, and the Foreign Minister's adoption of the Three Strikes and You're Out policy meant that they were fucked. First they had tried to quarantine his Chief Praise Singer's pet hyenas, called Liam and Noel after the Gallagher brothers, until Nasser reminded the Minister of

Defence of on-going negotiations to buy another 300 Hawks and the Home Secretary agreed the pets could be classified as entertainers and given work permits like Michael Jackson, Axl Rose and Courtney Love. They were hesitant about Oxford and Cambridge awarding him and his First Lady his 'n' hers honorary doctorates until Nasser showed the Prime Minister the *FT*'s *Niagra Survey* which confirmed that the country had more oil than Iraq. And even then they had to settle for degrees from Buckingham University as the Education Minister pointed out that the Oxford and Cambridge student unions were controlled by psychopathic cross-dressers, followers of Osama bin Laden, the criminally insane, communists, Old Labour pricks and friends of Gordon Brown.

The General's planned revenge against the Brits and the monkey eaters would be colossal in scale. He would use bacon, tomato and lettuce sandwiches with lashings of mayo as units of national account and convert his sterling balances to pork belly futures. And his *American* architects promised that his monuments would be seen from space, by the same Hughes Corporation satellite which located the world's greatest oil reserves under some fucking major league assholes who thought 'beauty', 'health', 'education', 'security' and 'long life' were better than crude! *'Did we fuckin show 'em!'*

Some building contracts were awarded to the Bechtel Corporation at the suggestion of retired General Colin Ploughman, former military aide of George Schultz when he was Reagan's Secretary of State and Daudu's command-ing officer at Fort Bragg, who bought him his first Elvis costume with resplendent sequins which sparkled with a green aquatic sheen, suggesting a new life form bred of the symbiosis of Graceland and Xanadu. Others went to Green and Branch after Mr Dick sent him a nice birthday present of $180 million when Burton Holly was awarded the $6 billion contract to build the biggest gas liquefaction plant on the continent. He even accepted Mr Dick's suggestion that the Elvis statue weigh a bit less than the Statue of Liberty 'so the American President wouldn't look like a fucking dork'.

Thus it was that the sacred Amuz Rock, in addition to bearing an Elvis statue visible from the International Space Station, was home to a replica of Graceland with the finest collection of sequined costumes in the world; a Grand Ole Opry museum with antique jukeboxes programmed to play digital recordings of every country and western song ever recorded in Nashville; an Afro-Disneyland with condemned political prisoners dressed up as Minnie and Mickey to appease Amnesty International and PEN; and the Rock Palace, bigger than the Sultan of Brunei's, where the General paraded his Henry VIII collection of wives for visiting American Presidents, British Prime Ministers, German Chancellors and a randy Lucasian Maths professor who occupied Newton's Chair at Cambridge and tried to synthesize *Rock Around the Clock Tonight* on his snazzy Korean-made PC.

Daudu did balk at the suggestion of Prophet Oluwole that he build on the rock the biggest cathedral in the world on the superb logic that he did not want God to overshadow Elvis. But in compensation for the Prophet, to whom he was forever grateful, he built him a temple *second* in size to St Peter's, having signed a protocol with the Vatican that His Holiness would beatify Daudu's beloved mother, making her the *shortest saint in Black Africa* provided he didn't make the Holy Father look stupid by building an oversized Basilica with boulevards wider than the Champs-Elysées and a runway long enough for Concorde to land in his hamlet with more sheep, goats and cattle than Catholics, full of cannibals and Evangelical Christians.

In recognition of the General's contribution to the development of the continent, the African-American Studies Department of Harvard University organized a conference at which the world's leading historians would compete for the $1 million prize, donated by the Burton Holly Charitable Foundation and the First Lady's Niagran Society for the Prevention of Cruelty to Children, to decide which of his acts was the highest expression of the African genius. Some mentioned his $106 million Taj Mahal of Chastity where Lynne Cheyney launched the slogan 'Say No to Sex' as the solution to Africa's AIDS problem. But the winner by acclamation was Andrew Martian who argued that by silencing Niagra's cows, the noisiest in Black Africa, the General had merited his accolade as the *Unique Miracle of All Time*. In *Great Battles of History*, volume twenty-five of his *Short Life of a World Statesman*, Martian had impressed historical critics with his contention that the General's blitzkrieg against the cows of Xanadu showed a tactical genius superior to that of Rameses the Great, Hannibal, Pyrrhus of Epirus, Julius Caesar, Napoleon, Shaka the Great and Donald Rumsfeld.

But enough of the pesky creatures remained loose in the rest of the country, causing traffic jams, looking stupid, annoying farmers, and contributing to global warming with uncontrolled farting. On a visit to his counterpart in the White House, Nasser Waddadda, the General's Karl Rove, came up with a radical solution. According to a cousin of a classmate of Karl Rove's grade school teacher who had met the uncle of a friend who knew Richard Perle's mother-in-law from a fat farm in Tuscaloosa, American environmental experts had discovered that global warming was not caused by gas guzzling SUVs, inefficient smoke-belching factories, gunsmoke from gangsta rappers in drive-by shootings, deliberations in Congress on the need for tax cuts, or contentions by Neo-Conservatives and Evangelical Christians that Saddam Hussein *was* a Weapon of Mass Destruction, but by the methane gas emitted by unruly cows. To undermine the Kyoto Protocol it was necessary to genetically modify the cows to fart nitric oxide (NO) rather than methane (CH_4) which would not only reverse global warming but save a hell of a lot on dental bills.

And thus it came to pass that General Daudu saved his people and continent from environmental catastrophe by slaughtering the rest of his polluting cattle and replacing them with clean ones retro-engineered on a small ranch in Crawford Texas to fart Laughing Gas. And since there were more farmers than cattlemen the General was a shoo-in to win the Presidency and both houses of Congress for the right wing of the Republican Party of Niagra.

NANNY

Delroy Moziah Kweku Chukwuemka Omowale Solomon was born in Nanny Town in the Cockpit Country of Jamaica, home of the Maroons, descendants of the Akan-speaking slaves who defeated their English masters and won their independence centuries before their fellow islanders. But unfortunately they blotted their copybook by agreeing to return escaped slaves to the plantations from which they fled. The role of betrayal in the black man's struggle for existence was something engrained in Delroy's psyche from a very young age by his father and grandfather, descendants from a line of storytellers who had maintained the tradition from their ancestors in today's Ghana and the Ivory Coast. Regardless of the Maroon's betrayal, the role of Nanny, the ferocious guerrilla leader, showed that Africa was the only continent where the power of *woman* was recognized, from the time of Hatshepsut, Nefertari, Nefertiti and the Nubian Pharaohs to Queens Jinja of Angola and Amina of Zazzau, Nigeria.

Delroy's father, Cudjoe, had descended to the plains of the capital city where he floated around the music scene dominated by titans such as Count Ossie and Don Drummond and was allegedly a minor character in *Brother*

Man, the seminal novel by Roger Mais. In his wanderings 'in town' he had met a *redibo* woman, the name given to light complexioned people who reminded Jamaicans of their Ibo slave ancestors from Eastern Nigeria. As he discovered later, she owed her beauty and her golden colour to the perfect blending of slave ancestors from the Fanti and Ashanti of Ghana, the Yoruba and Ibo of Nigeria and the indigenous Carib population, the so-called Arawaks who the first Spanish colonists thought they had exterminated. After failing to make it as a singer with Count Ossie's band his mother, who had taken on the Yoruba name Atinuke, became the first woman DJ to control a sound system at popular dances and is credited by some music historians with introducing the dub poetry which led to the rap phenomenon. (How she would react to the misogyny of modern rap and hip hop is another matter, although she was a very bright woman and would have recognized that the main audiences for these distortions of African music were middle-class white kids, prime-cut dorks and creeps traumatized by the materialism and confused sexuality of their parents.)

She was clearly the author of the lyrics made famous in the song 'The First Time Ever I Saw Your Face' as shown in the notebooks he found in her things after she died: 'The first time I saw you / I knew the sun, the moon and stars / Were your gifts to me / And the other doves in the sky.'

Atinuke soon found, however, that Music was a man's world, in which she had no long-term future, especially with the approaching birth of her child. So they returned to the Cockpit Country with its constant throbbing of drums, smells of roasting goat meat, ganja smoke, Scotch bonnet peppers, fever grass, ginger, stale sweat and white rum. In all his wanderings for the rest of his life Delroy always regarded the mist-shrouded land of the Maroons as home. When he was seven his mother separated from his father and accepted an invitation from an uncle who worked as a soccer coach at Howard University and emigrated with her son to the United States, then a combination of Mecca and Eldorado for the poor ex-slaves of the Caribbean.

In High School he excelled at both soccer and basketball and when his mother's uncle persuaded him to accept an athletic scholarship to Howard he was torn between the two and ended up not excelling at either. His main interest remained African music in the diaspora and he was fascinated by the figure of Stokely Carmichael, the pioneer of Black Power, who was born in Trinidad, naturalized as an American, graduated from Howard, but was threatened with deportation by J. Edgar Hoover for his 'un-American Activities'.

Later Stokely migrated to Guinea where he met the great African leaders Sekou Toure and Kwame Nkrumah and, to pay homage, took the name Kwame Toure. It was in Conakry, the Guinean capital, that Stokely met and married Miriam Makeba, the celebrated chanteuse from South Africa. Delroy would later dedicate to the couple his doctoral thesis, *The African Origin of American and Caribbean Music*, which was published by Lawrence Hill Books as *Out of Africa, All New Music*.

He thought of dedicating it to his father but considered this insufficient for the contribution Cudjoe had made to his spiritual development. With his hands crippled by arthritis, no longer able to make the *abeng* drums speak or to farm, barely able to build a spliff, Cudjoe made a precarious living telling stories of the great Maroon heroes and heroines such as Nanny, his namesake Cudjoe and others, such as Sam Sharpe and Paul Bogle, who fought the slave masters. As a major resource person in his research, Delroy saw no reason why he should not share his generous grant from the Ford Foundation with his disabled father who told him how the rebelling slaves communicated using the talking drums whose techniques they brought with them from West Africa. Music was important in mobilizing the people and Cudjoe taught his son the songs the slave master could not understand, songs which the leaders used to remind the people of what they had lost coming across the Atlantic and how they could regain their humanity by defeating the satanic powers which justified their crimes by appealing to a white god who created the black man to serve his children.

In Jamaica for his research, they attended cockfights where Delroy learnt further songs and traditions of Africa, the art of wrestling and stick fighting, to drink vast quantities of white rum without slurring his speech, drown himself with *mannish water* made from goat's head, balls and offal laced with conflagrations of Scotch bonnet peppers, and to smoke a variety of *sensimila* which grew only in the special soils of the Cockpit Country and would later be classified by an American Attorney General as a Weapon of Mass Destruction. Cudjoe took his son to old plantations where he showed him relics of the Yoruba, Ibo and Akan-speaking peoples who made up the majority of slaves to the island. Sometimes they were lucky and found very old people who remembered tales of the old times and the countries from which they were taken or were able to locate old drums, fifes, horns, gongs and stringed instruments made from gourds, cowrie shells and horse hide.

Cudjoe told him of the music scene in Kingston although he was still bitter that it had rejected his beloved Atinuke, one of the best talents he had ever known, so she was reduced to migrating to America to cook for white people. He told him of Alpha Boy's School, the orphanage for poor kids, which had produced some of the finest musicians in the world under the inspired tutelage of Sister Mary Ignatius. Years later Delroy could still recall the reverential tone that crept into his father's voice when he uttered the name of the nun, his red eyes and distended pupils lit up like a Jamaican sunset. 'See it, Del, dis a true African woman, Star.' He spoke of the young middle-class girl who, instead of marrying a big shot and becoming 'something' in the snobbish Jamaican society which looked down on poor people, took a vow to care for the weak and poor, God's precious little ones whom the world had abandoned. She knew the history of the island's music and musicians like no other and never closed her door to anyone. Cudjoe spoke of a Chinaman whom he referred to as another true African, a Victor Chin who ran VP recording studio and Randy's Record Shop where you could buy any record produced on the island.

But the old man told him that his education would not be complete without returning to the mother continent to find a gifted musician called Akintunde Ojo who had spent time on the island as a youth and was said to have inspired Roger Mais' *Brother Man* before returning home to influence a generation of musicians who blended the original rhythms of Africa with developments from the diaspora, allowing it to transcend itself with unique fusions from the western reaches to the centre and south of the continent. Young Ojo, an orphan from Niagra, formed a band at the age of twelve which played at weddings, funerals, and other ceremonies. His music, using traditional instruments, was so sweet that he was in high demand, making enough money to support his three sisters and four brothers in school.

He taught himself to read and his elder sister taught him to write and encouraged him to go to school himself later. This became possible when a very nationalist couple called Ransome-Kuti in neighbouring Nigeria took him under their wing after he had played juju music at the naming ceremony for their son Fela. Miraculously he made it to that country's premier university and enrolled in history because they had no academic course in the type of music he wanted. The academic environment was disappointing because the people were too rigid, too full of themselves, too know-all and cut off from the rich culture of their country and the rhythms of its existence. They had no music in their souls, felt no urge to sing when the sun was shining or the new rain sparkled on the throbbing vines of yams.

These black/white men and women drifted through life like zombies without living so that they had to seek paradise in an afterlife where they hoped to experience the pleasures they missed on earth. Always he felt as if he was trapped in a mausoleum where death had undone so many and the music within him was the explosive with which to resurrect them from their illusions of fear and greed.

Ojo immersed himself in Roger Mais' *The Hills Were Joyful Together* and felt even more uncomfortable in his marble halls of residence with uniformed servants to make them like white men and women when the only air he could breathe was that of the streets and the hovels of the dispossessed where he had grown up with his sisters and brothers. He searched for more books on the island and read the works of Marcus Garvey, the historical writings of Richard Hart, C.L.R. James, M.G. Smith's and Rex Nettleford's studies of the Rastafari, the chronicles of slave revolts from Toussaint L'Ouverture to Sam Sharpe.

He was intoxicated with the music of Count Ossie, Lord Kitchener, the Mighty Sparrow and other Caribbean practitioners in whose rhythms he felt himself reflected as in a mirror. From that time Ojo knew he could not be complete unless he followed his people to their new home and brought back the African seeds which they had planted under the searing Caribbean sun. Cudjoe told his son that the young African had pursued his goal with maniacal zeal as if he thought the world was about to end. He came with a tape recorder and carton full of cassettes and collected every song ever composed, every tune ever played on whatever instrument, interviewed Roger Mais and Peter Abrahams, studied the performances of Louise Bennet and other artists, spent time at Alpha with Sister Mary Ignatius

and her boy geniuses and gathered the most impressive
collection of ganja seeds ever put together in the history
of Jamaica. Some of his collection was now in the Jamaica
Institute and the History Department of the University of
the West Indies but the bulk had been taken back to Niagra
so the people there could see what their prodigal offspring
had achieved. Delroy had to see Brotherman to fulfil his
destiny as the prodigal son returning to Mother Africa.

Delroy filled his holdall with 45s recorded by Mamie
Smith, Blind Lemon Jefferson, Charley Patton, John Lee
Hooker, Howlin' Wolf, Blind Willie Johnson, Joe Turner,
Louis Jordan, Billy Holliday, Arthur 'Big Boy' Crudup,
Bessie Smith, Muddy Waters, Little Walter, Sonny Boy
Williamson, his mother Atinuke and other blues men and
women from Memphis, Biloxi and the delta around New
Orleans but found that Brotherman had no electricity to
use the portable player he brought. Telling him 'not to
worry' (like a true Jamaican!) he assured Delroy that there
were shacks nearer the main road with illegal connections
to the mains. There was also no need to worry about his
own recordings of Jamaican music since these had been
lent out to musicians like Fela who were looking for new
sources of inspiration. When they came round to jam he
would hear more than he would have from mere cassettes.
Roger Mais was a lousy artist and the sketches he made
of 'Brother Man' looked nothing like the man in real life.
In fact Brotherman looked more like Mais himself and
the choruses he wrote before each chapter were like tonal
snapshots of the Niagran.

On the hill surrounding the town they would gather to
parade the new musical styles amidst the ganja smoke
from Brotherman's imported seeds and the flames of
lanterns reminding him of the stars above the Cockpit
Country and the eyes of hawks and owls reflecting them
below. In the twilight he saw the shrunken images of the
polio-crippled children dragging themselves up the hill
from the streets where they begged or stole or sold bread

and cigarettes or small twists of hemp, feeding from dust-bins or fighting the pigs and dogs for leftovers, getting locked up, beaten or killed by sporting policemen or hunter-soldiers, and resting on the hard ground to hear the sweet new music which would one day conquer Africa and the World.

Delroy would look out across the rock at the centre of the world to the raging foam of the Atlantic which had once swept his people to a place they did not know and to which after five centuries they still did not belong. Brotherman told him about the statue of Jaja the King who fought the white man at his own game of trade and won, not knowing the rules of the game said *Niggers can not win*! And how he was swept away from his land to a variety of way stations until he ended up in the Caribbean and Delroy Solomon remembered his father's chronicle of the Great African Chief who brought news of what the people had left behind and how they came down from the hills as they would later for Marcus Garvey who was a Moore from the family whose roots were in Nanny Town which celebrated the power of the African Woman.

So he did not dedicate his book to Brotherman or his father because they were worth more than just a mention, worth as much as himself. Delroy gave over more than half his Introduction to them and used his advance to build his father a two bedroom concrete house in Nanny Town and to buy an old saxophone from a player in one of Coltrane's earliest bands for the fusion man of Africa and the Caribbean, the pioneer of *sensimila*, the first disciple of Jah, the Living God of Ras Tafari, in the land of Niagra.

The first time he saw the face of the teacher, Omolare, sun, moon, stars and sky collapsed into her being, his heart stopped together with his brain, his entire universe, future and all his hopes, and he knew then that without

her he could not be. Time, space and dimension were
sucked out of his existence and he could not see her shape
on the 'plump' side or her height of five foot two or her
round face in a skin as black as the braids of her hair. It
was her that the gods of Xanadu had used as a model to
carve the Amuz Rock 500 million years ago but she
exceeded their creation in the elemental force of her
bearing which was more stoical and impassive and without
haste than any rock could be.

Her stature shouted that WOMAN WOULD RISE AGAIN!,
confirmation of Sheikh Anta Diop's hypothesis that
matriarchy was the ruling principle of the continent, that
it would one day rise up to defeat the destructive forces
of patriarchy introduced by the Europeans and adopted
so slavishly by African men more in love with their own
cocks than Narcissus. She was Isis, Nut, Nefertari,
Hatshepsut, Nefertiti, all the Nubian woman Pharaohs
after the collapse of the last dynasty, Queen Jinja of
Angola, Amina of Zazzau, Nanny, Winnie Mandela,
Gambo Sawaba of Nigeria and Fela's mother, Mrs
Fumilayo Anikulapo-Kuti.

The first time he visited he could not see her sister
Kikelomo already taller standing next to her in all her
golden beauty, the frail orphan protected by the colossal
energy of her older sister who stood squat outside their
little house like the Amuz Rock guarding the green heart
of Africa. He did not know then what 'Kikelomo' meant
and was not seeing her but the portrait of his fifteen-year-
old mother painted by an insane one-armed Rasta who
poured so much of himself into his masterpiece that he
died of dengue fever shortly after as if the jealous gods
refused to have him paint another Swan. They said the
Catholic Archbishop was so smitten that he bought the
portrait from the starving Rasta and hid it in the sacristy
of the Cathedral where he took it out only on Easter
Sunday hoping that the Blessed Virgin would step from
the frame and lead him into the Paradise of the Ascending

Christ. In her gown of electric gold, green and red, Kikelomo was the picture of his mother freed from her mahogany frame and he wanted to worship her in honour of African Womanhood.

When he told Omolare that he would return from America and Jamaica to be with them all she said was, 'Until we see you, Del,' and there was neither hope nor doubt in those still eyes far deeper than the deepest crevasses in the heart of the Cockpit Country. And when he returned a year later with his job in the University her eyes had not changed as she presented him with their son who had his face and hair but the colour and profile of his mother's sister. She agreed on the names 'Antonio Maceo', after the Afro-Cuban revolutionary general who, like Simon Bolivar, lived and loved his exile in Jamaica, and taught him the dance for both male and female children when Brotherman and Fela brought their fledgling musicians to play at the naming ceremony. Then in the night they started working for the girl, having reserved the names 'Josina Machel' after the twenty-six-year-old revolutionary poetess from Mozambique, murdered in cold blood by the Portuguese secret police.

NO ORDINARY LOVE

by Kikelomo Nafiu

In the latest episode of her nightmare Grissom's icy blonde girlfriend works patiently on the head of the Unidentified Victim. As the concealed identity takes shape in the painful slow motion of dreamtime, Kikelomo studies the reactions of the engrossed spectators. Grissom has that quizzical look he puts on as the credits roll at the beginning, turning facetiously to the audience in a half-hearted salute to postmodernist disruption of the suspension of disbelief. Is he concerned that the revealed identity will question his judgement and put him on the spot with the iceberg whose knickers at once invite him in while freezing him out?

The women are a study in character and scene composition which would have made Kurosawa raise his glass of Irish whiskey in tribute: in her typical guilt-ridden way Jorja Fox grinds her teeth and bites her nails, shifting tensely from one leg to the other while the more brazen Marg Helgenberger stares brassily in that visual cocktail of nonchalance and calculation which vainly conceals her obsession with getting Warrwick into her bed. And Warrwick? For a moment Kikelomo thinks she sees a vague glint in his eyes as they shift momentarily from the slowly evolving brown head to the glacial visage of the iceberg. Does he in his male arrogance think he could defrost her

where Grissom has succeeded merely in lowering the
ambient temperature of her crotch? Quickly she shifts scene
to the delicate Nordic hands, which weave their magic like
the three Fates over resurrecting the Unidentified Victim,
taking Warwick's straying eyes from the imagined Venus de
Las Vegas under the unrevealing white coat to the head of
the stranger which is the matter at hand. Now that she has
restored him to his laid-back, Olympian unconcern she can
let her dream wander, however briefly.

The chill of the iceberg seemed to have frozen time and
she was back in the life of her beloved sister and her
husband Delroy whose temperament of unshakeable calm
was belied by a body of such immense energy that her
whole universe seemed to vibrate in his presence. There
he was shoving Antonio Maceo through the basketball
hoop for Omolare to catch. Trying vainly to teach the
gawky Joseph Mammamia how to shoot free throws. And
when he coached the football team she could not tell
whether his favourite was her husband Nafiu as sweeper,
his cousin Nuhu in left midfield, or the mysterious Ahmed
Abdullahi as lone striker. He was shown on the front covers
of all the weeklies and the features pages of all the Sunday
papers in traditional costume with the late chief of
Lidiziam, descendant of the great King Jaja, on the anniversary of the day his ancestor returned from his exile in St
Vincent to die among his own people who celebrated his
transition with drums and fifes and regattas and feasting
as their spirits accompanied him to the holy river in the
sky where the Agbani antelope drank in abundance among
the swaying grass.

There he was in the lead canoe behind the chief, their
tall heads bobbing above the surging waters like sentinels
above the deep who guarded the land from modern predators and their angry machines. This was the time of the
resurrection of the seed yams when the beautiful young

virgins paraded themselves so the young men who desired them would excel in making the greatest catches from the rich waters, build the highest yam hills and the sturdiest huts and show their school certificates to prove they were worthy of a wife they would cherish and protect. She remembered teasing her sister about her husband being tempted by such overwhelming beauty and Omolare for once was not amused by her mischief. But now in her dream it was she who was jealous and she covered the tempting bodies of the actresses with black, burkha-like garments which scarcely revealed their eyes.

A buzz in the CSI *scenario of her nightmare draws her back to the now trembling hands of the iceberg as the face of the Unidentified Victim, still in shadow, neared completion. Grissom's features are tight and serious as if his dull lust has been put on hold in light of the drama now unfolding. The women's profiles are grim as they try to hide their emotion at the unexpected revelation emerging under the firm caresses of the thawing Nordic hands. Even Warrwick is agitated and Kikelomo finds herself unable to calm him or to view the source of the wonderment and disturbance now unfolding to everyone but herself. She was no longer directing her nightmare, it is she who is being directed, as she finds herself in that stage of the dream where she experiences vertigo and nausea because she has lost control of her own existence and is floating in a world sucked free of gravity where time, space and oblivion interchange, two-timing and double spacing are possible where dimensions are abolished, singularities are the norm and Heisenberg's Uncertainty Principle is a sure banker.*

Everyone's being now revolves around the head which, because it is bigger than the entire universe, will take for ever and ever and ever before it completes the circle and lets her know the identity of her darkest secret. Then after she regains control and compresses eternity into an instance of dreamtime the head is there for all to see, filling the screen with the pensive features of Dr Delroy Solomon, her sister's husband. The suppressed screams wake her, her frozen body does not shake, and the cold sweat clings to her as she drags herself to the edge of the bed away from the warm body of her husband Nafiu, who sleeps peacefully, perhaps devoid of dreams. Antonio Maceo and Josina Machel moaned in their sleep but she was still a prisoner of the nightmare which followed into her waking twilight.

The very first time she saw that face she knew this was no ordinary love. She remembered the Sapphic ode exhorting the carpenter to raise high the roof beam for the advent of the warrior taller than Mars, nobler far than Mars. This was the man, the warrior she had awaited all her life since the death of their father who had taught them to dream, to reach beyond the stars into infinity, to achieve what mere mortals could not conceive, dreams that were more real than the real, more human than human. Here he was resplendent in all his majesty, mirror image of the war god Sango, veteran of the campaigns of the Carthaginian Hamilcar Barca, driving in the vanguard of his son Hannibal where his forces routed the Roman legions at the mesmeric battle of Cannae. He was Toussaint L'Ouverture, Henri Christophe, Samory Toure, Cudjoe, Abd el-Kadir, Shaka and all the Black Generals who fought to keep their people free. But his calm, distant and indulgent eyes belied the threatful physique and they were firmly fixed on the round figure of Omolare. When they strayed from her for an instant to survey the form of her little sister it was as if they were looking for one who was not there, a ghost in some distant past or longed for future he had encountered in his wanderings and experienced as beyond comprehension. He had hesitated before entering as if the roof beam was too low and Omolare, the shy and undemonstrative, had laughed as she pushed him into their little parlour with its tiny desks, Philips radiogram and small black and white television set.

Ever since she was a baby it was *her* people stared at, and when she was twelve, already tall as Omolare and growing breasts like green pawpaws, men devoured her beauty completely oblivious of the sister to whose plump body she clung. She was Omolare's golden mirror whom she polished with the finest oils from the petals of the lilies of the valley to a shine more radiant than the sun, braiding her hair into martial columns of black which shone above the ramparts of gold. It was her elder sister who, dressed in fading monotones of polyester, introduced her to the intoxicating cocktail of electric red, gold, cobalt, green and heliotrope of the dye makers of Rotterdam who transformed the raw white of Egyptian cotton into spectacular sunrises and sunsets designed to bedazzle the exotic natives of the steaming tropics. She was the Christmas tree in whose glow her sister did not even strive to shine, content to know that she had fulfilled her promise to their dying parents that Kikelomo would lack for nothing as long as she breathed.

Except that here she was now in love with the man of Kikelomo's dream with no chance of her sacrificing him too. There they were on the two-seater playing like small children, oblivious of the frowns of the youngster who regarded such behaviour as childish and unsophisticated as her usually reserved Omolare giggled till she cried, as Dr Solomon, who she had been told was a famous scholar, tickled her, made faces, and told the most outrageous jokes about the Pope, the American President, the Ayatollah Khomeini and their own criminal dictator, the already obscene and rapacious General Daudu.

The disdain at their childish behaviour, which they did not try to hide from her, hid the hurt deep in Kikelomo's heart that this was one good thing her sister could not sacrifice to her, even if she had the courage or the arrogance or the selfishness to ask. She found herself caught in revolving pyramids of hate, of the stranger who had come between her and the sister who was an extension of herself, and of the sister she loved more than herself or life who could not surrender the man she loved. So she hid the hurt together with the loneliness and the longing as her sister bloomed with his love and then with his children and he felt no self-consciousness as he patted her head or squeezed her shoulder or embraced her like a daughter or *his* younger sister with a love as pure as Omolare felt for her and not knowing the feelings that raged beneath the gold of her shining skin. And she could tell no one of her anguish, of her forbidden love.

It was only now after the *CSI* solution of her nightmare that she could acknowledge the nausea she felt after he moved into their little house instead of accepting the old colonial bungalow of cut stone the university offered – knowing the man she loved with all her soul was there wrapped in her sister's arms. Finding the ceilings too low and the space too confined for the three of them and their two children, he had come with an army of local carpenters, masons, electricians, butchers, cooks, students and musicians who, in the tradition of communal labour, added three rooms, raised the roof beams, then feasted on a cow, several sheep and goats, dozens of fowl, bags of rice, new yams and buckets of palm wine, *ogogoro*, Jamaican white rum, local beer and soothing millet drinks. Later they set up a neighbourhood work group to help others repair their dwellings, build a community centre, playgrounds for the children and mulch plots for organic rubbish.

It was there she first met her husband Rabiu, his cousin Nuhu, their comrades Ahmed and Joseph, and other students who impressed the local workers with their willingness to get their hands and bodies dirty, drink 'illicit' gin and smoke ganja with Brotherman, his trainee musicians and his band of crippled street urchins who looked clean and healthy despite their ragged clothes and matted hair. She did not know then that Rabiu was the one because she was impressed with the remote yet sultry passion of Nuhu and the mystery of Ahmed who was as tall and athletic as her brother-in-law but all were in the shadow of the burning passion she kept concealed beneath her angry responses to the teasing of Omolare and Delroy.

It was only when she entered the school and Delroy kept sending Rabiu to call her and ask if she needed anything that she began to feel that Rabiu perhaps could cure her of her sickness which, though he could not correctly diagnose it, Rabiu could see was tearing her apart from the silences, the downcast sleepy eyes, the refusal to see her own brother-in-law who every student like himself would die for. And when his feelings grew and became obvious he took the path of honour and approached her guardian with his friends and told him of his intention and his desire to have Delroy speak on his behalf. She was lifted by the irony of the man she loved so much she was afraid to be alone with him wooing her on behalf of one of his favourite students who worshipped him as a comrade and elder brother. But she liked and later loved Rabiu, though in an entirely different way, and thought marrying him would wean her away from a love she could not afford.

And the children would call her and Omolare 'Nana' and Delroy and Nafiu 'Baba' without discrimination, and when they went out together people always thought the children were hers and wondered who was their father. They would visit Brotherman at his hillside settlement and while the children played with the urchins and Nafiu and the others kicked footballs with the bigger ones, Omolare would take her by the hand and lead her to where Delroy sat smoking with the Rasta and both sisters would fall asleep leaning on one shoulder and she would dream of the forbidden fruits in Paradise.

At first she thought her miscarriages were due to her womb rejecting her husband's seed because she longed for another and she was tempted to approach a *babalawo* to find out if in their traditional system there was any possibility that a spirit had arranged for Omolare to bear her children with the husband she coveted.

But she loved her elder sister too much and Christianity, then the 'Scientific Socialism' of her brother-in-law, her husband and their comrades would have ridiculed her for her superstitions, despite Delroy's encouragement for the people to follow the path of the ancestors and his closeness to Brotherman and the small community of Brethren who worshipped his knowledge of their beliefs and their music. She became torn again when she thought of the role she had played in his death and that of her beloved sister. Even though the news of his visit to Lidiziam had appeared in the media the week before she still felt she should not have told Joseph Mammamia, who was later exposed as an agent of the Americans and State Security. Even now she could not look at the centre spread of the *Sunday Sentinel* where she had written the extensive coverage of the Festival of Returning with the pictures so revealing in their clarity and brilliance they could resurrect the village and bring its inhabitants and her beloved back to life.

Was the horror which followed the result of her not so ordinary, her forbidden, love which, in the tradition of her people, could take the form of evil jealousy, vengeful spirits which could destroy what she was doomed not to possess? Had she destroyed what she loved? Not finding answers meant she could not free herself from the guilt which crushed her like a thousand Amuz Rocks into the eternal, unyielding dust. *Now do you understand my anguish?* she sighed.

When Antonio Maceo cried out she felt his brother move inside her and was happy that now his father was no more it appeared she would succeed in giving them a companion. Feeling the new life freed her of her lethargy after the nightmare and she leaned over and kissed her sleeping husband before going to her children's room. They now lived in a modern bungalow owned by the *Sentinel* because she could not abide the ghosts of her beloved Omolare and Delroy whose presence became even stronger in her mind after their passing. But they had kept the old house which Delroy said he had built up so his wife would 'have somewhere to live in case anything happened to him' provoking the second bout of hysteria she had witnessed in her sister. It was now a shrine to the local community and rented to graduate students studying for doctorates in the discipline he had established in the university, using his tapes from the US, Caribbean, Nigeria, South Africa, Cameroon, the Congo and Niagra, of Brotherman and other roots musicians whose signatures would never appear on any contracts with EMI, Sony, or even the minnows of the recording industry.

'I'm so cold, Nana,' Antonio said, 'cold and thirsty.'

'Wait, my love, I soon come.' He was small for his age and she saw his lips were parched and his kaftan wet with night sweat while Josina slept like an angel. She returned with a towel, a glass of water and a dry kaftan and held him while he drank and his throbbing body relaxed toward sleep again.

'Where is Baba?' he asked in Hausa.

'Baba is gone,' she said in a distant tone and only awoke to the import of her answer with the alarm in his query:

'Gone? Baba gone too?'

Then she remembered her husband Nafiu sleeping peacefully in his bed and comforted his son:

'I meant Baba is gone to sleep, Antonio, he's probably dreaming of you and Josina and your baby brother.'

'What will his name be, Nana?'

'We don't know yet, darling, maybe Delroy.'

'Delroy? That's a funny name, Nana.'

'Yes, my love, maybe your brother will be funny too.'

She tucked the blanket so he would be warm in the night, turned out the light and returned to her bed. Nafiu was mumbling as if he was having an amusing dream but when she held him and pulled the covers around them he nuzzled up to her breast and was silent. She was gone almost as soon as her head touched the pillow and for the first time in ten billion years she experienced a long night of dreamless sleep.

CHAMELEON:
THE MANY COLOURS OF
JOSEPH MAMMAMIA

After seeing the American Consul to his bulletproof
Lincoln and jeeps full of American and Niagran Special
Forces, Joseph returned to his office, locked the door and
opened the wall safe from which he selected a half bottle
of Finnish vodka from his last trip to buy newsprint in
Ivalo. Remembering the sweating, bloated American pig
he wiped his hands in his kaftan then, when they still did
not feel clean enough, scrubbed them with the carbolic
soap in the bathroom he had added to the MD's office
after the print union was proscribed and no longer used
the adjoining room. Of course the pristine revolutionary
Rabiu and his idealistic comrades thought they were the
only ones who felt unclean when they stumbled into the
presence of the Honorary Consul they held responsible
for the death of their beloved Delroy Solomon.

They could afford to remain clean always, they were
born with silver feet in their mouths, the prestige of
learning and 'old' distinguished families, physical beauty
and charisma which allowed them to prance around in
revolutionary ecstasy without a care, always with others
like himself to do the dirty work. He was considered
unclean for 'selling out' to the degenerate General Daudu
and his American imperialist trailer-trash mentors, for

having partaken of their thirty-three billion barrels of crude reserves in delivering to them their main enemy, the representative of the King of Kings and Conquering Lion of the Tribes of Judah on Earth, the talisman of left-wing African Nationalism, Dr Delroy Moziah Solomon.

Before the first swig of vodka he took the Listerine mouthwash, Polo mints, and liquorice from his desk drawer – ready, in case of a visitor – to mask the faint odour that still overwhelmed his senses and self-image of the teetotalitarian born-again Christian, whose apostasy from the Left and 'betrayal' of his comrades people now blamed on a Pauline conversion to the True Faith. How could he let them know the real reason? They had not been born in the stranger's quarters in the town his ancestors had lived in for a millennium, son of a butcher so poor he had to rent his knives. His ancestors had been famous Islamic scholars long before the people of Rabiu, Nuhu and Ahmed rode in on horseback and declared them 'infidels' in order to push them off their land and into the gutters.

When the Europeans conquered the country his people had embraced the new religion, more out of vengeance than faith, hoping to rub the proud noses of their enemies in Christian shit. But in a manoeuvre unworthy even of a nation described as 'perfidious', the English had entered into a conspiracy with the old masters of his people in a 'Dual Mandate' or 'Indirect Rule' which allowed the old feudal oligarchy to push them even further into the dirt, occupying the lowest rungs of the social ladder in the 'unclean' occupations of butchers, barbers and shit carriers.

Never Again! had become his motto when his genius for learning the white man's knowledge had pulled him out of the slime. At the drop of a hat he would change sides so he would never again visit those hellholes his people had been consigned to for the past two centuries. He did not care whether they sneered at his contortions when he leapt from one branch of a toppling tree of power to another on the rise as long as he was above those on the way down. And he cared not for 'friends' or 'enemies' he did not recognize, understand or identify with but only his personal ambitions and the will to achieve them.

With an intellect that even his enemies described as formidable, he knew exactly what he wanted, knew that he had to conquer the fear so that he would prevail and triumph. So let the Rabius, Nuhus and Ahmeds sneer at his ideological 'apostasy', his revolutionary 'loss of faith'. What was their Marxism-Leninism but the latest religion of conquest?

He had grown up a shrunken thing until his fourteenth birthday when his limbs began sprouting in all directions like an unruly weed and remained uncoordinated, even today he had to watch his hand raising the vodka bottle to his lips so he wouldn't break his teeth. This ugly duckling would never grow into a swan despite the irony that he was living out a fairy tale more real than the real. Was this due to a genetic defect caused by his cattle-breeding nomadic ancestors marrying their first cousins to preserve the integrity of the herd? Whatever the cause, his hormones were all over the place, so his moods became as mercurial as his ideological flip-flops and his concept of himself.

He still kept his essays marked 'outstandingly brilliant!', 'sign of an incisive intellect!', 'I could not have done better!' which the late Doctor used to mark him out from his fellows who resented his domination of tutorials and debates. But why envy him his squalid intellectual triumphs? What he wanted was to be involved in their titanic struggles on the sports field where he could emerge triumphant and sweat-stained to see himself reflected in the golden eyes of the war god Dr 'Sango' Solomon and the sun goddess Kikelomo who reminded him of yellow bellflowers or the smell of lilies in new rain.

He could never once remember her making eye contact, even before she accused him of 'selling out' and shunning him for betraying her beloved. Did she think he did not know the intimate friendship she retained with her schoolmate, the equally beautiful Fatima, wife of the Commander of the Presidential Guards, despite the mortal enmity between their husbands? Or that she played Sade's 'No Ordinary Love' and Roberta Flack's 'The Very First Time I Saw Your Face' till the tapes wore out? Had Kikelomo heard the rumours about her and her dowdy sister? The two children looked like her and nothing like their supposed mother who was so round and black you could mistake her for a golliwog. Rumour had it that Gabriel, one of the General's Lebanese front men, became so besotted with Kikelomo when she was sixteen that he paid the President of Zimbabwe's Lebanese mistress to recommend a Zulu *sangoma* to block her fallopian tubes so she wouldn't have children or fall for any other man. But Fatima found out and stole $10,000 from her husband's briefcase to pay a Nigerian *babalawo* to reverse the spell and make Gabriel impotent. And this rumour, even if untrue, had made Joseph add the Lebanese to the long list of people he despised.

This was the man who complained to 'Florence Nightingale' on the BBC World Service that although people were accusing him of getting rich at the expense of the Niagran people he was worth *only* $770 million, causing the 'Rottweiler' of the airwaves to get the hiccups. He boasted that Niagran women were dogs to whom you just had to throw meat and had found wives and girlfriends from almost every country in the world for the General and his officers down to the level of platoon commander. He had offered his master his sisters and his wife but the General had refused the wife because she was too old and smelt of garlic. Did Gabriel think Kikelomo could be bought for his $770 million, the General's $15 billion, or all the money in the world? She would take it all, cut his balls off and stuff them in his mouth, then make him crawl and bark like a dog. And still he would not sniff her knickers.

Did the idiot forget what Kikelomo and Fatima did to his short-sighted brother Emile at the German Embassy reception when he mistook them for the Mauritians Gabriel had imported, and ordered a 'Protocol' officer to take them to Daudu? Their identical handbags hit his face at once, their matching sandals flew off as if rehearsed to kick sense into his crotch, then they dragged him by his greasy hair into the kitchen where Kikelomo cut his trousers off with a butcher knife while Fatima grabbed a kettle of boiling water and resisted the pleas of the entire cabinet, the diplomatic corps and Fatima's husband with the British Ambassador's wife in tow, until an old dish-washer raised his cock with her walking stick and said in Yoruba, '*My granddaughters, you do not cook a piece of rotten meat like this*'.

Of course not all rumours were true but how could such a plain thing as Omolare attract a former cham-pion athlete, part-time male model and renowned scholar? Their people had the most powerful charms in all Africa and it was said the older sister had squandered her life savings on the *babalawo* used by the General's midwife mistress – to prevent his wives having male chil-dren – to win the love of Delroy. But after netting her catch she found her womb could not hold his powerful seed and she had to mortgage her little house so the medicine man would transfer Kikelomo's womb to her to bear his children. Why else would they choose to live in that horrible slum when a beautiful colonial bungalow fit for the white man was available? Among the Ibo people she would have simply 'married' her sister and presented her to Delroy to bear children who would be legally hers. Did she take no responsibility for the tragedy which befell them because State Security suspected she was leaking

secrets to Rabiu and Delroy from the ravishingly beautiful Fatima who people mistook for that black American
Miss Universe?

Someone pressed the buzzer but Joseph ignored it,
wrapped the empty in an old newspaper, hid it in his metal
briefcase and took a new bottle from the safe. Rabiu was
certainly not the one to cast stones at him. He was fully
responsible for the death of Nuhu who was just a quiet,
pious Moslem boy until his wayward cousin tempted him
with the inflammatory *Wretched of the Earth, Civilization
or Barbarism*, and *How Europe Underdeveloped Africa*.
Rabiu led the demonstration protesting the clash with the
police in that Eastern village where he and Nuhu
composed the chants questioning the sexuality of the
President which provoked the shooting. And to add injury
to insult he had claimed in *Red Bull* that the General and
his American backers used Serbian mercenaries and gave
the names of the officers on the General Staff who planned
the operation with the American Special Forces commander and 'Mr Dick' from Burton Holly.

He closed his eyes tight as the raw vodka slithered down
the numb lining of his throat and he saw in brilliant light
the figure of the man whose death they blamed on him.
Was it not Rabiu, the star student trainee in journalism,
writing then under his own name in the *Sentinel* and as
'John Lennon' in *Red Bull* who had drawn attention to his
mentor and provoked the authorities with constant threats
of subversion? *Never wave the Red Bull before the General*,
his boss Professor 'Jerry Can' (because of his explosive
temper) Gotchakka had quipped.

Had Rabiu forgotten that his father, Justice Saleh, was
not called the Hanging Judge or the Hammer of God for
nothing? From birth he had marked out his only son to
follow him into the Law to compensate him in the sight
of God for the loss of his beloved daughter, Aishetu, who
was alleged to have run off with an Ethiopian. How could
he not hate Delroy Solomon, the man who had corrupted

his son and made him into one of the subversives he lived to annihilate? Did they think ice water flowed in his blood because of his devotion to duty and loyalty to his Commander-in-Chief? Did they think he would sit back and take lightly the cruel rumours that his lost daughter had become one of Fela's twenty-seven wives?

Rumour had it that the judge locked himself in his empty court to pass judgement on his nemesis, representing him in the dock with books by himself, Marx, Engels, Lenin, Mao, Fanon, Rodney, Cabral, John Pilger, Noam Chomsky, Joseph Heller, Pablo Neruda and Agostinho Neto. For the prosecution he piled up issues of the *Sentinel*, *Red Bull*, *Africa Confidential*, the *African Marxist* and the *Economist* Intelligence Unit's 'Profile on Niagra's Oil Industry'. The defence was represented by recordings of demonstrating students shouting obscenities at the General, his wives, mistresses, favourites and faithful Hanging Judge. They said he wrote up his judgement in his fine claustrophobic hand like print, had the twelve copies bound in expensive maroon leather by Smythson's of New Bond Street and presented them to the General, who confirmed it and assigned it to Disposal Units for execution.

Joseph started when he realized the new bottle was almost half empty. A fanatic teetotalitarian born-again Christian could not afford to swoon from the effects of alcohol, no matter how masked with odour eaters, although some unkind employees might attribute it to his spastic lack of coordination brought on by the contortions he went into to defend his indefensible General. Besides, he had to be alert after the offices had emptied so he could accompany the Men in Black in their search for subversive material. He thought again about Rabiu and Kikelomo as he replaced the bottle and locked the safe, of their contempt for him, the husband shielding their precious portrait from his eyes, the wife refusing to enter the building after she was sacked from the *Sentinel*, she not being a daughter of the Hanging Judge. With his eyes clouded with vodka fumes and his hands trembling from nerves he recalled holding the portrait as he would an infant to watch their smiling faces as they held their young children between them.

Even after all these years Delroy Solomon's eyes gazed straight into him in that quizzical splendour as if he knew what was inside, what he was, but could not afford to be. Delroy was the first man he thought he could trust with his secret, who would tell him there was nothing to be ashamed of, that all men and women had a duty to be true to their own nature, to look inside and find the truth that resided in the inner wo/man. He knew Delroy would protect him, praise his work even more lavishly, so that the others would not think he was unequal because he could not excel in sports. But would he feel as comfortable when Joseph's flailing arms and legs took him into violent contact as he feinted on the basketball court or ran at him in football? Thinking nothing of his confession would he be careful enough not to repeat it, so that he would not be stoned to death by both Christian and Moslem fanatics? Would his 'comrades' understand and not condemn him as a degenerate petty bourgeois with unnatural habits that he indulged at the expense of the glorious proletariat and peasantry? *These children of the aristocracy had a nerve prattling on about proletarians and peasants!*

Did they know what torments he was already going through because others knew what he could not admit even to himself? What choice did he have when the pipe-smoking Man in Black who would later set up Delbert Gower showed him the pictures of himself in the room at the Hyatt Regency Hotel? How could he not 'betray' those who would have stoned him to death for being what he had no responsibility in creating? The fault may have been in his genes, his parents, his culture, but certainly not in himself as he had fought a losing battle against it all his life. The Men in Black and their American masters had squeezed him, wrung him dry, forced him to pass on 'information' so demeaning his already low self-esteem sunk deeper into the gutter, till it came out on the other side of the universe of human dignity. Why did they keep asking him about what 'Kike' and 'Fati' were doing together in her husband's guest house, about whether 'Kike' and 'Del' were nothing more than in-laws? When the ultimate betrayal came he was so low he was already far below the radar of his self-abasement.

He had never doubted Delroy's capacity for understanding and accepting what was different until his minder from the American embassy began to peck and probe at his motives. Did he know that Jamaica was the most homophobic country in the world, that its African and Baptist culture infected *all* its people? Solomon was a macho man, drawn to the cult of the body and the glorification of the athlete. He had written and spoken about protecting and uplifting the poor, the workers, peasants, women, blacks, South Africans, Palestinians and all other people oppressed because of race, ethnicity, gender, religion or caste, but *never* those of different sexual orientation.

In the Burton Holly Guest House where they kept him there was a picture of the founder as a younger man when he was the star in the Directorate of Plans who had a reputation for *always getting his country*. 'Mr Dick' had a fascination with implements of torture and his world famous collection at the Metropolitan Museum went back to Roman times. There was a poster of one implement with a lapis lazuli handle – a cross between an egg-cup, a juice presser and a corkscrew – used for gouging out eyes. Now a division of Burton Holly, 'Advanced Medical Technologies', specialized in 'modern techniques of pressure and interrogation' and commissioned a study from the Herzovogina Consultancy on the influence of music on different ethnic groups, which found that people of African origin were most susceptible to country and western. Apparently they did not consider him of African origin because they kept playing the Beach Boys, Boy George and Queen after plying him with vodka whose queer taste he had attributed to its Estonian origin. The vodka and flashing pink lights from the stereo had already made him queasy before they started the video of the Jamaican student.

The boy's father, speaking the most horrible Jamaican patois, was shouting at his battyman son while brandishing pictures of naked white men he found in his school bag. When the other students started beating him with their books, lunch boxes and school bags the father joined in with his walking stick, egging them on with *boom boom, batty man, bye-bye*. His minders kept increasing the volume of the Beach Boys and telling him this was where Delroy was from, where he *was at*, and he shouting *Dr Solomon is not like that*. They had stripped the boy, his body was bathed in blood from his head and nose, then a girl who looked like Sade's daughter grabbed a pen knife from a teacher and when Joseph saw what she was doing he threw up on the carpet with the Green and Branch logo. The men were still talking about Delroy and now the boy's father seemed to have grown till he looked like Gary Dourdan, his son writhing on the floor with his genitals in his mouth, Joseph his mirror image. But still he said 'No, not Delroy,' and when the film stopped they gave him a simple test: '*Call your friend and tell him you were attacked on the Hill of David and Absalom by homophobic thugs who robbed you, stripped you and left you for dead to be eaten by jackals. If he comes to help it will prove you're right about him.*' They even offered a $50 bet which he still had enough dignity to refuse.

How was he to know it was a trap? In the state he was in he could not tell what planet he was on. After Delroy's murder Kikelomo got the tape of his conversation from Fatima and the Burton Holly Charitable Foundation had to spirit him out of the country to complete his doctorate at Yale, where Professor Harold Bloom described him as a 'fucking dork but outstandingly brilliant'. The first sign that something was wrong was the 'Breaking News' on NTV that the subversive Caribbean-American left-wing agitator, Dr Delroy Moziah Solomon, had disappeared, suspected to have run off with the young widow of the executed coupist Vatslav Powell, who allegedly knew the whereabouts of the $2.8 billion of gold bars hijacked on the national carrier transporting it from the Niagran reserves held in the vaults of the Bank of England.

Joseph knew the girl, a student who had attacked Omolare, the Doctor's wife, with a coke bottle after he rejected her advances and was destined to be 'wife' number seven of the General after he ordered Justice Saleh to find the girl's husband guilty of a capital offence the first time he set eyes on her at a reception for the American Vice-President. There was no way Delroy would have left his wife and family to run off with a woman described in student underground publications as the 'barracks' because of all the officers who entered her.

A revised bulletin was issued hours later that the Doctor had committed suicide on the Hill of David and Absalom after his scorched, headless, bullet-ridden body was found by passing motorists bound hand and foot with multiple stab wounds and a bullet in the back of his head. Joseph wept as he remembered the 'suicide' of Delbert Gower which he had been ordered to report by State Security in the *Sentinel*, only to be ridiculed by 'John Lennon' in *Red Bull*. It was the Voice of America, CNN, and the BBC Hausa Service which 'corrected' the story this time, denying that the body was that of Dr Solomon. 'In fact the so-called body was not even human but an unidentified primate, possibly a gorilla slaughtered for bush meat, a rare delicacy in these parts,' declared Dr Seamus Bothman, an Oxbridge expert on Niagran affairs, on all three stations.

But looking at it now, Joseph reasoned that Delroy had

in a sense committed suicide by publishing that series of articles in *Africa Confidential*, revealing the European bank accounts of the General and his family and the network of offshore companies they used to siphon off the wealth of the nation. 'He's asking for trouble,' Jerry Gotchakka had snarled over a carved mahogany dish of peppered goat head in the First Lady's guest house, built for the visit of the Queen of England. How could Delroy think he could get away with sending photos of so-called 'instruments of torture' to Amnesty International and the Medical Foundation Against Torture in London just before the President's state visit? Posters held by protesters on the Mall with the picture of Niagra's world famous sculptor being 'crucified' so upset the First Lady she had to be comforted by the Princess Royal and her killer dogs.

Of course Rabiu had to have the last word in the issue of *Red Bull* they published to mark the passing of *their* hero, with the mandatory dollop of bad poetry.

THE FELLING OF THE MIGHTY IROKO
by John Lennon

Dr Delroy Moziah Solomon was born in Nanny Town, Jamaica, brought up in a suburb of Virginia, USA, of parents whose genetic make up included indigenous Carib, African slaves, indentured Irishmen, Scottish overseers and English slave owners. Educated in the USA and UK in several disciplines, he credited his former DJ mother, a pioneer of dub poetry, as the main source of his knowledge, his father, a minor backing musician and his friend, Brotherman, founder of the Afro-Carib Fusion school of music in Niagra. This was a man of the world but uniquely a son of Africa.

Instead of sucking up to the generals and politicians like his other colleagues, he spent his time with his students in the classroom or on the fields of sport, with Brotherman and his band of urchins on the hills overlooking Xanadu or with his neighbours in the local community where he preferred to dwell, rather than occupy the stone house of some former colonial official built by the forced labour of Niagrans forbidden to enter its hallowed portals except as servants. This man lived the life of a Niagran and was certainly more worthy of the title than its privileged nationals whose burning ambition is to own a house in London.

Now this titan is no more, the Iroko tree has fallen, the bull elephant will trumpet no longer in the forest whose every leaf will weep at his passing. Niagrans were first alerted to this tragedy when government media announced he had eloped with a woman who had planned his assassination after he rejected her. A later version said he had committed suicide by binding himself hand and foot, emptying the magazine of an

M16 into his body, stabbing himself twelve times, then performing the coup de grâce by firing a single bullet from a 44 Magnum into the back of his own head, before setting himself on fire and decapitating himself. This form of 'suicide' was invented in the case of *Sentinel* founding editor Delbert Gower, and perfected in Kenya on Robert Ouko the Kenyan Foreign Minister who incinerated his own bullet-ridden corpse. The final 'correct' version was supplied to the international media by Shille and Coulton, the public relations firm employed by both the Niagran military government and the Burton Holly Corporation.

Our own investigations show that Dr Solomon received a phone call at 11.15 pm and informed his family that he had to go to the assistance of one of his students. A tape of this conversation now in our possession shows that the call was placed by Joseph Mammamia of the *Sentinel*, who claimed to have been critically wounded by attackers on the notorious Hill of David and Absalom and left for dead. The Doctor was met not by the supposedly injured Joseph but by his other student Zeinabu, the modern equivalent of Potifer's wife and a Disposal Unit from her future husband's Republican Guards, which specializes in 'clean up' operations after worker and student demonstrations, or staged coups d'état. The terror in Joseph's voice was genuine because for hours he had been plied with vodka and amphetamines by his minders in a Burton Holly guest house used to show snuff movies to Niagran torturers.

For those unaware of its provenance, the Hill is a sinister location which served as a place of human sacrifice before the coming of the white man. Even now traditionalists come there to sacrifice chickens, goats and sheep to their ancient deities. More modern practices are initiation ceremonies by wealthy right wing students influenced by their fathers' accounts of cult practices in secret societies such as Skull and Bones, to which the American President, the Chairman of Burton Holly and the Honorary Consul belong. The place was useful also because of the lime pits and hyenas, which disposed of the bodies of cult rivals. And this suggested to General Daudu that it was an ideal place for his Cemetery of Enemies, where unruly students, recalcitrant journalists and disloyal officers would find no final resting place because of the hyenas and sulphuric acid.

This best laid plan of mice and men was, however, rendered inoperative by the vengeful Zeinabu who insisted that the corpse be doused with petrol and set alight, not thinking that hyenas prefer their suppers raw. A poor woman rushing to sacrifice a 'special' American pig to see off the challenge of a junior wife's charms was convinced when the animal leapt from her arms and rushed into a copse that her co-wife's *babalawo* was indeed stronger than hers. Running after it to regain her honour and her husband's love she was shocked to find a much bigger sacrifice still smouldering in the bush. When her screams attracted passersby, the unknowing police took the body to the teaching hospital where the students recognized their lecturer. Unfortunately it was not possible to confirm this definitively at the time of going to press as a Green and Branch refrigerated truck with a black skull and cross bones arrived to remove the corpse and all the witnesses. *At the time of going to press it has not been confirmed that the head was packed in a cardboard box with pikes and dry ice and flown to the USA to be placed in the white marble 'tomb' of the Skull and Bones at Yale University.*

Joseph skipped the bad poetry about how at last the long-lost hero comes to rest and re-opened the safe to take a long, final swig of the throat-searing vodka. He was desperate to play his favourite Bob Marley tune '*One good thing about music / When it hits you feel no pain*', but was afraid the security men would hear. Yes, it was easy for Rabiu and the others to mourn their hero and vilify the Joseph who teamed up with Potifer's wife to destroy him. But what of him who had to mourn in secret for murdering the man he had loved more than all his ambition to gain the powers and glories of this earth? The Americans had challenged him to prove whether this macho man would protect a man like him and Delroy had responded by sacrificing his life to show that no oppressed and humiliated victim was too low to be worthy of his care. But having 'won' his bet he found himself like Pyrrhus counting the costs. *Do you understand my anguish?* he found himself asking over and over again, still longing for the music to kill his pain, the vodka having failed.

CHINATOWN
by Rabiu Nafiu (aka Robert Nesta)

Because what I have to say is so painful, even after almost twenty years, I'll have to temporize, get at it indirectly through allusions, smoke screens. My people are famous for covering things up, making horrors look enticing, using mirrors to mystify the experience of the reality. I am the scion of a conquering race who, like all predators, hide the truth of that conquest by blaming the victims. History after all is *the tale told by the winning side*. We laid waste the country with sword and horse but blamed Joseph's ancestors for *corrupting religion*. But as a so-called revolutionary I was supposed to have 'committed class suicide' and 'escaped the sins of my fathers'. Still I find myself asking: to what extent am I my father's son? It's so easy for people like Joseph, who don't understand my anguish, to answer, especially given the massive certainties of General Daudu's regime and American power and glory, represented by the Honorary Consul, Mr Armitage, his good friend and sponsor. What would he have done, even now he has abandoned the struggle, if he were burdened with being the heir of the Hanging Judge Justice Nafiu 'Sandra Day O'Connor' Saleh, right-hand man and black eminence of the most corrupt dictatorship on earth?

I consider myself a revolutionary by vocation and an investigative journalist by profession, both of which require probity, courage, the willingness and ability to reveal what lies hidden, uncover truth however bleak, enlighten the masses and enrich their political consciousness. But how can I take this noble stance, raise myself on a pedestal, present myself as the shining star of the revolutionary vanguard and journalistic

fraternity? How can I not blush when trainees look up
to me, and the NUJ awards me the Delbert Gower Prize
for the Best Investigative Journalist of the Year? How
could I stand there on the glittering, richly decorated
podium, shaking the hand of Jerry Gotchakka, who
showed deference to his greatest enemy because he was
the son of the Lord Chancellor, Solicitor General,
Minister of Justice and Attorney General of Niagra?

This was the man with the reverse Midas Touch who
turned everything I held dear into filth and dross, who
libelled my saintly uncle Aminu a 'senile old fool', and
his son Nuhu an agent of Marxist Fundamentalist
Anarchism. Delbert Gower's murder was all but guaranteed when Nasser Waddadda implicated him in a coup
attempt and arms smuggling after Joseph tipped off
State Security that he was about to do a cover on relations between the General's wife and the Okontino
cartel. And of course Delroy Solomon was not just my
mentor, best friend, comrade and benefactor, but was
married to my wife's elder sister. How was I, who should
be at least number three in their TOP TEN MOST WANTED,
to justify my continued existence, even 'prosperity', to
the widows and orphans of these lost comrades who
sacrificed their lives for what we believed in?

These people were not fools: they knew I wrote under
the penname 'Robert Nesta' in their government
controlled *Sentinel* after my father 'suggested' that I
stop using the name he had given me to abuse the
regime he worshipped. I never tried to disguise my style
or dilute its sharpness and readers told me that although
my picture was no longer there they could still see the
image of my hand holding the flaming pen above the
sword. Whenever there was a crisis in the country – a
near daily occurrence – the boys from the Hausa Service
at Bush House were on the phone, and even paid a fee
into an HSBC account I opened after a course at SOAS.
And Joseph, who had a genius for sniffing out the styles
of the General's enemies, suspected I had written the
series of articles in *Africa Confidential*, which revealed
General Daudu's European bank accounts and the web
of offshore companies he used to siphon off the nation's
wealth through bribes from Burton Holly and the

Russian debt buy-back. Yet here I am in this comfortable air-conditioned office, with a high performance
Japanese car, a wonderful colonial house of cut stone
and the most beautiful and intelligent wife and children in the world. What would you do in my position,
dear reader?

But to get back to what I promised at the beginning.
Do you remember the film noir *Chinatown*, starring
Jack Nicholson, Faye Dunaway and John Huston?
Despite the glitz of Hollywood it should come as no
surprise that a movie directed by Roman Polanski, and
with stars like Nicholson and Huston, should have some
pretty bleak undercurrents, which threatened to drown
the actors flapping about on the surface in a futile
search for what was happening. Even Nicholson, who
appears the epitome of *blasé*, seemed shocked at the
uncovering of the true relationship between Huston and
his daughter, played by Faye Dunaway. But was the
point of the story about incest or the corruption of
absolute power? Was the Huston character's sin that he
fathered a child by his own daughter, or that he had so
much power he could not be touched, and in fact could
decide who should live and who would die? After all he
appeared to love his daughter, and the lengths to which
he went to protect his daughter/granddaughter could
actually have won some sympathy from the type of
viewer attending a Polanski film. Would that I could
say the same about my own father.

First let me confess that I worshipped my sister
Aishetu and now, even after two decades of not seeing
her, still do, even though I know not where she is, what
happened to her child, or even if they are still alive.
There was no sibling rivalry, perhaps because we were
of different genders and separated by eight years. What
I remember most about her was her bubbly, outgoing
personality, and it was long after she had left, when I
looked in her photo albums (the ones our father had
missed when he destroyed all her possessions) that I
realized how beautiful she was. When I remember her
I think of singing not only because she had such a
haunting, ethereal voice, but because she reminded me
of Sade, Jennifer Lopez and Gloria Estefan. She was

always mimicking popular, usually sad, old songs like Paul Robeson's 'Old Man River', Bobby Darin's 'Moody River', 'River of No Return' by Marilyn Monroe in the film of the same name and Otis Redding's 'Sitting on the Dock of the Bay'.

Whenever I hear, or even think, of any sad song I think of my sister and her eyes like oceans on which my whole world floated. As I write this a pirate radio is playing 'Drive' by the Cars and I recall the days before the General decreed that we could only listen to Elvis and country and western, when Aishetu and I would crouch before our old Grundig radiogram waiting for the weekly Hit Parade, and how she burst into tears one day when Bob Marley's 'No, Woman, No Cry' made it to number one. At that time she rarely cried so it frightened me but later she cried all the time and I would become almost frantic when I saw her with dry eyes.

That was when the life went out of her eyes with the glisten of joy when we played together and they seemed to shrink till they squinted when she dared steal a glance at my face. Our mother seemed alarmed at first when her daughter started to lapse into moodiness, looking dull-eyed and exhausted even after spending most of her time after school and Koranic lessons in bed. Sometimes Aishetu would not answer her questions and her once clear and vibrant voice – described by a Yale classmate of our father as sounding like fine crystal – hissed like lisps from a harelipped person. I could feel my sister drifting away from me in her voice which no longer sang, her eyes without sparkle, her hands which once created universes of resplendent images with simple crayons now always crossed over her chest or rigid at her side.

I remember now how I would listen for my father's driver who revved the engine before killing it as his orderly rushed to open the door of the black Mercedes Benz. My father was a strict man and I suspected the driver kept the engine going to give the orderly time to reach the door as soon as the car stopped, though he told my father, when he protested, that it was to blow dirt from the carburettor. I would rush to meet him and though he seemed uncomfortable he allowed me to clutch briefly to his legs or hold his Koran. He was a strong man and I felt safe when I experienced the force, and saw how others cowered in his presence. I recalled not being able to distinguish between Father and God when I first came across the latter term. With him there to protect me no one could touch me, or make me feel pain. But I soon noticed that Aishetu was never there with me, and when I heard the engine I would look and see her retreating hastily to her room. When I asked why she never ran to the car with me, if she didn't love our father, I was met with tears or a tense silence.

In addition to her shrinking eyes with red tinged rims, I noticed other changes in my sister's physical appearance. As the first-born son who in our culture was supposed to keep his distance from our mother, I was never the object of her obsessive grooming and looking untidy was even considered a sign of manliness. With Aishetu it was the opposite and our mother treated her like a little ornament who needed constant decoration, polishing and meticulous care for the most minor detail of her appearance. Unlike me she had to be spotless at all times, carefully washed with moisturizing soaps, lovingly dried with big Marks and Spencer towels and anointed with the sweetest perfumed oils from the Lebanese Emporium. Our mother would do the braids of her hair herself though there were many women around who would have done it for free. And she was so skilled in applying eye shadow that people in the neighbourhood brought their daughters round when they were about to be married off.

Mother also chose the brilliantly white cloth for her wrapper when she was younger and then the stunning many-coloured Dutch waxes that would light her up like a Christmas tree during the festivals. But then I would catch her wiping away the eye shadow with a cloth when she thought I wasn't looking; she complained of headaches when mother wanted to braid her hair; would hide when it was time for her bath and found ways of soiling her new clothes, which annoyed Nana no end. I would hear mother complaining to our father, who kept silent or mumbled that it was her fault that their daughter was not being properly brought up since it was the mother's job in our culture and religion to teach girl children the art of obedience.

Then the quarrelling stopped and it was Nana who now seemed to collaborate with Aishetu in making her look as plain and unattractive as possible. Although we hardly played together anymore she would shout at me to 'stop behaving like a girl' and drag my sister, who looked more and more like a zombie, away to the safety of her own room. Sometimes I would hear Aishetu's screams and thought of going to her rescue but then I would hear our mother's voice berating my father and realize that she was having the same nightmare all the time as the sounds were always the same, in a guttural voice that was almost unrecognizable. By laying absolutely still in my bed I could make out some of Nana's words which were shouted at the top of her voice – 'haram', 'forbidden', 'hellfire', 'wickedness' and 'pray for your black soul'. But when my father did pray, trying to shout down our mother's harangue, it was a prayer for Aishetu – to stop Satan making her an object of temptation for pious men!

Although I am recounting these horrors here I still cannot think of my father as an evil man; and this image of him has still remained stubbornly fixed in my mind despite the incontrovertible evidence of my fellow comrades and journalists, and research by Kikelomo and myself, that he is at the centre of a diabolic 'judicial' process that sentences thousands of innocent people to death and unspeakable torture each year. This is a man I remember reading most of the books from Heinemann's African Writers Series, subscribing to the *New Yorker* and the airmail version of the *Guardian*, listening absorbed to *Laudate Dominum*, and the haunting rendition of a Puccini aria by Maria Callas, which reminds me of my sister whenever I hear it play. One day he showed me a picture of himself with a classmate, now a US Supreme Court Justice, at the National Opera in 1964, the black sheen of their rented tuxedos bright against the red of Maria Callas's gown.

It was from him I developed my interest in journalism, although he wanted me to follow him into the legal profession, when I stood outside his study listening to the Hausa Services of the BBC, Voice of America, DeutscheWelle and Radio Moscow on his short wave radio. He never raised his hand against me or my mother, and although what he did to my sister can never be forgiven in this life or the next, none of us can say that he ever denied us any material comforts which, in this world of gross materialism, I suppose can be considered a plus. So if my comrades and colleagues have enough courage the question they should ask me is: knowing your father as you do, do you consider him *normal*?

Reading the circumlocutions and procrastinations I've resorted to so far in this short piece I suppose you expect me to evade the question by asking what you mean by 'normal'. Or I could resort to religion, to the horror of my comrades, by saying that only God can truly judge. But judgement is the hallmark of my profession and I will give a qualified answer by saying that this man, the Hanging Judge, is normal like Hitler, who truly loved his dog, was normal. *Normal* like the butcher General Daudu who weeps when he hears Elvis's 'Fools Rush In', who broke down in hysterics when his mother died, despite scurrilous rumours that he had her killed to hide the fact that he was not born in Niagra. He prays to her embalmed body in its little gold coffin with raised Arabic characters in rubies and sapphires, in the rotunda of his Rock Palace, under the frescoes of himself at Graceland, painted on the gold leaf of the ceiling modelled on the dome of St Peter's Basilica, swearing she would never be placed in his twenty-two carat gold mausoleum in their native Cameroon before him. There she lies in eternal splendour, in intensely pink recessed light, surrounded by a thousand red plastic roses, enjoying 'I'm Sorry' by Brenda Lee, which young Daniel used to sing to her whenever he was naughty.

A far more interesting question would be why such *normal* men become capable of such evil. The tale I am about to tell has never been published before and I heard it only because the blind teller did not know who I was. As some of you may know, the General grew up

as a stable boy in my grandfather's household. While
there, according to the blind seer, there was some
'trouble' involving the younger sister of Uncle Aminu
and my father, and the stable boy was blamed and sent
away. (This aunt of mine must remain anonymous
because of the sensitivity of the rumour: she went to
school in America, married and converted to Christianity,
changed her name and never returned to Niagra. She is
now Professor of Post-Modernist Feminism and the
Fracturing of Identities at a West Coast University.)

It was Uncle Aminu who told their father the truth
so that his brother was punished and young Daniel
spared the injustice to his person and reputation. The
irony is that Daudu now hates my uncle who rescued
him from ignominy while worshipping the ground
walked on by my father. I still remember the first time
my father came close to hitting me, when he shouted
so loudly the servants came running from all over our
large compound, thinking that he was being attacked
by armed robbers. It was some years after my sister
disappeared, just before I was due to sit my West African
School Certificate exam, when an African-American
Moslem teacher of English Literature, one Muhammed
al-Bilal bin Baraka, recommended that I read Sembene
Ousmane's *White Genesis*. I had gone to answer a call
from my cousin Nuhu and left the book on a table in
the garden near where he parked, and by the time I
came out he was looking at it like some dangerous wild
animal, shouting to find out who was guilty of displaying
this offence against Islam and glorifying an apostate,
atheistic author who accused fellow Moslems of such
abomination against religion and nature. I swear that
if I had not been the guilty party he might have passed
sentence there and then.

But to come back to my story, which you must have
guessed by now that I put off because it was so painful:
I remember being so joyous when my sister who had
started looking like a stick insect suddenly began to
bloom. Her sunken cheeks flushed out and her eyes
started to grow again, although they appeared swollen
and always on the verge of tears. It was our mother who
now took a turn for the worse, her flesh seeming to

dissolve, only to attach itself to my expanding sister. Overnight her cheeks sunk like gashes on a dirt road, her eyes retreated, her fair skin shrivelled like a leaf and her once lustrous hair, which she no longer braided, went white.

It was the time when Daudu returned from a course in the USA, and was arrested for embezzling funds meant to arrange housing for men under his command. My father defended him and the case took up so much time he was hardly at home. But when he returned, having obtained an acquittal for his father's former stable boy, there was the mother of all rows as this man accused our mother of having brought up her daughter bad and insisting that she could not remain in the house to bring disgrace on a family with a thousand year reputation to uphold. I never saw my sister again and have spent the last twenty years of my life surrounded by rumours and her sketchbooks like Hieronymous Bosch's, seeing my sister in every beautiful light-skinned woman I meet on the road holding the hand of her child. Not long after that my mother returned to her father's house. She never married again but her former husband took the first of a succession of wives much younger than his own daughter. The last time I saw him, hearing falsely that he was gravely ill, I greeted a young girl I thought was my half-sister by patting her on the head, only to be rebuked by her husband who told me to show respect to my step-mother. And then I knew the rumours were true that he had no more children because his wives were so young they succumbed to *vesico vaginal fistula* and died in childbirth, or lived to envy the dead.

And this brings me back to *Chinatown* and the lesson it has taught me about the tragedy of my sister. Despite the crime he had committed the John Huston character recognized his daughter and took responsibility for his action through his willingness to love and protect her. Aishetu on the contrary was treated like an abominable criminal who was sentenced to exile and dishonour, to wander the world in search of comfort from strangers, she and her child sacrificed to protect the name of a 'distinguished old family'. In this way the story is more

like *White Genesis* than *Chinatown*. So why did I choose
Polanski's film rather than Ousmane's novella? Could
it be that *White Genesis* would have been much too
close to home, as the author predicted in his preface?
Perhaps now you understand my anguish.

REDEMPTION MAN

On the day of the coup there were no signs that something momentous was in the offing. It was not the Ides of March, there was no blind seer, no revealing entrails, no star or skulking Magi, not even a single witch to proclaim that the Sequined Terror of the General was about to end. As usual after the stress of work with the fanatic teetotalitarian Joseph, Rabiu branched by the Press Centre to share a Star beer with the other journalists. But in a country renowned for its scientific rumours, for which the reporter's watering hole should receive a clutch of Nobel Prizes for outrageous inventions in rumourology, there was not a peep. Instead everything appeared normal in a land where *normal* meant 'impossible' or at best 'extremely unlikely'. So he went out to get *tsuya* for Kikelomo, which was normal for him except that the Rasta boy was not there.

When Rabiu asked the meat seller for him he replied in a rather formal but enigmatic way that he had gone home early, that *people like him* sometimes needed extra sleep. Rabiu could never understand why the man appeared so cold and defensive when he tried to find out about the strange boy. He was surprised that such a wise, even-tempered old man appeared to get angry when he repeated the rumour that Bob Marley got his name from Delroy, who was struck by the astonishing likeness to the late reggae singer when he saw the boy with other urchins gathered to hear Brotherman play his Afro-Carib Fusion rhythm on his beat-up saxophone. While waiting for his *tsuya* Rabiu would glance furtively at him to see this likeness but could not, except for the colour: even his locks were more like the hair his mother used to braid for his sister and there was something definitely feminine in the slant of his face, like a cross between Sade's and Gloria Estefan's. If he had been with Delroy he should have remembered although there were so many street kids with matted hair.

He was struck by how protective the old man was toward the boy. Was he perhaps the child of some distant relation, whom even a man as enlightened as Alhaji Suleiman could not publicly acknowledge? Ahmed said how friendly the boy was, that he had a wizard of a girlfriend who read the most sophisticated books! But Rabiu knew his soft-spoken classmate had a wicked sense of humour, and the term *wizard* gave him away when he said that she came from Lidiziam: Daudu who knew not a word of Latin had instinctively followed the line of the Romans pursuing Hannibal when he ordered that the village be *completely destroyed* [Editor's note: *Carthago delenda est*]. Daudu's orders were very specific after being briefed by the Chairman of Burton Holly and the Honorary Consul that the 'rebels' put at risk the national economy, which was 90 per cent dependent on oil, and, by extension, the Liberator Daudu's place in history. In a copy of the order, which Fatima had passed on to Kikelomo, written in the Liberator's unsteady hand, it was stated: 'nothing alive should escape the hellhole of Lidiziam'. So they had slaughtered all the men, women, children, dogs, goats, chickens, then poured cyanide from the gold refining vats of Lone Star Smelting and Drilling into the waters and napalmed the trees. And *Platt's Oil News* reported that with the 'return of stability to the village, oil prices fell by a dollar a barrel, while shares in Burton Holly rose by ten dollars'.

He always looked out for the young Rasta who seemed like a brown extension of the rock he sat on, motionless as the cigar store Indians he saw outside American kiosks. But he had seen him move fast, dragging his bad leg like a doll from a fire, trying to get to the customer's car before the engine was killed. And this proved he couldn't possibly be the boy, Sergeant 'Idi Amin' Ogwu's son, who the torturer was rumoured to have sent with Nuhu's personal effects, which had almost killed his poor uncle with shock. Mallam Aminu spoke of a sweet, intelligent, very vibrant youngster, who had an innocent, almost supernatural air about him despite the grim tidings he conveyed. His uncle spoke of no physical or psychological defects, and this boy certainly looked more like twelve than twenty, although he was probably fifteen, the mild retardation making him look younger. It wasn't likely he would have contracted polio later in life, and he recalled Adama, the comrade in charge of health on the Central Committee, who spoke of the shame of Niagra that such easily cured diseases still killed and disfigured so many children of peasants and workers like young Bob Marley.

Recalling the boy's image now as he waited for the meat in the haze of wood smoke he saw the impossibility of his being Idi Amin's son. His bones were fine, almost like a bird, while most gorillas would pale in the shadow of the notorious torturer who, rumour had it, had gone to the mortuary to collect internal organs from Nuhu and the others, together with the bullets which killed them, for the General's trophy case. There was the innocence of Dostoyevsky's Idiot about the boy as he sat with his vacant eyes staring at infinities without care, incapable of stringing two thoughts together, but also of conceiving evil. For the life of him Rabiu could not understand what fascinated him about Bob Marley since he could not even use him as a character in his novel because he lacked credibility. He was feeling resentful that the old man was so uncommunicative to a man who prided himself as a good investigative journalist, who was almost a shoo-in for the ICIJ Prize this year, in recognition of his series of articles in *Review of African Political Economy*, on the fortunes made by Niagran generals from exploiting minerals and timber in Sierra Leone, Liberia and Congo where they served as 'peace keepers'. He was startled when the old man spoke to him in Hausa, still calling him 'teacher', although he knew he was a journalist.

'Here's your meat, *likita*, hope madam and the pickin enjoy.'

'Thank you very, very much, Alhaji,' Rabiu said, handing him the $50 bill and noting his strained smile.

'It's nothing, *likita*,' the old man said, handing him his change.

'No, Alhaji, keep it,' Rabiu said and then, when he refused, said 'give it to our little friend Bob Marley.'

'No,' the old man said, 'Bob is alright, he has someone to take care of him. Keep your money for your own people who need God's help!'

He was disturbed by the riddle of the old man's hostility, which he tried to hide with a sphinx-like display. Why did the absence of the young Rasta have such an impact on him? Heavily pregnant, freed of the kids who were with his uncle, and now rid of recurrent nightmares, Kikelomo was deep asleep when he arrived home.

Although he wished he could wash his mind of the smell of Nuhu's death as he lay on top of him, he did not envy his wife her new-found peace which was helping her keep this child to term. In his own dream he saw the sweep of his eyes on the slant of new rain then he was inside the eye sockets and they became a vortex and the pressure was inhuman on him and he could not breathe and his screams could not escape to drag his wife back to her own rollercoaster of cascading mirror images of terror. So to escape the horror he often stayed up late to watch the movies on the satellite channels from South Africa. Tonight there was a choice between *Chinatown* which he had seen many times and *Unforgiven* which he had never watched to the end because it had come on when Kikelomo still had *her* nightmares about the running man. But the experience with the meat seller and the mystery of the young Rasta pushed him toward his old obsession with Polanski's film. There was no parallel between the fiction of a powerful family destroyed by unnatural acts and the reality of a young boy who was a victim of poverty, alienation and disability. But both showed the pathology of class society, which destroyed the powerful as well as the impotent. As he watched the vulnerable young girl in the film he found himself thinking of the entrancing frailty of Bob Marley, and the unnatural way in which he blended with his environment, almost like an animal.

Then, just as Faye Dunaway finished saying 'my daughter, my sister,' the channel paused for a commercial on the super absorbent quality of the latest Tampax, he switched to the NTV news channel and beheld the face of Ahmed Abdullahi, wide as all the universe, staring from those haunting, dispassionate eyes, which he had once feared would win the love of Kikelomo. *No*, he said, *it can't be*. He felt himself being pressed back in his chair as, earlier in the day, he had tried to flee inside, as in his nightmare, from Joseph Mammamia leading the band of visiting Evangelical Christians from Crawford, Texas, sponsored by the Burton Holly Charitable Foundation, which was rumoured to have supplied the cyanide to cleanse the waters of Lidiziam of rebel fish. *No*, he said again, *not Ahmed*.

In his mind he ran through the images of the group of young revolutionary students who had made the University famous as the 'nest of radicals' when Delroy was alive. Joseph, the noisiest, had sold out to State Security, the Americans and Evangelicals. He was free to spout his own revolutionary slogans, although as 'Robert Nesta', because he was the son of the Hanging Judge. And they left Kikelomo relatively alone because she was his wife and her friend Fatima protected her. Nuhu and Delroy were dead and, like Delbert Gower, their corpses had never been returned to their families. *But Ahmed!*

He remembered the first rally where he saw the tall man in red fez and white kaftan near the back of the crowd. Chanting '*A luta contínua! A vitória é certa!*' Joseph was whipping them up to a frenzy when he paused suddenly and pointed a long finger on the end of his exceptionally long arm at Ahmed and screamed 'Agent! Agent! He's Lt Abdullahi from Military Intelligence!' The crowd froze in shock horror, its eyes widened as if it were a single individual, then moved as one toward the tall figure, who made no attempt to escape. Then Delroy, whom he had not seen on the fringe of the crowd, walked to the platform and took the mike from Joseph's trembling hands. He could still remember his words the way he remembered the little poems his sister used to write on the margins of her nightmare portraits.

'Leave the soldier alone, you're all young, you're all students, you all have a right to learn what is truth. How will we stop the soldiers killing the people and stealing from them unless we teach them to serve the people? Ideas are practical, not what exists only in the heads of individuals. As the most practical people in society, with the material power of life and death in their hands, soldiers are the most in need of popular ideas. How do you think the Portuguese people rid themselves of Salazar and General de Spinola? Their fascist leaders sent them to kill the people in their colonies but when they got to Angola, Mozambique and Guinea-Bissau they found on the bodies of "terrorists" they had killed the poetry of Agostinho Neto and Josina Machel, and the theoretical writings of Amilcar Cabral, named by his father after Hamilcar Barca, father of Hannibal, the Carthaginian general who defeated the

Romans at the battle of Cannae in 223 BC. They had been searching for what motivated poor peasants with AK47s, machetes and home-made hunting guns to take on the might of a NATO army and when they found it they turned their weapons against their own oppressors and their country became free.'

He remembered Joseph chewing his nails even more furiously, wiping the foam from his mouth with the back of his hand, as the wildly cheering students lifted their new hero on their shoulders and brought him up to the platform to present him to their teacher. But he never came to any more rallies and Joseph led a band of students who circulated posters with Ahmed's crudely drawn face on portraits of Herr Flick, the comical Gestapo spy from *'Allo 'Allo*. And here he was leading the khaki revolution, which overthrew the most odious military dictatorship in the world and promising as calmly as he used to greet them before Delroy's lectures *Democracy, Liberty, Equality, Fraternity, the Rights to Life and the Pursuit of Happiness.*

Perhaps he should have got a clue when Ahmed bought Delroy's old Volkswagen Beetle and became the first military officer in the history of Niagra not to own at least one Mercedes. He was also rumoured to have remained single because he said he could not bring children into a world where he could not protect heroes like Delroy and Nuhu. Rabiu's eyes were so fixed to the screen with Ahmed's face that he didn't hear Kikelomo walk up behind him until she pulled his ears.

'So you're awake?'

'How could I sleep when you're screaming like Joseph possessed by the spirits of America?'

'I didn't scream – and don't hassle me about Joseph – remember he fancied you!'

'Didn't you all? You always say you don't scream, even when you sleep.'

'I never scream in my sleep!'

'Yes, you do, that's why I moved the kids' room so they wouldn't think I'm strangling their father.'

'Keep talking rubbish – can't you see what's happening?'

'Yes, I can.'

'You sound so blasé. Aren't you surprised it's Ahmed?'

'Why should I be? Delroy always said he was the one.'

'Delroy said *that*?'

'Yes. Now it's you who sounded surprised. All the time Ahmed used to come to our house you thought he was chasing me.'

'It did cross my mind, but a woman like you is worth being jealous over.'

'Keep flattering – it *will* get you something!' she said, reaching into his pyjama top.

'Ahmed and Delroy used to sit on the veranda smoking ganja and drinking white rum, or with Brotherman and his crew composing music for the poems of Neto and Josina Machel. Delroy said Ahmed was always the first to strip off when it was time for communal labour, always consulted the people to find out what *they* wanted, unlike you idiots who came with ideas preset in concrete about what was good for the poor workers and peasants – they used to make fun when you guys spoke of "concrete" ideas for the masses. He was always impressed with the way Ahmed was able to communicate with the street kids. It was always so funny, those two tall guys sitting on the ground rapping with the crippled little ones and actually learning from them. So, no, I'm not at all surprised Ahmed is the one.'

'In a way I suppose he did it because he felt guilty about not being able to protect Delroy and Nuhu – we all did. I felt like I was being crushed by the Amuz Rock.'

'Not me, guilt is a male thing, that's why you're always killing each other.'

'You and your gender fascism, you and Fatima, you want it all –'

'Yes, we want it all, we deserve it after millennia of frustrated agony. Let's go, our baby needs some vigorous exercise.' She opened his pyjama top and was pulling him by the collar.

'You're crazy, you're nearly eight months pregnant!'

'All the more need for exercise.'

'And there's a revolution to celebrate!'

'You said it, Comrade Rabiu, what better way? Remember Josina's poem?' She was removing the rest of his clothes and as she pushed him to the bedroom she hummed Brotherman's tune of 'This is the Time'.

'You're mad,' he said, as she pulled him naked onto the bed.

'Yes,' she sang, '*Yes!* And tonight I won't let you turn off the lights. *Get up, Stand up, it's Revolution Time!*'

'Mad,' he repeated, 'I married a madwoman!'

HAVING A PARTY

The momentous events of 11 September 2001 created a moral dilemma for members of the Central Committee of the Marxist-Leninist Revolutionary Workers Party of Struggle of the Toiling People of Niagra (M-LRWPSTPN). On the one hand thousands of people had been massacred by a bunch of Islamo-Fascists from the reactionary petit-bourgeois feudal class of the Arabian Peninsula trained by totalitarian global imperial capital to crush the popular struggles of peasants and workers in Afghanistan and other neo-colonial outposts of Western Imperialism. On the other hand, in the finest example of dialectics since Comrade Engels continued to exploit the workers of his factories in order to liberate them, Comrade bin Laden, from the Saudi ruling class, had executed great vengeance on the Centre of International Capital, smiting the fascist warmonger Bush with furious rebukes. This was, however, only a secondary contradiction, which could be solved, in the finest tradition of Marxism-Leninism-Mao Zedong Thought, by writing an article for the *Review of African Political Economy* (*RAPE*).

The Primary Contradiction was the *beard*. How could the toiling masses of the M-LRWPSTPN distinguish the Islamo-Fascists of the Saudi Feudal Class from Comrades of Marxism-Leninism-Mao Zedong Thought if they all wore *beards*? This fundamental theoretical task was assigned to none other than Comrade 'Carlos', unique master of dialectical materialism and the most profound exponent of Mass Struggle since Comrade 'Bono'. [Editor's Note: In the finest tradition of Revolutionary Underground Struggle members of the Leadership adopted aliases or *noms de guerre* like the Georgian who called himself 'Stalin' ('Hammer') because it reminded him of what he did best, but also to avoid the jibes of comrades that Georgians, Tamils and Welshmen made poor revolutionaries because by the time you pronounced their elongated names to tell them to *run like hell* the fucking pigs would have crawled all over your ass. But in a subtle theoretical twist Niagran comrades *fidelized* their aliases after the fall of the Berlin wall when the Cubans promised members of the Politburo scholarships for their children and free health care for themselves. Thus Comrade 'Karl' was transformed into 'Carlos', Comrade 'Friedrich' became 'Frederico' and Comrade 'Vladimir', aka 'the Writer', adopted the nom de plume 'Vladimiro'.]

Comrade Carlos approached the task of the *beard* with the perspicacity in applying dialectics which had earned him an invitation to address the Party Congress of Albania in the glorious presence of Comrades Enver and Nexhmije Hoxa [Editor's Note: Pronounced 'Hojja'.] on the 'Universal Application of the Unique Experience of the Development of Class Consciousness Among the Workers and Peasants of Niagra to All Oppressed People in the Known Universe'. As an emotional Comrade Hoxa declared in a moving tribute after the four-hour disquisition, this was another unique example of the basic principle of Marxism-Leninism-Maoism-Hoxism i.e. *identity in difference* and *the unity of opposites*, which first appeared in the idealist posturing of that asshole Hegel's *Logic* and was transformed into historical materialism by the masterful dialectics of comrades Marx and Engels.

Applying the same principle to the *beard* the comrade
arrived at the same theoretical conclusions designed to
enrich Marxist thinking throughout the Continent. As an
undifferentiated category the *beard* was identical in so far
as it consisted of facial hair, but *opposite* in so far as each
individual beard had its own specific characteristic, which
distinguished it from the individual who 'sported' it. But
there was unity in the *purpose* and theoretical significance
of the hair-in-itself. While the crazies claimed that it was
against their religion to trim or shave the *beard,* every
comrade knew that *trimming, shaping, combing, sculpting
and conditioning* facial hair were the essence of revolutionary struggle. This created a practical problem for
distinguishing between Islamo-Fascism and Rastafarianism, an ideology of a section of the lumpen petit-
bourgeoisie, as the so-called Nazarenes also eschewed the
decoration of face as well as head hair.

But this was by no means the full extent of the Niagran
Comrade's contribution to the development of revolutionary theory. While other parties had struggled to come
to terms with the theoretical and practical problems
created by lack of funding after the so-called 'Collapse of
Communism', the M-LRWPSTPN solved *its* problem by
winning a grant from the Open Society Foundation. The
idea had been conceived and germinated after comrades
from the MPLA had addressed their Niagran counterparts
and denounced the NGO Global Witness as a 'bunch of
fairies who demand transparency in the finances of the
Angolan oil industry but refuse to publish the fact that
they are funded by crypto-fascist liberal pinko fucking
capitalist pigs'. It was Comrade Vladimiro who came up
with the ingenious scheme of applying for funds to
*Foster Transparency, Enhance Capacity Building and
Stimulate the Development of Civil Society in the
Governance of the Federal Republic of Niagra.* When they
received the reply, with the enthusiastic assurance that
the 'M-LPWPSTPN will contribute to the development of

democratic structures in Monteniagra', and a machine written and signed cheque for $35,000, the comrades declared party time and treated themselves to a 'banquet worthy of the masses'.

With this profound theoretical tradition to draw on the eighteen bearded and two clean-shaven comrades on the Central Committee had no problem assessing the significance of the military coup, disguised under the petit-bourgeois euphemism of 'khaki revolution'. The Plenary Report of the First Working Group of the Fifth Directorate of Theoretical Understanding was read by Comrade Rabiu Nafiu who, although beardless, was indulged because of his importance in the struggle to wean scions of the feudal ruling class from obscurantism to the clarity of the historical dialectical materialism of Marxism-Leninism-Mao Zedong-Enver Hoxa-Fidel Castro-George Soros Thought. His friend and classmate Joseph Mammamia showed more promise because he was from a genuine proletarian background, grew a beard in record time, shouted very loudly and had very long arms and fingers, which were crucial for Marxist-Leninist dialectical gestures. But unfortunately this young and gifted comrade had fallen victim to the dialectical idealist philosophy of Billy Graham, Jerry Falwell, John Ashcroft, Marceau Armitage, Richard Perle, Ahmed Chalabi and Rush Limbaugh.

Comrade Rabiu was expounding the theoretical line that the so-called 'khaki revolution' was a definite contribution to the bourgeois democratic phase of the national revolution, citing Lt Colonel Ahmed Abdullahi's overt allusions to the slogans of the French and American Revolutions. The masses were behind his movement, which had driven out the vicious military dictatorship, restored economic security and basic democracy to the people and set in motion the dialectical processes necessary to establish the basis of genuine bourgeois democracy.

But his comrades would have none of this. While they

were willing to humour him, because of the theoretical consideration that having him on the CC of the M-LRWP-STPN had pissed off his father, the Hanging Judge, and made his master, General Daudu, look like a prick, his defence of a petit-bourgeois putsch which replaced them raised novel theoretical issues of a very profound type. The Party would have to contemplate for a very long time to give any support. His citing of the petit-bourgeois counter revolutionary anarchist Dr Delroy Solomon with examples from Grenada under the revanchist, proto-Trotskyist, Maurice Bishop, and Burkina Faso under the populist crypto-fascist Thomas Sankara, further enraged the comrades who remembered the renegade, Rasta loving, CIA inspired, hemp-smoking, petit-bourgeois Doctor who had made the obscene reactionary remark that Niagra's so-called Marxist-Leninist comrades 'had their heads so far up the asses of foreigners that if it weren't for their beards the Russians, Chinese, North Koreans and Albanians would be chewing on their ears with their Kellogg's cornflakes'.

'No,' Comrade Carlos said, stroking his beard in a suggestive manner, 'this will not *do*. We cannot support naïve, petit-bourgeois soldiers without theoretical grounding in the revolutionary movement or a base among the proletariat.'

To which Comrade Vladimiro added: 'I'm not sure how Comrade Soros would view this so-called "khaki revolution" within the context of his newly developed theoretical reappraisal of Global Capital. Perhaps we need to make a new application to find out.'

Comrade Adama 'Beyonce' Adama, Radcliffe phi beta kappa, who was also tolerated despite her beardlessness because she was a woman, had sat open mouthed throughout the latest theoretical peregrinations and now shouted, 'If this is the way you boys get it up I'm *outta* here!'

THE JOLLY GREEN GIANT
by John Lennon in *Red Bull*

How did a revolution described by the *Washington Post* as 'almost like a tea party in its gentility' suddenly live up to its Maoist definition as 'a bloody act of violence by which one class seizes power from another'? How was the young leader of the 'khaki revolution', described by Gianine di Giovani, the *Sunday Times* foreign correspondent, as the 'Jolly Green Giant, a cross between Commandante Marcos, Thomas Sankara and Michael Jordan', ambushed on his way to his office on Friday 13 February in the middle of rush hour traffic and slaughtered in clear view of astonished bystanders?

Refusing the panoply of motorcades which made life more hellish on the crowded thoroughfares of Xanadu, Lt Colonel Ahmed Abdullahi, who still drove himself in his old Volkswagen to collect his beloved *tsuya* after work, was being driven in an official Mercedes with a lone bodyguard and his muscular ADC.

Some might regard this as naïve for the leader of a country of 130 million volatile people with a wealth of minerals coveted by other nations possessed of overwhelming force. In fact a correspondent of the *Washington Times* had somewhat peevishly condemned the modesty of the new leaders as 'political correctness gone mad, the posturing of liberal-leaning amateurs too wedded to the post-modernist need for New Age symbolic affirmation of popular display. As in the time of Napoleon it is still true that "men are led by baubles" – also by Humvees, Bradley Fighting Vehicles, brilliantly orchestrated motorcades and choreographed parades on the Fourth of July'.

This correspondent was obviously referring to the simple 'Ceremony of Rebirth' in which the young leaders stood before a cheering crowd of one million to pledge their loyalty to the people instead of the other way round. Each solemnly declared his/her assets, swore to uphold the Constitution and the sacred traditions of the nation, and the military members surrendered their medals and military regalia of dress uniforms from Anderson and Shepherd, ceremonial swords, polished swagger sticks and ornate gold braid. The man from the mouth organ of the Universal Church of the Reverend Moon, Christian Coalition, Republican Party and Moral Majority obviously preferred the good old days when General Daudu changed uniforms like football strips, almost bankrupted the country with the purchase of exotic medals and organized Nuremburg style rallies with the help of Shille and Coulton on the birthdays of himself, his mother, first son, senior wives, the Lebanese twins, 'Mr Dick' of Burton Holly, the American President, British Prime Minister and assorted 'favourites'.

In fact the civilian and military members of the Transition Council did not regard themselves as 'leaders' but 'facilitators of the democratic process', which so enraged the man from Rev. Moon that he denounced the 'ideology of the workshop' and quoted the imperial American Vice President who said, 'TALK SOFTLY BUT PACK A BIG FUCKING BI BOMBER'. Were Ahmed Abdullahi and his comrades (I use this term with a thousand apologies to Danny Finkelman) naïve to have left their 'big stick' in the barracks when they ventured among the people they claimed to govern, however briefly and gently? Were they correct in ignoring the advice of born-again revolutionary Comrade Joseph Mammamia, founder of *Red Tide*, that the 'revolution must wrap itself in armours of steel and be prepared to execute great vengeance and furious rebukes upon its enemies'? The fact is that the people loved it and felt secure that they too could travel to work without the threat of being run down, horse-whipped, shot or 'disposed of' by leaders so afraid of their people they could not walk alone among them.

But perhaps Danny Finkelman and Joseph Mammamia were right, because they are alive and Ahmed Abdullahi is not. And now it remains for us who survived to establish why and how he died. In the article quoted above the veteran *Washington Post* correspondent spoke of 'sources very deep within the administration' who referred to the Transition Council as 'not being politically toilet trained' and ordered the Directorate of Operations to 'dispose of the mess'. What could possibly have led to this cold-blooded directive by a very high-ranking administration official after initial favourable assessments by the State Department, major international media, and even the CIA?

According to Bob Goodall, writing for the website www.intelligenceonline.com, Jim Wood the station chief in Xanadu had written an effusive Field Assessment stating how closely the coup leader's opening speech resembled the American Declaration of Independence. His view was that the change of government would foster the American national interest by reducing the cost of doing business in Niagra, which had escalated with the increasing isolation of the previous regime, and the clamour for international sanctions, necessitating costly PR exercises and denial of trade opportunities. This regime, despite its mildly anti-American rhetoric, designed for public consumption, could be eased into more friendly directions by the promise of increased military co-operation and new American investments in the vital offshore oil blocs, which had tapered off because of public unrest. The ambitious blueprint for industrial infrastructure opened up new fields for American heavy industry. And the Agency had valuable assets within the junta, who could help shape its behaviour. In an extensive quote from the report www.intelligenceonline.com stated:

The strategic importance of the so-called 'khaki revolution' cannot be over-estimated. Given the need to diversify our sources of petroleum and reduce our dependence on supplies from the troubled Middle East, it is established American policy to supply 25 per cent of our needs from the West African region by 2005. To do so we need a stable environment, which can only be obtained through close co-operation with Niagra, the dominant regional power, which could discipline the whole of West Africa in US interests. Due to the mega-lomania, corruption and indiscipline of the previous regime and its 'Maximum Leader', the country was a source of instability, despite its 'pro-American' stance. Attempts to professionalize the armed forces with the help of PMCs were frustrated by General Daudu, who destroyed esprit de corps through neglect of the welfare of the lower ranks and the promotion of favourites.

Despite his 'leftism', which is more nationalist than socialist, Lt Colonel Ahmed is a superb professional soldier, whose austerity and willingness to share hard-ships with his men have made him the most popular officer in the history of Niagra. Through him it is possible to professionalize the military and make the country the focal point of American strategy. There can be no question of anti-Americanism because Ahmed shoots hoops with our defence attaché who played point guard at USC; he met Michael Jordan at Fort Bragg and still wears the t-shirt; and he's rumoured to have kept in touch with Earl Woods, Tiger's father, who spoke at the orientation for Abdullahi's PSYOPS course. (For the complete text click on www.bullredonline.com.)

The Agency also exposed the lie of Abdullahi's alleged relations with Al-Qaeda when newspapers all over the world printed pictures of the smiling colonel with a group of beards. When a Rasta man called Barracuda saw it in the *Jamaica Gleaner* he recognized himself (mistaken by the Pentagon's Office of Special Plans for Peter Tosh) with the group from the West Kingston ghetto of Tel Aviv, who had gone to demand the body of their guru, Dr Delroy Solomon, from General Daudu *long before the revolution*. The Yale-educated Barracuda, who was shacked up with a Nigerian superstar, demanded an apology from the paper which defamed non-violent, peace-loving Rastas by equating them with violent religious psychopaths who locked up their women, fucked little boys and bit the ears off camels, and threatened to burn down the place and kill everybody inside if they didn't. The very distinctive picture of the so-called High Priest of the Order of Niabinghi among the crowd was a dead giveaway. This former roots musician who sold tams and effigies of Haile Selassie outside the Ward Theatre in downtown Kingston had sparked a crisis in Jamaica/US relations when the Pentagon's Office of Special Plans interpreted Vela satellite photos of his billowing ganja pipe as a potential Weapon of Mass Destruction.

The Defence Secretary had just ordered the invasion of the country with 250,000 American troops and a coalition of the willing, and the installation of Ahmed Chalabi as Minister of Petroleum, when Condi Rice pointed out that the little shit hole of an island where Colin Powell's people came from did not have a drop of oil and had sold its only refinery to Daudu. The American Defence Attaché confirmed the story, stating he was with Abdullahi until the brethren lit up their pipes and he had to leave, while Nasser Waddadda and Jerry Gotchakka – who represented the government – inhaled but did not smoke.

On the contrary, Daudu did have a very profitable relationship with Al-Qaeda, for which he was paid $50 million by a young Saudi Prince in the Ministry of the Interior to declare Sharia law, praise Wahabbism, establish a network of Koranic schools and provide safe houses for Mullah Omar and Monica Lewinsky. To disguise the money trail the Prince routed it through CIA accounts in the Carlton Group which he had used to help the Taliban come to power, in order to build the American/Saudi pipeline through Afghanistan. The accounts were now used to channel money to the opponents of Hugo Chavez, John Kerry and Jean-Bertrand Aristide, and Nasser Waddadda convinced his American counterpart that the $50 million was to fight the youth who were blowing up Burton Holly facilities in the vicinity of Lidiziam.

Why, then, did the Directorate of Operations send James 'Gofer' Brown to Xanadu a month into the 'khaki revolution' with a detailed plan for destabilization and $69 million in two metallic Zero Halliburton suitcases? According to the *Washington Post*, alarm bells started ringing in the Vice President's office when both *Platt's Oil News* and *Energy International Briefing* reported a sudden spurt in the oil price unrelated to changes in OPEC policy or the situation in the Middle East or Venezuela. A source in the Elysée Palace with close ties to the French external aid agency in Africa told the website www.intelligenceonline.com that the source of the alarm was an interview by a minor official in the inside pages of *Red Tide*, an obscure newsletter with almost non-existent circulation, which stated the determination of the Transition Council that the Burton Holly Corporation pay compensation for the destruction of the village of Lidiziam.

Since the village was completely destroyed, and only those who were away survived, this would be purely symbolic. More important was the insistence of the survivors that, out of respect for their dead, no oil be extracted, but that the village be cleaned up and restored as a nature reserve to honour the souls of the 2,384 dead, whose preference for nature over wealth led to the original conflagration. There were reports in the *Sentinel* of demonstrations led by a diminutive, partially mute woman. The Council's action was in any event academic because rebellious youth from neighbouring villages had made the place a no-go area for the oil company, despite the brutal regime of Daudu's Disposal Units and their American 'advisers'. (For more details click on www.crisisweb.org.)

At a meeting of the Corporate Council on Africa in Houston, attended by all the oil majors, a tired and emotional Richard 'the Jackal' Burton, head of the Burton Holly Corporation, was overheard in the lobby of the Hyatt Regency hotel shouting 'if they fucking think a pygmy antelope and albino python are worth thirty-three billion barrels of crude they should have their fucking heads examined'. The Jackal was physically removed by his PA and two Special Forces bodyguards who later came back to explain to astonished journalists that '*there were twenty-seven Dick Cheneys in phone books in the Washington area*'.

Shortly after the CIA report, Al-Bilal, a hitherto unknown radio station based in Abuja, capital of neighbouring Nigeria, began broadcasting communiqués from a group calling itself 'The International Islamic Relief Organization' which accused the Transition Council of persecuting Moslems and appealed for the *Jema'a* to come to the aid of its brothers. Meanwhile 'Radio Voice of the Gospel' in Benin spoke of 'Islamic armies assembling in Chad, Niger, Northern Nigeria and Northern Cameroon to wage Holy War against Niagran Christians', and called on 'Apostle' Nwogu to raise Christian armies to embark on a crusade to defend the faith. Dr Norman Nwogu, a distinguished civil engineer, listed his 'religion' in his latest entry in *Who's Who* as 'agnostic' and with Ahmed Abdullahi, his fellow Councillor, had toured mosques, churches and shrines to assure Niagrans that the constant 'religious' riots orchestrated by the previous regime to distract the people from its crimes belonged to the past. But here was Radio New Dawn referring to the Lt Colonel as 'Sheikh Abdullahi' and demanding that he pick up the mantle of his distinguished religious forebears as the Last Imam of Xanadu.

The fact is that there were 'Islamic' armies but their motivations were American $100 bills, not the *hadiths* of the Holy Prophet Mohammed (Peace Be Upon Him). According to the *Washington Post*, a Hausa-speaking pony-tailed special forces officer, with a single gold earring and silver stud in his tongue, drove his Jeep Cherokee with canvas bags full of money across the West African savannah to purchase whole units of the armies and security forces, with their total complements of armaments. Meanwhile another officer embarked on a similar mission in the more forested regions to recruit 'Christian' soldiers for the new crusade. Gofer Brown had issued instructions that any officer refusing the offer should have his hometown or village targeted with a 'daisy cutter' bomb, then be offered half the amount.

At the same time the Voice of America and *Washington Times* were quoting very highly placed administration sources as 'warning Sheikh Ahmed Abdullahi to cut his ties with Al-Qaeda, *or we'll fucking do it for him*'. These 'ties' were presumably deduced from the report that the Oxford-based International Islamic Relief Organization, which called on the

'Sheikh' to 'wage Jihad against the infidels', was said by MI5 to be a front for the bin Laden network. But as John Pilger, the British journalist, disclosed in an article in the *Daily Mirror*, a spokesman for the relief organization denied any connection with Radio Al-Bilal, which it denounced as a CIA asset designed to 'wage propaganda war against Moslems in the new Crusade of infidels, Christians and Jews'.

Meanwhile sources within the *Direction de la Surveillance du Territoire*, the French intelligence agency, reported special forces from a task force based in the Bight of Benin landing in the Delta to occupy the deserted village of Lidiziam. Pilger concluded that all on- and offshore sources of oil in the West African region were within range of American bases in São Tomé and Benin. It was from one of these bases in Cotonu, capital of the Republic of Benin that, according to a report by Guillaume Degas in www.intelligenceonline.com, a special forces 'snatch squad' was despatched to retrieve the body of Lt Colonel Ahmed so that, in the words of James Gofer Brown, 'the sons of bitches won't even find the head of his dick to fucking worship'.

According to the wife of a high-ranking official in the former government, the Americans were faced with a dilemma when they collected the mutilated corpse of the late Ahmed Abdullahi. Despite the three magazines of the MI6 rifles emptied into his body he still had a faint pulse, raising questions about the American government prohibition against assassination of its enemies by American citizens. The solution was to fly him to the HQ of Lone Star Smelting and Drilling where the Belgian vet in charge of the company clinic applied a lethal injection of ketamine. When the doctor certified that he was dead, and thus beyond the remit of the 'assassination directive', Gofer Brown authorized his Special Forces team to dismember the body before dissolving the pieces in the sulphuric acid vats of the mining company. So far rumours that he removed the head and packed it off to the Skull and Bone 'tomb' in New Haven on pikes in a heavy-duty cardboard box stuffed with dry ice have not been confirmed. (For further discussion click on www.military.com.)

In a moving tribute to the late revolutionary, John Pilger wrote in the *New Statesman*:

They called him 'Madiba' because of his striking resemblance to the young Nelson Mandela in his boxing days. I first saw him at the opening of the Delroy Solomon Refuge for Homeless Children, converted from the former Afro-Disney Theme Park built at vast public expense by the dictator General Daudu. What struck me was not just the grace and agility of this six foot five inch man but the ease with which the young urchins danced around him as they dribbled the ball on the makeshift basketball court. Before the game they had lined up to touch his Michael Jordan jersey, signed by the great man when he joined a game on a visit to Fort Bragg, where young Abdullahi was pursuing a PSYOPS course. He neither intimidated nor patronized his little friends, exchanged insults, abused the referee, or complained when fouled by a dreadlocked opponent who barely reached his waist.

And now he is dead because, mistaking the nature of the new American Dream, he politely asked for freedom for his people when the only liberty now allowed is the freedom of Burton Holly to extract oil at the cheapest price.

Ahmed Abdullahi is dead now because he wanted to free his people while others, more powerful than himself, wanted free markets for other people's resources. As in the time of Thucydides, 'rights are in question only between equals in power so that the strong do as they will and the weak suffer as they must'. For centuries they have ripped from our loins our men, women and children to die during the Atlantic passage or for the survivors to envy the dead. They have stolen our gold, silver, copper, iron, diamonds, palm oil, gum Arabic, cola, uranium, cobalt, coltan, molybdenum, amethyst, sapphires, rubies and zirconium and now want to rob us of the ability to honour the 2,384 souls of Lidiziam, to desecrate their remains in order to make way for their inhuman drilling machines.

For a few glorious weeks we were free of the numbing rhythms of Garth Brooks, Tammy Wynette, Marina McBride, Hank Thompson, LeAnn Womak and Loretta Lynn, free to listen once more to our heroes Fela Anikulapo-Kuti, Bob Marley, Sade, Shata and Aretha Franklin. When Brotherman and his boys jammed at the opening of the Delroy Solomon Orphanage, even the children wept until he reminded them that they should rejoice at being alive and free of the odious dictator and his Yankee masters. But now the General is back big time, with the latest hits from the Grand Ole Opry, and 'Courtesy of the Red, White and Blue', the Redneck anthem, is number one on Radio Niagra. His Elvis statue is still there, because the Transition Council said they had more urgent things to do than remove the heaviest statue in Black Africa. His 'Frescoes of a Visit to Graceland' are still on his gold-leafed ceilings because the sign painters were too busy converting his 'Grand Ole Niagran Opry' to the African House of Youth. Only the tiny jewelled casket with his mother's remains was not there to greet him, because the late Ahmed Abdullahi declared that the old woman deserved a proper burial and accompanied her home on her final journey to her birthplace in Cameroon, which Daudu could not because his constitution declared that no one whose grandparents were not born in Niagra could seek political office or rise above the rank of sergeant in the army.

His American patrons decided that the son should not be outshone by the brilliance of his mother's internment and, citing the 'danger of Al-Qaeda' (from Richard Armitage of the State Department), accompanied his chartered 747 with a squadron of F16 fighter jets equipped with Sidewinder missiles and B1 bombers kitted with JDAMs. Following in the footsteps of Leni Riefenstahl, Hitler's camerawoman, Shille and Coulton organized a Triumph of the Niagran Will, and put on a fireworks display which required a full month's supply from three major Chinese factories; when Anderson and Shepherd failed to produce all the dress uniforms required, Gofer Brown was forced to raid the stores of

Sandhurst, West Point and Annapolis to dress his new legions in the jackets of the old.

And proud he should be of the shining legions of Niagra, embellished by the purchased Jihad armies from Niger, Chad and Northern Nigeria, and the equally resplendent Crusaders from Benin, Cameroon and the Nigerian South. The crowd of illiterates, swept from the streets at fifty cents a shot to salute them in the renamed General Daudu stadium, were supplied with ballpoint pens by Shille and Coulton to fill in the assessment forms for their magnificent labours. And the dead of Lidiziam can sleep no more because PSYOPS Units in the Special Forces were ordered to play 'Courtesy of the Red, White and Blue' at full volume wherever they went in the delta in snazzy new Humvees and Bradley Fighting Vehicles with blacked-out windows.

When will they ever learn that the young women, men, and even the flowers, killed in the battle of Lidiziam, will one day rise again. That those who have fallen will get up, stand up and pay homage to Bob Marley, Nuhu Aminu, Delbert Gower, Omolare and Delroy Solomon, Ahmed Abdullahi and the 2,384 restless souls of the forgotten village? May their souls rest in perfect peace while those who murdered them ponder their next heart attack.

BOOK III:
REDEMPTION MAN

THE BALLAD OF
BILLY BOB LIOTTO

Crouched behind the mustard coloured skip, eyes closed to the eruptions of dust and smoke, forehead pressed to the ground to avoid shrapnel and hands covering his ears to keep out the sounds of rockets, missiles, sirens, shells and machine gun bullets, Bob Marley did not hear the men coming till the hand grabbed his neck from behind and the fingers joined in front. He had seen fingers like those on the hands of a gorilla on the mountains of Rwanda in the wildlife book by David Attenborough that Ahmed brought back from the BBC shop, but the gorilla's looked more gentle, more human. At first he thought the hand was Idi Amin's but the smell was different and there really wasn't time to think because he was yanked from the ground like a rabbit and turned round to face his captor who held him at some distance so he could have a full appraisal of what kind of terrorist Al-Qaeda scumbag he had picked up.

His thumb was pressed up under Bob Marley's chin so Bob was forced to look up and what he saw was a black mountain in forest green khaki like Lover's Leap where the hanging plants flowed over the side toward the hissing foam of the Atlantic full of the breath of countless slaves from days of old. The giant's eyes danced like blackened,

sea-tossed coconuts in lakes of red flame to the music of
'Courtesy of the Red, White and Blue' as he smiled at his
leader. Even from a distance Bob Marley was drowned in
the American's raging odours of sour mash whiskey and
hotdogs smothered in relish, ketchup and mustard, making
a blinding mélange as he felt the air being squashed out
of his smarting breast plate and his brain turning blue.

'Well, well, what the hell you got there, Hissene?' The
white man had a scraggly yellow beard and hair like a
woman's tied behind with a red, white and blue kerchief
with fifty American stars. The Redneck Anthem was
coming from a Walkman connected to an ear with a tiny
diamond stud, he wore pale blue jeans and a red Atlanta
Falcons t-shirt, his eyes grey like the underside of a cobra's
neck.

'It is certainly one of them, Monsieur Billy Bob,' Hissene
boomed, in a voice far deeper than the engines of the
Humvee full of Special Forces soldiers doing high fives to
the theme song of 'Born in the USA'. 'What do you call
yourself, *sir*?' When Bob Marley did not reply, his puzzled
eyes appearing to say he didn't understand Hissene's
accent, Billy Bob asked kindly, 'Won't you tell the nice
man your name, *sir*?'

'Bob Marley,' he whispered with his last breath as the
fingers tightened round his neck.

'Speak up, *sir*, we can't hear you,' Billy Bob said in the
singsong of the Voice of America's 'special English'.

With his eyes almost exploding and his eardrums
expanded beyond their limits he managed to squeeze some
air from his blood back into his collapsing lungs to repeat,
'Bob Marley.'

'*Bob Marley*, eh? Perhaps the *garçon* thinks we make
the joke,' the Chadian chuckled.

'Show the "garson" what we think of Bob Marley,
Hissene, my man,' Billy Bob said, adjusting the earphone
above the diamond stud. Suddenly Bob Marley felt himself
flying as the giant swung his hand back then spun to gain

momentum and slam Bob's face into the skip which exploded into all the stars in all the galaxies in all the parallel universes and he felt relief as his brain disintegrated and became one with the metal and the asphalt it concealed and he felt no pain nor the smell of burning pig fat mixed with the blood flowing from his mouth, nose, ears and forehead nor the cold stream down the inside of his leg. There was just the cold, black, emptiness of space where he floated in search of the lost souls of Agbani's people and other forgotten dead.

'This will teach him to joke about serious thing, eh Monsieur Billy Bob?' But Billy Bob, now that his earpiece was firmly in, had surrendered himself to the ambrosia of sound and as the notes of the Anthem approached crescendo he reached the ecstasy of hillbilly heaven which had eluded Gatsby. Almost in a trance, he replicated the gestures of Hannibal Lecter in his cage under the blinding Atlanta lights as he serenaded the beauty of Mozart's *Eine Kleine Nachtmusik* and feasted on human flesh, and turned, moving with the grace of the ballet dancer his faggot of a father had once wished he would become. Hissene followed him toward the Humvee dragging the terrorist behind him like the straw dolls his sister used to make in Sarh, Southern Chad, where the shiny crimson berries made a dye more haunting and intense than fresh blood.

Bob Marley wanted to be unconscious again when Hissene tossed him into the vehicle and he felt the metal floor reach up to meet him but the blood in his nose was choking him and he kept retching in a state beyond sleep where the nightmares were more real than the real and he saw/felt the body of his father Revelation rising up with the force of the bullets then falling across him and his mother praying to God to make him normal and the hands of Idi Amin Ogwu on his head promising money for his paints and the bloodstained clothes of Mallam Aminu's son and Barkono's drunken rants and the feel of the rifle slug and the spectres of Agbani's people floating in her nightmares as he struggled to hold her down in the nice little hut they'd hoped to expand with the money from the paintings Ahmed brought from London and put in the bank. When Hissene tossed him in he fell on his face but he heard Billy Bob's voice saying they didn't want him to die before they got him to talk and a boot turned him on his back so he wouldn't drown in his own blood.

He saw others in the car but they were ghosts on the flickering black and white television screen of his mind, spectres on the black underground river where no one could forget the victims of Lidiziam who had jumped into the bottomless sinkholes gashed out of the earth to escape the burning stench of napalmed sweat, wraiths twisting with the rolling liquid metal floor of the vehicle bumping on crater-like potholes which shamed the still moon without colour as the band played on and on. There was a man smaller than Hissene or Billy Bob fiddling with a box and he thought in the cold twilight that the sound of the Anthem was coming from this because the earphones now hung from their necks like the stethoscopes on the doctors who floated into and out of his consciousness as he recovered from the wound inflicted on him by Barkono in the General Daudu University Teaching Hospital.

'How much you gonna give him, Bobby Joe?' Billy Bob asked, scratching his ear with the diamond stud.

'Gotta start low and build up.' Bobby Joe had a crew cut and in the dimness and his black and white vision Bob Marley could not see the colour but his hands stood out clear and sharp in the gloom because of their purpose and the precision of their calibrations on the quietly humming machine and it registered on his brain that this was no record player.

'What the fuck you mean "start low", Bobby Joe? We ain't got all fuckin day, man.'

'It's you say you don't want him fuckin dead yet. Me, I don't fuckin care whether some fuckin nigger live or die.'

'You sounin just like fuckin girl, Bobby Joe. Give him enough so he talk, and *fast!*'

'Ain't goin to talk slow or fast if you kill him, you an that big nigger sure do a job on his ass aready. Where you get the gorilla from anyway? Don't look or soun like one of ourn.'

'I say shut the fuck up and feed him some, Bobby Joe.' Then when the thin man moved, holding the machine like it was brimming with some precious liquid he didn't want to spill, Billy Bob said *'Wait!'* and, with the big hunting knife strapped to his thigh, cut away Bob Marley's clothes till he lay naked on the cold metal floor with the wound in his side from the spear of the Roman soldier plain to see.

'Start with his fucking toes,' Billy Bob said, taking the relish, ketchup and mustard being passed round to garnish the hotdog he held up like a trophy as he hummed along to 'Courtesy of the Red, White and Blue' on speakers big as fucking ammo boxes.

Bob Marley lay there like a corpse on a slab but when the electricity flowed like the waters in the Black Delta of Lidiziam from his toes through his peripheral nerves then to his spine and his numbed brainstem his back arched and his legs kicked out, almost slamming the electrodes into the angel face of Bobby Joe.

'Fucking Nigger!' he snarled, checking to make sure his state-of-the-art machine was still in top shape.

'Now you will tell us the true name, no?' Hissene asked, but the man on the floor did not reply because the current had fused his tongue to his palate. As a good Moslem the Chadian could not abide the pork meat of these infidels and his French instructors who were true professionals would never eat like this on a job or play the foul music. 'Higher,' Billy Bob mumbled with his mouth full of hotdog, relish and mustard on his lips, and Bobby Joe adjusted the voltage and gingerly touched the electrodes to Bob Marley's groin. This time his lungs expanded and the air rushed in then out again in a scream so piercing the General could have had him shot for making his sirens sound like a ballad of his hero Elvis and his body twisted like the contortionists Agbani said performed on the Day of the Reawakening when new yam vines burst from the black loam of Lidiziam.

'Turn up the music,' a quiet voice said from the dark of the farthest corner.

Bobby Joe turned the knob to maximum but when he pressed the electrodes into Bob Marley's scrotum there was no scream just the sound of his bowel evacuating.

'Gross! Stinking nigger!' Bobby Joe shouted, stumbling as he was caught between holding his nose and protecting his precious machine.

'How the fuck does this nigger expect a man to eat in this atmosphere?' Billy Bob asked, throwing the stub of the hotdog into Bob Marley's face. The near miss with the computer-controlled machine angered the operator and his hands were shaking as he tried to turn the knob, then when he realized it could not go further his hands shook more violently and he pressed the electrodes on either side of the head of his victim's penis.

'Take that, you fucking nigger!'

'Is he now dead perhaps?' Hissene asked.

No one answered but from the passenger seat in front a very cultured Ivy League voice requested: 'Now that the young gentleman will no longer scream, perhaps someone could lower the volume of your very wonderful music just a tad?'

'Yes, siree,' Billy Bob said. Bobby Joe was still pumping the juice from his machine into the crotch of the prostrate figure jerking convulsively as all the dials read 'maximum'. Beads of cold sweat had coated Bob Marley's body and, as it shook with the electricity, there was a spray of hot vapour-like smoke mingled with the stench of burning flesh.

'Whoa! Bobby Joe, we already eat, we don't want no

barbeque now!' Billy Bob was standing over them and, as the thin man withdrew the electrodes and replaced the machine in its black leather case, unzipped his jeans and pissed all over the steaming body on the gunmetal floor.

Then for the first time the *Washington Times* reporter embedded with the troops started screaming at the gross indecency of a grown man urinating in public. His publisher, the Reverend Sun Myung of the Unification Church, would never tolerate this in an organization which regarded cleanliness as superior to godliness and supplicants had to strip, shave all body hair, pass through a modified car wash machine and drape themselves in white sheets and hoods before entering his Presence.

'O, my God,' moaned the Ivy League voice as someone turned the volume of 'Born in the USA' to max on the big gunmetal speakers.

MIGHTIER THAN
THE SWORD?

Under the loose floorboards of the temporary office Rabiu heard the soldiers throwing furniture around, drawers of filing cabinets being opened, ransacked and hurled to the ground with such force the dust of termites gorged on unseasoned wood swept over him and he held his nostrils to stop himself sneezing. He was afraid their heavy boots and the falling metal cabinets would break through and land on his head but perhaps the boards were kept in place by the cracked grey linoleum which was nailed down at three corners. The men swore in Hausa and French and from their accents he knew they were from the south of the Chad Republic. There was at least one American but he remained silent after his instructions to 'take the fucking place apart!' and from the earpiece of his Walkman Rabiu could hear the faint lyrics of Bobby Womak's 'I'd Be Ahead If I Could Quit While I'm Behind', a favourite of the General's which was number two on the Niagran charts after 'Courtesy of the Red, White and Blue'.

After the takeover and General Daudu's flight, the workers had dismissed the management of the *Sentinel* and voted out Joseph Mammamia as MD despite the Comrade's declaration that he had remained a revolutionary all along, only pretending to be the General's lapdog to 'fight from within the belly of the beast'. While they voted Rabiu 'Team Leader of the Editorial Board' they nevertheless warned him to 'forge simple words the people can understand, words that will enter like embers into people's souls'. (He knew it was a quote from somewhere because Delroy had used it in a tribute to the late Comrade Samora Machel but he couldn't be sure from where: perhaps the Angolan Comrade Mário de Andrade, or Marcelino dos Santos of Mozambique. He doubted it was Josina Machel, whose style was less assertive.)

After directives from the Transition Council that pictures, tributes, praises, paid adverts and birthday greetings to members were banned, the *Sentinel* and other publicly owned papers reduced newsprint by 75 per cent and increased circulation five-fold as writers gave free rein to their creativity in expressing matters about hunger, health, schools, housing, jobs and public transport which were of interest to the toiling masses. Things had got so bad that on Friday 13 February when General Daudu celebrated his tenth year in office, his silver jubilee of marriage to his first wife, and tenth anniversary of the 'suicide' of his predecessor, the entire 256 page issue was devoted to portraits of the General with sponsors which read like a Who's Who from the IAC *Company Intelligence*. The most popular were Daudu with the Queen and Duke of Edinburgh waving to ecstatic members of the British Conservative Party from the balcony of Buckingham Palace (twenty-seven times), and Daudu with the American Vice President with Richard 'Mr Dick' Burton and Garth Brooks in the Rose Garden of the White House (nineteen), paid for by the Burton Holly Foundation, Zapata Oil, the Lone Star Smelting and Drilling Company, Harken Oil and the Carlton Group.

Traders in need of wrapping paper eagerly looked forward to the numerous birthdays of the General's first son, his favourite wife, or the anniversaries of his countless acts of heroism which had led an emotional Joseph

Mammamia to declare in a front page *Sentinel* editorial
that our Supreme Commander was indeed the *Unique
Miracle of the Twentieth Century*, not that pygmy General
Ibrahim Babangida of neighbouring Nigeria who was
deemed unworthy to lick Daudu's hand-stitched boots
from Swaine & Adeney (which supplied polo equipment
to the Prince of Wales and his two delightful sons).

As all good things do, this one too came to an end
when the satirical English magazine *Private Eye* published
a slanderous rumour that General Daudu's portraits, taken
by the Bond Street photographers Richard Kay, contained
a spell which caused the viewer's penis and left testicle
to shrink. (Rumour had it that the right remained intact
because Hauwa, the General's daughter, a real tearaway
and red sheep of the family, pursuing a course in Post-
Modernist Dream Images in Post-Independence African
Shamanistic Literature at Stanford, had described her
dad's favourite marabout from Marrakech as a *'shrivelled
up piece of dog shit'*.)

Rabiu had fought hard to keep the paper on a steady
centrist course in line with the moderate posture of the
new government, fending off the yapping of Joseph
Mammamia's ultra-left *Red Tide* and his own Party's stolid
and supercilious denunciation of 'armchair petit-bourgeois
democratic "revolution"' in *Red Flag*. *Red Tide* had
published a full-page photograph of a smiling Honorary
Consul presenting a letter from the American Vice
President to Ahmed with the provocative caption 'WHY
ARE THESE MEN SMILING?' The paper demanded the
nationalization of all means of production and distribution, including bars, brothels, restaurants, petty trade and
crafts, while *Red Flag* hinted broadly that the 'revolution'
was made in the USA, and that it had identified at least
six of the twenty members of the Transition Council,
including one of its co-leaders, as CIA agents of influence.
This was confirmed by the internet site www.bullred-
online.com which published the Chief of Station's Field

Appraisal entitled 'Regime Change in Niagra'. He had also learnt from Kikelomo of Fatima's complaint that the Americans were bloody ungrateful for refusing her husband a visa so she could be rid of him, after all he had done for the bastards. He was being held under house arrest 'for his own protection' and she wanted Kikelomo to promise she could come live with them in case Ahmed turned nasty and decided to shoot her husband who had sent him a gift package with a charred goat head with a note saying 'see your friend' after the first reports that Delroy Solomon, whose country's national dish was curried goat and rice, had been burnt to death.

Which is why the counter-coup came as a shock despite warnings in *Red Bull* of American Special Operations Forces landing in Nigeria, Chad, Niger, Benin and Cameroon, Combat Search and Rescue facilities being established at the Nigerian airbase in Makurdi, an aircraft carrier group harbouring outside the oil town of Port Harcourt and the promise of a State Visit to the President of São Tomé, who had granted permission to establish a naval facility and renamed his capital after Laura Bush. The operation was so sudden it caught everyone off guard and even Joseph Mammamia, who was busy organizing a demonstration of oil workers against the reactionary government of Lt Colonel Ahmed Abdullahi, was detained until he convinced the Honorary Consul that he had been only acting as an *agent provocateur*, 'boring into the belly of the revolutionary beast to destroy it from within'.

Soon he was not only restored to his old job but made deputy to Jerry Gotchakka as Minister of Women's Affairs, Culture, Enlightenment, Education and Sports. The *Red Tide* became the *Crimson Tide*, and his old paper became the *Red, White and Blue Sentinel*, which kicked off with a rousing campaign against the Terrorist Threat, Al-Qaeda and same sex marriages.

Rabiu was on his way home to Kikelomo, who was due

to give birth any day, when the BBC Hausa Service stringer in Xanadu broadcast a report of unusual troop movements across several borders, AWACS flights in Niagran airspace, and the jamming of radio and television signals all over West Africa. As he approached their gate he saw two jeeps, a Humvee, a black Cherokee and a red Mustang with whitewall tires. As he turned right, away from the house, he saw the roadblock manned by black soldiers with a lone ponytailed white man in t-shirt, jeans and cowboy boots leaning against a beat-up Land Rover with his MI6 slung over his shoulder, reading a *Mad Magazine* and chewing on a McDonald's *Royale*. The soldiers who checked his papers spoke with accents and, when he replied to their questions in French and Hausa, they let him through without searching his car, angering their American patron who did not want to interrupt Martina McBride's rendition of 'The Star Spangled Banner'.

He called Kikelomo on their land line and when she answered 'everything's gonna be alright' he knew it wasn't and called her mobile and they spoke in Fifek since they knew the Men in Black had purged all speakers of that language after the destruction of Lidiziam. She told him: 'Fatima came over to help and also to avoid her drunken husband and was inside having her bath when we heard a deep Southern American drawl shouting to open the door before they smashed it down and when I went in my bathrobe with the wet sponge in my hand I saw this ponytailed blond man leading a group of soldiers I recognized as Southern Chadians from their tribal marks. With my big belly and my eyes bulging as if the tears were waiting to overflow he was looking more and more confused and I decided to enter his head and play with his mind. When he asked for my husband I looked angry and said you weren't at home despite the state I was in and asked if he and his kind people could search for you so you could help about the house as the baby could come any minute and before he could finish saying no, that won't be possible, I looked at the men and asked if they were there to collect relief supplies because of the famine in their country. Then the puppy ran out of the bathroom – you know how he jumps up and makes a nuisance of himself when you're trying to take a bath? Now he was all over Meatloaf's legs as if he wanted to fuck him and I remembered the Faulkner story where a politician put jimson weed on his opponent's trouser leg so the dogs came and pissed on it and he lost the election because people said they couldn't vote for a man who dogs mistook for a tree. I let the puppy enjoy himself for a while and put on a Blanche Dubois act, sounding so frail and vulnerable before scolding the puppy, picking him up so he almost licked the quivering red blancmange face. I told him I knew the soldiers with him preferred dog meat but would they manage with goat and I was laughing so much inside tears did start to fall and Meatloaf beat such a hasty retreat he bumped into the Chadians and called them stupid fucking niggers. I knew this Redneck would have killed you if he caught you but his knees turned to jelly when confronted by a three-month-old puppy. The values of these people! I could just see into the pea he had for a brain saying WE AMERICANS DON'T KILL DOGS, WE KILL PEOPLE! I didn't know Fatima had opened the bathroom door and was listening and she laughed so much she choked and turned blue and I had to slap her hard on the back with the sponge.'

Most of the co-op escaped and they started a cat-and-mouse game with the new authorities to keep producing the *Sentinel*, adapting the plugs on their laptops to work on car batteries when they couldn't find a place like where he was hiding now, e-mailing articles to each other and laying out the pages before sending one of the street kids to sympathetic private printers, or sometimes even to workers in the regime's own print works. Comrade Adama called it *guerrilla journalism* because the American PSYOPS teams and their foreign mercenaries chased the street kids who distributed them, tying sales to the bread, toothpaste and cigarettes they sold in traffic. But the kids were too smart for them, taking piles of Joseph's papers which nobody wanted and hiding the *Sentinel* inside, acting theatrically like real little conspirators as they peeled back the cover of the government rag to reveal the forbidden news. The Americans tried to trace their mobile numbers but they had comrades in Signals who cloned their phones with secret numbers reserved for their superior officers in State Security, and there were a lot of disgruntled Niagran Men in Black ready to declare war on America after listening to Tammy Wynette's 'Stand by Your Man' at full blast for thirty-six hours non-stop while being forced to eat hotdogs and drink Dr Pepper cola. He started, almost bumping his head when the American switched to Tammy's song, there was a tap-tap like a rifle barrel hitting the floor just above his head and a voice mixing a Southern drawl with its own Hausa-inflected French called the American over.

'What the fuck you want, nigger?' the Redneck asked.

'Look here, sir,' the Chadian implored and Rabiu was so enraged he felt like smashing through the rotten, termite infested floor, tearing his head off and stuffing it down his fucking throat. Despite all the sophisticated ideological training the Party gave in understanding other cultures, nationalities and ethnic groups, he had always had an irrational dislike of Chadians which started when his sister Aishetu used to scare him with a picture of François Tombalbaye, the late Chadian leader, saying, 'If you don't drink your porridge you'll grow up to be as ugly as this one!'

'I still don't fuckin see nothin,' Captain 'Trent Lott' screamed.

'*Here*, sir,' the Chadian repeated, banging the gun barrel for emphasis and Rabiu started breathing easy, numbing his body and mind to whatever awaited him while avoiding a return to the fatalism of his youth where he would mutter *ikon Allah*, God willing.

HIGH FLYER

Bob Marley was suspended by a pole slung through the shackles holding his arms and legs behind, which hung from the reinforced concrete ceiling by giant meat hooks. His last memory after waking from electric sleep was of shadows sliding a needle with yellow liquid out of his arm, the smell of stale urine, then the sound of Elvis Presley's 'Suspicious Minds' at unbelievable volume synced to a technicolour display of strobe lights like endless explosions of fireworks among bright galaxies of stars and he felt his body light with whatever drug they had given him penetrating the light till his body was but a weary unbright cinder in the infinite festival of fireflies.

He could tell he was not far above the ground because as he drifted in and out of consciousness he could judge the level of the toilets flushing in the neighbouring cells and the squeal of the rats scurrying across the floor leaving imagined, minute, rising trails of dust in their wake. The pain was not in most of his body which was numb except for the points where the current had concentrated feeling and in his eardrums which had almost exploded and between his eyes which felt like a needle had been pushed in to draw out his brain. The darkness was intense except when he dreamt and there was a blinding column of light on which Agbani descended but was always just out of reach as the light dispersed over the fleeing people he had painted and when he heard the screams he could not tell if they were in the next cell where they came with the flushing of the toilets and curses or in the village where the dead and the dying struggled with the brightness of the paints and the light and the gently flowing water of the crystalline streams. He dreamt of his paints which were alive now and no longer needed him and could create what they wanted without the pain or the odour of burnt flesh, sweat, piss and shit. Time no longer existed, he was there for a moment, for eternity, suspended in unbounded space where pain could expand with the odour forever and ever till they too no longer existed.

Sometimes he felt a tingling in the arch of his back and thought sensation was returning but when he shivered without volition he heard the whirr of tiny wings flapping and the hiss of cockroaches feeding on his ripening sores. Then he knew precisely how close he was to the ground when the rats started reaching up to gnaw at his navel and groin and he drifted back into the relieving unconsciousness and the ecstasy of forgotten nightmares. Time was *now* and he could not tell if it was past or future when they tied him in a red, white and blue harness which they slung from a ceiling fan with giant gunmetal blades like a helicopter turning counter clockwise to the revolving strobes with purple and pink lights and the soundtrack of 'Born on the Fourth of July' exploding in all directions and as the motion approached the speed of light he felt his body dissolve until it became one with the molecules of his vomit. But he could not tell if it had already happened to him because of the overwhelming feeling that it was about to again, for ever and ever.

Then he was awake again to the sound of new rain but it was directed in a single stream which propelled his body in all directions as the water sought out hidden corners of his being and there was the sound of heavy boots shuffling about and then he realized there was light in the cell but his eyes were blindfolded. The jet of cold water cut through his face and hair but he could not see the flow of dissolved blood or feel the wounds opened anew until the flow ceased and he felt gloved hands holding his wrists and ankles and opening the locks of the shackles and felt nothing as he fell flat on the floor and his limbs were so stiff they remained in place behind and he heard the voice of Hissene saying, 'Let's go, *garçon*, we don't get all the day,' and when he did not move he felt the shape of the toecap as the boot landed and his body jerked away from his ribs but again there was no pain or again when it landed twice more and, no longer prisoner of the bar, his back now flat, his arms and legs sliding to the wet floor where the cold was soothing, it was a bit more comfortable and he could sleep.

Then he dreamed of the old white woman who came with Billy Bob and said, 'In my professional opinion this is no Al-Qaeda operative, officer, his beard is too sparse, not enough body, the texture is not right, not fuzzy enough,' and Billy Bob replying, 'It's orders, ma'am, Professor Herzovogina, the Office of Special Plans says a beard's a beard, he's male as you can see, he's in the wrong place at the wrong time, and therefore constitutes a clear and present danger to the security interests of the United States of America.'

When Bob Marley was half awake he saw himself tied to a hard wooden chair with his hands again cuffed behind and his head bowed and although his eyes were almost completely shut the orange jumpsuit was so bright it shone like all the sunrises in the history of the world and all the moons shining above the spirits of Agbani's people and he could not look up when he heard Hissene speak. He had no idea how long the man had been talking or what he said but now his words, though he attempted to make them more soothing, cut through his shattered eardrums like broken glass. There was an urgency so

intense in the voice that Bob Marley found himself almost
compelled to listen when sleep did not succeed in
dragging him down into the valleys of Lidiziam where rare
white orchids would not bloom again, Agbani antelopes
would roam no more, nor albino pythons inspire hope
and fear. *'The Americans were right, garçon, you are the
true believers who are most hard to break, who believe
Allah will give you the strength to resist but in the end no
one can resist Hissene. Why won't you tell us your name?
What harm will that do? Telling us you're "Bob Marley" is
so méchant. Perhaps you want to protect your friends and
their networks. To what purpose? For all you know we have
already persuaded them to talk. Then where will that leave
you? We could be friends, you could tell me about yourself, the hopes and fears you experience in movements like
yours, which require such devotion, so much self-sacrifice.
Look, I will tell you a little about myself, how normal I
am, so you'll see you can trust me, confide your secrets,
which I will be bound by my code of honour to respect.
Perhaps you had parents who loved you, whom you abandoned for a higher calling, the irresistible obligation of the
demand by the Almighty. Look, I had a sister once who I
loved so much but I left her behind for the higher eroti-
cism of the military. We used to play under the shades of
date palm trees near the waterholes among the wild red
and yellow bellflowers which I used to decorate her hair
like garlands of the gods —'*
Bob Marley's head had dropped farther forward and
as the air forced itself through the dried blood in his
broken nose it sounded like snoring. He could not see
the big man approaching nor feel his fist smashing into
his face and driving the chair against the raw concrete
where it broke into pieces. 'This will teach you how
impolite it is to fall asleep when someone older talks to
you, *garçon*.'
The opening door caught against the man on his side
still tied to the broken chair but the thin man was in a

surprisingly chirpy mood after learning of his return to his unit in Fort Bragg, and he was beating out the rhythm on his new clip board as he whistled Elvis's 'Don't Step on my Blue Suede Shoes'.

'How your patient doin, Hissene?'

'Not good at all, Monsieur Bobby Joe. Like you said, a very stubborn one, he'll need perhaps the special measures.'

'You'll have to "measure" him some other time, you've got to clean him up now, pass him through the medics, make him look fit enough for inspection. Niagrans in the States been raisin hell, someone from the legal department's comin round to make sure we're respectin his constitutional rights!'

WHEN I FIND MYSELF IN TIMES OF TROUBLE . . .

In the coffin-like space under the rotting floorboards Rabiu found that all the pains, cramps, pins and needles, nausea, suffocation and claustrophobia flowed out of his body with his decision not to resist, to surrender to gravity or whatever force of nature chose to possess him. He lay with his arms by his side and his palms upwards, his legs slightly parted, his breathing even and easy as he allowed the involuntary muscles controlling his lungs to kick in and save him the energy of inhaling/exhaling. Was this the basis of what ignorant Westerners referred to in his people as 'fatalism' but which was very realistic, even rational, as in his present case? Time and space were no longer absolute or relative but just there, irrelevant, and he found himself floating without movement in a space without dimension and a time of *now* without progression as his brain froze with his body in the unspeakable and incommunicable twilight of an horizon without beginning or end, beyond cognition, beyond care or belonging. The men above were no longer there in any meaningful sense, not even as abstractions, not ideas in his head, which was not there, but their voices and the sound of their rifle butts hitting the floor with accompanying wisps of termite dust were mere extensions of his cryogenic body which had long ceased to be.

'I still can't see what the hell you talkin about,' the American said.

'Here,' the Chadian said, 'look.' He held up the minuscule remnant of a joint between thumb and forefinger as if resentful that the American Special Forces who had thought of everything, including Military Ready-to-Eat meals with pork fat, had not provided surgical gloves to protect him from this abomination. 'This is why we fight,' he continued, 'to protect our young ones from the foreign ideas and illicit drugs being spread by the infidels. With this in their blood they disobey, blaspheme and that is why we must kill them now, kill them again and again till the land is pure and free for the *Jema'a*.' He held the tiny stub and shook it with such force that the remnant of ganja spilled onto the cold, grey linoleum and he jumped back with such alacrity to avoid the contamination of the evil weed that he bumped into the American, spilled his hotdog, and knocked over his M16 which he grabbed, crouched in full combat mode, as if to lay waste the inspiration for John Lennon's 'Mother Mary'.

'They use this shit to finance terrorism,' Captain Trent Lott said, 'they sell it to little kids to buy weapons of mass destruction to kill innocent Americans and when the kids grow up with their brains deformed they headfuck them with anti-American shit so they become suicide bombers and go round blowin up evythin that's why we gotta kill em all an blow up all the caves an dingy little shit holes like this where they hide cause they don't like the light where we Americans live so the whole fuckin world can see what we are, the values we protect, the fuckin one dolla-a-gallon gas we'll fuckin kill for.'

'This was a false alarm, Capitan,' the Chadian said, 'no one's been here. You should find the one who told you, get your thousand dollars back and kill him.'

'The Niagrans are big pieces of shit, *mon capitaine*, one

can never trust such people, they don't behave like good Moslems,' another Chadian said. The vision of the evil ones financing terrorism by selling weed which they feed to tiny babies who grow up to blow up everything was exercising his mind and there was a tremor in his voice, showing the depth of his hatred for these infidels, his desire to kill them all. He felt the pressure in his brain, skull, sinuses, blood vessels and main nerves straining to burst out of his bulging eyeballs, and the Captain thought he was having a heart attack. But Goukooni was a deeply religious man, who truly believed that if he didn't burst out of this hellhole to search and destroy his Niagran enemies in the street he would turn his weapon on his 'comrades' and slay them all like sheep in celebration of the festival, beginning with the white, porcine American infidel who did not know it was *haram* for Moslems to eat so-called MREs, which consisted of ground cockroach wings with baby shit and crushed bat heads steeped in bacon grease.

Rabiu heard them kick the door out as they trampled from the room stirring new clouds of termite dust which again forced him to hold his nose to stop himself sneezing. The surreal calm in his body left with them and he could once again feel its weight and pain and he was determined to leave after a while but still was not back in time or able to see if it was night or day. He thought of Kikelomo alone, about to give birth to their first child. *First?* Antonio Maceo and Josina Machel were *their* children now, just as if he had fathered them and Kikelomo had given birth and they loved them truly because she loved her dead sister more than herself and they both loved Delroy, and the children looked more like her than their biological mother Omolare. He could see them now running free in Mallam Aminu's house in garments of blinding white as the old man looked over them, protectively, swearing never again to lose any of his own to his devil of a brother and the evil one he had once saved from ignominy and oblivion.

They said Nuhu and the others were still alive when they took them to the morgue and Mallam Aminu had pleaded with his brother Nafiu and his master to spare his first born and he was prepared to break all the laws of man but not of Allah, to give his life in exchange for Nuhu but while they promised to spare him Daudu had already sent the beast Idi Amin Ogwu to lay his hand upon him to squeeze out what little life was left and up till today all he saw of his son were his torn clothing, note books, ball point pens and the Holy Koran with the pages missing because the General's marabouts swore they would protect him from the vengeful souls of his enemies. Were Nuhu's remains in the trophy room under the Rock Palace or in the cold marble of the 'tomb' in New Haven?

So he feared not for the children but for Kikelomo who was probably still with Fatima whose husband was busy protecting his master and liaising with the Pentagon's Office of Special Plans to go in search of enemies and destroy them so the oil would be free for Burton Holly. Kikelomo wanted him to be there at the moment of delivery when his eyes would be the first to see the resurrection of the seed which had died so many times before in the wasteland that had been her womb. He wanted to be there like the great explorers who first gazed over vast mysterious oceans and endless savannahs and scaled unassailable peaks or stood in awe before magical beasts and supernatural people but without the hubris of 'discovering' what had been there before time or beginning. And the scream of rebirth would drown in his head the cries of Nuhu pressing his life into him as he lay below, of Delroy when the flames bit into his flesh, of Lumumba dissolving in his acid bath and the multitude of children weeping for their main man Ahmed Abdullahi who was lost. As a member of the Party he was officially an atheist but at the birth of his child he would weep and thank God for His Gift and for sparing his wife. Surely the comrades could not grudge him this act of regression?

In his enhanced state of nervousness his senses were light and subtle and he heard the soft padding of feet moving above with stealth that was infinite across the fading linoleum. It was the sound of an animal that could see in the dark, a big cat, though not a predator, moving relentlessly toward his hiding place. It was not Captain Trent Lott and his circus, this one was too full of loneliness, of purpose that could not be deflected, invincible and remorseless. The American and his charges from the wastelands of Sarh had seen too many episodes of *Hawaii Five-O*, *Miami Vice*, *NYPD Blue*, *Homicide*, and *24*, and could not enter or exit a room without kicking the door down, shouting their obscenities in the name of law, order, motherhood and apple pie. Then the Mystery Man was right above him, silenced feet wide apart as he bent to lift the linoleum, then the rotting planks and, unable to think of anything to do, Rabiu let his body go again into saving oblivion as the torch flashed into his face and he saw the polished black hands of *iroko* that were totally without mercy.

LOST ON THE UNBRIGHT CINDER

The light shone bright and sharp into his distended pupils but Bob Marley did not see it. He did not see the doctor in white with a green mask or feel his cold thumbs propping his eyes open so the blinding light could enter his soul. He had not felt it when they untied him as he lay on the floor, the Chadian complaining about the broken chair as he threw him on the gurney to take him to the military hospital. And he did not hear the conversation between Dr Barton Scott and Captain Billy Bob. All he could hear was the whining of electric drills mixed with Berlin's 'Take my Breath Away' but could not tell if the echoes were making holes in his wrists and ankles, if it was happening to him now, had been, or was destined to be repeated for all eternity.

'What the fuck you boys do to him? It's a fuckin' miracle he's still breathin'.'

'It wasn't me, Doc, those different niggers sure hate each other's guts.'

'*Niggers*, Captain? Thought that went out with separate facilities in the military.'

'We're Special Forces, Doc. Different rules.'

'Whoever did it, you're in charge. He's got three broken ribs, a stress fracture of the right hip, cracked skull with excessive haematoma, broken nose, one burst eardrum, several teeth missing, a cracked palate so he'll be fed by a tube for the rest of his short life. I'll have to make a report.'

'No can do, Doctor, this is a top-secret mission, usual rules suspended for foreign terrorists connected to Al-Qaeda. You've got to get him in shape for the inspection.'

'I told you it was a miracle he's still breathing. You can't expect two miracles in a fuckin' day. Keepin' him alive will be tough enough.'

'We brought him to you 'cause they said you was the bee's knees, the miracle worker, Doc, we gotta get this one in motion so he can talk the talk, even if he can't walk the walk! Come on, do your magic, lay your healin hands on him, make him whole again. The future of the whole nation's in your hands, we gotta get his secrets before his people strike again. Maybe if I play you "Courtesy of the Red, White and Blue" . . .'

'No!' the Doctor said hurriedly, 'You don't want to kill both doctor and patient.'

The man in the blue Lacoste polo shirt and beige Ermenegildo Zegna linen suit looked from the Doctor's notes to Bob Marley who was slumped in a wheelchair. 'What the fuck is this?' he asked, waving the notes in the face of Captain Billy Bob Liotto. 'Every fucking thing's blacked out. What the hell's going on here? And will you *please* turn off the "Ballad of Billy Joe"?'

'This is a classified mission, sir, including medical reports. Our commander said it was authorized at the very highest level by the Pentagon's Office of Special Plans **For the Eyes Of the Vice President and Secretary of Defence Only.**'

'You mean Special Forces can tell the CIA what we can and can't read?'

'That's what the man said, sir. He thought the report

could give comfort to the enemy if it fell into the wrong hands.'

'This man looks barely alive. Can you tell me what's wrong with him – or is that classified too?'

'No, sir. I'm authorized to tell you that he suffers from a nut allergy. We didn't know this when we fed him his MRE. The reaction was most severe, sir, he looked much worse an hour ago.'

'I find that hard to believe, he must have been dead then.'

'Close, sir, these nut allergies are a bitch. He should soon come round.' The Captain took a syringe from the pocket of his danshiki, sprayed a golden arc of urine coloured liquid into the air then stuck it in Bob Marley's left arm.

'What're you doing, Captain?'

'The last of the anti-allergy injections, sir. See, his eye's blinkin awready.'

'He said he feelin great, sir. How the English say it? On top of the world.' When the CIA man asked the questions he could not hear Bob Marley's answers and Billy Bob bent over and put his ear close to his mouth then gave the man his answer.

'There's nothing you want, sir?' he asked, with his silver Mont Blanc pen poised over his blue clipboard.

'He's a bit peckish, sir. Maybe a fat sirloin steak with a nice Caesar salad.'

'You sure that's what he said, Captain? His mouth hardly moved.'

'Yes, *sir*. A drippin sirloin steak, live if possible.'

'Get out of the way, Captain,' the man said, moving closer to Bob Marley whose face turned paler, aching with agony at the mention of bloody meat and he bent forward as if to retch. The CIA man felt nauseous and his nose twitched with the logo on his polo shirt when the stench of disinfectant and stale blood hit him as he strained to hear the forced whisper.

'What the hell – he said he doesn't eat meat because he's a *Rasta*. What the hell's going on, Captain? No one said anything about Rastafari.'

'It's the hair, sir, the Chadian grabbed him from behind and said his hair felt natural, that's how the Al-Qaeda boys like theirs, without conditioners or fancy trimmers like the lefties. We could see this boy had never been inside no fancy salon.'

'So you almost killed him because you couldn't tell the difference between a Rasta and Al-Qaeda?'

'That's our rules of engagement, sir. No presumption of innocence here, the mission's too important to take chances. Besides we didn't do it, the fuckin Chadians did.'

'We have to clean him up some before we hand him over to his own people. Get his clothes, Captain. We can't let the Niagrans know we've been holding a Rastaman as a terrorist suspect, it would make us look like a bunch of fucking dickheads.'

'That all the clothes he got, sir. We had to destroy his when the MRE spill on them. We can't afford none of them allergy attack again.'

'Okay, Captain. My son's a fourteen-year-old at Andover. His clothes will fit this young man. Here's a note to my wife, and buy him some underwear from the commissary on the way.' He gave a fifty-dollar bill to Billy Bob who called on his radio and the Thin Man came to relieve him.

'These dangerous terrorist suspects must be guarded by Special Forces at all times, sir. The future of our civilization depend on it.'

He came back with a monogrammed suit carrier of very fine leather which Gary opened to reveal an ensemble which made Billy Bob and Bobby Joe say *gee whiz!* A navy

blue J. Press blazer with gold buttons, grey flannel
trousers, grey ribbed socks, tanned Ferragamo brogues,
pastel blue Brooks Brothers button down shirt and a red
and black Turnbull and Asser tie like the ones Diana
bought for Charles.

THE WRESTLER OF CONSCIENCES

The man reached in, held him by the upper arm and Rabiu felt as if he was on a cushion of air. The hand circled his arm as if it were a child's and held him till the cramp flowed out of his legs, the nausea from his stomach, the ringing from his ears and from eyes suddenly freed from the claustrophobic dark the nightmare images of the unknown. To his surprise Rabiu found that the man was almost the same height though twice as broad, the width of his shoulders, the near absence of waist or hips, and the tree trunk arms and thighs made him look like a blown-up Mike Tyson in his prime. His waist, smaller than Rabiu's, was surrounded by pawpaw-yellow rifle-propelled grenades like ripening cocoa pods, a 9mm Beretta pistol in a holster, and an AK47 with 'Guitar Boy' carved into the wooden stock like a water pistol in his hand. He had never seen him without sunglasses before but could see even less in his eyes now they were bare and felt the pressure of his fingers lessen on his arm as he recovered his balance. He did not speak until Rabiu had recovered and was steady on his feet. 'Good to see you're okay comrade,' Ahmed's ADC said.

'How did you find me here?'

'Your wife told me.'

'Even Kikelomo doesn't know this place.'

'She does now – when the men raided your place she got one of the street kids you let sleep in your servant's quarters to follow them on her moped. After what she did to Meatloaf they were too confused to notice a kid on a motorbike.' He had never seen the ADC smile before and was moved to say: 'Yes, my wife has that effect on people.'

'You should know, but her fame is spreading in the barracks. The Chadians were almost pissing themselves with laughter after the way she castrated the American Special Forces guy who rushed in like Rambo then out like Sergeant Bilko. They think these guys like them because of the $100 bills and the cheap American goods they can buy in the commissary but they tip us off about most of the raids and we have comrades from Chad. One of them knew you were here from your Aramis aftershave but created a diversion to confuse the Good Old Boy.'

'It was just before I let go in my pants – then even the Redneck would have known.'

'Kikelomo and Fatima inspire many of our women in the barracks. They say the Brigadier is, the only officer to defy the General – all he has to say is "But, sir, what will I tell Fatima?" There are stories about what they did to the Lebanese twins who didn't know who they were and tried to pick them up for Daudu. I remember the first time I met the two of them together, Ahmed went to work out with Dr Solomon and the American Defence Attaché at the Xanadu Sports Club.'

'I heard about it, I was in São Tomé following up a report that the Americans were building a base there to control the oil in the sub-region.'

'Your wife and her friend turned up to buy soft drinks with a bunch of street kids they were tutoring. Then they saw her brother-in-law and his friends and offered them a game with the kids so Dr Solomon agreed but said they should split up so there would be one woman and one kid on each team. But the women said no, they would play by themselves with their students. Then your wife said I should be the referee, she spoke to me in Fifek and I should have started worrying then because no self-respecting *man* from my area spoke that type of raw dialect. I must confess I've never seen anything like what happened next.' He was still shaking his head at the memory then remembered Rabiu had been there a long time and gave him a plastic bag with bananas, tangerines and a can of Jamaican Ginger Beer.

'Where was I? . . . Yes, they taught the kids to run straight at the men and keep the ball low and screamed bloody murder and blasted me when I didn't call foul when the *men* failed to get out of the way. After barrages of insults in several Niagran languages and threats to report me to my *wives* (I have just one!), I found myself calling "foul" almost every other minute, disallowing perfectly good goals and expelling my own master from the game. I've been in combat and never felt as shell shocked, but this was nothing compared to Ahmed and his friends who were shaking and sweating as if wishing they had taken on the Bulls with Michael in his prime.

'But the trouble was just beginning. There's a rule in the club that members should shower and change after games before coming to the bar but since the women had come in tracksuits they had nothing to change into and no intention of showering in a male only club so they went to the bar and ordered for themselves and the kids. The head barman was very light-skinned – fairer than you – and treated even rich Niagran members with a certain disdain. When Kikelomo ordered he sucked his teeth and told her in his most supercilious English accent that he didn't serve women and told them to get rid of the *"dirty little niggers"*.

'Kikelomo grabbed him by the collar and began pulling him across the bar while Fatima poured a bucket with ice, water and champagne over his head and screamed for the kids to get their hockey sticks from the car to beat this "albino cockroach till he shit his pants". The expatriates and some of the older Niagrans had already fled, knocking over furniture, while the other barmen and waiters hid under the counter and tables. They had almost stripped the man naked and his face was a mess and his head was bleeding when Ahmed and the others rushed in to beg the women to calm down while at the same time looking for an escape route in case they turned on them. They stopped only when the man started bawling and prostrated himself on the floor, begging them to spare him.

'The irony was his wife was a cook and she was there with all the women cooks, waitresses, cleaners and even some prostitutes who normally waited outside the gates for drunken members, they were hooting and cheering on the two to "beat some sense into that bloody pig of a man who thinks he's white". The English chairman of the club, an executive of Shell, wrote them a personal letter of apology and promised to admit women in future. So, knowing what type of woman you're married to, when she told me to send my men to look for you I decided not to take chances but to come myself.'

'Wise move. Did Ahmed ever tell you how she refused to join the Party? When we were interviewed, she told the Chairman of the Politburo he was full of shit and looked liked Homer Simpson but without Homer's brain or charisma and asked what kind of woman would marry such a fucking pompous ass? Which hurt him a lot because his wife had just run away with an African-American Special Operation Forces captain who came to instruct the Niagran Presidential Guard in counter-insurgency.'

'Definitely not a woman to mess with. Trouble is if I screw up with you I'll have to answer to *my* wife too, Kikelomo and Fatima are her heroines. These guys are still watching the place so I'll have to handcuff and blind-fold you when I take you out.'

'No sacrifice is too great for the revolution, to quote Comrade Mammamia. Ahmed never told me your name, comrade.'

'Which do you want, my Hausa name? Call me *Mai Magani*, "Medicine Man".'

They had come out of the building and were walking towards Mai Magani's Pajero when they saw Meatloaf and his Chadians sitting in two Humvees and a Bradley Fighting vehicle listening to Elvis's 'Ain't Nothin' But a Hound Dog' at full volume.

DRESSING DOWN

Gary tried getting Bob Marley to walk but like a baby his knees buckled whenever he moved a foot forward. They had succeeded in getting him to stay upright to get the new clothes on but Billy Bob and Bobby Joe stayed close to catch him if he fell while Gary checked that they fit properly. The jacket and trousers were a bit loose but that was okay for kids his age, Ricky had told him it was the fashion when he wanted to send them back for alterations. But the length of the sleeves and trouser legs were unacceptable as they hid the cuffs and dragged on the floor. So he sent for Seyi, the tailor who did alterations for the local branch of Rossini's, the Bond Street boutique where affluent Niagran and Nigerian men shopped while their wives were kitted out at *Place Vendôme* on nearby Conduit Street where Mrs Thatcher bought her heavily padded power suits with shoulders like Al Capone's.

Unlike his colleagues, who thought everything Niagran was crap, Gary had a keen appreciation for the tailor's genius. Without being cynical, he decided to play a trick on Barlowe Clunes who had said 'if you want to destroy anything sacred or precious give it to a nigger'. Clunes had asked him to pick up a cashmere and wool Cerutti 1881 suit when he was in London to see *The Doll's House* with his parents who were passing through on their way from Tashkent. He bought the suit for himself, picked up a length of the same cloth from a shop on Regent Street and gave the suit, cloth, Cerutti label and Clunes' measurement to Seyi who built a suit for Clunes in two days. The bastard was so impressed he said how *superior* Italian tailors were to American and British, because the fucking unions and high wages had destroyed the Anglo-Saxon working man's pride in his work.

Seyi took one look at the youngster and started to work with the sewing machine he brought on his Vespa. In no time at all he had the sleeves shortened with just the right show of cuff, slightly less than half an inch for that shade of blue. That was how people of Gary's class wore their cuffs so social inferiors would not feel embarrassed by their Pathek Phillipe watches or think they were surreptitiously checking the time.

With the trousers just below the belly button the leg now fell to the roof of the heel in back and just over the tied laces in front. Gary swore under his breath when they said they could not find Bob Marley's personal possessions and was not placated by an absent minded Thin Man who remembered that all he had on him at the time of his arrest were pencils, sketching paper, a red, green and gold wool cap, a red leather charm bracelet and under two US dollars in Niagran currency. Asked where these were now the crew-cut started saying, 'These niggers –' but under Gary's withering stare changed it to, 'These people are like vultures, sir, they took it all.'

Gary removed two $100 bills from his monogrammed calfskin tan billfold and was about to put them into Bob Marley's breast pocket when Billy Bob warned him, 'You sentencin that boy to death, suh, they kill him for $5.' Distressed at such depravity among the lower orders, Gary reluctantly removed one of the $100 bills and patted Bob Marley's pocket to encourage the kid to buck up, remembering fondly how, at his age, his lacrosse coach at Andover would cheer him up with a punch in the solar plexus which produced instant paralysis and a call to FUCK FEAR! in the cold November rain.

He saw the two Rednecks waiting, experiencing withdrawal symptoms from his cutting off their supply of Toby Keith and Martina McBride, and had a sudden blinding flash of insight into the malaise of the American Way of Life. As leader of the free, Anglo-Saxon world, the country had lost its natural right to rule by its abdication of the simple courtesies and ancient refinements once embodied in the old New England families. He reminded himself to read that *New Yorker* piece his father recommended in his last letter. The title went something like 'The Coarsening of Western Civilization: Why Bin Laden Hates Us', written by some major league asshole with a fucking Kraut-sounding name like Carsten Wanker.

The boy had reminded him of the time he was in Jamaica trying to get over Yvonne and deciding whether to work for Payne Webber, where his father had spent twenty-five years as head of the legal department, or Morgan Stanley where his elder brother Burton was already being talked of as a future CEO. So he chose neither but settled for the undemanding job of Counsel to the CIA to protect the Agency not from legal liability in the countries it fucked over but from no-brainers like John Kerry in Congressional Oversight Committees who thought that a basically unaccountable institution with such power would be further beyond blemish than Barbara Bush. How the man made Skull and Bones and won the Purple Heart he could never fathom. He had heard of the singer Bob Marley from Yvonne but nothing prepared him for the size and excitement of the cortège as it passed through the exuberant multitudes on its way to inter his remains in his village of Nine Mile. He was sitting on the hill overlooking Discovery Bay by the heart-shaped pool of the grandiose villa which

upper class islanders saw as status symbols and tried to
outdo each other in garishness and inutility. His parents
owned a much bigger compound next to the Pershing's
near the Round Hill Hotel which he had visited from
before he could remember but this was like a transplant
from the Hamptons, functional to the point of sterility,
where even a pool would have been considered vulgar.
Sarah was not a bad girl, in her red bikini she was even
attractive in a cheap, young Elizabeth Taylor sort of way,
bronzed by her genes and the heat of the Tropics. He had
met her at Bryn Mawr not long after the split from Yvonne
and her endless chatter, without even pauses for 'really?'
or 'is that so?', was more distracting than Prozac. But she
was obsessed with the Great Gatsby, thought of herself as
Daisy and him as Gatsby, a fucking irony for a Jewish
princess whose father made money from selling textiles
and electrical goods to the local coloured people. Then a
sound system in the procession started playing 'One good
thing about music / When it hits you feel no pain' and
suddenly the enormity of what he had lost hit him. He
had met Yvonne at his brother's apartment on Park Avenue
where she gave piano lessons to their twin girls to pay her
way through Juillard. Her renditions of Brahms and Chopin
were competent rather than spectacular but it was when
he heard her sing the *Laudate Dominum* that he realized
she had a voice with more range than Maria Callas or
Victoria de los Angeles and a soul bigger than the fucking
world. He did not experience the trouble he anticipated in
pursuit of her because she neither encouraged nor discour-
aged him, taking everything in her stride the same way she
sang 'The Very First Time I Saw Your Face'. She said her
people came from Jamaica originally, from St Elizabeth, near
Colin Powell's people's home. He told her about the house
near Round Hill and she said she had a cousin who was a
barman at the hotel and knew all the houses where he
worked at parties from time to time and had a friend called
Dick Pershing who died in Vietnam and Gary thought this

must have been the classmate from Yale Burton talked about. He remembered as a boy sneaking off to the servants' house where he was intoxicated with the rhythms of Lord Kitchener, the Mighty Sparrow, Count Ossie and Don Drummond. Later still he sampled the rum punch, had his first taste of weed and was taken to watch the *Johnkunnu* masquerades and drink white rum at the all night parties where the sound systems and lascivious dancers did serious damage to his narrow moral WASP perspective. Garfield Payne dreamt of remaining in Paradise forever and even on the coldest November day at Andover, Yale, then Yale Law School where his performance was unspectacular, the sunshine of his vision lit up the New England gloom. And now here she was, the reverse of the cynical and capricious Sarah, the answer to his dream, the perfect woman in a world of imperfection and mediocrity. Here she was, a product of countless races, with more genetic diversity than all his relatives of three centuries put together with grandiose names like Bingham, Whitney, Biddle, Payne, Forbes, Warren, Bush, Winthrop, Burton and Davenport splashed over all the preposterous old *faux* Greek and Roman buildings in the Ivy League and Wall Street. There was nothing *faux* or 'old' about Yvonne and she treated him just as she would have some clerk from her Jamaican background she met at her Baptist church. The problem was his own people and he looked forward to introducing her with a mixture of defiance and trepidation. But to his astonishment his parents *liked* her and his mother even teased that *he* was the one making a fantastic catch. It was the reaction of his brother and his wife, however, which killed it for him. His hatred for Burton had nothing to do with sibling rivalry – they were ten years apart – but because he was perfect, a clone of his father Burton Payne III. At Andover he did five sports and played golf and lacrosse at Yale where he graduated *summa cum laude*, was a Whiffenpoof and tapped by Skull and Bones before going on to Harvard Law where he grad-

uated in the top ten and was on the editorial board of the
Journal. Like his mother Amelia, Burton's wife Emily went
to Smith and was so into good deeds, so concerned about
the less privileged, so wholesome she made Laura Bush
look like Nexhmije Hoxa or that Serbian bitch. He knew
they were too cultured to refer to her race or social
standing but at least he expected to be counselled, in the
subtlest way of course, about possible cultural incompat-
ibility. Imagine his horror therefore when he learnt that
his perfect brother and sister-in-law had taken Yvonne as
one of the family because she too was perfect, did not
drink, smoke, or have lovers and was a regular church-
goer. *He* was the black sheep, the outsider, with subversive ideas about the American Dream to which the rest of
the world's people like Yvonne aspired. For the first time
in three centuries a member of his family had tried to
branch out on his own, to break away from the narrow
circle of families who married each other like nomadic
cattle herders to keep their property intact only to find
that his bastard of a brother and his perfect wife were
bent on turning his intended into a fucking civic lesson
on how to be an American. Gary woke to the realiza-
tion that his people would kill his would-be soul mate
with niceness and, without the imagination to tell the
truth, left her with the impression that he had come to
accept the conventional wisdom that rich White Anglo
Saxon Protestant men could fuck but not marry poor black
Jamaicans. And it almost killed him when he went to tell
her and she started to sing '*One good thing about music*'
and, seeing the stricken look on his face, apologized for
singing their song at such a time. His nieces, who later
joined the Unification Church and then became aides to
Paul Wolfowitz and Douglas Feith, never forgave him for
driving away the only human being they'd ever met in their
young lives. Deciding that if his people were going to
accept his choice of spouse he would give them one of
their own, he married Holly Davenport Winthrop Burton,

an analyst at Morgan Stanley, whom he had hated since childhood and swore never to marry if she were the last woman on the planet, who had confessed to a friend at a gym on Lexington Avenue that rather than fuck that prick Garfield she would stuff her cunt with C4 explosives, sew it shut, then shoot herself. He remembered her now, a totally impractical porcelain doll lost in the huge leather chair in his mother's study as she waited for a servant to collect her after violin lessons in the adjoining Brownstone on 71st Street between Park and Lex. She had been conceived on one of her father's trips between installing General Suharto in Indonesia and Colonel Cab Calloway in Niagra when her mother mistook him for one of her lovers. In the Directorate of Plans he was known as 'Dowser' because of his genius for discovering dictators who could serve the interest of his father's oil company. His wife spent her time between the arrival of cases of vintage whiskey with her lovers and playing golf and made sure her husband paid for all three although the whiskey was from a distillery on the Isle of Wight which a maternal grandfather had bought for $20,000 during the Great Depression because he liked the single malt. When Dowser arrived in Djakarta he found the Station had prepared a list of Chinese the size of *War and Peace* for Suharto to eliminate but, knowing how tough the Chinese Communists were, he had his people trawl the phone books to pick out every tenth Chinese sounding name so the General would have a cool million to play with to draw the Communists' attention to his will and resolve. After the leftist civilian government was removed in Niagra Dowser instructed General Calloway to appoint Colonel Daudu, his flamboyant tank commander, Army Chief of Staff and gave him a list of 137 leftists in the military, academics and the media who had formed the core of the previous regime. But 'Danny Boy' was pathologically thinskinned and added the names of everyone who had slighted him since he was three and instead of handling the problem discreetly in the privacy of the barracks, staged a spectacular on a public beach at low tide so by the time the last batch of two hundred were unloaded the tide was rising and many drowned and had to be shot under water, and for months after the satellite analysis division was trying to discover the cause of the sudden efflorescence of red algae off the West Atlantic coast.

Garfield's mother was mildly surprised when he told her his plans because Holly had told her mother she never thought she could hate a man as much as her father until that smug bastard Garfield came along. He had sacrificed what he had with Yvonne for a marriage which, while there was no love or illusion, had a wonderful complement of mutual indifference and no pain to kill. And here was this fucking Rasta boy, whom the degenerate Rednecks had almost beaten to death, bringing it all back home. If he had had the guts to marry Yvonne, despite his people's enthusiasm, this could have been his son. No one could understand his anguish as he hummed their song under his breath and, lucky for Bob Marley, Garfield Whitney Bingham Payne had ridden to his rescue.

HANGING OUT
BETWEEN THIEVES

Bob Marley was supported by two enormous Chadians who followed Billy Bob Liotto down the long corridor of the State Security Annexe at the Rock Castle. In his right hand Billy Bob held the syringe containing the urine-yellow liquid, called the 'Donny Rumsfeld' because it allowed American forces to fight wars on three fronts – against the Iraqis, North Koreans and Colin Powell. After the long corridor they entered an atrium with an ornamental pool filled with fat koi carp, compensation from the collapsed Bank of 'Criminals and Cocaine' International, where the General had lost one hundred million dollars of his Pension Fund.

Because his deposits were second only to those of Sheikh Zayed bin Sultan al-Nahyan of Abu Dhabi, Aga Hasan Abedi, founder of the BCCI, had built a branch in the grounds of Daudu's Rock Palace, which the *Lahore Times* described as the finest example of Islamic architecture since the Alhambra Palace in Spain and the Taj Mahal in India. But the Islamic architecture was nothing compared to a financial structure which spanned the cocaine cartels from Colombia to Panama, Mexico, Peru, Bolivia, Chile, Niagra, Nigeria and the United States.

With Colonel Danilo Gonzalez of the Colombian police,

General Daudu steered the US Drug Enforcement Agency to wage wars on their enemies in the Medellin, Cali, Tijuana and Abuja cartels until their own Xanadu and Northern Valley Colombia cartels achieved a monopoly which was run from offices in the BCCI complex, a stone's throw from the DEA office which had decorated Gonzalez and Daudu for 'their selfless dedication and willing sacrifices in the war against drugs'.

The protected status of the branch and its great liquidity made it ideal for the Directorate of Plans to channel money to the Contras, Unita, Renamo, Inkatha, the Moslem Student Society and the Lord's Resistance Army.

After the collapse of the bank, Richard 'Mr Dick' Burton, now Chairman of Burton Holly, suggested to the General that his company's subsidiary Green and Branch transform the facility into a regional centre for the war against drugs and terrorism as it had done in Djakarta, Riyadh, Kuwait City, Baghdad, Tashkent, Caracas and Mexico City. After the refurbishment, cells in the underground annexe were described by Amnesty as 'chicken coops without frills'.

There was an oriental bridge across the pool and, on either side, palm trees on islands around which the carp circled, fascinated by the reflection of the golden RPG-shaped fruit. Bob Marley's feet were dragging and his head hung limply as the men practically lifted him over the wooden planks of the bridge. His eyes were closed when they took him to the reception area on the other side where two Men in Black saluted and pressed a buzzer under the desk. The man who came to meet them had the build of a long-distance runner and smoked a pipe like the one in the ad for 'Black Gold'. He wore a navy blue Cecil Gee blazer, white shirt, red Armani tie from the last day of the Harrods sale, and smiled at the men without removing the pipe, which kept puffing out hazy, blue, sweet-smelling smoke like signals from an earlier time.

'Arab is he? Al-Qaeda?'

'He ain't no more Al-Qaeda than my granpaw's dawg. Ain't all up here,' Billy Bob said, pointing to his temple. 'If he was one of ourn, people'd be makin jokes bout his ma and pa!' He handed over the red file with TOP SECRET in black crossed with an X and the long-distance runner called on his mobile, still with the pipe in his mouth. 'Bob Marley!' he whistled as he opened the file and this time he removed the pipe. 'So our men were wrong all the time, they said he was tall – over six feet, round eyes, thick lips and a good set of teeth. No wonder they couldn't catch him.' After a pause he replaced the pipe and mused: 'But then these Al-Qaedas, according to Professor Herzovogina, have miraculous powers due to the Sufi mysticism they practise. *Maybe* he could shape-shift from five feet two inches to over six feet.'

Two other Men in Black came out from a door behind the desk and took Bob Marley from his Chadian and American guardian angels. 'Guard this one well, gentlemen, as if your lives depend on it, because they do. Here we have the ideological engine room of the Niagran "Revolution", the combination of Robespierre, Toussaint L'Ouverture, Mao Zedong, Che Guevara and Thomas Sankara. None other than "Bob Marley", aka "Rabiu Nafiu", "Robert Nesta" and "John Lennon". These are aliases we *know* but such a slippery customer could have dozens of others. *You*, Ismaela, cross reference all these aliases with "Robin Hood", "Brotherman", "The Scarlet Pimpernel", "Ho Chi Minh", "Trotsky", "Norman Tebbit", "Geoffery Howe", "Ann Widdecombe" and all the others we haven't been able to match.' Ismaela had come from a side passage and saluted.

'Yes, sir,' he said. He wore a white kaftan and red fez, his face was pockmarked and he had yellow, scaly skin like dried eucalyptus bark.

'And you, Kola and Pius, take good care of him, *remember he has to be alive to talk.*'

His head was still buried in the file but he looked up briefly and pointed at them by swinging the pipe in his mouth.

'Yes, sah!' they shouted and, as they saluted, Bob Marley started falling but was caught by Ismaela's bony hand.

'Idiot!' he said. 'Na be our masta say make you take good care of am?' As he walked away with the pipe man the ones at the desk buzzed again, the door opened and they descended into the dark, cavernous interior. Now they were gentler, caressing his arms with their fingers. For the first time they were appreciating the softness of fine new wool. Kola was almost the caricature of torturer, tall, bony, with a pinched, saturnine face which blended like wallpaper into the gloomy type of setting where the best work was done in his chosen field. To inflict pain and experience its effects, to listen constantly to screams and pleas for mercy, death rattles and the crack of snapping bones without flinching, required a type of face and constitution that fit Kola Omisore like a Saville Row suit.

But the touch of the wool, the cut of the blazer, and the smell of the fine leather suit carrier which still clung to it like the pipe smoke of his master, caused his features to soften and there was the hint of a smile on his face, a patina of vulnerability, even human weakness, not unlike the moment of climax with a vanquished prisoner. Normally his skeletal hand held the prisoner in such a death grip that the flesh melted like liquid into the bones of his upper arm. But the rich feel of the cloth had a hypnotic effect on him, profoundly affecting his sense of values. Even without appreciating the elevated status of 'J. Press' in Gary's social milieu, Kola knew value when he felt it and treated the sleeve with a reverence approaching awe.

Everyone knew that the Niagran security forces were grossly underpaid. In fact Nasser Waddadda had argued convincingly that this was necessary to 'incentivize them

to put more effort into their work'. As a result all had
second jobs and Kola's was that of Evangelist because his
build was impressive in a flowing white robe and his long
arms trembling in the wide sleeves had an intoxicating
effect on women acolytes especially, who invested in his
ministry to win their fortunes in money or rich husbands.
If his son could dress up like the convict now was, he
would be inundated with envelopes from mothers seeking
the extortionate school fees charged by the network of
schools owned by the wives of senior officers. His boy was
handsome and already conscious of the effect he had on
women and Kola daydreamed of him marching
triumphantly on the red carpet up the steps to the stage
where he preached, perfectly oiled, seraphic in the vest-
ments of the White Man, accompanied by the serenity of
'Come, Let Us Gather at the River'. So when he sighed,
'*My pickin go look fine fine in dis suit,*' there was reverence in his voice.

At which Pius sucked his teeth and growled, '*Dis suit
be like God sef make am for my own boy.*'

It was Hannibal Lector who said incisively that 'one
covets what one sees', agreeing with St Augustine who
spoke of the 'sins of the eyes', and located the essence
of Western epistemology from the time of Plato in the
sense of vision when he wrote '*noli foras ire, in teipsum
redi, in interiore homine habitat veritas*'. Pius Obodo
clearly belonged to this tradition because at the sacri-
legious mention of his pagan colleague, his face too
underwent a profound transformation. Unlike Kola's,
his features were cherubic which, he argued in his self-
assessment for performance-related pay, was a distinct
advantage – convicts were disarmed by his engaging
smile and so unprepared for being whacked in the face
with a concealed knuckle-duster.

But now the cherub flew out the window at the thought
that this bloody apostate wanted to parade his heathen
son in these divine garments. As a good Catholic he kept

his soul pure with daily confession and constant reminders that his blasphemous colleague would burn in the hottest corner of hell. As a man of exquisite moral sense there was none of this anti-Christ Evangelism for him. He and his equally devout wife prayed several times a day, with giving of alms, that their beloved son Emeka would pass the exam for the Military Academy, become a General and be even richer than that conman Daudu. The interview was in a week and his wife had been pestering him for months to get the money for an *oyibo*-style suit. But how could they with the pittance he earned as a security man at the Burton Holly HQ or his wife's trade as an Avon Lady which actually *lost* them money. And now to hear the ranting of this foolish ant! Pius sucked his teeth again, this time with emphasis.

'God no be blind, Pius, you boy like you sef, na real balloon man, im no fit fine *oyibo* clothes.'

'*Oyibo* no make clothes for skeleton, Kola; make I bring Emeka here for try.'

They had rested Bob Marley into an armchair so they could argue the merits of their cases and Kola reacted instinctively, slapping him when spittle trailed from his mouth toward the lapel of the blazer. But Pius was more thoughtful, wiped his mouth with his copy of the *Spicy Girls* and rested his head back into the torn upholstery with its overpowering odour of vinyl.

'Okay,' Kola said, 'make you say we toss – head or tail?'

'Head!' Pius said.

Kola tossed the coin, caught it and shouted '*Tail!* You lose!'

Pius grabbed his hand, tore it open, and when he saw the head he screamed 'Cheat! Na head, I win.'

'Na you change am, Pius, make we toss again.'

'Okay, but na me go do am dis time.' He allowed the coin to drop on the cold concrete floor and when it came to rest the head was clearly visible to both. Now it was Kola who sucked his teeth as Pius did a jig round the armchair and carefully removed the blazer. When he found the $100 bill in the inner pocket he was so excited he lost his senses and shouted, and Kola pounced on him.

'Na you get de clothes, de money na for me,' he shouted, grabbing at Pius' hand to wrestle the money away. A shadow darkened the angelic face as Pius feared his Bushman of a colleague would damage the precious garments, the key to his family's success as producers of a future Commander-in-Chief. In keeping with H.L. Nieburg's axiom that 'the rational goal of the *threat* of violence is the accommodation of interests, not the provocation of actual violence', Pius, therefore, made an offer he thought his friend could not refuse: 'Make I give you twenty dolla.'

'Na be you don craze,' Kola said, now threatening actual violence to the sacred garments. 'Give me my hundred dolla.'

'Thirty!'

'Hundred!'

'Forty!'

'Hundred!'

'Fifty last!'

'Hundred!' Kola said but saw that Pius had put the convict and his clothes out of harm's reach and was guarding them with his ample body. So with his face restored to normalcy, Kola accepted defeat without testing Nieburg's concept of the rational goal of *actual* violence which he defines, unsurprisingly, as 'demonstration of the will and capability of action, establishing a measure of the credibility of future threats, not the exhaustion of that capability in unlimited conflict'.

'Na God sef go judge you, Pius, gi me my money.'

'When Idi Amin Ogwu come make we go see dat Hausa money chanja.'

When Idi Amin arrived with Bobby Joe he looked the same as when Bob Marley saw him last, so many years ago. But in his green and white prison uniform he could not do the comparison because he lay back in the tattered armchair with his eyes closed and his tongue hanging out. The giant was telling him about his mother who still loved him and his brothers and sisters who had never been told of the brother they had lost, or even knew they had. A cloud of disappointment, possibly anger, shadowed the great face at the failure to respond and he turned to the Thin Man by his side with a mixture of resentment and wounded pride.

'He use to be one fine pickin,' he complained. 'Im modder teach am sense well well. Dese bad companion dey lead im fom de path of righteousness.'

'Maybe dis will bring im back to de straight and narrow,' said Bobby Joe in a remarkable imitation of a Niagran accent as he squeezed a yellow arch into the air and pumped his Donny Rumsfeld restorative into Bob Marley's limp right arm. 'De boy need de orange juice!'

Bob Marley shook like the engine of an old car starting for the first time on a fine mid-winter morning and his eyelids moved in rapid bursts as at the onset of a wet nightmare. The drug was like a stone dropped in a pond, stirring memories in no order of time, so when confronted with the image of Idi Amin it was that of years ago when he saw him off at the motor park with the package of bloodstained clothes for Mallam Aminu and fixed in his mind as in wax was a frame of time with his mother waiting for him at home and he found himself wanting to ask the giant for the money he promised to buy him paints and the new house, white with green roof, of cut stone, they would move into with his mother. But he found he could not speak, his words were empty echoes and it was the giant who spoke, promising he would take him to see his mother and the other pickin if only he would tell them about all his friends in the Revolution he was leading to fight the General.

There was no point lying, his mother was a good

Christian who taught him to tell the truth at all times, the Security had a big file on him with all his aliases like 'Rabiu Nafiu', 'Robert Nesta', 'John Lennon' and all the others he used to write bad things about the General and his gofment. They knew about the prize he got from the newspaper boys, his plotting with the late Lt Colonel Ahmed Abdullahi to overthrow General Daudu, the monies he received from him to bribe other journalists to write lies about America, his party number with the kamanists.

Bob Marley had a hard time focusing on Idi Amin and his image kept flicking in and out like a black and white TV set with a bad tube. His eyes had turned inwards and he was seeing himself inside out because his body was no longer his but belonged to the yellow fluid which he now saw like globules of amber right down to the molecular level coursing through the veins and the heads and faces of Idi Amin and the others who hit him or hung him upside down or shocked or injected him were there in the bright spheres which glowed like cinders or sparkled like diamonds or exploded like fireworks or erupted like volcanoes when the pressure of the juice built up and a whole universe of cold, unspeakable and incommunicable emptiness which had inhabited him darkly since the hand of the man closed round his throat that day outside the Post Office was annihilated to rise anew in the cold fire which overwhelmed him now. But he could not see images of Agbani or his mother or Ahmed or the meat seller because his loved ones were never in his nightmares. And when he even wanted to think their names he could not because his tongue was a dead whale inside the prison of his mouth, its hump lodged in the cleft of his broken palate, all the sound on one side of his head big as the globe away from his shattered eardrum which felt like needles before but was now part of the general numbness which was his body where the drug entered with a rush and he was caught up in the current and flung into another dimension where all the senses were one.

'Is de drog dese young people take,' the giant sighed, shaking his massive head in regret.

'We get de same problem in de States,' the thin Special Forces man said. 'Me sef I don get younger brudder who take drog overdose. He almost kill my modder when she divorce from my paw.'

'Sorry, sah,' Idi Amin commiserated, 'de kamanist bring de drug to make de young one dem not obey. See dis boy now, him could be teacher or clerk now if not for de drog.'

'After we kill de kamanist and de Al-Qaeda make we kill de drog dealer.' They saluted when the Pipe Man entered with Bob Marley's thick file.

'How's our young man coming along, Captain Ogwu?'

'Not good, sah, de boy stubborn pass Job sef.'

'Even with you, his stepfather, Captain? A tough nut, tough indeed. And here it says in his file that he has a nut allergy which has had such crippling effects on him.'

'He'd break quick if we gave him to the Egyptians, sir. Arabs are the best at this bisnez.'

'But we have no Arabs here, do we, Mr McVeigh? So we have to rely on our trusty *iroko* trees like Captain Ogwu here. Don't mistake his gentleness, it's a family thing!'

Idi Amin flushed with embarrassment at this accusation of 'gentleness' and tried to explain. 'Na be *you* say "take care he got to be alive to talk," sah. Im no strong enough.'

'A joke, Captain Ogwu. But on a more serious note we have to pep him up a bit to complete his interrogation. His confession must be ready by tomorrow, Judge Nafiu will deliver the verdicts in two days' time. Mr McVeigh?'

'He have enough for today sir, another dose could kill him.'

'A risk we have to take, some risks are worth taking, don't you agree, Mr McVeigh?'

After Bobby Joe gave him the shot they could see his head jerk up and his body begin to shiver and inside his head Bob Marley felt the torrent raging high, lifting him above the mountains of the moon, now one of the

shiny yellow globules possessing his body, blending it with
the universe which would live inside him forever. He
felt the giant's hand on his upper arm, lifting him perhaps,
but up and down were the same and when he stumbled
he could not tell whether he was falling or rising into the
sky to his father Revelation whom he could not see because
of the yellow globules blocking his sight. He was floating
but could not tell if the man was carrying him or dragging him across the cold concrete because there was no
feeling in his legs and the numbness was the same sweetness as tobacco smoke.

'Sit him before the mirror,' the Pipe Man said. 'Cuff
him behind so he doesn't fall, and hold his head so he
can see.'

Bob Marley could feel the rush of liquid through his
veins and his eyeballs pushed out forcing his lids to open.
He sat before a glass and could see through because there
was nothing there but a light which shone brighter and
more glorious than the sun. Then the woman entered with
two children and the light was extinguished because her
beauty was even more radiant. He might have seen her in
a previous life and she looked like the woman he saw with
Brotherman, Ahmed, Delroy and his wife. She and her
friend taught him and the other *Outkastes* how to fight
and he remembered their smells but that was before the
time in the chicken coop with the strobe lights and the
pliers and the music and then the urine yellow liquid
which arched like McDonald's so he saw her through a
haze and did not know her anymore. She was as beautiful
as Agbani but golden and full with the child they had
always wanted and her face was thrown back so her cheekbones were moons which orbited the sun of her face
standing high and haughty above the dominions of the
earth. From the way she held the hands of her children,
he could tell not even the giant or the man with the pipe
would dare touch them because she was a lioness and
would tear off their faces and rip out their insides and

smash their windpipes and bury what was left of them in the sawdust of their minds.

'Your wife Kikelomo and your children Antonio and Josina, Mr Nafiu,' the Pipe Man purred between perfectly formed puffs of smoke. 'Tell us what we need to know and no harm will befall them.'

Despite his love for Agbani, Bob Marley wanted to possess them, this tall golden Princess with her children like suns and the baby he and his wife longed for but could not have because of what the soldiers did to her in the village where they had fallen from the skies like locusts and consumed the land and the people and now here was the yellow stream which flowed through his veins and his consciousness creating this goddess and his children out of the flood.

'Take your time, Mr Nafiu, but the sooner you confess the sooner they will be home – and of course the sooner *you* can join them.'

Idi Amin was rumbling and the Pipe Man puffed some paternal smoke toward him to show his sympathy. He was resentful that the useless boy he had kicked out of his house so he could have his mother to himself had found such a fine woman and rich-looking children and now had the temerity to deny them because of the drugs, godless kamanism and refusal to confess to his crimes against the General.

'What's bothering you, Captain Ogwu?'

'Dis boy he stubborn pass Job, sah, he deny im own family, dat not de African way, sah. Africa man always want him wife and pickin.'

'Foreign ideologies, gentlemen, that's the problem when foreigners impose their beliefs on others. A clash of cultures is always fatal.'

'That's so true sir, family values are what make America great but not all immigrants know that, sir. The result is a clash of civilizations. We believe firmly in the melting pot but oil and Coca Cola just don't mix.'

The Pipe Man blew an appreciative ring of smoke,

pressed a buzzer and suddenly the light went out in the room with the sun goddess and her children and there was a prolonged scream of a woman blended with those of children and the shrill whine of a frightened dog as both Bobby Joe and Idi Amin reached for their weapons, letting go of the chair with Bob Marley which crashed forward. 'Relax, gentlemen,' the Pipe Man said, 'you never heard of PSYOPS?'

When they lifted the chair the beads of sweat on Bob Marley's forehead were like the golden globes of liquid and his lips and fingernails were blue. Bobby Joe wet his index finger and held it under his nose and when he felt no breathing checked the pulse at his wrist, throat and temple.

'Fraid we might have lost him, sir.'

'Nonsense, Mr McVeigh, State Security never lost a convict on my watch and it's not happening now. Call the Doctor to revive him, he's got a confession to make tomorrow. The Doctor killed so many black people under apartheid it's about time he resurrected one. We want him bright-eyed and bushy-tailed come the dawn.'

LIDICE

'Howdy, pardner,' Meatloaf shrilled as the Captain emerged from the building with a blindfolded and shackled Rabiu. 'So at last you've brought us the "Soul of the Revolution".' He had switched off Toby Keith and was approaching to take custody of the prisoner.

'This one's mine,' the Captain said. 'It's *personal*, not business.'

Meatloaf kept moving forward until he saw the Captain's eyes narrow and his grip tighten on the upper arm of the prisoner. He got his name from his bulk but while he weighed as much as the nigger the distribution was entirely different. He enjoyed watching cartoons on the Nickelodeon channel and one of his favourites was the inflatable weightlifter who fell over when his chest and shoulders got too big for his spindly legs. But there was no danger of that here as the guy, like all niggers, had a narrow waist, no hips to speak of, but thighs like oil drums on concrete column legs set in boots like shiny flat-bottomed boats.

He was a life-long supporter of the Dallas Cowboys from the time he worshipped the quarterback – third after Elvis and God – and remembered that day in the cold November rain when the Cowboys had a shot at making

it to the Super Bowl. They had a slim lead at the tail
end of the fourth quarter when the Packers' defensive
linebacker hurdled the Cowboys' defence like it wasn't
there and planted his size sixteens in the quarterback's
groin causing a turnover and a crippled quarterback. That
was the end of that. Later the quarterback claimed he
shouted 'Nigger!' before the play just to rile the defensive line and meant no harm because all his team mates
were niggers. The linebacker was built like this guy but
he wasn't five feet away and with his helmet and face-
guard on you couldn't smell the hate. And, even more
important, he wasn't holding a rifle in his hand like a
child's water pistol with the RPG like a slowly ripening
fruit pointed at his head.

'Yeah, man, we can't always play it by the book. You say
it's *personal*? Who am I to pass judgement?'

'Don't let thees Niagran gorilla push you around, sir,'
said a Chadian who did not seem to have followed the
dialogue because his head was buried in an *Asterix* comic.

'Shut your fuckin mouth, soldier!' Meatloaf screamed,
almost shrinking to avoid the Captain in case he decided
to move on the idiot. 'You're free to go, sir. Sure you don't
want an escort?'

'I said it's *personal*, I don't need your escorts.' Meatloaf
winced as he saw the steel grip bite into the man's arm
and the sudden propulsion which almost lifted him off his
feet. With his exquisite moral sense he reflected ruefully
on the unfairness of the world – if it was him who did
that to a nigger they would call him a fucking cruel
Redneck.

As they approached his Pajero which was parked about
two hundred metres away they heard 'Brother,' and the
Captain turned to see the African-American in Chadian
uniform running toward them.

'You guys shouldn't be collaborating with these fucking
cruel Rednecks to suppress our African brothers, Captain.'

'I'm not, brother, I told the man this was *personal*. Now

run back before he thinks we niggers are plotting to under-mine motherhood, apple pie and Dick Cheney.' Inside the vehicle Rabiu was still blindfolded and shackled. 'In case of roadblocks,' the Captain said.

'You could've been more gentle with the brother, *Mai Magani*.'

'Your brother, maybe. If Meatloaf wanted to catch us out he wouldn't send a fellow Cracker. State Security is full of bearded "comrades", including friendly "African-American" and "Caribbean" people who are so in love with the struggle. Ahmed used to give the names of all his agents on campus to the late Dr Solomon.'

'What's the point if you can't trust anyone?'

'You trust who you have to, Comrade. Your wife seems better at this than you.'

'No doubt about that – but can you trust yourself? I felt your grip tighten, and you were moving forward when that Chadian provoked you. How'd you know that wasn't a set up?'

'The "Chadian" was the one who saved your ass, Comrade. He diverted attention with the remnant of the joint he took from his pocket so they wouldn't get to that corner and notice the boards were loose or the smell of your lousy Aramis aftershave. His father is even more reac-tionary than yours, he's the Paramount Chief of their part of Chad, from a family which collaborated with the French from the very beginning when they converted to Christian-ity and helped suppress the resistance. He was a playboy screwing French socialites while doing his degree at Vincennes when he read *How Europe Underdeveloped Africa*. He had heard how Kikelomo broke the collarbone of one pipe-smoking security man while under house arrest when he opened the door without knocking as she was changing. He also read an article of yours on *Post-Modernism and Class Struggle* in a collection by some "philosopher" in Paris and wanted to make you cringe the way he did when he read your favourable appraisal of "thinkers" like George Soros and Jacques Derrida: that's why he kept knocking on the floor to make you soil your trousers.'

'You two seem to know it all, you're so bloody cynical. So what made you join the struggle? Was it Ahmed?'

'I gave the late Comrade Cabral's *Weapon of Theory* when he was agonizing about how to change the system while he still was an essential part of the machine. Remember Lidice?'

'No,' Rabiu said.

'It was a small village in Poland. When Reinhardt Heydrich, the German Governor, was executed, Hitler ordered that Lidice be wiped from the map, never to rise again since his Reich would last a thousand years. The village was flattened, all the inhabitants slaughtered and even the name removed from the maps. But Hitler lost and Lidice is now a flourishing little town. I'm from the former ruling house in Lidiziam, I was away at Fort Bragg mastering counter-insurgency and explosives making when they destroyed my village. I escaped being flushed from the army because we all used aliases and Ahmed pulled the information from my file so Daudu's witch-finders would not know I was due for culling.

'Jerry Gotchakka, Daudu's Goebbels, told him about Lidice after the American and British Special Forces guys were executed for murdering innocent civilians and suggested how well the destruction of the village would play when he rearranged his postponed visit to the White House if he transferred his PR account from Scraatchy and Scraatchy to Shille and Coulton which paid him a retainer. Ahmed found out later that the idea came from a memo sent by your super-revolutionary comrade, Joseph Mammamia, who had a precocious talent for betrayal. Yes, I trust very few people, I'm cynical, even paranoid, and use so many aliases I sometimes wake up wondering who the fuck I am. But it's justified because I'm one of a truly endangered species, a rare survivor of Lidiziam. The day

Ahmed was killed I begged the Nigerians to kill me too but they said the Americans only paid them to kill the "Big Rabbit" so I swore upon his corpse to avenge him together with my 2,384 kinsmen and women. No, I have no intention of dying before I've killed as many of my enemies as possible.'

Rabiu could feel they were turning corners, perhaps to shake off pursuers, because the road to the border was straight and, through the blindfold, he could sense the waning of the light.

'Relax, Comrade, I think someone's following us.' The Pajero slowed down, sped up, slowed again, then turned and stopped. 'Sit tight,' the Captain said and Rabiu heard the door open, running footsteps, the squeal of tires as the other car braked and tried to reverse. Then there was a single loud explosion which he assumed was an RPG, the staccato of automatic fire, then three single shots. When the man was in the car again and the door closed and his breathing was even Rabiu asked 'What happened out there, Comrade?'

'They won't follow us anymore,' he said. The car was bumping along a rough dirt track and there was the sound of vegetation scraping the sides. 'We're here, Comrade.'

Rabiu rubbed his eyes and then his wrists as the blindfold then the shackles were removed and he saw the Captain had not addressed him but was speaking into his mobile. It was dark but after the blindfold he could make out individual *iroko* and mango trees and suddenly he realized how hungry he was. But before he could ask if he could fetch some mangoes the man arrived on his Vespa without lights and threw himself on the ground at the Captain's giant feet.

'Welcome, Comrade Jaja,' he greeted as the Captain took a Beretta from its holster.

'How many times must I tell you I'll shoot if you keep prostrating to me, Isaac?'

'You can't, master, then who would ferry your passengers across the border?'

'You appreciate the ironies of our feudal socialism, don't you, Comrade Rabiu? This is Comrade Isaac, another survivor of Lidiziam.'

'Rabiu Nafiu, Comrade, I used to write a column for the *Sentinel*.'

'I know you, Comrade, everyone knows you. You're Kikelomo's husband.'

CONFESSIONS OF
AN ALIAS

'How's our young friend, Mr McVeigh? Bright-eyed and bushy-tailed I hope,' the Pipe Man asked, switching his gaze between Bob Marley and his file.

'Good as he can be under the circumstances, sir.'

'Not good enough, not good enough at all. He must be able to sign a confession.'

'Way he is now, he won't sign nothin, not for a long time, if ever, sir.'

'That's where you're wrong, Mr McVeigh, we have ways of making them sign. You can confirm at least that he's still alive?'

Bobby Joe checked Bob Marley's breath, then his pulse: 'Yes, sir, but just barely – excuse me, sir – I don't see what difference this makes.'

'All the difference in the world, *all* the difference. Niagra is a nation of laws, we always have a representative at the Court of Justice in the Hague and our Attorney General, chairman of the tribunal which will convict Bob Marley and his fellow conspirators, is the foremost expert on military law on this planet. Know why he is called Justice "Sandra Day O'Connor"? His background so matches that of this legal eagle on your own Supreme Court that had he been an American he would surely be in line to replace your own Chief Justice Rehnquist when he retires.

'Last April the learned Justice wrote an article entitled *"Military Tribunals and International Law"* for the *Harvard Law Review*, the journal of his *alma mater*, and I am happy to report that this seminal work forms the legal foundation for the military tribunals with which your government will convict the evil followers of Mr bin Laden in Guantanamo Bay. Being a stickler for legal procedure the Attorney General devoted a whole paragraph to the subject of confessions in his brilliantly drafted Decree 419 on *The Conduct of Military Tribunals*, the core of which is that "a confession can be rendered invalid if it is proved definitely and beyond all reasonable doubt that the convict was deceased at the time of signing".

'The Doctor did a splendid job in reviving the convict yesterday or all our good work would have been rendered irrelevant under the terms of Decree 419. Now we need just a final push with your restorative tonic to really crown our achievement.'

'Not advisable, sir, the man's so past it I couldn't put the hair from a frog's back between him an death.'

'O ye of little faith! Don't you believe in God?'

'Of course, sir, I'm an American soldier!'

'Then you know that "God moves in mysterious ways, His wonders to perform." In the Higher Realms of Duty and Patriotism He expects us to rise above the humdrum.'

'I'm religious as the next man, sir, but this is an experimental drug, the FDA won't approve it for Americans until it's been tested on foreigners and terrorists. We don't know its full effects – one Arab we tried it on sang "Suspicious Minds", though he didn't know no English. This guy has it up to his eyeballs, even the Doctor was surprised he wasn't dead yet, an he's killed enough niggers to know a dead one when he see one.'

'Faith, Mr McVeigh, faith, and the commitment to the

advancement of American science and technology. Take this as a challenge, not a catastrophe, a birthday present to the Federal Drug Administration.'

Bobby Joe took a syringe from the pocket of his kaftan, saluted the morning with the golden arch of its spray, then inserted it into the inert arm of the man slouched in the wheelchair. Bob Marley's eyelids opened to reveal dilated pupils in an expanse of polished glass, his head nodded sagely and his limbs began to jerk.

'Welcome back, Mr Marley, or shall I call you "Rabiu", "Robert", "John" or . . .' he paused and laughed and the others roared in chorus. 'Mr McVeigh and you, Kola and Pius, the procedure requires that the confession be witnessed by me as the supervising officer and three others, of which at least two must have grandparents born and bred in this country. Is that clear?'

'Yes, sir.'

'If any one of you have reasons why this confession should not proceed, speak now.'

When they remained silent he pulled up a chair in front of Bob Marley who was still nodding and jerking, smiled, and extracted three sheets of typewritten foolscap paper from the file, swinging his pipe from side to side so as to speak from both corners of his mouth.

'If you're unable to speak, Decree 419 allows for answers to be indicated by gestures, winks, nods, nudges or movements of the hands. The beauty of this legal instrument is its respect of commonsense: "here silence shall mean consent".' Then the Pipe Man proceeded to read the document in the special English of the Voice of America, pausing at the end of each paragraph to ensure that the confessor understood and nodded in consent.

ODERINT DUM METUANT

TRUE CONFESSION

THIS IS THE TRUE confession of Rabiu Nafiu, alias 'Bob Marley', alias 'Robert Nesta', alias 'John Lennon'. I confirm that I am of sound mind and understand the spirit of Decree 419.

Although I was born of a good family with every prospect of amounting to something and contributing my penny's worth to the society which made it possible for me to prosper I was led astray from an early age into betraying the values of my family, my religion, my country and Commander-in-Chief.

I have a beautiful, submissive and obedient wife who loves me and blessed me with two beautiful children, a boy and girl, with another on the way, but instead of thanking my Creator and Commander-in-Chief for these blessings, I have, with great ingratitude, neglected my family and showed disloyalty to my Benefactors.

I now recognize that Communism, Islamic Fundamentalism and all the other foreign ideologies which led me astray and which I slavishly followed from the time I was an impressionable adolescent, far from being panaceas for the nation's ills, are evil doctrines which destroy virtue, promote vice and undermine decency, obedience and good faith of vulnerable young people like myself.

In his book, *The God that Failed*, volume thirty-three of the abridged Autobiography written by Andrew Martian, General Daudu, the great Niagran Patriot explained how Communism, Al-Qaedaism and other atheistic ideologies had destroyed the nation's faith in him and thus brought its economy to the brink of collapse. The Niagran armed forces had also been demoralized and lost its *esprit de corps* and sense of mission by renegade elements which refused to obey his orders.

I apologize unreservedly to my Commander-in-Chief for the part I played in these nefarious activities which I now recognize as a disgrace to God, the Authorities and the Unique Miracle of all Time. I apologize for the minds of all the people I poisoned with my 'writings' in the *Sentinel*, *Red Bull*, and other publications which should have borne a health warning because they have the mark of the beast.

My role in the recent uprising against my Commander-in-Chief is established beyond reasonable doubt as defined in Decree 419. I was recruited to this foul purpose by the renegade traitor, the late Ahmed Abdullahi, who bought subversive books for my wife and paints and brushes which I used to create forbidden images which tended to show General Daudu in a bad light, undermine his dignity, question his wisdom and detract from his prestige.

This Evil Genius also opened an account in my name at the HSBC which was used to finance the recent coup attempt, including the PR battle spearheaded by the Australian journalist James Bulger, who writes slanders against Niagra and her Commander-in-Chief for the *Daily Mirror*, a front paper for the National Communist Party of Great Britain.

Using the paints, brushes and canvas supplied by the Arch Traitor, Ahmed Abdullahi, I resurrected the village of Lidiziam which, according to Decree 1941 of 23 August, had officially ceased to exist. I now recognize that this evil act was designed to spread disaffection among the people, bring the Authorities into disrepute and scare away tourists and American investment in the oil industry.

For all these acts of treason against the State, the Nation, the Commander-in-Chief and the Attorney General of the Federation I hereby plead guilty to the following offences as defined in the preamble to Decree 419:

1. Subversion
2. Aggravated Treason

3. War Against the State
4. Spreading Disaffection and Disrepute
5. Questioning the Authority of the Military Government
6. Revealing State Secrets to Foreigners
7. Being an Agent to Foreign Powers
8. Undermining Virtue and Promoting Vice
9. Bringing General Daudu and his family into disrepute, and
10. Disturbing relations with friendly foreign powers.

I fully understand that all these crimes carry the death penalty and take full responsibility for committing them, absolving the government from liability in any future mass action suit filed by American human rights lawyers.

I swear by Almighty God that all the above admissions were freely made by me and are the Truth, the Whole Truth and Nothing but the Truth, so help me God.

Rabiu Nafiu, aka . . .

The Pipe Man rested the paper, patted it with satisfaction, then blew smoke redolent of John Denver's ballad to West Virginia's Blue Ridge mountains over it. 'Satisfied, Mr Marley, sir?' Bob Marley's body was still nodding and jerking and he took this as a YES!

EASY RIDER

'Hold tight, Comrade,' the man called Isaac said. In his white kaftan, ragged blue sweater and cheap plastic shoes he looked like a typical *okada* driver.

'I'm okay, Comrade,' Rabiu said, adjusting his buttocks to sit more comfortably on the mangled seat of the old Vespa which bumped like a rodeo donkey on the path.

'Maybe it's okay for you, sir, but Comrade Jaja ordered me to take care of you. What I said about his not daring to shoot me was a joke. If anything happens to you I'll continue riding when I get to the Nigerian border. If you've seen *Pulp Fiction*, the Comrade quotes Ezekiel 25:17 with far more conviction than Samuel Jackson. And then there's your wife Kikelomo, the only person I know who makes my master quake. He said to make sure you're alright or she would pursue him like the Yoruba goddess of doom to the farthest reaches of the universe. So, *please* hold tight, sir.'

'I'm sorry, Comrade, it's just that I didn't want to hurt you by holding too tight on this track. Where did you go to school?'

'Same as you, Comrade, I studied French and was well into my Honours thesis on the *Poetry and Politics of Aimé Césaire* when they expelled us for demonstrating against

Cheney, the CEO of Halliburton, when he came to discuss resuming oil exploration in Lidiziam with the General. "John Lennon" had written in *Red Bull* about the secret visit, published the full agenda and the fact that when the man was in government he'd opposed sanctions against apartheid and the release of Nelson Mandela, supposedly saying they should *"hang the fucking nigger"*. And he supported terrorist movements like UNITA, the FLNA, FLEC, Inkatha and Renamo. We were the lucky ones, twelve of our late colleagues were not. We were inspired by your uncle, Mallam Aminu, his late son Nuhu, Dr Solomon, Comrade Ahmed and your wife. Knowing the role your father plays in the regime we also thought you were the classical example of Cabral's idea of *class suicide,* we admired your courage. Comrade Jaja and his master Comrade Ahmed put us up in your wife's old house and paid us to teach the street kids to read, write and do basic arithmetic, as well as organize to defend themselves.'

Isaac fell silent and Rabiu could think of nothing to say as he tried without success to get even an inkling of where they were going. They were travelling without lights, the flickering points of stars serving only to accentuate the darkness and the vast emptiness of the sky. Sometimes a tree appeared suddenly and he thought Isaac would have nothing to fear from Jaja or Kikelomo because neither of them would make it. From the blurs and shadows of the branches overhanging the track terrible squawks and screeches of unseen birds disturbed by the uneven drone of the Vespa shook the air out of which mirages from his past floated in swirls of memories carved from the dust.

He could not have found his way walking in the gloom and wondered how Isaac was able to drive the machine at thirty miles an hour. Although he hated stereotypes he thought this might be the reason they called people from his area 'Hawkeyes' or 'Cat People' because they were able to see in the dark. Rumour had it that the reason the oil majors had been unable to start operations in Lidiziam

was the ability of the people to creep up on the American
and British Special Forces in the dark and slit their throats
– despite the foreigners' hi-tech night vision equipment.

How could he explain to the Comrade that the reason
he was reluctant to hold him tight was that he knew his
father's role in the destruction of his village and people?
As a politically conscious cadre of the only surviving
authentic Marxist-Leninist Party on the Continent, he
should be able to overcome personal prejudice and see
things objectively but could never see himself being so
solicitous for the life and welfare of a man whose father
had been responsible for the slaughter of 2,384 members
of his extended family. Jaja was undoubtedly right to blame
Jerry Gotchakka and Joseph Mammamia for their version
of the 'Final Solution', but knowing Daudu, he would never
approve such an important operation without consulting
his closest friend, the Attorney General, the 'Amuz Rock'
of his regime.

A decision to lay waste a whole village, destroy everything in it and then to poison the land and waters so
nothing could ever live in it again smacked of his father's
compulsion to be perfect, totalitarian thinking, his God
complex, self-righteousness, absence of self doubt and the
relentless pursuit of his enemies, alive or dead. He remembered as a child running to his mother after his first lesson
in Koranic school shouting, 'The Mallam was talking about
Baba.' As the teacher described the attributes of the
Creator, citing the Koran and Old Testament, the picture
emerged of a tall, upright, all-knowing, omnipresent,
violent, vengeful, vindictive and remorseless man, who
thought he could do no wrong.

His father was *God*! When his mother understood the
enormity of what he was saying she burst into tears,
washed out his mouth with carbolic soap and Listerine
mouthwash and began chanting verses from the Koran to
guard against Allah's retribution for this act of blasphemy.
The fact that he was too young to know what he was saying

was even more serious: *it meant Satan had entered the mind of the child and made him mouth the abomination that a mere man could equal the glory of his Creator*. So she sat him down and warned him that she would die if he ever repeated what he said of his father. And to make doubly sure she had paid the Mallam $100 to pray for the sanctity of his soul and purchased an amulet from the marabout who, at her husband's suggestion, the General had brought from Noudadhibou at colossal public expense to help cure his piles. But despite Rabiu's promise to his mother, which he had sworn long before he reached the age of swearing, the more he read the books of the Jews, Christians and Moslems, the more he saw God in the actions of his father.

Adam, Eve, Job, the Egyptians, Persians, Moabites, Hittites, Ammonites, Philistines and all the men and women He had condemned to pain, suffering and destruction were His creatures whose destinies He had known from all eternity and hence was responsible for their actions, but still they were punished for their 'sins' of disobedience. How could a creature as puny as man be guilty of disobedience to an Omnipotent and Omniscient Master? Millennia before Hitler and the Likud God had sanctified collective punishment against innocent men, women and children, 'smiting' them alongside the 'guilty' who asserted their God-given individuality against an Unforgiving Creator who told man that individuality was his or her defining characteristic.

His father had sentenced the people of Lidiziam to the same fate that God had inflicted on Sodom and Gomorrah and inflicted unspeakable cruelties on his own daughter as God had inflicted on the Prophet Isa. But God had belatedly taken responsibility for his handiwork and, in the doctrine of the Christians, had even recognized his 'Son' as God and raised him up to the right hand of His Father. Like the father in *Chinatown*, God appeared to love the creatures he had made to suffer, sought to make amends through acts of restitution. On the cross Jesus had cried out to the Father who had forsaken Him by preferring common thieves but was rewarded for his suffering by being recognized as the Saviour of Mankind.

Where was his sister now? For years he had heard her crying but her only reward had been to be expelled into the exterior darkness because of the sins of *her* father. Where was his father's child/grandchild now, his own brother/sister or nephew/niece? The Attorney General would not recognize them and, if he did, would probably draft a decree to punish them for defaming his image and subverting the Majesty of the Law. He himself could meet his sister's child and not know him/her from a stranger. What was it Tom Wolfe had said in *Look Homeward Angel*? In the biting cold of the wind and dust and insects on the sputtering Vespa he felt the words he thought he had forgotten on those long, lonely nights when alcohol and marijuana had not been able to obliterate the image of his lost, beloved sister and her unknown child: *'which of us has known his brother, which of us has looked into his father's heart? Which of us has not remained forever prison-pent? Which of us is not forever a stranger and alone?'*

Like his father the Americans also suffered from this divine *hubris*, absolute self-righteousness combined with absolute power and lack of self-knowledge. It was not true that absolute power corrupts – God, the Americans and his Father could have used their power for good if they had been honest and enlightened. Instead power and hypocrisy had blinded them, rendered them cruel, remorseless and machine-like, capable of the most bestial megalomania, like the plagues on innocent Egyptians, the genocide of Native Americans and the slaughter of Lidiziam.

He had often wondered at the close friendship between his father, who hated Christians and Westerners, and Mr Armitage, the Honorary Consul, the transplanted Texan who regarded Moslems, Blacks and Arabs as vermin. The American worshipped the Attorney General's 'formidable intellect', his triumphs at Harvard Law, his iron will, his appreciation for power, his *reputation for uprightness and incorruptibility*. When Burton Holly had a legal problem Armitage never bothered with expensive partners at Baker and Botts, whose CEO he claimed was a slimeball for bribing the referee in the Yale/Princeton game, but strolled over to his friend, the 'Legal Eagle' where, between musings on the importance of family values, the affinities between Islam and Puritanism, Penn Warren's *All The King's Men*, or a bowl of millet porridge, he would deliver a judgement of magisterial clarity and authority.

When Armitage wanted to marry a nomadic Fulani (*Bororo*) woman from Niger, who had accompanied her father when he came to work as a watchman at Armitage's house, it was his friend who made all the arrangements, riding his white horse deep into the Sahelian bush to negotiate how many cows, bags of millet, salt, sugar, pieces of cloth, big embroidered gowns, CFA francs, sets of jewellery and shoelaces had to be given as dowry. And as a good friend and *Toronkawa* Fulani himself, Nafiu Saleh paid all. After the success of his friends, the Chairman of Burton Holly and the President of the United States, Armitage could never return home where his failure would be magnified, but was made to feel at home by this man of such comprehensive authority and compassion he could have faced his maker without blinking.

The Vespa hit a branch in the road and as the wheels twisted Rabiu tensed his body for the fall. But Isaac rose on the seat, rode the bucking motion and kept them upright. The rough cotton gown he wore had let in the wind and dust and cold but by holding so tight to the comrade he felt the cold beads of sweat slide down through the dust on his cheeks like tears in new rain. Isaac had come with a complete set of faded, dirty grey, local cotton clothes like those of a petty trader crossing the border to buy soap, sugar and Maggi cubes in neighbouring Nigeria. Rabiu had surrendered his own clothes and been teased by Jaja who said fifty-five-year-old small-scale smugglers would hardly wear Calvin Klein boxer shorts or Church brogues, especially since the latter company had been taken over by Prada! The clothes, including the local underpants, had the musty, sweat-stale smell and feel of having been slept in over long periods and journeys. Another courier would take his clothes and some foreign currency across while, tied around his waist under his clothes, as would be expected of a petty smuggler, was a money belt with 20,000 Niagran dollars. A comrade was waiting across the border with the ticket from International PEN, the writers' organization.

When he came out from hiding under the floor he had tried to brush off the termite dust but Jaja said to leave it as it added at least ten years to his age. With the dust, insects and eroding wind whistling past the Vespa, Rabiu's only worry was that the American Special Forces and State Security men on both sides of the border would doubt that a man so old would still be plying his trade! He constantly thought of Kikelomo but never worried about her or their children. Kikelomo could take care of herself and all around her. With her around his father would never have got away with what he did to Aishetu and his sister would now be happily married with a whole gang of nieces and nephews for him to pet because she had longed for children ever since they made wonderful Giacometti-type dolls from pale straw which they dyed with henna.

He had often wondered, even worried about Fatima's almost dog-like devotion to his wife, her willingness to betray her husband and his most intimate secrets which helped to undermine the odious regime of his beloved master. Once, she had driven herself to their house in her Honda Celica looking all dishevelled, her eyes red with tears and bleeding from her mouth and nose. After hugging and kissing her, Kikelomo told him to fetch warm water and a towel to tend to her friend's wounds. Then she took the keys to the Celica and drove off.

Fatima was the daughter of a powerful chief in neighbouring Nigeria. Her father had sent her to the famous girls' school across the border because she was bright and rebellious, having refused to marry a tributary chief, her first cousin, whose children were her best friends. As a lonely fifteen-year-old she moped around, homesick, lonely, unable to concentrate and with a poor appetite. But it was when loneliness turned to depression that her classmate, one year her senior, noticed her.

Fatima confessed all the problems she was suffering from: a family which blamed her for 'disgracing' them, a strange school to which she had transferred at her age, a strange country with different customs and diet and no close friend. But these paled beside Dr Kunle Obofumi, their Nigerian Latin teacher, who said he would *fuck her even if she shut her pussy with superglue*. Rabiu could still see the hurt and anguish in her telling as he massaged her face. All the excuses – that she was a virgin, had a fiancé back home, a genital deformity which mutilated uncircumcised penises, a father who castrated and impaled child molesters as her ancestors did in the old days, or was a girlfriend of the head of State Security, a certified psychopath, Elvis impersonator, manic depressive and sadist, only excited him more. He kept calling her to his office, threatened her with expulsion if she refused to come, abused her people for marrying their close relations when she slapped his hands away from her breasts, and bruised her wrists when he held and tried to kiss her.

When she went with Kikelomo to confront the man tears flowed down his cheeks as he laughed and laughed, telling them he would *make a nice cunt sandwich by fucking them both at the same time*. When a shocked Fatima burst into tears, Kike told her to dry her eyes, took her by the hand and led her out of the office. The man had a wife from Ulster, a secretary who had paid his school fees when he was a student at North Bank Polytechnic and tried to impress his Niagran colleagues with a Mrs Slocombe accent straight out of *Are You Being Served?* Kikelomo took Fatima directly to the Administration Building where the woman worked, told her about her disgusting husband, then plotted his humiliation.

Expatriate friends had told her about seeing her husband's car outside the girls' hostels and Paradise Hotel but she always dismissed them as frustrated English spinsters jealous of her handsome and athletic husband who coached the school volleyball team and could give it to her *six* times a night except on Sundays when they fucked all day. But these girls were young, gorgeous and seemed capable of throwing her through the second floor window if she messed with them. So they planned that Fatima return to Obofumi's office, face tear-stained and full of remorse, to apologize for her lack of manners in refusing the requests of an elder and the atrocious behaviour of her thuggish friend who had had the temerity to call him a *dried up piece of dog shit child molester who picked on little girls because his dick was so shrunken from screwing old men for money he couldn't satisfy his white slut of a wife who was getting it from the cook and garden boy.* Confronted with her fragile beauty, the Latin teacher made an appointment for that night because he feared he couldn't hold it in longer.

At the seedy hotel Fatima begged him to turn off the light and let her wait outside until he undressed because she was too shy, having not done it before, and fearing she might faint as her friends told her he had such an enormous cock. When he called to say he was ready his voice was so choked with emotion he began to cough and he was almost retching when the three women rushed him in the dark and began tearing into him with *bulalas*, the rawhide whips soldiers used to torture demonstrators, called 'bull pricks' because of their shape and capacity to hurt.

Dr Obofumi's people had a reputation for being superstitious and he felt convinced now that the girl was a spirit as he had long suspected because mere humans could not be as bewitching as she and her insane friend. How else could she be hitting him with six different hands, the blows coming from every conceivable angle but landing unerringly on his prick? He fainted when they turned on the light and he saw his wife with the same look on her face as when she climaxed and screamed, '*Dr Paisley forever! No Surrender to the IRA!*' He did not see when they left with his clothes and locked him in.

Shortly after, his wife divorced him and he returned to Nigeria where he now heads a women's charity funded by the UNDP and the Scandinavian governments to fight against HIV/AIDS, child prostitution and genital mutilation. [Editor's Note: Dr Obofumi has now won election to the Nigerian Senate and heads the committee to promote women's affairs.]

When Kike returned she was smiling grimly and, as Fatima rushed to embrace her, she gave her what appeared to be a jam jar wrapped in yesterday's *Sentinel*, threw the keys on the centre table, and whispered, '*He'll never lay hands on you again.*'

'Almost there,' Isaac said, 'remember, don't *look* fifty-five, *be* fifty-five, more if you can make it. And *be* as submissive, servile, subservient and pathetic as you can. The Special Forces and State Security guys are animals, predators who can smell fear but also pride, courage, bravado, intelligence, wit, decency, power and resistance. To convince them how low you are think of wallowing in dog shit, sleeping with a mad woman as some of our rich men do at the behest of sorcerers. Think of working twenty-hour days in the Lone Star mines, being pissed on by American Marines, answering "yessah!" to Mr Armitage and the General's degenerate acolytes. Put yourself in my place and think what the Hanging Judge would do to such a worm.'

What would a proud woman like Kike do in such a situation where she had to become all she was not and had never been? How would such a beautiful princess who conquered all that was in her way, turn into a frog to jump on the orders of those gnats she hated and despised? He knew and loved his Kike and knew she would do what had to be done, would stoop to the enemy to sink her teeth into his groin and shrink into herself to leave space for her bloated opponents to burst themselves on the spear-points of their hubris. She knew well the art of Sun Wu-Tzu to win the most glorious victories without a fight. So demeaning himself was a triumph.

When the Vespa stopped Rabiu's body and mind were so numb he was hunched over, covered in dirt and insects, his hair and eyebrows grey under the hand-woven bonnet the nomadic Fulani wore and he had so absorbed the lessons Jaja and Isaac had drilled into him that he felt a very unhealthy seventy-five, with shallow breathing, swollen prostate, stiff joints, trembling hands and feet shaking in his cheap plastic shoes. But the tremor was what would be expected from a man as low as himself in the political food chain. When the State Security man and their Special Forces handler came into view he did not allow himself to see them but kept his eyes so low on the ground they could crush them beneath their heels if they so wished. He did not need to look up to see the giant billboard on the Niagran side with YOU ARE NOW LEAVING THE GREATEST BLACK COUNTRY ON EARTH!

He also knew that on the Nigerian side was an even bigger sign with YOU ARE NOW ENTERING THE GREATEST COUNTRY ON EARTH!!

He felt exalted, almost euphoric, in his lowliness.

APOCALYPSE NOW:
JUDGEMENT DAY

'*Get these men out of my court!*' The words shot out like
a hurricane on a day of majestic calm when even the
finest hair on a new vine would fear to tremble lest some
avenging god of the weather condemned it for *lèse majesté*.
Weary journalists witnessing the final stage of the latest
military tribunal looked up from their notebooks, their
biros frozen above blank pages; guards armed with Uzis
and MI6s tightened their grips on the triggers, faces
creased in expectation; and even the convicts awaiting
judgement tensed flayed, pierced, aching, broken, torn,
wounded, burnt limbs at this outburst which had the
impact of God bypassing the tablets of stone and ordering
Moses to tell the Israelites by megaphone to *stop pissing
Him off*.

Justice Nafiu Saleh was not the type of man to shout
and regarded a raised voice in his court as an act of sacrilege heinous as blasphemy, treason, presumption or forni-
cation. Convicts appearing before him were coached by
lawyers to whisper and be *asked* to 'speak up' rather than
talk loudly and have their predetermined sentences
doubled for contempt. They themselves were coached in
the Niagran Law School on procedures when appearing
before his tribunals: no eye contact with His Honour;

correct declension of the head, beginning at the shoulders; limited hand movement; correct titles for even the
most minor officials; wig smaller than the Judge's; black
shoes polished to such a shine you could check your wig
and gown in them. But to make doubly sure, there were
huge mirrors at strategic points so that transgressors who
provoked the wrath of His Honour with a sleeve wider
than the regulations permitted would not be tempted into
the even more incriminating offence of admitting *they
were ignorant of the law*.

Now here he sat in his disturbed majesty, thunder and
lightning shooting from his brow, showing the uninitiated
just why he was called 'Chicken Hawk' and the 'Justice
Sandra Day O'Connor' of the Niagran Bench. His achievements at the Harvard Law School and his definitive contributions on Military Tribunals and Natural Justice to its
Journal had established him as a Legal Eagle, with his
eagle's beak like the prow of some ancient galleon riding
loftily on an ocean of horsehair. Of course the danger of
metaphors, similes and all other forms of analogical
thinking should be obvious to all but the thickest, truly
major-league asshole among you. There *was* a big difference between the chicken hawk and the Judge: for the
most part the chicken hadn't the slightest clue about what
was about to hit it, while convicts knew full well, but
knew equally they *could not do a fucking thing about it*.

So who yanked the chain of this man who famously
announced to a panel of the Bar Association with the
temerity to challenge his ruling that 'Judgement is Mine'?
Although the American Special Forces had handed over
Bob Marley to the Niagrans they were requested to accompany him to the tribunal to administer the Donny
Rumsfeld to keep him alive until he was sentenced to
death in accordance with article 69 of Decree 419. But
no one had bothered to brief Billy Bob and Bobby Joe
about the sartorial etiquette of Justice Saleh's court, which
most definitely did not include Tampa Bay Buccaneer

t-shirts, torn jeans, white Air Jordan trainers with red and blue *swoosh*, shampooed beards, sweat bands, floral ribbons in the hair, or trailing earpieces of Walkmans percolating the simian twang of 'Don't Look Up My Skirt / Unless You're Serious'.

After a relatively restrained, '*Who are these men?*' the Pipe Smoker had approached the Bench with sufficient deference, holding his unlit pipe in his hand and whispering to His Lordship that this breach of protocol was necessitated by the requirements of National Security and the beautifully crafted article 69 of Decree 419 that the convict be kept alive until sentenced to die thus preserving His Court's power of life and death. Somewhat mollified by the deference of one who showed the consciousness of his own inferiority the Judge made the kind suggestion that these requirements could be met by the scruffy individuals handing their elixir of life to properly attired Niagrans and getting the hell out of His Court. But here Billy Bob blotted his copy book by approaching the Bench *without permission* and *murdering* the Queen's English right there in the Court of a Man whose prose had been described as the 'Platonic form of economy in legal drafting' by none other than the editor of the *Harvard Law Review*.

'No can do, yo Honah, this is a classified Amhurrican drug, can't hand it over to no furriner.'

Contrary to popular opinion that the Judge lacked a sense of humour, Justice Nafiu Saleh, within the limits of judicial propriety and Islamic jurisprudence, often squeezed in what could, by the more discerning aficionado of legal nicety, pass for a joke. Rather than dismiss the hirsute young man as a 'redneck', 'cracker', 'infidel', 'American' or 'imbecile', and sentence him to twenty years' hard labour for contempt, he constructed an amalgam of comedy and law which could serve as a precedent for future forensic jurists in *Law and Order*.

'I'm sorry, young man, as *you* are the foreigners here,

you *must* hand over your drug to a Niagran officer who has had the courtesy to dress properly for My Court.' (His friend Mr Armitage was in court on behalf of the State Department to ensure that Justice was seen to be done, but didn't count as he was a honorary citizen married to a woman with more tattoos than Ozzy Osbourne.)

According to a Sun Wu-Tzu lookalike in a Shanghai game show, 'There is a fine line between stubbornness and stupidity which the unbright, for very obvious reasons, cannot recognize.' Without rushing to judgement on the delightful Billy Bob, the unbiased observer could conclude that he had come very close to this line, if he had not already crossed it. But Justice Saleh was the Judge, and when Billy Bob said: 'What'd the nigger say?' it was clear he could not be allowed to cross back over. 'Take this man out and shoot him then bring him back so I can sentence him to death!' the Justice screamed at his orderlies.

This explosive situation (literally since the Niagran soldiers competed with their American counterparts to see how many RPGs they could fit between hip and shoulder) was saved by the Honorary Consul who rushed to placate his friend by pointing out that not *all* Americans had the benefit of a Yale undergraduate education, memberships of DKE and Skull and Bones, plus a masters from Harvard Business School, and so could not be held to the same standards of civilized conduct as the President, the finest Judicial Brain in the world and his humble self. Then in true diplomatic fashion he approached the offending citizen of Mobile, and explained in his most avuncular tone that these were *friendly* foreigners and thus almost as good as Americans. He should therefore apologize most humbly to the Justice Sandra Day O'Connor of his nation's judiciary.

After which the Judge uttered the immortal words at the beginning of this chapter.

The men in question having been got out of his court,

the good Judge then turned his formidable attention to the Pipe Man and the convict whose custody appeared to have been handed over to him. At the outset it should be stressed that his Worship did not approve of this man. In all his perusal of scriptural and judicial texts he had never discovered a precedent for a man allowed to keep a pipe in his mouth, even if he did not actually inhale, at a tribunal of such importance, where the guilt of convicts was confirmed beyond reasonable doubt. But alas matters were never as simple as this.

Remember the paradox of Epimenides the Cretan who said that all Cretans were liars? If this statement is true – the brighter of you will get my drift here. . . . Our Judge faces the same dilemma: *how could he, the Judicial Authority who had established the C-in-C as Legally Infallible, ban the Pipe Man from his court when the Man with the Pipe billboard was General Daudu's favourite ad, a cornerstone of his business empire, starring his beloved younger brother?*

So his judicial solution was the Solomonic/Clausewitzian/ Maoist displacement of judicial targeting by humiliating the fucking Pipe Smoker *by other means.* 'Why is this convict not shackled to the others and why is he allowed to insult the dignity of My Court and the authority of My Commander-in-Chief by slouching in this unmanly manner?'

The Pipe Man made the judicial error of opening his mouth to answer the Judge's question and was slapped down with furious rebukes.

'Get this convict upright and shackled with his co-conspirators in the dock or join them yourself, *do you hear me?*'

Quicker than it takes to say 'round up the usual suspects' Pius and Kola had grabbed Bob Marley on either side and the Pipe Man, after displaying the compulsory golden arch from the syringe, pumped him full of the Donny Rumsfeld. Shackled between a hefty Lance

Corporal and a weedy Lt Colonel, Bob Marley nodded vigorously to the rhythm of the yellow molecules.

After his two hour summary of Decree 419 the Judge received the bound volume of his judgement from an orderly who had held it gingerly throughout, like Moses with the stone tablets, as if awed by the feel and smell of expensive leather. For the Westerner brought up in the unruly atmosphere of the courts where lawyers were allowed to talk through their assholes, the court of Judge Saleh was a breath of fresh air. Like a Japanese kabuki play nothing was left to chance, each person knew his role, every syllable was arranged in its ordered place.

Almighty God who is Omnipotent and Omniscient had created the world and all that was in it and knew from the beginning of time what would be when the final trumpet sounded and Judgement was passed upon the unbelievers and unworthy. To think that a man could change what God had ordained was an act of blasphemy and treason. Since the General could not rule without the Authority of the Most High it meant that his Acts were the Law and those who deviated would be called to Judgement and condemned. He, Justice Nafiu Saleh, was His mere instrument whose task was to see that God's will and the General's prevailed. Arguments for both prosecution and defence were, therefore, vetted by him before being bound, and it was his duty, ordained by the Most High, to ensure that confessions were in accordance with His Law.

Although Justice Saleh, like his neo-con friends in America, did not believe in Mr Darwin and his evolutionary horseshit, his military law did not spring full blown from the *Harvard Law Review*. After cleansing the country of the atheistic government of Murtala Aminu, Mr Richard Burton, recognizing the importance of government based on the rule of Law, had commissioned a future Supreme Court Justice to draft a Fundamental Military Law whose only drawbacks were secularism and imprecision.

Depriving itself of Divine status opened Military Law to potential challenge while imprecision meant that it was theoretically possible for an accused to be 'proved' innocent. Which came to pass in spectacular fashion when several enemies of the state escaped judgement and fled to the United Kingdom where they were feted in the *Guardian* and *Voice* newspapers, allowed to prattle on the *Today* programme and the World Service, and to hang out with promiscuous atheists such as Lord Avebury, Michael Mansfield, Tony Gifford, Helena Kennedy and Eddie the Eagle.

Luckily for the nation and the Burton Holly Corporation this gowned crusader had flown to the rescue with arguments from Saudi Arabia, Pakistan, Sudan and Afghanistan to plug the legal loopholes and make Niagran Military Law the template of what would later fry the assholes in Guantanamo Bay. And discovery of even more oil off the coast of Lidiziam persuaded their British hosts to transport them to the Central African Empire where the Emperor Bokassa had them for some delightful breakfasts, lunches and gourmet dinners.

As he read the verdicts of guilty and the sentences of death without the right of appeal, he was buoyed by Bob Marley's nods of approval, which showed a precocious judicial sensitivity in one so young. But when he came to Bob Marley, the 'convict of a thousand aliases, the engine room of the revolution, etc. etc. etc . . .' his mien changed abruptly from the patriarchal look of Ibrahim and Musa to the vituperative wrath of Leviticus and Ezekiel, as he questioned the sincerity of the nodder, wondering whether it was a cynical but futile ploy for mitigation of his mandatory death sentences. 'The youth of today!' he sighed to himself. 'Will the convict Bob Marley please stand?'

Since Bob Marley could not even sit, his perceptive neighbours lifted him up and kept him in place as the Judge read his 'confession' and sentence from the volume whose new leather smell reminded General Assizer, his military assistant, of McAfee's, the little shop in Knights-bridge where he used to buy his boots until the anarchy of Thatcherism forced it out of business. Now not even the vastly more expensive hand-lasted products of Lobb, Berlutti and Swayne & Adeney could provide him with such comfort by accommodating the bunion on the joint of his left big toe.

Suddenly Assizer was distracted from the pain of his bunion by the dramatic pause of His Honour, who closed his book of judgement, removed his pince-nez, looked down at the polished Brazilian mahogany of his table and appeared in genuine distress. The consternation of the members of his panel was shared by all in the court except Bob Marley who appeared spaced out. One should remember that this was the original 'Iron Man', the regime's 'Amuz Rock', to whom emotion was as alien as deviance, sex or mercy. As the Guardian of Justice this was a weakness he could not afford. Did the Prophet Suleiman show emotion when he judged his people? Did Hitler allow himself to falter with pity or regret when he had to do what was necessary to solve the Jewish Problem? But clearly there were matters of far more serious import, capable of breaking the iron in a man, undermining his resolve and reducing him to the weak will and emotional flabbiness of feminized, western, secular man.

But here was the Iron Judge apparently so reduced, and even the hardest hearted convict must have been moved by the vision of the Amuz Rock near tears, as if some Evil Genius had slipped a tube full of Kryptonite up his Judicial Ass. Then, with superhuman effort, he pulled himself together and with great dignity proclaimed:

'All decent people in this room know the depths to which the convicts on trial here have sunk in depravity and degeneration, breaking their most sacred duties and obligations to their God and Commander-in-Chief. They have betrayed loyalties, oaths of obedience, patriotism, the dictates of religion, commitments to their families, and refused to avoid sexual deviance, promote virtue or give tithes to the poor. They have wantonly raised their hands against the Commander-in-Chief and, because the duty of obedience to legally constituted Authority is sacred, against Almighty Allah himself. Most heinous of all they have sought to disrupt relations with our friends overseas ordained by the Almighty.

'None of this, however, compares with the misdeed of one "Bob Marley", the so-called "Man of a Thousand Aliases" and "Engine Room of the Revolution". We all know the damage done to the image of the Commander-in-Chief and our nation through the poisonous words he has pumped out in obscene publications such as *Red Bull* and the foreign-based *Private Eye*, the *Daily Mirror*, *Guardian*, *New Statesman*, the significantly titled *RAPE*, and the so-called *Africa Confidential*. We all know of his dissemination of the evil doctrine of Rastafarianism, which promotes idol worship of Haile Selassie and Bob Marley, ganja smoking, child abuse and blood sacrifice.

'But no one could begin to imagine that a fellow human being would sink to the depths of this young convict you see before you, nodding like an idiot, undoubtedly the result of drug abuse, which the journalists at the back of the room, because of their obsession with liberalism and secularism, blame for the fall in standards of behaviour and civil conduct we see demonstrated in this little happy-go-lucky monster who mocks his impending death with such carefree abandon. While this indifference to his own death may be forgiven by the God Who created us all, however, no one can forgive the vicious attempt this young criminal has made to besmirch the reputation of one of the oldest families in this country.

'As you all know the "Confession" made by the convict and read out in this court is a sacred document, the last will and testament, so to speak, of a man led astray, through which he bequeaths to his God and Commander-in-Chief the Truth of his whole life, action and behaviour. This is an act of exculpation through which he unburdens himself and seeks forgiveness from Divine and Secular Authority, uniquely combined in the Person of His Excellency General Abdu-Salaam bin-Sallah-ud-Deen bin Sani-Ibrahim al-Daudu, the Unique Miracle of the Century. Only the most depraved would eschew this final opportunity to come clean with his soul and seek admission through the golden arches of Paradise, albeit through a side door.

'But did this malevolent wretch, this evil spirit weed, this shrivelled orange peel, this desiccated piece of camel dung, this son of a thousand whores, this so-called "Bob Marley" seize this opportunity with both hands and run with it towards this last chance saloon of Redemption? No!! Instead this unrepentant convict used his sacred confession as a means of defamation of a man from whose sandals he was unworthy to lick the dust, as the Hittite king said to the Pharaoh Rameses II.

'Although the confession is a sacred, legal document, I found myself unable to read the section where he claimed to be "Rabiu Nafiu", in case this act would confer judicial legitimacy on such a libel. As you know, the real Rabiu Nafiu has been led astray by evildoers such as the late Dr Solomon and Lt Colonel Abdullahi, he may have lost his soul to Marxism-Lennonism-Mao-Zedong Thought and married a blaspheming infidel. BUT HE IS MY SON. Now look at this straw of a man, this insult to the creative genius of the Almighty: HOW COULD ANYONE IN HIS RIGHT MIND MISTAKE BOB MARLEY FOR MY ONLY SON?'

The orderlies cocked their guns and prepared to evacuate the court – shooting the convicts and journalists if necessary – in case their master succumbed to his tears. If any of the bastards thought they could get away with a headline like 'WE SAW THE HANGING JUDGE CRY' they'd better fucking think again.

'And for this outrageous final act of blasphemy of claiming to be my son, in addition to the five death sentences already conferred on him, I hereby sentence the convict Bob Marley to a further forty-nine years at hard labour, in solitary confinement, without the possibility of parole.'

Then he noticed that the convict had slumped once more, struck his gavel with such force the shock waves vibrated through General Assizer's bunion as he shouted 'Guards!' and the Disposal Units prepared to fire.

But the Pipe Man's reaction time was superior to that of any orderly, as it should be for a former champion athlete who still worked out in the hi-tech gym of the Lone Star Bakery owned by the Burton Holly Charitable Foundation. He grabbed the two remaining syringes of the urine-yellow drug and, holding one in each hand with the taut screen style of a Clint Eastwood gunslinger, approached Bob Marley. Then, holding them up at the last moment, he sprayed the golden McDonald's arches with the panache of the Archangel Gabriel opening the Gates of Heaven to the multitudes of the Redeemed, or Saddam donating his sword arms to create the Sacred Arch for Don Rumsfeld and Dick Cheney to make their Triumphal Entry into liberated Xanadu.

With the drug inside him Bob Marley had felt like water over a low flame with the molecules in motion but below the threshold of boiling with a low throbbing that could not translate into sound or vision there was the twilight of neither day nor night which was like the screen slashed across his brain as he awaited the latest episode of his nightmare in which he was one with the fleeing victims of Agbani's village shadowed by the locust clouds about to blossom into death. Then he felt the dull jab of the needles in both arms and as the flood of yellow pumped into him he felt himself rising as the screen lit up and suddenly he could see all that was and had ever been and would always be, the men to whom he was shackled who bore him up above the wide expanse of the world, their faces of such clarity he would never need to paint them to let them be, the Pipe Smoker beaming at him with a bright, metallic intensity and the Judge, Master of his rapidly expanding Universe, with the visage of God and all His Avenging Prophets of Old, surrounded by angels in green khaki worried by the swell of bunions and the stench of those about to die.

When they raised him up he was in front of a mirror and for the first time since he was captured he saw what he had become and could not recognize what he saw. His head was bald, the size of a football, and under the power of the drug the memory floated to the surface like dead leaves in a pond of one man holding his neck with his rubber-gloved hand while another broke a Dr Pepper Cola bottle and scraped his head till the blood flowed into his eyes and ears and he was seeing the bare walls with the American flag through a yellow haze and the sound of his screams were lost in Berlin's 'Take My Breath Away' and the prison of his shattered eardrums slowly filling with the unseen fluid and he remembered at the meeting to discuss the painting of the ceiling of the Rock Palace the tall man, Rabiu, who always stared at him strangely, reciting the words of emptiness for Brotherman to put to music:

> In the still corner of an empty room the blind man sings a tale no one can hear, and the Brethren urging him on with 'forge simple words that even children can understand, words that will enter like embers in the people's souls'.

He could remember it all now as the Donny Rumsfeld rose in him, flooding his soul and overflowing into eternity, the images rising on the flood with the lightness of butterfly wings. There was a vision of his mother weeping like new rain on the vines and the rainbow of her face reaching into Paradise to be one with her Beloved Son. But to get to her he had to retrace his steps on the reversing carousel of time through the horrors of the grey steel door four metres wide opening onto a grey corridor without end which led to an underground car park of raw concrete then through another grey steel door onto another passage through a gate made of steel bars onto the final corridor which led to the cells like chicken coops without light or life, black as death or the red blood of the dying and then the screams, the screams which would not end, the whimpering in the night and then the silence of the dead and dying. The blood fell in the darkness like the petals of wild flowers, flowers for the dead, *flores, flores, flores para los muertos*, then there was the water on the stripped-naked ones but there was no healing in this baptism which removed the scabs from the sores so there was no protection when the rats, roaches and mosquitoes came for supper or when the blindingly hot, grit-filled air was flushed into their tired faces and they could not breathe or see when the stabbers came and pierced their genitals with hot knitting needles or the beaters with nail-studded planks hitting their backs and shoulders or the shitmen who emptied the buckets over their heads or the grillers who forced them to stand on hot metal plates or the *dan daudus* who forced Sun bottles up tensed anuses or the rising waters in the cells where the shit floated around the shine of bobbing heads like petals below the bloody graffiti 'Flowers of Evil'. Then he felt a cotton bud in his ear he could not tell if left or right and on the ripple of its soothing sensation the yellow fluid his being had become floated his mother on a sunbeam, her voice golden with the melody of the green mermaid, her hands like solid honey and her odour of crushed orchids. Then all the sensations were compressed into a point without dimensions which when it exploded created the universe of pure sound into which the waters of Lidiziam flowed with their billions of barrels of oil, the waters of all the oceans, of all the solar systems and the galaxies and he was floating through all the dimensions of sound till he felt a hook wide enough to embrace the earth pull him down then fix him to wood and the nails being driven into his wrists and ankles were no more than mosquito bites and a man swearing 'these fucking DFID nail guns are not worth spit' and the ones the Americans used to make their barracks in Lidiziam went right through his flesh like butter and it was the ones from France outsourced to Shanghai that were ideal for the procedure and he felt himself hanging in the sky.

But he was no closer to the rainbow of his mother's face and there was a strange emptiness he was seeing for the first time of the new vine whose yellow bellflowers he would not see on the following Saturday in the house closed for mourning. But the mirror was lying, he could not be what he saw, his face like a balloon with scars all over and his eyes on different levels seeing double, his mouth without teeth and his tongue so swollen it stuck through the split of his upper lip under the nose flattened between the mounds of braised flesh where his cheek bones had been. The thing he saw in the glass was not him, not 'Bob Marley', not the lover of Agbani, the friend of Ahmed and the meat seller. He could not be this rotting vegetable in the absurd suit of green and white with the shackles of grey steel round his neck, hands, waist and ankles, and scores of other men even more battered than himself. Was this distortion from the mirror or his swollen, dislocated eyes?

Then the pressure from the drug rose to a climax and suddenly he could see himself and all he had been as he was and Agbani was embracing him, anointing his head with oil, parting his locks and massaging his scalp before they swam like mermaids in the crystal waters of Lidiziam where the silver fish danced with the reflections of the white lilies of the valley and the rare pygmy antelope crouched over the bank to sip from the liquid ambrosia. This mirror was real, it was big and bright enough to reflect all it saw in proportion, their naked bodies golden in the light of the dying sun which flooded the waters with its radiance and convincing the wild doves that this was a perpetual dawn where they could sing forever and ever. Agbani's love had redeemed him, he was whole again, able to gaze at himself without fear or shame or the distorting mirror they had put before him.

Then she held him in her healing arms and they became one and he felt himself rising and when he was alone again he was above the slope of Nine Mile with the multitudes at Bob Marley's funeral and he gazed down at his friends Ahmed and Dr Solomon, Charlie Bronson, Mr T, Kilimanjaro, the Balloonman, Jairzinho, Harry, Ade and all the other *Outkastes* drifting in the pale smoke of the finest *sensimila* in the world. But he could not save them, nor could he save the souls who from the Beginning he had been destined to paint, to make them *more real than the real, more human than human*. Then he opened his eyes wide enough to all the splendours of the world and there among the endless crowd he could not save he saw his mother calling out to him in songs he could not hear, her eyes beseeching, hands raised toward her brown dove which flew just out of reach as Idi Amin Ogwu gained on her to keep her from him and as in his worst nightmares he found himself frozen as nemesis closed on what he most wanted and he thought he would wake any minute but now the enormous hands were almost embracing her and he knew he would never wake again and had to reach her there and then and he succeeded in slowing time so the space between his mother and those grasping prisons of the giant's arms increased and he felt the lightness of her being as she rose up to him and they were flying, two brown doves, wing tips touching, without hindrance through a cloudless sky toward the sunlit arches of paradise.

First they flew above the canopies of trees bunched like sculpted green sunlight and when they reached the sea they turned right toward the bosom of Africa from whence they came and islands of coral reefs were polished jade encircling the souls of all who had died coming over who joined them now in formation through night made light by soaring fireflies and mornings bright as friendship when the sun rose from beneath the sea. There were white flakes like snow and he thought it was because they were flying so high but when they came closer saw they were petals of the white lilies pouring down from Okontino's tower onto Harry's coffin, onto the massed ranks of Mallam Aminu's followers, onto Kikelomo and Fatima like twin emeralds and Candace hidden in her white shawl of mourning, but he had not seen them then because all the *Outkastes* lay on the coffin insisting they be buried with him since they had died when they could no longer hear his voice until Brotherman played Harry's song and they saw him rise in his white linen suit and he was cradled in his mother's arms as they were lifted radiant and serene into heaven. Then it was there after the petals of white, Africa, the emptiness that was not there, and they were gazing above an endless horizon, brilliant in the freezing sunlight at the entrance to eternal dawn. 'Mother,' he said, 'Mother,' and she dipped her wings and his ears became whole again to hear her say, 'Home at last, my son, we are home at last.'

Bob Marley was so light the men shackled to him on either side could hardly feel his weight but they were aware at the almost imperceptible change when his hands began to chill and strove to exert just that more effort to keep him upright so they would not hang him twice as the executioner had done to Ken Saro-Wiwa in Nigeria. Then with the skill of the contortionist for which his people were famed Lance-Corporal Ito, another survivor of Lidiziam, reached up his twisted, swollen fingers to close Bob Marley's scorched blue lids over unreflective eyeballs, protruding like a dead frog's which no Princess would kiss again.

EYES ON THE PRIZE

'The International Consortium of Investigative Journalists are here tonight to award the Carlos Alberto Cardoso Prize of $50,000 for the journalist who has done most to advance the cause of transparency in government and financial transactions, to expose injustice, corruption and the secret manipulation of power. The man after whom the prize is named was one of us, a journalist in Mozambique who tried to expose the financial dealings of very powerful individuals, which led to the collapse of a bank and serious damage to the stability of the whole national economy. Carlos Alberto Cardoso was brutally murdered, the man arrested for his murder was mysteriously freed, and now, after a national outcry, the trial is underway of cronies of the son of the President for this act of infamy.

'Over the years hundreds of journalists have been murdered for their devotion to the truth, and three of these are competing for this prize posthumously. Norbert Zongo was an investigative journalist from Burkina Faso and editor of the weekly newspaper *L'Indépendant*. He was murdered in 1998 for investigating individuals close to the President, Blaise Campaoré, who himself was implicated in the murder of his immensely popular and charismatic predecessor, Thomas Sankara. His killers were never arrested.

'Igor Aleksandrov was a prominent Ukrainian journalist working for the independent television company Tor. On 3 July 2001 he was beaten with baseball bats as he entered his office and died four days later at the age of forty-five. He was the eleventh Ukrainian journalist to be killed in the last six years and his "offence" was to have produced *Rez Retushi* (Without Censorship), which featured investigative reporting of government corruption and organized crime.

'Another name on the shortlist is that of the late Georgi Gongadze, whose decapitated body was found in a forest near the town of Tarascha in November 2000. He was an outspoken critic of high-level corruption on his internet news site, *Ukrainska Pravda* (Ukrainian Truth), and extremely critical of President Leonid Kuchma and his entourage. The murders of these two heroic journalists remain unsolved because they were killed by those who are in charge of the police and judiciary.

'I am happy to say, however, that our fourth contender is alive and well, though sentenced to death *in absentia* by his own father, the Derry Irvine to the Life President of Niagra. Rabiu Nafiu, writing under the name "Robert Nesta" and other aliases, has laboured to expose the regime, of which his father is the acknowledged *éminence grise,* in his local paper, the *Sentinel,* as well as in *Private Eye, Africa Confdential,* the *Guardian, Review of African Political Economy,* the *Nation, Monthly Review, Liberation* and the *Christian Science Monitor.* His memoir, *Double Trouble,* for which he had a contract with Heinemann, will now be translated and published by the Harvill Press following disagreement concerning the commitment of the former to Africa after its decision to put an end to the African Writers Series started by Chinua Achebe.

'But the prize goes to his wife, Mrs Kikelomo Omolare Rabiu Nafiu who, writing under the pen name "John Lennon" in *Red Bull* and other underground publications, has had, in the opinion of all the judges, the greatest impact on the life of any nation, and this includes such classics as Woodward and Bernstein's *All The President's Men*. Although a mother of two, expecting a third, Kikelomo has found time to expose the financial criminality of a regime described by Transparency International as the most corrupt on earth. In a ground-breaking series of articles in *Africa Confidential* she has unravelled a network of fraud, corruption and money laundering that runs through all the Western capitals, South America, the Middle and Far East, Kenya, the Ivory Coast and Nigeria, accounting for about a third of the $300 billion earned from oil over the past twenty-five years, and now lodged in private bank accounts and off-the-shelf companies. Accompanying lists and diagrams also show the names and nationalities of the companies and executives who bribed Niagran officials and the banks which facilitated their theft despite the laws of their countries which were not enforced.

'To Amnesty she has supplied graphic videos of political prisoners being tortured, as well as a catalogue of the instruments used and their countries of origin. Despite the horrors of the realities she has revealed, Kikelomo has an irrepressible sense of humour which constantly bubbles to the surface. While researching the fate of Niagra's most famous conceptual artist who was imprisoned for making an "inappropriate portrait" of the First Lady, she discovered that many of the seismic maps of deep-sea oil blocs for which the majors had paid billions in signature bonuses had been drawn by the artist on the orders of Nasser Waddadda, General Daudu's Peter Mandelson.

'A nuclear physicist dismissed from the university after complaining of the lack of equipment, he turned to conceptual art based on his knowledge of quantum mechanics and string theory. But he had been detained indefinitely when Andrew Martian, the regime's spokesman and official historian, claimed that the artist had "used minimalist techniques to demean the prestige of the First Lady".

'Kikelomo was also responsible for posting on the internet documents which exposed how the Burton Holly Charitable Foundation used impoverished Niagran Evangelical Christians as guinea pigs to test genetically modified wheat and tilapia in its campaign of 'the Loaves and Fishes' which led to investigations into Burton Holly by a US Congress alarmed by its similarity to the Tuskegee Syphilis Project which still rankles with African-Americans.

'At present she is on the run, pursued by the security forces of Niagra and its major Western allies who blame her for the agitation of young women who are held responsible for preventing the exploitation of the oil fields in the destroyed village of Lidiziam.

'And here to receive the cheque for $50,000 on her behalf is her husband Rabiu Nafiu, aka "Robert Nesta", the journalistic "Bob Marley" of Niagra.'

HOME ALONE

'It's been over two weeks since we last heard from my wife Kikelomo,' Rabiu Nafiu said. 'But wherever she is I know she will be fighting to the end. Street children acting as lookouts near the cave complex where she and her sisters are hiding speak of "toy planes" overflying the area – these we presume are American surveillance drones. They also speak of "bats" flying high, which sound like stealth bombers. We also hear of battle ships from the American base in Equatorial Guinea, whose President promised to rename his capital after Barbara Bush, positioning themselves off the Niagran coast, from which Lidiziam will be in range of cruise missiles, Hawk jets, and F16s. When she hears of this award I'm sure Kikelomo's reaction will be that this is a victory of the Niagran people, for all the mothers whose sons have gone, fighting to make their lives go forward, to make their husbands live up to their duties as partners, to create a better future for their children. She will want the $50,000 to fulfil our dreams of honouring the memories of our sister, brother and mentors, Omolare and Delroy Solomon, by completing the refuge for orphans and battered or abandoned women, which we started building in their names. Kikelomo has never been one to fight for ideas that exist only in the heads of individuals, but is prepared to accept the necessary sacrifices to see that justice is done on this earth. Although we have long given up religion because of the injustices it has been used to foster, you will forgive me if I ask you to pray that she succeeds in her battles, wherever she may be at this moment. Again, I repeat: she will fight to the end.

'To the names of journalists murdered I would also like to add those of Dele Giwa and Bagudu Kaltho in neighbouring Nigeria, with whom we compete to see whose dictator is more corrupt and odious. In 1986 Giwa, editor of the weekly *Newswatch* magazine, was blown up with a parcel bomb following rumours that he was about to expose drug dealings of the family of the dictator, General Ibrahim Babangida. In 1996, during the dictatorship of General Sani Abacha, Kaltho of *Tell* magazine was burnt beyond recognition, allegedly for being caught with a book by Wole Soyinka, the Nobel Laureate, a vocal critic of the regime. The official line was that the reporter was blown up by a bomb he was carrying on behalf of Wole. Heard that one before? Think of Walter Rodney in Guyana, Robert Ouko in Kenya and Delbert Gower and Delroy Solomon in our own country. Without appearing to blow our own trumpet, I must pull rank and claim the prize for dictatorial tackiness for our own *Miracle of the Twentieth Century*. Generals Babangida, Abacha and Abdusalaam are clearly not in the same league as our own General "Danny Boy", who has the finest collection of Elvis memorabilia in the world, and stood up at a White House Reception to sing Lefty Frizzel's "You're Humbugging Me" with such Grand Ole Opry angst it brought tears to the eyes of Presidential *Svengali*, Karl Rove, described affectionately by Colin Powell as "the man with the brillo pad for a heart". Now our two countries are engaged in a ferocious contest to woo the arms and wallets of our almighty American friends. After the Nigerian President offered to rename his country

"Almajiria" after Alma, Colin Powell's wife, General Daudu trumped him by promising to change our own capital to "Buckleyville" to honour Donald Rumsfeld whose favourite grandniece owns a Vietnamese potbellied pig named William F. Buckley Jr.

'Please allow me to complete Andrew Martian's explanation of why the nation's foremost conceptual artist was detained and tortured for his "inappropriate portrait of the First Lady". Inspired by string theory which posits that the universe is made up of vibrations of one dimensional energy "strings" of infinite length the artist was short-listed for the Turner Prize but lost out to Tracy Emin in the finals when the judges could not find the works which, in accordance with the theory, were theoretically "non-existent". According to Martian: "The First Lady approves of the Theory of General Relativity and Quantum Mechanics, and has no objection to the iconography of Bracht, Giacometti and Gaudier-Brzeska. But, like Laura Bush, she thinks that String Theory and Same Sex Marriages are contrary to Morals, Decency and the Right Wing of the Republican Party." [Editor's Note: Allegations that Lord Scraatchy bought the work for £250,000, insured it for £500,000 and then burnt down the warehouse, were left out on legal advice.]

'I must confess that my welcome here has been so warm that I have been tempted to ask for political asylum and join the millions of fellow Africans who were forced to seek a life here because of the depredations of the Mobutus, Amins, Bothas, Bongos, Abachas and Daudus of Africa. At first I woke up in the night sweating because I could not hear the staccato of machine gun bullets and explosions of rocket propelled grenades which the General Disposal Units use to ensure that people here have enough oil to run their debt-fuelled consumer economy of junk food, neon lights, reality TV, expensive appliances and obese people. This passed and then I started to sleep soundly without the fear of Men in Black breaking down my door to serve the death warrant signed by my own father. For entertainment no film or nightclub could beat the thrill of sitting on top of the Number 11 bus and seeing the life of a great city pass by – without the fear of a Prime Ministerial convoy threatening with intimidating sirens to annihilate everything in its way. And walking along the Thames from Chiswick Bridge to Hampton Palace is better than a stroll through Heaven's Gate.

'The British people have been so generous that I cannot believe they elected successive Prime Ministers who sold the General the arms he needed to massacre his own people and threaten his neighbours. Niagran and other African exiles confirm the assistance they have received from people like Baroness Whitaker, Diane Abbott and Lord Avebury. I was even given the opportunity to see my beloved Arsenal defeat Chelsea by a delightful MP called Tony Banks. Imagine my horror when I discovered that this man who looked nothing like a serial killer, lawyer, accountant, real estate agent, Peter Mandelson or a Tory was in fact *a Chelsea supporter*!

'Being among the Niagran communities in Peckham, Haringey and Tottenham is just like being at home and it is with genuine regret that I refuse the offer of women, all of whom have heard of Agbani, Kikelomo and her friend Fatima, to send them pots of fiery *egusi* and *edikang ikong* soup. Their genius in creating a vision of Niagra from the best bits of our country, without the Generals and their First Ladies, keeps hope alive that one day the true, African Niagra of all its peoples will rise again, so that the cleaners, mini-cab drivers and security men with Ph.D.s in biochemistry who toil here will return home.

'Of course these beautiful and sentimental impressions of your country are not the whole story. Yesterday I read in *Africa Confidential* that the General had bought a new toy, a Boeing 767 so luxurious a Saudi

Prince would blanche at the iciness of the solid 22 carat gold Presidential toilet seat, which can't be very kind to Daudu's piles. The plane was purchased through a Liechtenstein-based company set up by the Khadouri brothers for the General and his First Lady to acquire majority shares in a budget airline operating out of Stansted Airport. Although Boeing would have sold the plane for $40 million, with a further $10 million to "configure" it to Presidential standards, the twins bought it through another off-the-shelf International Business Corporation, on which six members of the British Establishment sit as nominee directors, for $150 million.

'Yesterday the editors of *Africa Confidential* and *Private Eye* treated me to lunch at Rules, the Covent Garden restaurant favoured by Charles Dickens, Graham Greene and John Betjeman, then we took the Stansted Express to view the wonder of the gold-plated 767 with the green Presidential seal and bold, black PRESIDENT OF THE FEDERAL REPUBLIC OF NIAGRA. Apparently one of Daudu's daughters by a long-term mistress was marrying a Colonel in the Special Presidential Guard and the Lebanese twins had promised to "organize" some girls for the stag night, which they did with a lunch at their $30 million Chelsea mansion, with food flown in on the Presidential jet from their three Michelin star French restaurant in Xanadu. According to the Curator of the British Library the double fronted mansion houses a collection of pornography which is "probably the finest in the world". The gossip columns of several tabloids reported that the credit cards of the "Protocol" officers from the Niagran embassy almost melted from overuse as the "girls" went on a shopping frenzy at the exclusive boutiques on Sloane Street in Knightsbridge.

'A security man who was a comrade from secondary school escorted us to a vantage point from which we could see why the *Economist Intelligence Unit* had calculated that Niagra spent 7.5 per cent of its GDP on "entertainment", more than its combined budgets for Health, Education and Welfare. Twenty-five brand new Mercedes 600 limousines followed the twins' gold Rolls Royce *Silver Cloud* right up to the tarmac where "Protocol" officers waited to open the doors and BAA porters to unload the Louis Vuitton suitcases which, even at a distance, overwhelmed our senses with the smell of new leather. I heard a gasp of disbelief when the twins emerged in their Francesco Smalto silk ensembles of blinding cerise double-breasted suits, ruffled *eau-de-Nil* shirts with Theo Fennel emerald and ivory cuff links, hand-painted Hermes ties with the iconic image of Marilyn Monroe above the heating grate and square-toed Star Vito Artioli hand-lasted ankle boots, made from purple stained baby alligator skin.

'After the third bottle of St Emilion during lunch I had tried to describe the twins but the editor of *Private Eye*, who had seen all the Batman films, complained that I was taking the piss out of them by describing the Joker played by Jack Nicholson. Even when seen with their own eyes they insisted these were actors going to entertain the General's guests, refusing to believe when told these were barely literate itinerant traders I knew as a boy when they came to beg transport money from my grandfather's palace, which explains why they take their shoes off and make obeisance in my father's presence, while treating the General as an ordinary potentate. I could see the disappointment on Patrick's face when he saw that the men he had written so much about were not evil geniuses but part clown, part pimp, part *parvenu*, and 100 per cent psychopath. Were these the men who allegedly helped Ahmed Chalabi steal $125 million in Amman, invest $500 million of General Daudu's "Pension Fund" in rebuilding Beirut and collar the oil market in Niagra? Or persuaded successive British Prime Ministers to keep supplying fighter jets and military air control systems to a country which banned its own pilots from flying?

'But we all forgot about the twin clowns when the "girls" began to unfurl like petals from the maroon limousines with their identical Louis Vuitton handbags and beauty cases, and platinum Mimi So ankle bracelets with two carat red diamonds. My comrade from the Men in Black had tipped us off to buy all the day's tabloids and we almost came to blows trying to identify from the "exclusives" and gossip columns the Page Three Girls, grade D celebrities, aristocratic "It" girls, surgically enhanced and subtracted "models", footballers' girlfriends, superstars of the X channel, several regulars from *Readers' Wives* and *Asian Babes*, undergraduates reduced to penury by the government's education policy and a Downing Street adviser on Cultural Diversity who hoped to be the first openly declared transvestite in New Labour's modernized House of Lords. They were guaranteed to make this party the Mother of all Stag Nights and the Africa Editor of the *Financial Times* had told us during dinner at the Africa Centre the evening before that the latest development on the Chelsea Embankment had been bought out by a Nauru holding company fronted by the Khadouri twins, so those "girls" who were lucky and hit the jackpot would earn one of the most exclusive addresses in the world for a weekend's work.

'Not all of our national proclivities have these humorous aspects, however. Considering the bestiality of military regimes and their obsession with secrecy, it is surprising that they should meticulously record their crimes. For example, the present Ethiopian leader could pay off his country's debts and abolish future famines if he sold all of General Mengistu Haile Mariam's videos of his "Red" and "White" terrors to the thriving communities of sado-masochistic cannibals, aristocrats, lawyers, estate agents, heavy-metal rock stars, right-wing journalists and neo-conservatives in Western Europe and North America.

'In our own case Niagra has an archive of nearly 30,000 videotapes, record of forty years of military dictatorship with its massacres, targeted assassinations, tortures and rapes, and this has sparked a civil war between Nasser Waddadda, who wants to release them on internet pornographic sites, and Jerry Gotchakka, who thinks they should be distributed as snuff movies. A trial sample sent to the Danish capital has already sparked gang wars between the Hell's Angels and Bandidos, the rather laid-back Scandinavian excuse for tough guys. A brilliant young economist who worked for Joe Stiglitzt and General Daudu, then succumbed to alcoholism after leaving in disgrace to teach at the Yale School of Management, had written a memo on the possible exploitation of the tapes, using the Central Selling Organization for diamonds as an entrepreneurial model for pornography.

'The real jewel of the crown in our terror archive is undoubtedly *Red Mist*, the one shown to firing squads before executions, initiation ceremonies for our Men in Black and "special" parties for diplomatic wives. When the CIA staged the coup to bring General Cab Calloway to power they gave a list of 3,000 probable "leftists" to Colonel Daudu and ordered him to shoot them on the famous beach as a warning to the others. But Daudu was late because he was consulting Prophet Oluwole and before they were halfway through the tide had come in and the prisoners were up to their waists in water but Daudu insisted they continue because the Prophet said they must be "extinguished" before the end of Friday the 13th of February when the moon was in the house of Jupiter. When the red hot barrels of the AK47s and F16s of the executioners began to fizzle and jam Daudu was nowhere to be found, having left to distribute the widows to his troops. The Captain ordered them to fire from the beach-front hotels but the range was too great. So he ordered the Serbian pilots who were playing basketball with the American Special Forces to take them up in their Apache helicopter gun ships and shoot the convicts with Barratt Light sniper rifles but when he saw this was slow he ordered them to switch to .50 calibre machine guns. Then the Serbs, intoxicated by the smell of churning blood and brain under water, started firing rockets which made red fountains when they hit and white ones when they missed, a triangle of electric colours against the sky blue of the Atlantic. The videos were called *Red Mist* because of the vapour which rose with the souls of the three thousand in the setting sun, to which was later added the sound of Guns n' Roses' 'November Rain'. I know this for a fact because the Captain, now a Brigadier, Daudu's second-in-command in the Disposal Unit, later married my wife's best friend and entertains the British Ambassador's wife, in the national security interests of his country in cementing relations with the United Kingdom.

'Although tempted by the quiet life here I love my country and want to return. Before even being informed that my own father had sentenced me to death *in absentia*, Joseph Mammamia, a former comrade, had issued a statement accusing me of making it up to con the British into giving me political asylum, and I was roundly denounced by the *Mail, Express, Sun, Telegraph* and *News of the World* for trying to steal benefits out of the mouths of the British taxpayer. My friends in the Hausa Service gave me a chance to deny this rubbish and even "Florence Nightingale", the Princess Royal of the World Service, interviewed me, though belatedly.

'But my decision was finalized when I heard that my wife was now ahead of me on NIAGRA'S TEN MOST WANTED. On behalf of Kikelomo and all the other fighting women of the world, I say thank you and "Respect!" The Struggle Continues! Since we have come together to pay homage to her courage, commitment and compassion it is only fitting that we should end with her words of defiance when she was informed that her father-in-law, the Hanging Judge, who received an honorary doctorate from Cambridge, had sentenced her to death *in absentia* with a price of $10 million on her head: *"All that I've tried to do is hold up a mirror so that you can see your own reflection. If you do not like what you see, breaking the mirror will change nothing. Neither will cutting off my arms. Killing me will achieve even less. The truths of men and women cannot be dissolved in their blood."'*

Descending the steps of the Virgin Airways 747 at Lagos airport, Rabiu did not think of Benito Aquino of the Philippines, or any other exiles shot down or arrested on their return. His mind was clear of everything except Antonio Maceo, Josina Machel, Kikelomo and their expected child. The Pipe Man with two Men in Black stood by a new Peugeot station wagon without number plates on the tarmac holding a brown envelope. 'Good evening, Comrade Rabiu,' he beamed, handing him the detention order.

In the front seat reading Helon Habila's *Waiting for an Angel* by the overhead light was a slender white man in a beige Cerutti 1881 linen suit. He flipped a Camel cigarette from a gold case and lit it with a matching lighter with the initials 'G.P.' But as Rabiu was about to enter the car he felt an enormous hand close over his upper arm and turned to see Captain Jaja, Comrade Isaac in a lieutenant's uniform, two lance corporals and a Nigerian lawyer, Gani Fawehinmi. 'We'll take care of the convict, *sir*,' the Captain said. And as the man opened his mouth, his pipe almost fell out as the Men in Black prostrated to Jaja who sucked his teeth, gripped his pistol and pulled them roughly to their feet. 'Don't shoot us, comrade, we have young families,' the Men in Black grinned. The Pipe Man was still standing by the open door of the Peugeot as the men marched toward a black VW combi. Then Jaja took the envelope from Rabiu, perused it briefly and handed it to Isaac who marched briskly to the station wagon.

'Put *this* in your pipe,' Isaac said, handing him the order, 'and smoke it, *sir!*'

EPILOGUE

'THE MOTHER OF ALL VICTORIES'

written for *Granta*
by Kikelomo Rabiu Nafiu

UNDERGROUND IN THE dark womb of the cave complex
on the outskirts of Lidiziam the nucleus of a new people and
nation is being nurtured. We tell night from day only by the
pale light from concealed entrances and odd cracks in the
roof covered by vegetation above. It was not our choice that
our little community of fighters, formed over the past few
weeks, be made up of women: our men are in exile, in prison,
or dead. It is the cruelty of our oppressors which has elevated
us to the status of 'Mothers of the Revolution'. In my own
case this should be taken literally – a week ago I gave birth
to Delroy Solomon Rabiu Nafiu, thanks to the extraordinary
skills of our leader Agbani whose grandfather taught her the
arts of local medicine which enabled our people to survive
for millennia before the coming of the Europeans. Believing
that victory is certain for those who fight for justice and
freedom, we sincerely hope that one day he will be able to
look into his father's heart and provide companionship for his
brother Antonio Maceo and sister Josina Machel.

Our existence as 'cave women' was not planned but began
when some of us accompanied a group of architecture
students to survey Lidiziam, intending to build a suitable
memorial for the 2,384 dead. Nneoma, the national student
leader, daughter of one of the members of the former Transition
Council, had launched an international campaign to gather
resources and received very favourable responses, including

a letter of support signed by a hundred leading architects and published in the *Guardian*, *Politiken*, *Washington Post*, and *Le Monde*. Central to any memorial would be the extraordinary series of portraits of the village painted by Agbani's husband Bob Marley on pieces of cardboard, old plywood, and, in the last few days before his capture, on the canvases brought him by the late Colonel Ahmed Abdullahi.

Agbani said that she would tell him what the village looked like before and it would be just as if he was taking the images directly from her brain and imprinting them on whatever material he was using. When I first saw them my body was covered in cold sweat and the goose bumps were as big as my waist beads because I had never seen anything so *real*. Agbani, who was watching me intently, confessed that she too, although she was closer to him than she had been even to her father, felt the same way because she was seeing things in her own village where she was born, and in the people she had known and loved, that she had never noticed before. When the panels were lined up in order, it was almost like a motion picture of the history of Lidiziam.

I certainly would not want to compare Bob Marley's creation to Picasso's *Guernica*. The great Spanish painter was a genius, a sophisticate who intended his great painting to make a statement about unjust war, terror, genocide, evil, the horrors of capitalism and its bastard offspring, Fascism. Bob Marley was an innocent, a boy-man not capable of good or evil, but only of existence. He loved Agbani, felt her needs, and translated them into images *more real than the real, more human than human*. And because of the purity of his creations, their transcendent innocence, they were fitting monuments to immortalize the dead of Lidiziam.

But as soon as we started losing ourselves in intimations of immortality we were rather rudely reminded of our own mortality and led to recall Delroy's counsel that '*the irony of existence is that in order to be immortal we must first die*'. We had seen the surveillance drones the kids referred to as 'toy planes' overhead as we were arriving and then scouts we left to watch the roads into the village reported columns of American Special Forces, British Special Boat Commandos and Niagran Disposal Units approaching from several directions in Humvees, APCs and Bradley Fighting Vehicles, followed by white Green and Branch refrigerated trucks with black skull and cross bones, the so-called Skull & Bones on Wheels. They described vehicles like fire engines, which we figured were gas dispensers, flame throwers and self-propelled howitzers with uranium tipped shells. To make Fatima even more depressed before she ran away, her husband had told her of the Americans bringing in supplies of Agent Orange, Zyclon B, Sarin and VX gas, anthrax, small pox and botulin spores to make sure no one would ever be tempted to live in the village again. There were also Daudu's Ukrainian-made 'Black Marias', equipped with pikes on which shackled prisoners were impaled when tossed around on country roads.

Inspired by the Romans who spread terror by lining the main thoroughfare with the bodies of Spartacus and his comrades after their rebellion, the Death's Head Special Unit from the Third Marine Commando came equipped with laser-guided, computer-controlled crucifixion machines and Spanish crosses made of unvarnished pine. We knew what to expect if they caught us – on Valentine's Day Fatima's husband sent her thirty-three videotapes of the torture of Bob Marley, in a box covered with red hearts and tied with a bow, with the helpful suggestion to '*share with your friends*'.

Agbani is our leader, our inspiration, the one who keeps our hopes alive, and without her we would never have found the shelter of these caves, much less survived in them. After the death of her beloved Bob Marley and so many of our comrades, some of us despaired and resigned ourselves to the death-in-life of survival, under a numbing dictatorship narcotized by American fast foods, designer drugs, PSYOPS slogans, and country and western music. But mumbling words only her late companion had been able to understand, using sign language or writing in her script so fine we still mistake it for printing, Agbani crafted the message of why we must fight, and keep fighting, to avenge our men who had died, and protect those who survived so they could become good husbands, lovers, partners, fathers, sons and brothers again.

For the first time we learnt what really happened to her in Lidiziam on that day of infamy when General Daudu and his American and British masters decided that the village should go the way of Carthage, Sand Creek, Wounded Knee, Benin, Guernica, Lidice, Deir Yassin, Odi, Zaki Biam, Ambike, Setif, My Lai, Kolwezi, Oradour, Pijiguiti, Wiyiramu, Sharpeville, Soweto and all the other towns and villages which imperial powers decided had to be destroyed to 'encourage' others to obey. The night before the villagers were kept awake by sonic booms from Hawk fighter jets, hallucinatory red, white and blue flares, and PSYOPS teams blasting obscene country and western lyrics such as 'Shove your hand down my blouse again/These ain't no plum tomatoes'. The next day the sleep-starved villagers were still disoriented when the Americans started playing the more soothing rhythms of Johnny Cash, Jim Reeves, Waylon Jennings, Merle Haggard, Don Anderson and Willy Nelson, which many used to enjoy even before the General became an Elvis Impersonator and banned all other music.

At first they were disconcerted by low-flying Hawk jets and clouds like locust swarms but as the red, white and blue parachutes descended they thought of flowers and a carnival atmosphere was reinforced by sounds of fiddles and sunbursts of brilliant Chinese fireworks. Some were actually cheering until the Hawks started firing missiles, the paratroops landed and they saw the dreaded insignia of the Special (Death's Head) Commandos of the second Parachute Regiment, trained by North Koreans and Israelis. But by then the killers were firing their F16 and Galil assault rifles, targeting men, children and old or pregnant women. Young women were left free to run toward the exits out of the village only to find that these had been blocked off by American and Israeli Special Forces, British Special Boat Squadron and black-clad Niagran Disposal Units. These elite forces remained relatively disciplined and relaxed, even trying to cheer up the women by telling them that the Commandos were there to pick out notorious criminals who were terrorizing the village, after which the women could return to their homes and families. Few believed them.

Maddened by the orgy of killing, crack cocaine, methamphetamine, GBH, Jack Daniels, Dr Pepper cola and the hypnotic sounds of Appalachian bass fiddles, the Commandos descended on the women like hyenas, not bothering to undress them but slashing their clothes with bayonets and serrated hunting knives. Although there were enough to go round, they fought each other with fists, knives and gun butts so the women were overwhelmed not only by the ferocity of their lust and insanity but the spectacle of their gaping wounds and stench of blood. After raping one woman they would attack their comrades raping others, so many victims suffered the double death of violation and being caught in the crossfire.

Young girls like Agbani were prized because of the belief that the blood of virgins bestowed special powers and cured chronic venereal diseases or HIV. Because she was so beautiful, several men were seriously injured fighting over her until a Captain Piltdown of the Special Boat Squadron persuaded them to call a truce, cast lots, form a queue by name, rank, or serial number and 'enjoy' her in an orderly manner. She lost count of the men at seven and was semi-conscious when the American lieutenant Kali, aroused by the fiddles, the misty taste of moonshine and screams of rape, demanded his turn. But even in her exhausted, semi-conscious state Agbani refused his demand for oral sex and, when he persisted, prying her mouth open with his bowie knife, she bit his penis so hard it was held together only by a pink flap of skin.

Enraged, he jumped up, grabbed his rifle, and before the

British Captain could restrain him, thrust his bayonet twice into her mouth, knocking out four teeth, splitting her tongue and palette, then three times into her pelvis, lower abdomen and vagina, destroying her entire reproductive system. She bled so much her skin became as pale as the Europeans and when her eyes rolled back and they could not find a pulse they cast her on top of the corpses of those lucky to have passed on before. But this was the daughter of a long line of warriors who had fought and won against would-be conquerors long before the Europeans. When she regained consciousness she put branches and earth over the mound of corpses to at least protect her fellow women from the indignity of the jackals and vultures then began treating herself with the roots and herbs as her grandfather had taught her.

She had to find clean water as the streams had been poisoned with cyanide, rotting corpses and Agent Orange sprayed on the crops to ensure the village and its precious oil would never again be disturbed by the presence of humans. She recalled these caves where her people had taken shelter in the past, where there were underground streams and pools of pure water and stockpiles of dried coconuts, yams and wood. It was here that she recuperated because surveillance planes flew over, and surveyors and prospectors from Burton Holly made the rounds of the village in protective suits. When she felt strong enough she embarked on an odyssey down the creeks and through the forests until she got to the nearest towns and then to Xanadu. But her people, even close relations and those her father had schooled and set up in business, wanted nothing to do with her. She was a ghost, the destruction of the village, celebrated in the government and Western media as a 'triumph against terrorism', had been so thorough no mere human could have survived. She was mumbling incoherently, like they imagined from their nightmares a ghost would, and her wounds were so horrific she could not have survived without sorcery, and was no longer a woman as she could not bear children. So she had no recourse but to resort to life on the street where she met Bob Marley and the army of orphans and other homeless children created by the cruelty of the dictatorship.

After the murder of Bob Marley it was from these disinherited ones that Agbani recruited the first members of what we now immodestly call our people's army. Many had graduated into the sex trade, some had become cart pushers, porters, touts in the motor parks, conductors, street peddlers and petty criminals. Programmes started by Delroy, Omolare, Brotherman and Captain Jaja had taught some to read and write, apprenticed others to traders and craftsmen. All were in a position to spread the word about Agbani and her new warriors, and even those who had made it to school and become teachers, journalists, soldiers or other important members of society were now reminded of what it had been like to live on the street. Agbani told an ancient tale of her people in which warriors were denied their wives and lovers unless they were willing to fight the enemy and we recognized the universality of the theme of Aristophanes' *Lysistrata*. Our women now told their men to fight or practise celibacy: 'No Backbone no P----y' as our placards put it delicately! Our first strike was a brilliant success as women at all levels denied their husbands cooking, nookie, and forced them to iron their own underpants to impress their 'other' women.

Mallam Aminu, who was sceptical about Ahmed's military coup, now supports us with his millions of followers: he had little choice as his own wife told him to warn his *mujahiddin* that Allah was not a Niagran Man who declared it right to beat up and cheat on his wives. A 'renegade' daughter of the President had edited the Brigadier's video to show people how an innocent Bob Marley had been treated as an Al-Qaeda militant by the Americans and a terrorist mastermind able to shape shift from five foot two to six foot one by the Niagrans. Sympathetic journalists took up the story and the word spread all over West Africa that an army made up predominantly of women was on the move. The Hausa Services of the BBC and VOA ran features and left-wing journalists such as John Pilger and Robert Fisk speculated that one of Che's promised 'many Vietnams' might be in the making, though in a most unusual form!

A biography of my late sister Omolare, entitled *Get Up, Stand Up!* by a journalist from *African Concord* in neighbouring Nigeria, gave further impetus to the movement. There were reports, even in the heavily controlled government press, of women in high places bawling their eyes out when they read the emotional account of Omolare's death:

> So profound was the impact on the African audience of Omolare's entrance into the General Daudu National Stadium, packed to the roof with revellers gathered to celebrate the visit of the American Vice President, that few noticed she was stark naked. Not so the British and American soldiers, businessmen and diplomats who tittered about the ubiquity of streakers or who snickered like the Israelis about the craziness of the unpredictable *shiksas*. But among the Africans who knew the meaning of a middle-aged married woman with the stretch marks of childbirth parading her nakedness there was fear, premonition and awe as she made her appearance under the triumphal arch at the entrance of the stadium modelled on the sword arms of Saddam Hussein at the entrance of Baghdad, in tribute to General Daudu's former 'Eternal Friend'. Although censored by the *Sentinel* and all the other government media, all had read the horrific account of her husband's death by 'John Lennon' in *Red Bull*, the guerrilla underground paper, and many swore after the event that they saw Dr Delroy Solomon, spitting image of Gary Dourdan, the African-American actor, down to his 'pimp roll' (Tom Wolfe), marching beside his wife. They had the sensation of the Amuz Rock uprooting itself and moving toward the platform where General

Daudu was enjoying his triumph of a visit by the American Vice President and the Chairman of Burton Holly, despite sanctions by the UN, EU, OECD, IMF and World Bank, and condemnations by the US Black Congressional Caucus, UN Commission on Human Rights, the State Department, Amnesty International, PEN, The International Consortium of Investigative Journalists and Transparency International for incessant massacres, targeted assassinations, unique methods of torture and running the most corrupt and brutal dictatorship in the world.

For the Niagran officials, Daudu included, the consternation was near panic, because many of their wives and mistresses had been Omolare's classmates, their children were being taught by her, and her husband's assassination had raised his cult status to the level of Guevara, Mandela, Fanon, Rodney and Cabral on the nation's campuses which the more intelligent of their children insisted on attending, spurning automatic entrance to the University of Buckingham in the UK. Many were paralyzed with fear and foreboding as they recalled the occasion when Mrs Fumilayo Anikulapo-Kuti, Fela's late mother, laid siege to the palace of the tyrannical Alake of Abeokuta with an army of shrivelled, stark naked grandmothers, forcing his abdication before the unrest could spread to the rest of neighbouring Nigeria. They were acutely aware of the abomination represented by the woman marching with such remorseless intensity of purpose up the red carpet meant for Kings, Presidents, Prime Ministers, Lebanese billionaire pimps and the Chairman of Burton Holly, representing a nemesis they could not escape. Even the American Vice President, his entourage, and secret service agents were caught in the grip of the emotion and were fidgeting in their expensive seats as their armpits drowned in cold sweat. But there was an American Special Forces man who was under orders to snuff out any threat to the security interest of his nation and the first shot from his Barratt Light sniper rifle hit her in the chest. But she kept moving forward even after a second and third shot to the head, and when the fourth shot rang out she still fell forward on her face.

But by then no one noticed because women were charging toward the sniper's nest, some toward the royal box with the General and his American guests, but the majority toward the body of Omolare Delroy Solomon as she lay, face down, arms outstretched, on the bloodstained red carpet. They wrapped her in their own clothes, carried her in triumph on their shoulders, fighting to touch her exposed face with eyes wide open, dry, clear, and, despite the vehement protests of her family, forced Daudu to grant her a state funeral in his gaudily decorated FIELD OF MARTYRS AND HEROES where he buried the predecessor he assassinated on Friday the 13th of February with full military honours.

[Editor's Note: Claims by Seymour Hersh in the *Atlantic Monthly* that John Allen Mohammed was ordered to shoot after Richard 'Mr Dick' Burton passed a note with '*black widow*?' (suicide bomber?) to the Vice President must be treated with scepticism as the graphologist used to authenticate the writing was the same employed by the Pentagon's Office of Special Plans to prove that the Strategic Arms Limitations Treaties were not signed by Ronald Reagan but by Nancy's Futurologist in San Luis Obispo, hence worth diddly squat.]

Even today the wives, sisters and daughters of high ranking members of the regime go on pilgrimage to pay homage at Omolare's tomb, and one of the President's wives persuaded Hilary Clinton to visit and dedicate a copy of *It Takes A Village To Raise A Child*. The regime has never recovered from this demonstration of the moral power of the African Woman, confirmation of the primacy of matriarchy demonstrated in the works of Cheikh Anta Diop, and it was from this time that Daudu and his advisers attempted to harness this power through a series of frivolous and tragicomic measures, designed to better the lives of the nation's women, but which gave further opportunities for stealing to his wives and mistresses who rushed to form chapters of the Association for Better Wives for Husbands.

When Agbani led the first group of sex workers, cleaners, beggars, street children, cripples, the unemployed and other lumpen elements to Omolare's tomb, she was surprisingly joined by a sizeable group of society women, including Candace, one of the estranged wives of the General, two ex-ministers, permanent secretaries, and the leader of the official Niagran Association of Women. Candace, plucked from school at fifteen by a Lebanese pimp to join the General's harem in exchange for a 'dowry' of a low cost DFID two-bedroom house, and a distributorship for Guinness stout, soon became tired of living in a golden cage suffocated with luxuries. Always first in her class, with ambition to become a gynaecologist while her boyfriend Jairzinho played for Arsenal or AC Milan, she begged her husband to let her continue her studies after the birth of her sons. But when he exploded in derision that *a man in his position could not let his wife be fucked by half-starved lecturers and fellow students,* and she defied him and gained admission to the School of Preliminary Studies, the General took swift revenge: she was cut off from her children, held under virtual house arrest in a guest house built for a visit by the Queen of England, and later found out in a routine medical that she had been sterilized by a Belgian doctor hired by her husband to check his wives for venereal diseases he might have passed on from his Indian, Inuit, Mauritian, Jamaican and Pakistani call girls.

Candace became devoted to Agbani who was with Jairzinho on the street, and joined us in the cave complex as an intelligent, inventive and hard-working comrade. But Daudu had killed something inside her and, deprived of alcohol and painkillers, she would lapse into bouts of depression, repeating the homilies she learnt from the missionaries in school about death coming like a thief in the night, and all of us disappearing *in a moment, in the twinkling of an eye, at the last trumpet.* She had nightmares of Jairzinho hanging from a meat hook with nose sliced off and eyes gouged out, and of stealth bombers sneaking up on us, dropping their smart bombs so silently we would not be able to tell death from sleep, or dreams from reality.

Then one night she disappeared and only later we found out her mission from the note she left concealed under a jam jar where Fatima kept her 'souvenirs'. She had discovered where the doctor had his surgery in barracks near Lidiziam, occupied by American, British, Australian, Spanish, Polish, Danish, Jamaican, Turkish and Pakistani Special Forces. Taking advantage of a captain in the Presidential Guard, who was besotted with her from their school days when he played inside left beside Jairzinho, she obtained ten kilos of PETN military explosives which she strapped to her body and, disguised as a heavily pregnant officer's wife, waddled into the Belgian's office next to the main mess in the barracks at dinner time. Although this was a great blow to our enemies, our opposition to suicide bombing, on the grounds that it contradicted our humanist philosophy, and that the lives of a million 'enemies' are not worth one of a liberated woman's, caused us to issue a communiqué claiming responsibility, using the letter head of Rabiu's former 'Marxist-Leninist' party, which we called the 'Boy George Liberation Front' after their benefactor, who financed them under their new name of 'Democratic Alternative'.

Fatima finally abandoned her useless husband who bears the same name as my own Rabiu. This drunkard and wife-beater had been warned repeatedly, and after very extreme action had been taken against him we thought he had changed his ways. But like his master Daudu whom he worshipped, he could not. After the last beating which damaged the hearing in her left ear, Fatima kept quiet and went out and bought two bottles of Scotch, aged in Cuban rum casks, which cost US$120 each in the Duty Free Shop run by Daudu's senior wife. This was his favourite and she knew that once he saw the bottles he could not resist finishing them both. Keeping out of his way to avoid total deafness, she waited until she heard his snores like the electric saws the Disposal Units used to 'clean up' leaders of 'coup plots', took out the old scalpel we used in our college biology classes, pulled down his *Sloggi* briefs and removed the one testicle I left, in an act of misplaced charity, the last time he broke her cheekbone. Now we have both in the jam jar we labelled 'The Keeper of the Crown Jewels' and 'Souvenirs of a Man of Power!'

We maintain contact with the outside world by disguising ourselves as peasant women. I am particularly effective with Baby Delroy strapped to my back which helps in recruiting, as no African woman can resist coming up to pat him on the head or offering me gifts of money or farm produce. But our principal means of communication are the street children Agbani picked up from the old haunts she occupied with Bob Marley and the *Outkastes*. The best are those trained by Brotherman to liberate food, clothes and other necessities from expensive shops owned by the Lebanese, Indians or wives of top military officers. I would like to use this medium to thank the American Defence Secretary for his commissary's generous gifts of Pampers, gripe water, baby soaps, oils, talcum powder and wipes which Baby Delroy compliments for their delicacy! *Thank you, sir!*

The kids are under the care of Adama 'Beyonce' Abdullahi, widow of the late Colonel Ahmed, who abandoned the 'George Soros Party' not only because her former comrades refused to support her husband's 'khaki revolution' but because its leader, 'Pancho Villa', with his revolutionary moustache, betrayed him to the American Special Forces hit squad led by James Gofer Brown, in return for a visa and a bungalow in Jamaica, in the borough of Queens, New York. The successes we have been able to achieve as 'cave women' have helped pull her out of her depression and, now that she heard her father Adamu Adamu was arrested and extradited to Guantanamo Bay on charges of 'links to Al-Qaeda', she's ecstatic.

Apparently a CIA computer expert was running a program on 'Gum Arabic', one of the businesses Osama bin Laden used to launder money when he controlled the economy of Sudan. As grandson of an immigrant from Sudan, home to three million people of Niagran origin, and the undisputed 'Gum Arabic King' of our country, the Yanks put two and two together and got her dad's 'link with Al-Qaeda'. Beyonce is particularly pleased because he was one of the African busi- nessmen used to launder CIA money through the BCCI and then the Carlton Group, for Renamo, UNITA, Inkatha and other murder groups, facts she revealed in *Red Bull*, and was denounced for 'petty bourgeois adventurism' by her former party when she offered to 'bump off' her father, who threw the occasional bone to his former comrades from his days as a student revolutionary, by sponsoring their kids or girlfriends to study at the University of Buckingham where Margaret Thatcher was Chancellor.

Some government publications, and even sympathetic foreign ones such as the British *Guardian*, have referred to us as 'Amazons'. As you know, Amazons were Greek warrior women, possibly mythical, who defeated men by cutting off one breast so they could aim their arrows better. The Romans who invaded Scandinavia with the intention of raping the women after killing the men complained of powerful women assaulting them with battleaxes *before* they got to the men. And in the neighbouring Republic of Benin there were supposed to have been a race of very powerful women, organized in a matriarchy with a warrior queen, who fought as well as any male-dominated society. As you can see from the enclosed photos of Agbani, Beyonce and Fatima, we are far from being 'Amazon' in the sense of muscle-bound wrestler types. These comrades could be beauty queens, movie stars or catwalk models if our intention had been to sell our bodies and become slaves in the beauty trade. While we appreciate the sympathetic coverage of progressive male writers, Naomi Klein and Germaine Greer were right to point out that 'feminist' was not equivalent to 'dowdy, moustachioed Amazons with varicose veins, bad breath, and hairy armpits'. *Hello, boys!*

Many women like myself and Fatima are here with young children and we avoid the usual stress of individual mothers by going back to our African tradition of raising them in common, instilling love and respect for *all* mothers, brothers, sisters and, when the time comes, fathers. From the ashes of a society destroyed by a monstrous regime, we hope that a new future will rise.

Round the clock we are bombarded by PSYOPS teams blasting out Toby Keith's 'Courtesy of the Red, White and Blue', Andrew Card's 'Shove your hand down my blouse again', Berlin's 'Take My Breath Away', and other American 'patriotic' music, threatening us with search-and-destroy missions, chemical and biological weapons of mass destruction, smart bunker-busting bombs and tactical nuclear weapons. But we know their threats are baseless, because while our lives are worth nothing to the powers-that-be in Washington, London, Crawford and New York, we sit on treasures they value more than life itself, or the love of their wives and children, in the form of billions of barrels of oil so near the surface it costs a fraction of that below the desert sands of Saudi Arabia and Iraq to produce.

We can thus feel more secure from American J-DAMS and nuclear tipped shells than the Vice President with his dicky heart, hidden from the world in his secret bunker in DC. Now that friendly media in the West have enlightened the public to the fact that we are not hairy-legged, drug-crazed terrorists out to blow up the world but working mothers trying to guarantee a future for our children, Presidents, Prime Ministers and Chancellors will have to explain to their wives and daughters why they're trying to murder us just to continue providing dollar-a-gallon gas for their SUVs, and multi-billion dollar profits for the Burton Holly Corporation. *Come on, sisters, take a look at your dudes in the White House, Number 10 and the Elysée. How would you feel if our husbands were dropping 2,000 pound bombs on your kids? Why not tell them to replace the damp squibs in their Y-fronts with the weapons of mass destruction they're trying to fuck us with?*

The beat of *'One good thing about music,/when it hits you feel no pain'*, reminds us of the singer Bob Marley's birthday and we've planned a little surprise for Agbani who celebrates this as Little Bob's birthday too since we aren't sure the exact day he was born. Yesterday she said she heard from Elean Thomas, the Jamaican poetess, that they had located Bob Marley's birth mother, Aishetu, who lives in a small, thatched, daub-and-wattle hut in Nine Mile with her loving Rasta husband, who was in a very joyful mood now that the government, despite Yankee threats, has finally recognized the religion of Jah and legalized the sacred herb. Her advice is that we leave Aishetu alone with her family for the time being as the trauma of the death of her first born could rekindle the horrors she fled when she was a poor abused child. I can't wait to tell Rabiu that we're proud aunt and uncle to six beautiful Rasta children whose photos I'm looking at in wonder by a column of light which coils itself like a golden snake round the roots of a giant fig tree.

The piercing eyes and long hair of the eldest remind me of Rabiu's cousin Nuhu, and the quotation he wished inscribed on his tomb, which remains unfulfilled because Daudu's henchmen had 'disappeared' his body: *wherever death may surprise us let it be welcome, provided our battle cry has reached even one more receptive ear, and other hands reach out to pick up our weapons, and other voices intone our funeral dirge with new cries of battle and victory and the staccato of machine gun bullets.* (You must forgive me if I don't get this word perfect, editor! I believe it was from Che.) But why am I thinking of death when I can see, in the dappled light from above, the fresh, healthy faces of Bob Marley's half brothers and sisters, and the bright smile of our own Baby Delroy gurgling happily like one of the springs trickling from the walls of the cave? We owe it to ourselves and our cause to celebrate life, and not succumb to thoughts of the possibility of instant death, which kills us many times over while we still live, gifting our enemies victories they cannot win through smart bombs and poison gas.

These somewhat defiant but morbid thoughts remind me of poor Candace who some comrades criticized for undermining morale with her so-called obsession with death. Whenever we looked at the bright side and appeared to be gliding over rough edges, she would tell the story of the scorpion who tried to persuade the little dog to take it across the stream. 'But you're a scorpion,' the dog replied 'you'll sting me to death and we'll both drown.' 'No,' the scorpion argued persuasively, 'I may be a scorpion but I'm not a fool. I won't sting you if my own life depends on it.' So his reservations swept away by this immortal logic, the little dog took the scorpion on his back and swam easily against the current but when they reached the middle the scorpion stung his companion and they began to sink. 'Why?' the little dog asked with his last breath. 'I *am* a scorpion,' his companion replied, '*I couldn't help myself.*'

Was Candace right in thinking that our faith in the good sense of our enemies in the White House, Downing Street, the Elysée Palace and the Reichskanzler's office, was misplaced? Who are these men but political scorpions? These are people who killed millions and, more importantly from their point of view, spent a trillion dollars to guarantee supplies of titanium for their nuclear submarines and to prevent the fall of illusory dominoes in Vietnam, then coined the celebrated phrase *'it was necessary to destroy the country in order to save it'*. They kill their people by preventing simple laws against tobacco, guns, junk food, country and western music, talk shows, reality television, Evangelical Christianity, unsafe cars and pollution.

The worst that can be said of Candace is that she had the terrible courage of her convictions and was willing to pay the ultimate price for 'victory'. But like Pyrrhus of Epirus we must ask ourselves how many such victories we can afford, when our finest women sacrifice their lives to 'defeat' poor men and women who will be joyfully replaced by rulers committed to the perpetual machines of death and destruction they use to rule our lives. Just now I'm distracted by Suzy humming the *Laudate Dominum* to her three-month-old daughter. Suzy was a child prostitute whose mother, also a prostitute, died of AIDS when Suzy was five. But determined not to die like her mother she saved the money she earned from NGO and oil company workers, whom she insisted wear condoms, enrolled in a course at the Royal Academy, and showed so much promise that she was taken on as a trainee flautist by the London Philharmonic Orchestra. But when she read about us in an article by Diane Abbott in the *Voice*, she decided she had to return home to be a part of the history of her country.

Josina Machel was about my age when she died but by then had written the lines which guarantee her immortality:

> This is the time we were fighting for
> Our guns are light in our hands
> The reasons and aims of our struggle
> Clear in our minds
> The blood shed by our heroes
> Makes us sad but resolute
> It is the price of our freedom
> We keep them close in our hearts
> From their examples new generations
> – revolutionary generations –

Are already being born
Ahead of us we see bitter hardships
But we also see
Our children running free
Our country plundered no more
This is the time to be ready and firm
The time to give ourselves
To the Revolution.

What brought Josina to mind was the sight of Agbani teaching the young ones about the history of her people of Lidiziam, of her great warrior ancestors, including King Jaja, and how to use the ancient wisdom of the people to help present and future generations protect themselves from annihilation. We all have segments of this course, to impart what we know of the history of our people, and the whole programme is co-ordinated by Professor 'DuBois', Rabiu's aunt, who decided to return from her self-imposed exile after she read articles by Angela Davis, Gloria Steinem, Noam Chomsky and Naomi Klein about what we are doing here to make our country fit for human beings to live in again. We call her Hafsat, her original name, and it's incredible how strong she's become since the horrors of her childhood. She spent years in therapy on the West Coast but it was not until she took a year off on the advice of an academic exile from apartheid, and spent time with a *sangoma* in Natal, that she was able to put the pieces of her life together and become whole again.

She visited the Western Cape and Southern Namibia to experience the sites where our mother, the original Eve, gave birth to all of us. To Hafsat feminism was not just an academic discipline but a principle of existence and she modelled her life on the women she studied, who domesticated plants and animals, laid the basis for civilization and made us human while men played silly games 'hunting' animals little different from themselves. Even biologically she considered men defective with their vulnerable Y chromosome, which made them insecure and therefore prone to constant violence and the need to dominate.

Knowing how strange these ideas would seem in our present patriarchal world she has expressed them in science fiction. In 'Men Without Pricks', dedicated to the science fiction writer Philip K. Dick, she argued that the aspiration of Western feminists was simply to join or supplant their men in dominating and exploiting other men and women. In the second volume of the trilogy, 'World Without Men', women have inherited the earth after pollution caused by permanent Republican governments in the United States destroyed the Y chromosome. But in a plot twist worthy of Walter Mosley, a group of White Anglo-Saxon genetic technicians were caught trying to reconstitute the male chromosome through recombinant DNA splicing, so they would return to the best of all possible worlds where they exercised power without responsibility in the shadows of their sleazy scuzbag husbands. The final volume was the 'Pretzel', where the WASP women have succeeded in recreating a race of particularly feeble-minded, violent and greedy men who keep threatening to kill everybody and destroy the world if they are not given all they demand. Then a group of revolutionary young women develop nano-technology which turns male genitalia to pretzels when they think of women's breasts and crotches while the women are trying to discuss serious issues of relationships, society, home and family. The stupid men, incapable of telling their pricks from their pretzels, choke on the pretzels while watching holographic Democratic politicians fucking interns in a futuristic right-wing Drudge Report. Unfortunately our male-dominated publishing industry has shown little interest and we're waiting for some sisters to make that editorial cut on their male bosses so we can have a true feminist voice, not a continuation of patriarchy by other means.

But what if Josina died in vain? Three decades after her death Carlos Cardoso was murdered by powerful men, members of the ruling family in Mozambique, the country she fought to liberate. Is history repeating itself as the heirs of the revolution act out the tragedy begun by the Portuguese secret police, who murdered her to keep her people in chains? Even if this is so we must still press on. Future generations will not forgive us if we give up. Pessimism will guarantee defeat and threaten the future of our children, while indifference will hand our enemies victory on our bent black backs if we bend our knees or open our legs to them. Perhaps we can take heart from the fact that these killers have been punished while their predecessors probably got medals from their masters.

In London we hear that Rabiu is the overwhelming favourite to win the prize named after Comrade Cardoso. When we complete our Refuge for Abused Women and Orphans with his prize money, we will name assembly halls and dormitories after Josina, Carlos, Little Bob Marley and other martyrs of the Revolution, who died before their time. We have made tremendous progress on this and other projects with money 'liberated' from their fathers and husbands by wives, daughters and mistresses of the President and his cronies. One, an undergraduate from the University of California at Davis, said her father would never miss the $250,000 she took from his bedroom at the Rock Castle because there was at least half a billion dollars there in American, British, German, French and Swiss currencies. Fatima and I helped ourselves to several Louis Vuitton cases packed with $100 bills from one of her husband's walk-in closets, which we invested in schools, crèches, soup kitchens, shelters and defence measures. We also hear of offers from Renzo Piano, Norman Foster and Tadao Ando to design the refuges, crèches, clinics and kindergartens we hope to build in future.

But enough of business: a cocky little Rasta kid, who resembles one of Bob Marley's half-brothers, has just embarrassed Agbani by asking a question she can't answer! But instead of getting all serious and trying to wiggle her way out of it, she's just laughing with them, till the tears fill her eyes. She's a truly great one, and though she's much younger than most of us, we tease her when she gets a bit bossy, calling her 'Mother Hen'. And that's part of the surprise we plan for her, to celebrate the birthdays of Bob Marley and her own Little Bob. We've organized a sketch called *Chicken Inna Yard*, based on a short story by Jamaica Kincaid and a poem of Elean Thomas, about a group of hens who have to fend for themselves because the jealous and cruel masters have killed all the beautiful cocks. Beyonce will play the Mother Hen and the sketch will be directed by Binta, the President's other daughter who studied film-making at UCLA. I will be part of the chorus – tonight I'm in charge of taking care of the young ones and their cries will make good background music against the constant drone of British Hawk fighters and American Stealth bombers.

But it would be wrong if I gave the impression that Agbani is some kind of uncool person, precocious beyond her years. She has this little guitar made from a calabash, plywood and old piano wire by Harry, one of her late comrades from the street. Bob Marley had painted a fantastic green mermaid on it with squiggles like hieroglyphics under it saying *'Island in the Sun by Harry Belafonte'*. Whenever she played a song – and she played beautifully if tragically, with each note evoking her longing for her dead husband – she always claimed that it was first sung by her people in Lidiziam. We ignored her until one day Fatima and I started teasing her when she explained that 'The First Time Ever I Saw Your Face' was actually from *The Ballad of the Green Mermaid*. Fatima and I laughed about her ancestors creating the world, Lidiziam being the garden of Eden and her people inventing the wheel, sliced bread and the mobile phone. She kept singing and playing and her profile, against the flame of the torches, was like the beautiful images of women we see on the walls of Egyptian temples. Then later, while Fatima and I were relaxing on a swing, after handing Baby Delroy to Beyonce in the crèche, Agbani crept up behind us and *bit our asses!* Of course she knew the caves so much better than us that we couldn't catch her to take revenge.

Just then there were a series of co-ordinated explosions more powerful than any we had heard before, which rattled the pots on the fires and knocked rocks and soil from the walls and roof. This was followed by a wailing more intense than a thousand sirens, which almost burst our eardrums, and a bagpipe version of 'Take Your Breath Away'. Then there was a whooshing sound as if a bomb had burst a cavern containing all the waters in the world, in a repeat of the Great Flood. Hafsat just smiled enigmatically and sighed 'men' as she paused from peeling the yams for our evening meal. She has much to smile about as she's the one responsible for Mallam Aminu's support: she's first cousin of his wife who grew up in their household and the women never forgave their men for not being able to protect her, Aishetu and Nuhu from the cruelties of their relative, the Hanging Judge. I personally think 'toys for boys' and wonder what the world would be like if Hitler, Idi Amin, Emperor Bokassa, Daudu, Rabiu's father, their American and British friends, and all the other legitimized mass murderers, had developed into ordinary serial killers like Jeffrey Dahmer and Harold Shipman, rather than political psychopaths.

But life must go on, we must show commitment and compassion to the end. And above all courage. Whatever happens we must be brave, comfort each other, live. The solidarity we have shown so far must develop into love, from these lonely caves among the ghosts of the village of Lidiziam to the rest of Niagra, Africa and the world. If we can succeed in teaching the new generation what we have learnt from these years of struggle, we women and our children will be free to declare to all the world:

This is the end of mutual incomprehension and cruelty between men and women
    This is the end of women remaining silent while being beaten by men, or women of higher rank

This is the end of men or women being forced to sell their bodies, of indignity being heaped on the citizen, of all exploitation by men or women

This is the end of genital mutilation and other forms of abuse of our daughters

This is the end of the exploited and humiliated being forced to sing the praises of their oppressors, of being dictated to by foreigners

This is the end of religions which preach the worship of hate-filled, vengeful, indifferent Gods

The end of all self-hate and mutilation

This is the end of false happiness and megalomaniac, egocentric illusions.

This is . . .

ACKNOWLEDGEMENTS

Allusions are too numerous to mention but I would like to thank the following: Gabriel García Márquez for his *The General in his Labyrinth*; Agostinho Neto for his poems *Sacred Hope*; Josina Machel for her poem 'This is the Time'; Amilcar Cabral for his *Weapon of Theory*; Caligula for his horse and George W. Bush for his cabinet.